"I have no intention of

Olivia's words hit Josh like a sucker punch, and he had to bite back the oath on the tip of his tongue. Yet when it came to the Princess, the very first hotel built by his grandfather, it was difficult not to let his emotions come into play. To see the Logan Hotel banner flying over the Princess again had been his dream for as long as he could remember. And once again, that dream remained just out of reach.

"Please hear me out," she told him.

Josh nodded, settled back in his seat.

"I want to see the Princess returned to her throne, Joshua. Once I see that happen, I'll turn over the reins. From the day your grandfather signed her over to me, she's been run by a Jardine."

"But your grandchildren have no interest in running the Princess. The only other Jardine left to run it is you," Josh pointed out.

"Not necessarily," Olivia told him. "There is another alternative."

"Do you intend to tell me who this mysterious Jardine relative is?"

"My granddaughter. Or I suppose I should say, my *other* granddaughter."

Metsy Hingle
The Wager

MIRA

ISBN 1-55166-826-2

THE WAGER

Copyright © 2001 by Metsy Hingle.

All rights reserved. Except for use in any review, the reproduction or
utilization of this work in whole or in part in any form by any electronic,
mechanical or other means, now known or hereafter invented, including
xerography, photocopying and recording, or in any information storage or
retrieval system, is forbidden without the written permission of the publisher,
MIRA Books, 225 Duncan Mill Road, Don Mills, Ontario, Canada M3B 3K9.

All characters in this book have no existence outside the imagination of the
author and have no relation whatsoever to anyone bearing the same name
or names. They are not even distantly inspired by any individual known or
unknown to the author, and all incidents are pure invention.

MIRA and the Star Colophon are trademarks used under license and registered
in Australia, New Zealand, Philippines, United States Patent and Trademark
Office and in other countries.

Visit us at www.mirabooks.com

Printed in U.S.A.

My heartfelt thanks go to the following people who helped me give life to *The Wager:*

Dianne Moggy, Editorial Director of MIRA Books, for believing in me and this project. Without her support, this book would never have been written.

Karen Kosztolnyik, my editor, whose support, guidance and patience were invaluable to me in the writing of this book.

Tara Gavin of Silhouette Books for her support and endorsement.

Linda Hayes, friend and former agent, for her years of encouragement and advice.

Karen Solem, my agent and guiding force, for her enthusiasm and support.

Sandra Brown, my dear friend and mentor, for her encouragement and support.

Dave and Judi Burrus, dear friends and hoteliers, who introduced me to the business of luxury hotels.

R. A. Jardine, banker and friend, whose surname served as inspiration.

Linda Kay, Hailey North, Rexanne Becnel, Erica Spindler and Karen Young, fellow authors and friends, for their support and encouragement.

The remarkable, talented staff at MIRA Books for their support and expertise.

And as always, a very special thanks goes to my children and family whose love and understanding enables me to spin tales of love, hope and happily-ever-after.

For Jim
My husband, my lover, my friend

Prologue

The sound of skidding tires and metal crashing against metal finally stopped. So did the screams. Lying in the rain beside the mangled car, Laura Harte opened her eyes and listened. But all she heard now was the steady beat of the August rain and the distant hum of traffic from the San Francisco road. She drew in a breath and winced at the sharp ache in her ribs.

Then she caught it—the metallic scent of blood. Tamping down on a spurt of panic, Laura struggled to sit up and gasped as white-hot pain shot through her shoulder. Her stomach pitched. Her vision blurred, but not before she'd noted the odd angle at which her arm hung. Gritting her teeth, she managed to half walk, half crawl from the twisted car to the side of the dark road where her mother lay in a crumbled heap. The fear that had bolted through her when she'd seen the lights of the truck coming at them hit Laura again as she stared at her mother's pale face. "Momma, can you hear me?"

Her mother's eyelashes fluttered. "Looks like I ruined your big celebration," she said, but the grimace that followed diffused the lighthearted remark.

"I don't care about the awards banquet," Laura soothed. Right now she didn't care about her job, the promotion, anything—only her mother and the ragged sound of her breathing. "You're going to be all right. Just hang on while I go get help."

"No. There's not enough time," her mother said, her voice raspy. She caught Laura's hand, held it. "There are things I need to tell you…things I should have told you a long time ago. About me, about your father."

"Shh. Don't talk anymore. You need to save your strength." Biting back the panic threatening to choke her, Laura tried to keep her voice calm as she said, "You can tell me all about your great romance with daddy again later. Right now, try to lie still. I'm going up to the road to flag down help. We need to get you to a hospital."

"T-too late for…hospital."

"No, it's not," Laura insisted. She didn't care if her mother was a nurse. She was wrong. It wasn't too late. It couldn't be too late. Then she heard it—the squeal of sirens—and nearly wept with relief. "Listen! Do you hear that? Sirens! That means help is on the way. All you have to do is hang on a little longer."

Her mother squeezed her fingers, but her grip had grown weaker. "I'm sorry, baby. I always thought I'd have more time," she said, her voice thready. "I need to tell you about your father…to explain…"

"I know all about Daddy." *Did her mother's insistence on talking about her dead husband mean the injuries were even worse than she feared? Hadn't she read somewhere that when a person was dying their thoughts focused on the past?* No! Her mother was not dying, Laura told herself as tears ran down her cheeks and mingled with the rain. To comfort herself as much as her mother, Laura repeated the oft-told tale. "Daddy was a navy aviator who came to the base hospital where you worked as a nurse. He was the most hand-some man you'd ever seen, with beautiful blue eyes and a kind smile. The two of you fell madly in love and after a whirlwind courtship, you got married.'' The beautiful, tragic tale of her parents' romance cut short by her father's death in Vietnam had been as much a part of her life as breathing. Her father may have died before she was born, but Laura had grown up loving him.

''We were so much in love,'' her mother whispered.

''I know,'' Laura said softly, growing more terrified with each moment by her mother's labored breathing and the gray cast to her skin. Then she heard it—voices calling out, footsteps. ''Over here,'' Laura cried out. ''And please…hurry!''

''Laura,'' her mother gasped. Her fingers tightened. ''Remember I love you.''

''Momma, don't—''

''Promise me you'll go to Paul. Tell him—'' A harsh cough stopped her.

''Don't talk anymore,'' Laura ordered, alarmed by her mother's coughing and the pain in her dark eyes. The hand that held hers seemed to have grown colder.

''Go to Paul. Tell him I said to give you the key to the second box. And please, try to understand, dar-ling,'' she said, her voice growing weaker still. ''Try to forgive me.''

''Momma, you're not making any sense. What key? What box—''

But it was too late. Her mother's eyes closed. The hand holding hers went limp. And then came that an-guished animal scream of pain. It wasn't until much, much later that Laura realized that the scream she'd heard that night had come from her.

One

"**Y**ou don't have to do this."

Laura looked up from the second safety-deposit box she was about to open into the solemn hazel eyes of Paul Shaw, her mother's attorney and oldest friend, the honorary uncle who had seen her through the bleakness of her mother's funeral. "Yes, I do. It was the last thing…" Her voice broke, and Laura swallowed past the lump in her throat at the mention of that terrible night. "It was important to her."

Reaching across the table, her uncle covered her hands with his own. "It's only been a few weeks since the accident. You've barely recovered physically, let alone emotionally. Going through the rest of Juliet's things now is only going to upset you. Why don't you wait a few weeks? Give yourself a little more time."

But going through the remainder of her mother's legal papers and documents would be painful whenever she chose to do it, Laura reasoned. She still didn't understand why her mother had needed a second safety-deposit box or why her uncle had been listed as a signer and not her. But whatever her mother's reasons had been, they no longer mattered. *She* needed to do this for herself, Laura admitted. Once she had, maybe she'd be able to put the nightmare of her mother's death behind her. "I'd rather just get it over with now."

For a long moment, her uncle said nothing. He simply stared at her, his expression somber. "I guess you're right," he said finally, and released her hand.

Laura lifted the lid on the metal box, fully expecting to see more bonds, stock certificates and legal papers. Instead there was only a single manila envelope with a file folder inside it. After opening the folder, Laura frowned at the faded newspaper clipping of her father. Since Richard Harte had been killed shortly after marrying her mother, there had been very few pictures of him. And in those rare photos that she and her mother did have of him, he was dressed in his navy uniform.

But not in this photo. In this black-and-white shot, her father wore a tuxedo. And the bride standing beside him was not her mother. Stunned and more than a little confused, Laura glanced up from the news clipping to her uncle. "I didn't realize Daddy had been married before," she said. She would have sworn she'd known everything there was to know about her father. But then again, Laura reasoned, she could understand her mother not wanting to share this bit of information with her.

Setting the clipping aside, she picked up the next item—a birth announcement dated nearly twenty-eight years ago from a Mr. and Mrs. Andrew Jardine upon the birth of their son. There was a second announcement from the same couple dated three years later announcing the birth of twin daughters. Laura frowned again, puzzled as to why her mother had kept these announcements and why they were in her safety-deposit box. "I don't remember Momma ever mentioning anyone named Jardine. Does that name sound familiar to you, Uncle Paul?"

"He was...an old friend."

At the hesitation in her uncle's voice, uneasiness began to stir inside Laura. Telling herself that she was imagining things, she reached for the next newspaper clipping. This one was less faded, and her father didn't look quite as young as he had in the previous one. Once again he was dressed in a tuxedo and standing with the other woman. With trembling fingers, Laura smoothed out the piece of paper and read aloud the caption beneath the photo. "Mr. and Mrs. Andrew Jardine at the Krewe of Rex Mardi Gras Ball in New Orleans." Suddenly the room started to spin. Her legs nearly buckled. "This can't be right," she said, her voice barely a whisper. "There's been a mistake!"

"Laura, honey…"

Frantic, she began digging through the rest of the folder's contents. There were more newspaper clippings, announcements, magazine articles, all accompanied by photos of her father—*her* father, the man whose picture sat in her living room, the father she had been told had died before she was born. This man couldn't be her father, Laura told herself as she tried to stifle her growing panic. Her father was dead. Richard Harte had died twenty-nine years ago, while this man…this man had clearly lived far longer, long enough to have a wife and a family. She repeated the words to herself like a litany as she dug through the rest of the newspaper and magazine clippings, the articles and photos all bearing her father's image—and all identifying him as Andrew Jardine. A sob tore from Laura's throat as she spied the clipping dated only a dozen years ago of this smiling man who so resembled her father with his arms wrapped protectively around two young girls. "Andrew Jardine and twin daughters at school fund-raiser," the caption read.

Pain ripped through Laura like a storm. She

squeezed her eyes shut, curled her hands into fists. How many times growing up had she wished that her father had survived that plane crash? That he'd been there to see her grow up—to carry her on his shoulders, to teach her to dance, to sit beside her at the father-daughter banquets at school? And how many times had she consoled herself with the knowledge that had he lived, her father would have loved her, been proud of the person she had become?

Opening her eyes, Laura stared at the face in the news clippings. This man wasn't her father. He only looked like him, she reasoned. Her mother would never lie to her—certainly never about something so important. Sucking in a breath, she told herself there was a simple explanation for the resemblance between the two men. There had to me. "Uncle Paul, who is Andrew Jardine? And why...why does he look so much like my father?"

"Laura," her uncle said, his voice heavy with anguish, "Andrew Jardine *is* your father."

Laura flinched, the words hitting her like a blow. She stared down at the damning news clippings, the images of the father she'd loved and never known. No, she wouldn't believe it, refused to believe it. "You're lying," she accused, her voice hitching. She wrapped her arms around her middle. "He's not my father. My father was Richard Harte. His plane was shot down in Vietnam, and he died before I was born." She knew the story by heart, had listened to her mother's tales about their great romance, the idyllic marriage cut short by her father's untimely death. This man couldn't be her father because that would mean...

"Listen to me, Laura. There never was a Richard Harte. Your mother made up the name. Your father was

Andrew Jardine. And he didn't die in Vietnam. He died in New Orleans about five years ago."

"You're lying!" Sobbing, she glared at him through tear-filled eyes. "Why are you doing this to me, Uncle Paul? Why are you making up such horrible lies?"

"It's the truth, Laura. I swear it on your mother's grave. It's the truth."

Oh, God! He was telling the truth, she realized. All these years, her mother and her Uncle Paul had lied to her.

Which meant her life had been a lie.

She wasn't Richard Harte's daughter.

There was no Richard Harte.

The heritage, the good name she'd been so proud of all her life, they weren't really hers at all.

Hysteria bubbled inside her. How many choices had she made based on who she'd believed herself to be? How many times had she found a relationship lacking because the man had not measured up to the sterling image of her father? When all the while her father had actually been... She choked back another sob.

"I'm sorry, honey."

She thought of her mother, the person she'd loved and admired most in the world. *How could you, Momma? How could you have lied to me all these years?*

"I know what a shock this is for you, finding out this way—"

"Do you, Uncle Paul? Do you really have any idea how I feel?" Another bolt of pain ripped through her. Her heart ached as she stared at him—the honorary uncle she had loved and trusted all of her life. The man who had perpetuated the lifetime of lies her mother had told her. "I thought you loved me," she told him, her voice breaking.

"Laura, I *do* love you. I've always loved you. You're like a daughter to me." He gathered her to him, patted her back the way he had when she'd been a child and had fallen and skinned a knee.

For a moment, because the ache inside her was so great, Laura took comfort in the feel of his sturdy shoulder beneath her cheek, the familiar scents of peppermint and pipe tobacco that she'd always associated with him. She wept, remembering how she'd crawled into her uncle's lap as a little girl and listened to stories about his adventures in the navy and his close friendship with her father.

And not a word of it had been true.

The admission was like a knife in her chest. She lifted her head, took a step back and stared into his eyes. "How could Momma do this to me? How could you?"

"Neither of us meant to hurt you. Please believe that. Hurting you was the last thing either of us wanted."

Laura mopped her wet cheeks with the handkerchief he offered her, then she clenched the white linen in her fist. "All these years I believed my father was a hero, that he and my mother had been deeply in love, devoted to each other." The smiling face in the clippings on the table seemed to mock her as Laura recalled the child she had been, how each night she had gotten down on her knees and prayed for this man she'd believed to be in heaven watching over her. And all the while...all the while he hadn't been in heaven. He hadn't even been dead. He'd been alive and raising a family in New Orleans.

Pain ripped through her at the sight of him with his arms around the twin girls. She pressed her palm to her breast, trying to ease the ache in her chest. When her mother had died in her arms that night on the dark, wet road, Laura had been positive that nothing could ever hurt her so deeply again.

She had been wrong.

Learning of her mother's deception and then having the memory of the father she'd loved stripped away from her was every bit as wrenching. It was like losing both of them all over again.

"I'm sorry, Laura. I'd sooner cut off my arm than hurt you."

But he had hurt her…terribly. So had her mother. Wrapping her arms more tightly about herself, Laura ignored the twinge in her left shoulder, the reminder of the accident that had left her with a separated shoulder, bumps and bruises, but had taken her mother's life. Oh, God! She swallowed back the spurt of anguish that came as she thought of her mother asking her to forgive her. *This* was what her mother had tried to tell her that night.

"Please, try to understand."

"I don't understand. I can't," Laura countered. She looked at the jumble of clippings and photos on the table. "And I don't know what to believe anymore."

"Believe that I love you," her uncle told her, his voice softening. "And believe that from the moment your mother learned you were growing inside her and until the day that she died, she loved you, too."

"Is that why she lied to me all these years? Is that why *you* lied to me?"

He brushed his fingers along her damp cheek where the last of the bruising from the accident had begun to fade. "It wasn't my place to tell you. It was your mother's."

Laura stepped away from his touch. "And she chose to deceive me."

Her uncle sighed. His hand fell to his side. "Juliet didn't set out to deceive you. She only meant to help you. If you believe nothing else, believe that."

"Why should I?"

"Because it's the truth. You were so smart, even when you were just a little thing," he explained. "You were barely able to talk when you starting asking questions about your father. Where was he? Why did the other daddies pick up their kids from school, but your daddy never came for you? You were so eager to have a father that you even asked me if I'd be your daddy." A pained expression flitted across his face for a moment before he continued. "Anyway, your mother was worried about you. And she felt guilty for not being able to provide you with the daddy you seemed to want so much. That's when she started telling you the stories about your father."

"You mean the lies about my father, don't you?"

"She only did it to protect you. She didn't want you to think that your father hadn't wanted you."

But her father hadn't wanted her, Laura reasoned as she looked at the photograph of him with his daughters and felt that sharp sting of rejection. "My mother should have told me the truth."

"She wanted to—especially as you grew older. But she was afraid that you wouldn't be able to forgive her, that you might even hate her."

"So instead she let me believe in a father who never even existed," Laura accused. The all-too-familiar ache that she had lived with since her mother's death welled

up inside Laura again. As much as she had loved her
mother, right now, she almost hated her. And the admission both shamed and angered her. Above all, it
hurt. So much. So very much. She wanted to scream
at her mother and demand she explain. At the same
time she wanted to bury her face against her mother's
shoulder, to hug her close and breathe in that combination of talcum powder and the rose scent that her
mother wore. The tears spilled over once more,
streamed down Laura's cheeks. "How could the two
of you do it, Uncle Paul? How could you make up
those stories? How could you let me love someone who
wasn't even real?"

Her uncle washed a hand down his face. For the first
time he looked old to her, Laura thought, as though the
very life had gone right out of him. He picked up an
aging photo of the handsome navy officer and the dark-
eyed brunette and traced the worn edges with his index
finger. "He *was* real, Laura. Not everything was a lie.
Twenty-nine years ago your father really was my best
friend. We were flight buddies serving in the same unit.
And your mother really was a WAVE nurse working
at the base hospital in San Diego when she met Drew."

Drew. Hearing her father referred to by the strange
name shook Laura. Andrew Jardine was her father—
not Richard Harte. She clamped down on the churning
in her stomach that came with the realization. This was
something she had to face, a problem she had to deal
with, she told herself. Drawing in a deep breath, she
reminded herself that she dealt with problems every
day in her job as the assistant general manager at the
Ambassador Grand Hotel. She would deal with this
problem as she would any other—by listening, gathering information and analyzing the data. Then she

would decide how to proceed, how to deal with the fact that she wasn't the person she'd thought she was.

"I was with Drew when he met Juliet for the first time. He was recovering from knee surgery and hadn't been cleared to drive yet, so I took him to the hospital for his first physical therapy session. I remember it like it was only yesterday," he said. Her uncle continued to stare at the photograph. "Drew and I were sitting in the waiting room, joking about how he had to get his knee in shape so he could dance at his wedding that summer. Then we heard this angel's voice calling his name. When we looked up, there she was. This vision with wild dark hair and sparkling brown eyes. I think Drew fell in love with Juliet right there on the spot. And Juliet...well, she felt the same way about him."

"Did she...did my mother know he was engaged?"

"Yes," Paul admitted. "Drew was honest with her. He told Juliet right from the start about Adrienne."

Laura's heart sank. *Her mother had known he was an engaged man. And the two of them had had an affair, anyway.* She felt the bitterness of disappointment as she digested that information. Only now could she admit to herself that she had been hoping for some plausible explanation, some tale about them being star-crossed lovers, anything to excuse her mother's actions. She had wanted, needed to believe that the relationship had been innocent, that she hadn't been a mistake.

As though he knew what she was thinking, her uncle said, "Don't judge them too harshly, Laura. They tried to fight their feelings for each other. But Drew was at the hospital three times a week for more than two months for therapy and Juliet couldn't very well claim that she was unable to do her job because she was in love with her patient. She was a WAVE nurse. She didn't have that option.''

"She could have walked away from him. And he could have left her alone.''

"You don't know what it's like to be in love, really in love, the way they were,'' her uncle told her. "That type of love, it doesn't happen for everyone. If you're lucky, it might find you once. And when it does, it grabs you by the throat and takes charge of your heart and soul, and it refuses to let go.'' The smile he gave her was fleeting. "Even if you're able to walk away from it, how you feel about the other person doesn't change. You don't stop loving him or her. Juliet and Drew could no more have stopped loving each other than you or I could stop an earthquake from happening. Your mother was in love with Drew, and he was in love with her.''

"Then why didn't they do the right thing? Why didn't he break his engagement and marry my mother if he loved her so much?''

Paul rubbed a hand across his brow as though his head were aching. "It was complicated. The Jardine family is an old, distinguished family in New Orleans. Things were done differently in the South, particularly back then. Drew couldn't just break off his engagement because he'd fallen in love with your mother. There were other people who had to be considered, other families whose livelihoods were dependent upon his marriage to Adrienne.''

"You make it sound like a business merger.''

"In many ways it was. Drew's family was in the hotel business and so were the Duboises—Adrienne's family.''

That bit of news came as a shock to Laura. Then she

remembered the newspaper clippings with the photo of
Andrew Jardine accepting an award in front of a hotel.
A shudder went through Laura as she thought of the
career she'd chosen in hotel management. *Had her
mother encouraged her interest because she'd known
about the Jardine family's business? Or had her choice
of profession served as a painful reminder to her
mother of the man she had loved and lost?* Either option left Laura feeling sick inside.

"Drew was an only child with a widowed mother.
He had responsibilities to her, to the other members of
his family, to the people who worked for them. He
couldn't just walk away from those responsibilities."

"So he walked away from his responsibility to my
mother instead."

Her uncle shook his head. "It wasn't like that. He
wrote to his mother, telling her about Juliet, that he
loved her and wanted to break his engagement to Adrienne. Naturally, his mother was upset. Adrienne and
Drew had grown up together, had been childhood
sweethearts. Her parents were old friends and Olivia
Jardine, your grandmother…"

A shiver went through Laura as she heard the woman
referred to as her grandmother. She'd never had a
grandmother. And though she'd often wished her
mother had had an extended family, she didn't want
one now—not this way.

"…Olivia loved Adrienne like a daughter, and Juliet…well, your mother was a stranger and not even
from the South. Olivia insisted Drew come home to
discuss the situation before he did anything. So he did
as she asked. He went back to New Orleans, and then
he sent for Juliet."

"What happened?" Laura asked, her curiosity overriding her hurt and disappointment.

"I'm not really sure. Neither Juliet nor Drew ever told me exactly what went down."

They didn't need to because she had a pretty good idea of what had transpired, Laura decided. Olivia Jardine hadn't wanted anything to do with her son's bastard child. Had her father wanted her? she wondered. Obviously, he hadn't. She had been a mistake, the unexpected result of his fling with her mother. The realization left her feeling hollow inside. Turning away, Laura spied the clipping on the table of her father and his children. And as she looked at the photo of the Jardine family, Laura thought of her own life, all the years she had ached to know him, to be loved by him.

"Only your mother and Drew know what happened and why Juliet came back from New Orleans alone."

"Unfortunately, they're gone now and can't tell us," she said, her voice hoarse with the effort it took not to cry. "But here I am—their shameful mistake."

"Your mother was never ashamed of you. She never considered you a mistake."

"Somehow I doubt that the Jardine family would agree with her."

Two

New Orleans, Louisiana

"It's about time you showed up."

Handing his coat to the houseman, Josh Logan glanced across the elegant parlor at Olivia Jardine. Despite the business rivalry between their families that spanned more than half a century, Josh admired the crusty old gal. "Good afternoon to you, too, Duchess."

"Don't call me by that ridiculous name," Olivia reprimanded, pinning him with crystal-blue eyes that belied her eighty-one years. "I dislike it. And I dislike to be kept waiting. I called you over an hour ago."

"And I came as soon as I could," Josh countered as he made his way over to the iron-willed woman who had been at the helm of the Royal Princess Hotel for as long as he could remember. Even seated in the wheelchair, Olivia Jardine remained a formidable figure. With her head held high, her spine straight and diamonds winking at her ears, she reminded him of a queen. The royal moniker he'd tagged her with twenty years ago when he'd been a brash teenager still fit her perfectly. He could almost understand how a fiery, younger Olivia had managed to ensnare his grandfather's youthful heart. But to this day, he still didn't understand how Simon Logan had let his feelings for Olivia cost him the Princess Hotel.

"Considering your interest in the Princess, I'd have thought you'd be more eager to meet with me."

Josh's heart stopped, then started again at the mention of the Princess Hotel. It had been because he was so eager that he had deliberately waited after receiving Olivia's summons. "I'm always eager to see you," he said smoothly. "And as I said, I came as soon as I could."

Olivia arched her brow. "Your grandfather could charm the skin off of a snake with his pretty words. I see you've inherited his charm as well as his looks." Leaning forward slightly, she stared at his face out of eyes that seemed to measure him. "Tell me, Joshua. Have you inherited Simon's spirit of adventure as well? Or do you shy away from taking risks?"

Josh smiled at the challenge in her voice and considered some of the more outlandish deals he'd pulled off over the years for Logan Hotels. "Oh, I've been known to take a risk or two," he said evenly. "Of course, the prize would have to be worth the risk."

"I assume you'd consider the Princess a suitable prize?" she asked smoothly.

Yes! Josh wanted to shout the word aloud, to pump his fist in the air. He did neither. And though it took every ounce of control he possessed, he managed not to give any hint of the excitement humming in his blood. This was it. The moment he had looked forward to for more than half of his thirty-three years—making good on his promise to his grandfather to reclaim the Princess Hotel.

As though it were only yesterday instead of almost

twenty years ago, he remembered standing inside the lobby of the Princess with his grandfather....

"If only you could have known how it felt to own her, Josh, my lad. To see this vision in your head take shape, to watch mortar and glass and brick come together, to see the dream you've carried inside you come to life and create this thing of beauty. Ah, and she was a beauty, my Princess—even before I lost her to Livvy and she fancied her up with those antiques and expensive whatnots. All a body had to do was walk through her doors, stand on these polished marble floors in the lobby to know it, too. One look up at those crystal chandeliers gleaming like giant diamonds or a whiff of those pretty flowers stuffed in the giant urns, and a person felt like he was royalty. That's why I named her the Princess."

"Let's buy her back," Josh urged.

"Oh, I'd like to, lad. Believe me, I'd like to. It's been my dream for as long as I can remember. But I'm afraid Livvy won't sell her. I've asked more than once, but she loves the Princess as much as I do. No, I'm afraid the Princess is lost to us."

"But it should be yours. You built her," Josh argued.

"Aye, I did, lad. But I lost her fair and square. She belongs to Livvy now—not to us Logans."

"I'll get the Princess back for you, Granddad. I swear I will. Someday she'll belong to the Logans again. I promise."

And that day had finally arrived. The rumors had been circulating for months in the business community that the old luxury hotel was taking financial hits in the fiercely competitive New Orleans market. The fact that Olivia was slowing down and had refused to turn over the reins to anyone had made selling the property the logical thing to do, Josh reasoned. Olivia Jardine was a shrewd businesswoman—shrewd enough to know that the only person likely to pay her top dollar for the aging hotel was the family of the man who'd lost it to her in that crazy bet fifty-six years ago.

"Am I to assume from your silence that you consider the Princess worthy of a few risks?"

"Given my most recent offer to buy the place, I think you already know the answer to that. I take it you've had a chance to review the offer?"

"I glanced at it," she said, her tone noncommital, her expression inscrutable. She maneuvered her wheelchair over to the antique table and pointed to the chair opposite hers. "Do sit down, Joshua. I'm getting a crick in my neck looking up at you."

Josh did as she instructed and took the seat across from her. "It's a good offer."

"It's a *fair* offer," she corrected him. "Tell me, Joshua. Just how badly do you want the Princess?"

"Bad enough to pay you more than it's worth, but not enough to kill you for it."

Her mouth twitched, and for a moment Josh thought she might actually smile. She didn't. Instead she said, "I appreciate your honesty. It's one of the things I've always liked about you."

"Thank you," Josh said, eager to end this cat-and-mouse game that Olivia was playing with him.

"So I'll be equally honest with you. I have no intention of selling the Princess."

Her words hit him like a sucker punch, and he had to bite back the oath on the tip of his tongue. Reminding himself of his first rule in negotiating with an opponent—to never reveal what he was feeling—Josh managed to keep his expression neutral while frustration churned inside him like acid. It was a skill that he'd honed in his eight years as head of acquisitions for Logan Hotels and one that had paid off handsomely for him and his family. He'd dealt with tougher negotiators than Olivia Jardine and for hotels of far greater value. Yet when it came to the Princess, the very first hotel built by Simon Logan, it was difficult not to let his emotions come into play. The Princess had always been more than brick and mortar and stone to him, Josh admitted. He'd fallen in love with the place as a boy while listening to his grandfather's stories. To see the Logan Hotels banner flying over the Princess again had been his dream for as long as he could remember. And, once again, that dream remained just out of reach.

"You have a good poker face. I'll give you that."

"Are we playing poker, Duchess?"

"In a manner of speaking." She paused. "But before we go over the rules of this particular game, I could use a brandy. Why don't you pour us each a glass?"

Josh did as she asked, filling the heavy crystal glasses with the expensive vintage while he reined in his emotions. After he handed Olivia her glass, she took a sip, then leaned back in her chair.

The urge to toss back the brandy was so strong, Josh deliberately drank slowly, savoring the bite of the liquor and wanting to wash away the taste of disappointment in his mouth. When he reclaimed his seat, his emotions were in check once more. Deciding there was no point in pushing Olivia, he remained silent and waited for her to continue the game.

"I'm sure by now you've heard the rumors that the Princess is losing money."

He had. Despite the size of the city, New Orleans remained very much a small town in many respects. There was little that went on in the business or personal lives of its more prominent citizens that stayed a secret for long. And the Jardines had always been news makers. "I've heard the Princess has been feeling the pinch from the competition."

Olivia snorted. "You and I both know that the Princess has been feeling more than a pinch. I've lost a small fortune keeping the doors open this past year alone. And I'm sure you also know that my family and financial advisers believe I should sell it."

"Maybe they're right, Duchess. I've offered you a good price. Why don't we save ourselves some time and dispense with the game-playing. Just tell me straight-out what price tag you've set on her."

All humor faded in an instant. "There isn't a price tag," she told him. "The Princess is not for sale. At least not at this time."

"But—"

"Hear me out," she said, lifting her hand.

Josh nodded, settled back in his seat.

"When your grandfather built the Princess it was with the intention that she become the grand lady of New Orleans. After Simon...lost her to me in that foolish bet, I made sure that she lived up to his dream. I turned her into the finest hotel in this city," she told him, an intense light in her eyes. "I want to see the Princess returned to her throne, Joshua. Once I see that happen, I'll turn over the reins."

Josh couldn't help it. Hope stirred in his blood again. "If it's help you need, I can recommend a good management company, put together a team for you and help you turn the place around before you sell it to me.''

Olivia shook her head. "I don't want some stranger running the Princess. From the day your grandfather signed her over to me, she's been run by a Jardine.''

Josh sighed. "Katie told me she offered to take over running it for you months ago, and you turned her down.''

"Katherine already has her hands full running the Regent. And before you suggest Alison, it's out of the question. She has enough on her plate taking care of her daughter and helping her sister.''

"And Mitch isn't an option," Josh added, referring to Olivia's grandson.

"Mitchell made it clear years ago that he wasn't interested in the hotel business. Besides, it appears his security business is doing quite nicely.''

"That leaves Adrienne.''

"My daughter-in-law would be the first one to tell you that she's far too busy with her charities and social functions to even consider working at the hotel, let alone trying to manage it,'' Olivia informed him.

"The only other Jardine left is you," Josh pointed out.

She sighed. "And as much as I hate to admit it, I'm getting too old to deal with the daily demands of running the hotel.''

"Which brings us back to my suggestion—bring in an outside manager to get the hotel back on its feet before you sell it to me. It's your only option.''

"Not necessarily," Olivia told him. "There is another alternative—one that would keep operation of the Princess in Jardine hands.''

His curiosity piqued, Josh couldn't shake the feeling

that the old gal was up to something that he wasn't going to like. "Do you intend to tell me who this mysterious Jardine relative is, or am I supposed to guess?"

"My granddaughter. Or I suppose I should say, my *other* granddaughter."

"All right. You've got my attention, Duchess," Josh said. "You care to explain that?"

"It's quite simple. I have a fourth grandchild."

Before Josh had time to recover from the shock of that statement, Olivia continued, "Recently I learned that Andrew has another child. A daughter, the result of a…a liaison that Andrew had with a young nurse in San Diego before his marriage to Adrienne."

Speechless, Josh could only stare at her. A Jardine with a child out of wedlock? While the rest of the world might have entered the new millennium, in this tight-knit corner of the South the moral climate remained stalled in another century—particularly when it concerned a member of one of the city's most prominent families. The social mores simply didn't allow for an admission to anything as potentially scandalous as the existence of a love child. And while, personally, he didn't give a damn what the city's holier-than-thou upper-crust members thought or wrote about him in their gossip columns, Olivia Jardine did care. She always had. A member of the city's old guard, she lived by a different set of rules. So did most people in her circle. And Olivia had always insisted her family toe the line of responsibility that came with their good name. "I don't know what to say."

"I don't expect you to say anything. For now, I'd just like you to listen."

But as he listened, Josh couldn't figure out why on earth Olivia had decided to tell him about what must surely be a great embarrassment for her. Nor could he believe that she could seriously be considering bringing this supposed granddaughter into the family fold.

"The girl's name is Laura Harte. She's twenty-eight and lives in San Francisco. She works for a hotel there as an assistant general manager."

"She's in the hotel business?" Josh asked, and wondered at the odds of Olivia's illegitimate grandchild being in the same field of business. More than likely, the girl had been steered into that particular career direction by a clever mother with eyes on the Jardine fortune, he decided. Otherwise, he'd have to chalk up the ironic twist of fate as a coincidence. And he didn't believe in coincidences.

"I understand your reaction. I had a similar one when I first heard," she explained, evidently detecting his skepticism. "That's why I hired a private investigator and had her checked out. Here's a copy of the report."

Intrigued and still unsure why Olivia was telling him all this, Josh picked up the file she'd slid across the table. Opening it, he shuffled through the paperwork. Quickly he scanned the detective reports, birth certificate, old school and employment records. But when he came to the photograph, he paused. With four beautiful sisters and a healthy appreciation for the feminine gender in general, he was no stranger to striking women and had been involved with more than a few.

Laura Harte was definitely a striking woman.

It was her hair, he reasoned. The color of a summer sunset—dark flame shot with gold. The wild color seemed at odds with the no-nonsense style she'd chosen. And there was something about the angle of that stubborn chin that reminded him of Olivia. So did that in-your-face confidence he read in her blue eyes. Then there was her mouth. It was too wide for her narrow face, he reasoned. But her smile…her smile was part siren, part angel, he decided, and felt the inexplicable tug of desire. This was crazy, he told himself, whooshing out a breath as he dropped the folder back onto the table top. Definitely not his type. He liked petite blondes with curves—not tall, skinny redheads.

"The girl lost her mother a couple of months ago," Olivia told him. "According to the information I received, she's only recently learned the truth about who her father was."

"It's an interesting story and I'm glad that you felt you could share it with me. You have my word that I won't say anything."

"I never thought you would. But sooner or later, the word will get out."

"Not from me," Josh assured her. "But what I don't understand is why you told me? You've apparently already made up your mind to have this Laura Harte take over operation of the *Princess.*"

"I told you because I need you," Olivia informed him, an odd note in her voice. "In fact, my entire plan hinges on you."

"Me?"

"Yes. I need you to go to San Francisco and meet with my granddaughter and convince her to come to New Orleans to meet her father's family."

Caught off guard by the request, Josh asked, "But why me? I mean, it would seem more appropriate to send a family member. Maybe Mitch or Katie or even Alison? After all, this woman is *their* sister."

"Half sister," Olivia corrected him. "They don't

even know the girl exists yet. And when they find out, I'm not sure they'll welcome the news.''

She was probably right, Josh realized. As Olivia's heirs, the Jardine siblings stood to inherit a fortune. Regardless of how sizable the inheritance, the sudden appearance of another sister would mean a cut in the others' shares. Josh took another swallow of his brandy, felt the smooth heat at the back of his throat and tried to imagine how he would feel if he were Mitch, Katie or Alison. How would he feel if he were to learn that he had another sister who was the result of an affair his father had had years before with another woman? Try as he might, the idea refused to compute. Probably because he still had both of his parents, and they were clearly in love with each other. On the other hand, the Jardine trio had lost their father years ago. Knowing how much they had all worshiped the man, Josh suspected the news that their father had had feet of clay would not be welcome—especially not by Katie. Of Andrew's three children, Katie had been the one closest to her father. ''When do you plan to tell them?''

''When the time is right. In the meantime, I need you to go to San Francisco and convince Laura to come to New Orleans.''

Josh shook his head. ''You don't need me, Duchess. Considering the state's forced heirship laws, this Laura Harte stands to inherit a fortune as your granddaughter someday, as well as a portion of her father's estate. My guess is one phone call from you telling her that will be all the convincing that she'll need.''

''I did call her, and the girl informed me that she'd been well provided for in her mother's will and that she had no need or interest in the Jardine money. She also said she had no interest in meeting me or in establishing any type of relationship with her father's other children.''

''Obviously she's not nearly as bright as those reports indicated.''

''Or perhaps she's smart enough to realize that material wealth isn't nearly as important as most people believe.''

For a moment Josh thought he saw pain flicker in Olivia's eyes. Despite the headaches this woman's refusal to sell the Princess had caused him over the years, he couldn't help but feel sad for her. Growing up in a family far less reserved than the Jardines, Josh didn't stop to consider his action. He simply reached across the desk and squeezed Olivia's fingers. ''Whatever her reasons for refusing, the loss is hers, Duchess. She could have learned a great deal from you.''

''Thank you,'' she whispered, and withdrew her hand. She straightened her shoulders, her expression as stern as her voice, then said, ''But I have no intention of accepting her refusal. That's why I'm sending you to San Francisco, so you can convince her to come.''

Josh shook his head. ''Count me out, Duchess. This is a family matter. I'm not about to get involved. Maybe you can send one of your attorneys and let him or her explain to Miss Harte exactly what it is she's saying no to.''

''I want *you* to go, Joshua.''

''Duchess—''

''I want your opinion of the girl.''

''Why? It looks to me like you've already checked her out thoroughly,'' he told her, motioning to the file folder.

She dismissed the report with a wave of her hand.

"I'm not interested in the opinion of some overpriced detective or lawyer who will candy-coat things and tell me what they think I want to hear." She leaned forward. "I want *your* opinion."

"I appreciate your confidence in me," he said, and meant it. "But I don't see what my meeting her could possibly tell you that you don't already know."

"Modesty doesn't suit you any better than it did your grandfather, Joshua. I've heard you have very good instincts when it comes to people. I want to know if my granddaughter has inherited more than the Jardine eyes. I want to know if she's got the grit of a Jardine and can be trusted with the Princess."

Because he didn't know what to say, Josh remained silent.

"Will you do it? Will you go to San Francisco and convince Laura to come to New Orleans?"

Torn between his own desire to reclaim the Princess and the anxiety he heard in Olivia's voice, Josh opted to be honest with her. "You know I want the Princess. My helping you bring this Laura Harte here to run it would be like cutting my own throat. You'd only end up turning it over to her. The smart thing for me to do is not to help you and let the place continue to bleed money. Eventually you'll have to cut your losses. And when you do, I'll buy the hotel."

"But that's where you're wrong," she informed him. "I told you, I'm not interested in selling the Princess. And I assure you, I am not going to change my mind."

Frustrated, Josh said, "Then I guess we're both wasting our time."

"Oh, sit down," she ordered when he started to rise. "I said I wouldn't sell you the Princess. But if you'll help me, convince my granddaughter to come home to run the hotel, then I'll give you a chance to win it.''

Josh narrowed his eyes. ''Win the Princess? How?''

''The same way that I won her from your grandfather.''

''I'm listening,'' Josh told her, intrigued even though he tried not to be.

''If my granddaughter turns out to be the woman I believe she is, I'll turn over management of the hotel to the two of you. You'll have six months to turn the operation around. At the end of that time if the hotel shows a profit, no matter how small, I'll sign over ownership to Laura and—''

''Forget it. I'm not interested in working for you, Duchess. And I'm not interested in a partnership with your long-lost granddaughter,'' Josh countered, sure he knew where Olivia was heading. ''I'll buy the Princess from you right now. Name your price.''

''You're just as pigheaded as your grandfather was,'' Olivia accused, her mouth tightening. ''For Simon it had to be all or nothing, too. That's why he insisted on that foolish wager with my father. If Simon won, I would break my engagement to Henry Jardine and marry him. If I won, Simon would sign over the Princess Hotel to me and get out of my life forever.''

''And you won.''

''Yes, I won,'' Olivia said. Wheeling over to a secretary situated in a corner of the room, she opened a drawer and retrieved a small package before returning to where Josh waited. She placed a deck of cards bound with a faded gold ribbon in the center of the table, then lifted her gaze to Josh's. ''I'm offering you a similar wager, Joshua. I'll give you a chance to win back Simon's Princess. Convince Laura to come to New Orleans, to work with you and turn the hotel around. If you're successful, at the end of the six months, the two of you will draw cards just as your grandfather and I did fifty-six years ago.''

"And the stakes?'' Josh asked, unable to believe what she was offering him.

"The deed to the Princess.'' She loosened the ribbon from around the cards, placed the deck in front of him and met his gaze once more. "One game. High-card draw. Winner takes all.''

"It sounds almost too good to be true.''

"I asked if you were a risk-taker. You assured me you were—if the stakes were right.''

The stakes *were* more than right. They were downright incredible. He shoved a hand through his hair.

"Joshua?''

"Six months isn't much time to turn a hotel operation around,'' he argued as he began to analyze the pitfalls in the crazy scheme. "What if we can't pull the hotel out of the red that quickly?''

"Then all bets are off. I keep the Princess.''

"And there's always the chance that even if we succeed in pulling the hotel out of the red, that Laura will win the card game.''

"True. But I can't help thinking you might have better luck convincing Laura to sell you the hotel than you'll have with me.''

Of course, she was right. Still, it was too easy, Josh thought. The way she had laid out the plan, the worst thing that could happen is he'd be right where he was now—without the Princess. On the other hand, he could win and end up owning the Princess for nothing more than a little of his time and effort. Or he could find himself negotiating with Olivia's granddaughter to buy the place. He thought of the woman in the photograph again, remembered the unshakable confidence in those blue eyes, that stubborn take-your-best-shot tilt of her chin.

"I must admit, I expected more eagerness on your part at a chance to win back the Princess."

She was playing with him, Josh realized as he rubbed at his chin. "Unlike my grandfather, I try to look before I leap."

"Then why don't I see if I can help you make up your mind?" she replied calmly. Her lips curved slightly, and he knew she was about to put him between a rock and a hard place. "Either you go along with things as I've laid them out, or you'll have to wait until I'm dead before you get another chance to bring the Princess under the Logan Hotels banner."

When he still hesitated, she said, "Just so you know, I had my annual physical last week. Despite whatever rumors you may have heard and the fact that I might use this chair occasionally, my doctor claims I'm in excellent health and could live another twenty years. And if you think that I won't be able to sustain the losses at the Princess, you'd better think again. The other Jardine properties and investments are even healthier than I am."

"You're a hell of a poker player yourself, Duchess."

"So I've been told," she replied.

Josh thought of his grandfather again, remembered the way the older man's face had lit up whenever he'd spoken about the Princess, the way his eyes had glowed with pride as he'd talked about building the hotel. And he remembered the promise he'd made to him all those years ago.

"What's it going to be?" Olivia asked.

He was crazy to even consider this, Josh told himself. His grandfather had been dead for more than five years. Did it really matter if he kept his promise now that he was gone?

It mattered, Josh admitted. He'd made a promise, and his grandfather had taught him that a man always lived up to his promises. He stared across the table at Olivia, and couldn't help but feel that he was about to make a bargain with the devil, a bargain he would come to regret.

"Do we have a deal?"

"Yes, Duchess. We have a deal."

And as he tapped his glass against Olivia's to seal the bargain they'd made, Josh's gaze fell to the open folder on the desk where Laura Harte's picture stared up at him. There it was again—that slam-in-the-gut punch of attraction. And he couldn't help wondering if he had inherited Simon Logan's impulsive streak after all.

Three

"**Y**ou had no right to contact her, Uncle Paul," Laura said, still reeling from the call she'd received from Olivia Jardine three days earlier. She stared down at the Caesar salad she'd ordered in the hotel's café and recalled how the older woman had practically ordered Laura to come to New Orleans.

"I'm sorry. I never meant to upset you like this."

At the expression on her uncle's face, Laura immediately regretted her sharp tone. "I know you meant well. But you shouldn't have contacted her."

"I was worried about you," her uncle explained. "I'm *still* worried about you. Look at you. You've lost weight. There are shadows under your eyes. I hate seeing you like this."

"I'm fine," Laura insisted, even though she knew that in the two months since the accident, her injuries may have healed, but the pain of her mother's deception and the shock of learning the truth about her father had taken its toll.

"Then how come the only time you leave your apartment these days is to go to work? And why can't I even remember the last time I saw you smile?"

"Maybe because losing my mother and then finding out everything I believed about myself was a lie hasn't exactly left me in a mood to party or smile lately."

Her uncle visibly flinched.

"I'm sorry, Uncle Paul. That was uncalled for," she said, and reached for his hand, shamed that she'd hurt him with harsh words. "I shouldn't be taking my frustrations out on you."

"It's okay." He gave her hand a gentle squeeze. "I know this hasn't been an easy time for you."

No, it hadn't been easy. It had been a nightmare. And even though she'd told herself a hundred times that nothing had changed, that she was still the same person now that she'd been before learning the truth, she didn't *feel* the same. She felt different, as though she'd been stripped of her identity, of who and what she was.

"You've been dealt several blows at once. That's why I contacted Olivia Jardine. I thought that perhaps…maybe if you were to meet your family and—"

"They are *not* my family," Laura informed him, snatching her hand free. "My name is Laura Harte— not Jardine." She reached for the glass of tea with unsteady fingers. She refused to think of Andrew Jardine as her father or any of his relatives as her family.

"Laura, if you'd just—"

"You'll have to excuse me, Uncle Paul. I really do need to get back to work." She tossed down her napkin and stood, eager to retreat to her office and put an end to the discussion.

Her uncle frowned as he rose. "Will I see you for brunch on Sunday?"

Pain swift and sharp hit her as memories flooded back—memories of the Sunday brunches shared with her uncle and her mother for most of her childhood and a great number of her adult years. It had been a lovely ritual, but now it, too, was a part of the past. "I'm afraid I can't make it. I promised the Realtor who's going to list mother's house that I would finish packing up this weekend so they can begin showing the house next week."

"You're selling Juliet's house?"

The devastation in her uncle's voice matched his expression. She'd long suspected Paul Shaw's feelings for her mother ran much deeper than those of a friend. Losing her had been as difficult for him as it had been for her, Laura realized. She touched his arm. "It's for the best, Uncle Paul. A house needs to be lived in."

"But it's your home, too."

Laura shook her head. "It hasn't been for a long time now. It's too far out for me to commute every day. And you know I work crazy hours and weekends. The house is being neglected, and it shows. Mother would hate that. It's better if I sell it to someone who'll take care of it properly."

"Juliet loved that house."

"I know." Her mother had adored the country cottage, and she'd spent countless hours tending its gardens. But each time she'd been to the house since her mother's death, Laura found herself missing her mother more. "She's gone now, and I have to let her go. We both do, Uncle Paul. We need to get on with our lives."

"Yes. You're right, of course," he said, his voice sad but resigned.

"Listen, I'd better get back upstairs before they send out a search party." She kissed his weathered cheek.

When she started to withdraw, he held on to her. "I really am sorry. About…about everything."

"I know," she whispered, and gave his cheek a pat before stepping back. She was sorry, too—sorry to have the fantasies she'd believed about her parents shattered into a million pieces.

Some of her thoughts must have shown on her face because her uncle caught her off guard when he said, "Maybe it would be a good idea if you were to talk to someone...a professional—"

"No." Laura stepped back from him, eager to escape. The last thing she wanted was to share the shameful truth she'd discovered. How could she possibly tell anyone that the father she'd worshiped all her life had actually been a philanderer? A man who had abandoned his pregnant lover and child so that he could marry his society bride and father three legitimate children? Anger welled up inside Laura again—toward her mother, toward the man responsible for giving her life. How she wished that she'd never learned the truth, that the secrets had gone with her mother to the grave.

"But—"

"Thanks, Uncle Paul. But really, I'm fine."

Only she wasn't fine, Laura admitted the next afternoon as she rummaged through her desk drawer for a file. Her fingers stilled when she spied the framed snapshot of her parents. Her heart ached at the sight of the photograph that, until two months ago, had sat on her credenza. After learning the truth about her father, she'd banished the picture to the back of her desk drawer, hoping to banish with it the ache of betrayal. It hadn't worked, she realized as she retrieved the photograph. Grief and anger warred within her as she stared at her mother's young and smiling face. "Oh, Momma, I miss you so much," she whispered, tears filling her eyes.

She traced the edges of the small pewter frame and

thought of all the years her mother had spent alone. Wasted years in which her mother had turned away suitors, claiming she had found and lost the only man she would ever love. Laura squeezed her eyes shut and recalled her mother's voice, the dreamy look on her face whenever she'd spoken about her fairy-tale romance, her great love and loss.

And it had all been a lie.

Just as her childhood, her very identity, had all been rooted in that lie.

Opening her eyes, Laura stared at the face of the handsome navy lieutenant with his arm wrapped around her mother.

Her father.

Not Richard Harte. Not the dashing hero she'd loved and respected and longed for all of her life. Her father was the wealthy, irresponsible Andrew Jardine—the man who had so carelessly discarded her mother and gone back to his society life. It wasn't fair, Laura thought as anger burned in her heart toward the man. *He* had led a full life. *He* had had a wife, other children. While her mother…her mother had been left with a life built on lies and a child to raise alone.

The intercom on her desk buzzed, jarring Laura from her thoughts. She shoved the picture back into the desk drawer and reined in her emotions. ''Yes?''

''Hello, sunshine.''

Laura smiled at the sound of Nick Baldwin's voice. The general manager and owner of the Ambassador Grand and her boss for the past year, Nick was smart, charming and one of the nicest men she'd ever known. He was also one of the best-looking—a fact that was not lost on the hotel's female guests or staff.

''How's my favorite assistant GM this afternoon?''

Laura chuckled at his remark. "I'm fine. And in case you haven't noticed, I'm your *only* assistant GM," she reminded him.

"That's right! How on earth could I make a mistake like that?"

"Beats me."

"Maybe it's because you do enough work around here for two people."

"And maybe I'm wondering why you're laying it on so thick," she teased.

"Just stating the facts."

A rush of gratitude spilled through her at Nick's praise. He was a great boss, one who never failed to let her know she was appreciated. He was also a dear friend and had proved so often during the past couple of months. She could think of few people who would have done what he had—handling the arrangements for her mother's funeral, insisting she take as much time as she needed before coming back to work even though the hotel was extraordinarily busy. And there had been genuine worry in Nick's eyes last week when he'd expressed concern about how she was holding up. Yet as much as she liked and respected Nick, she hadn't been able to tell him the truth. She wasn't sure she ever could tell him or anyone.

"Laura, you still there?"

Shaking off her gloomy thoughts, Laura attempted to recapture the happy mood Nick's call had sparked. "Right here and worrying because I have a feeling that you're about to drop some major catastrophe in my lap."

"You're a cynic, Ms. Harte."

"Hardly, Mr. Baldwin," she said with a laugh. "I distinctly recall the last time you were laying on praise this thick. It was just before you told me that the hotel was overbooked and I had to find fifty rooms pronto.''

''An honest mistake. Besides, I wasn't the one who failed to block the space in the hotel's main system.''

''Yes, I remember whose fault that was,'' she conceded. She was sure that Nick remembered, too. The fault had rested on the very attractive, man-hunting reservation agent in the hotel's sales department who had been so busy trying to catch Nick's eye that she tended to let minor things like her job slide.

''The important thing to remember is that it all worked out okay.''

It had. Thanks to her scrambling like mad and absorbing the cost of those extra rooms at a neighboring hotel. The unexpected expense had played havoc with her budget, but she'd taken the hit to preserve the goodwill of the account.

''You got a few minutes?''

Laura eyed the file folder on her desk. ''I was about to go over the meeting room charts for the cardiologists' convention that's arriving tomorrow before I sign off on it. After that, I'm free.''

''Great. How about coming by my office when you've finished?''

''Sure.'' She paused, worried over her last conversation with Nick. She didn't want to get into another discussion with him about what he perceived as her unhappiness lately. ''Was there something in particular you wanted to see me about?''

''Actually, there's someone that I'd like you to meet.''

A prospective client, Laura guessed, and felt a measure of relief. Perhaps it was just what she needed—the challenge of a tough new account to sink her teeth into and get her mind off of her own troubles. "Give me ten minutes to wrap this up and I'll be there."

Josh sat across from Nick Baldwin and listened to his old college friend's side of the conversation with Laura Harte. In many ways, he and Nick were a lot alike, he thought. They both came from families whose fortunes had been made in the small luxury-hotel business. They both had grown up knowing that one day they, too, would be a part of the family business. And they both had been part of a dwindling breed of hoteliers who still retained ownership of the family hotels. Many family-owned chains like the Fairmont had done as its owners the Swigs had done—sold their interests to some Saudi prince or hotel conglomerate. The Logans hadn't. Nor had the Jardines. And neither had the Baldwins—at least not voluntarily.

From what Nick had told him when they'd been at college, Big Jack Baldwin had managed to gamble all four family hotels away before his son hit eighteen. But from what he knew and the buzz in the industry, Nick had not only reclaimed the hotels lost by his father, he was on his way to buying more. And although Logan Hotels far outranked the Jardine and Baldwin family operations because of the number of hotel properties they held, all three families remained part of the elite group of hoteliers whose name was synonymous with luxury. Given what he'd seen of the Ambassador Grand, Nick was maintaining the tradition.

Josh grinned as he thought back to the first time he'd met Nick—a dozen years ago when the two of them had both been enrolled in the university's hotel management program and working nights for Logan Hotels. He'd have sworn the two of them had had absolutely nothing in common. He'd pegged Nick as a West Coast prick whose rich family had used their connections to get him a job. In turn, Baldwin had pegged Josh as a dumb-wit Southern boy who didn't know squat about hotels. They'd both been proved wrong. After several minor clashes, the two of them had been sharing drinks and dreams. The friendship had waned due to time, distance and Nick's romance with Josh's sister. But he'd decided to use what remained of the old friendship, anyway, as a means to reach Laura Harte. Instead of approaching Laura with Olivia's request at her home, he'd opted to do so on neutral turf. He'd also wanted to get a chance to see her in action.

"She'll be here in a couple of minutes," Nick said as he hung up the phone.

"Thanks," Josh said, dragging his thoughts back to the reason he was there—to try to convince Laura Harte to come to New Orleans and meet her family. Too edgy to sit, he stood and began to prowl the spacious office. He stopped in front of the window and admired the view of the bay. "I owe you one."

"I'll settle for you telling me what this personal business is you want to discuss with Laura."

Josh paused. Turning, he studied the wary brown eyes of his old friend. "I can't. You'll just have to trust me when I tell you that it's personal and I'm here as a favor to a friend." Yet even as he said the words, guilt plagued him. He seriously doubted that Olivia could be classified as a friend. At the admission, he once again cursed his decision to take Olivia up on her crazy offer. *Why had he allowed himself to be talked into this mess?* Just as quickly as the question formed, so did the answer—*the Princess*. He wanted her. He had from the very first time his grandfather had taken him to the hotel. His chest tightened as he thought of his grandfather, the vow he'd made to one day reclaim the Princess. That vow was the reason he was here, Josh reminded himself. He hadn't been able to turn away a chance to win her back.

"At least give me a name. Tell me who this friend of yours is?"

"Come on, Nick," Josh said with a sigh. He walked back across the room to stand before his friend. "Listen, I tell you what. After I talk to Ms. Harte, if she wants to share the context of our conversation with you, she's free to do so. But it'll have to be her call. Until then, I'm asking you to back off."

Nick frowned. His fingers curled around the pen he'd been fidgeting with since hanging up the phone. "All right. I'll back off—for now. Just remember what I said. Laura's been through a lot lately. She's been sort of fragile since her mother was killed."

"I understand. And I promise, it isn't my intention to upset her." Yet if what Olivia had told him about Laura Harte's reaction to the older woman's phone call was accurate, Josh suspected that the lady might very well be upset when she discovered why he was there.

"Then make sure you don't. Because I'm warning you, Logan, you upset Laura and I am going to be one unhappy guy."

Josh narrowed his gaze. "What gives, Nick? Something going on between you and Laura Harte besides business?" For some reason, the idea of his friend being involved with the woman whose photo he'd studied repeatedly since that night at Olivia's left a foul taste in his mouth.

"You know me better than that. I have rules about mixing business and pleasure, remember?"

"Yeah. But I also remember a time when you broke those rules with my kid sister."

Heat flashed in Nick's eyes. He pushed back his chair and strode over to the windows that overlooked the bay. When he turned around, his expression was once more inscrutable. "That was a long time ago. It wasn't anything serious."

"Tell that to Faith. She blamed me when my folks shipped her off to intern at the London hotel that summer. She didn't speak to me for months."

"She was just a kid."

"Yeah." For the first time, Josh wondered if maybe he'd been wrong all those years ago. Could Nick have been more serious about Faith than he'd thought? When he'd first gotten wind that his best friend was romancing his baby sister, he'd been furious. He'd been sure Nick was just toying with Faith since he knew Nick was like him when it came to women—he enjoyed them but wasn't interested in commitment. After he'd torn a strip off of his friend, he'd gone to his father and spilled the beans. "Faith thought she was in love with you, and she blamed me for busting you two up."

A haunted look came across Nick's face. He turned away, stared out the window once more. "It was for the best. Anyway, I heard she got married."

"Unfortunately, I wasn't around to check out the scumbag until it was too late and she married him. But I did make sure I was around to help her pick up the pieces when she came to her senses and divorced him."

The hand Nick had jammed through his hair stilled. He turned around. "Faith's divorced?"

"Almost a year ago."

"I hadn't heard," Nick said. "I'm sorry things didn't work out for her."

Josh wasn't sure what to make of Nick's reaction. Was it possible that his friend had actually been serious about Faith?

"Listen, about Laura...I don't want you to get the wrong idea. She's a terrific lady. Smart, really sharp. She works hard and has a real feel for the business. She's good. Someday she's going to make a hell of a GM. But there isn't anything personal going on between us. We're friends. Good friends. But that's all."

Before he could stop himself Josh asked, "What about a boyfriend?"

Despite his casual tone, Nick frowned. He eyed Josh closely. "None that I know of—or at least no one serious. Laura's career has always been her primary focus. What makes you ask?"

Josh shrugged. "Just curious."

Nick hesitated a long moment. "Well, just remember what I told you. Laura's been through a rough time and is kind of fragile right now. Her mother's death hit her hard, and the poor kid doesn't have any other family."

Only Laura Harte did have family, Josh thought in silence. It might not be a family she wanted or accepted, but blood was blood. Nothing could change the fact that Laura Harte was a Jardine. And as a Jardine, she had a family—a grandmother, three siblings—and she was his key to finally getting back the Princess Hotel.

Four

Laura adjusted the lipstick-red scarf around her neck, then smoothed the skirt of her black dress just before the elevator dinged and the doors zipped open.

Exiting the elevator, she forced a smile on her lips as she approached the desk of Nick's very pregnant assistant. Although Jennifer Simmons was only four years younger than her, the difference might as well have been forty. The other woman had not only married her childhood sweetheart, but she was also expecting the birth of her first child. Whereas she...she had yet to meet any man she could imagine a long-term relationship with—let alone marriage.

"Hi, Jen."

"Thank you, God," the other woman said, lifting her eyes heavenward before she beamed at Laura. "I was desperately in need of a break, and here you are— giving me the perfect excuse to take one."

"To hear your boss tell it, you don't usually need an excuse."

Jen crinkled her nose. "Who are you going to believe? Me or the slave driver?"

"You, of course," Laura said, grinning. "So how is the little mother-to-be feeling this afternoon?"

"Like a blimp with legs. But the champ here is doing great," she said, smiling as she smoothed a hand over her burgeoning middle. "In fact, I'm convinced this little guy has a future as a football or soccer star."

"Still kicking up a storm, hmm?"

"Do fish swim? Why I—" Jen gasped and clutched her stomach.

"What is it?" Laura demanded, suddenly alarmed. Fearing the baby was coming, she grabbed the phone and started to punch in 911. "Hang on. I'm calling the—" She stopped at the burst of laughter.

"I'm sorry," Jen told her, wiping tears from her eyes as her laughter subsided. "If you could have seen the look on your face."

Her heartbeat once again normal, Laura primly returned the phone to its cradle. "I'm glad one of us finds this amusing. You nearly scared me half to death, Jennifer Simmons. I thought you'd gone into labor," she accused, but had difficulty acting royally miffed when she wanted to laugh, too.

"I really am sorry," Jen said again, the last of her giggles fading. "Although I have to admit there is a part of me that wishes I had gone into labor."

"Well, I for one am grateful that you didn't. You'd be in worse shape than Scarlett O'Hara when she went into labor, because I don't know anything about birthing babies."

Jen laughed as she was meant to do. "Oh, I think you'd manage just fine."

"Well, I'd just as soon we not find out—especially not two months early."

"Don't remind me," Jen groaned. "I can't believe I still have two whole months to go."

"It'll be here before you know it."

"I certainly hope so. I can hardly wait for this little guy to arrive. I want to hold him in my arms so bad.

So does Bob,'' she said. ''I know it sounds sappy, but we love him already.''

''It doesn't sound sappy at all. I think it sounds sweet.''

''It is,'' Jen confessed. ''But you'll find that out for yourself someday when you're expecting one of your own.''

A lump formed in Laura's throat. Would she ever know what it was to share that kind of love with someone? To feel a new life growing inside her? At twenty-eight, she was no stranger to men. She'd dated her fair share but had never been serious about any one of them. She'd told herself it was because her career was her major focus. But deep in her heart, she knew the reason had less to do with her career focus than the fact that none of the men she'd dated measured up to the man her father was. Or at least the man she'd always believed her father to be, Laura corrected herself.

''Laura? Are you all right?''

''Hmm? I'm fine,'' she said, shaking off the sad thoughts. ''It's just been a long day.''

''I know what you mean. This is the first time today the phone hasn't been ringing off the hook.''

''Speaking of phones, Nick buzzed me a few minutes ago. He said there was someone he wanted me to meet.''

''Oh, terrific,'' Jen said, her face beaming. ''You can get the scoop on TDH.''

''TDH?''

''Tall, dark and handsome,'' Jen explained. When Laura simply stared at her, the other woman sighed. ''Tall, dark and handsome as in major hunk. When I returned from my doctor's appointment and stuck my head in Nick's office to tell him I was back, I saw him.''

"Him?"

"The hunk," Jen replied, shooting her a warning look to pay attention. "He didn't have an appointment scheduled. And the reception desk said when Nick came back from his lunch meeting, the guy was with him. The tongues in Marketing and in Reservations have been hanging out since he walked into the hotel. Everyone's dying to find out who he is.''

"Probably a potential client," Laura reasoned.

"Whoever he is, he is one gorgeous male specimen. He's also unattached.''

Laura blinked. "How on earth do you know that?''

She held up her left hand, wiggled her ring finger. "No wedding ring," Jen explained. "I checked.''

"Need I remind you that you *are* married?''

"Yeah, but I'm not dead. And there's no reason I can't appreciate a good-looking guy with a great tush.''

Laura arched her brow. "I wonder what Bob would say about you checking out the guy's tush.''

"Hey, I was checking him out for you," Jen defended herself. "But now that you're here, you can go on in and check him out for yourself," she said, and pressed the intercom button to announce Laura's arrival. "Just remember—no drooling.''

Laura didn't drool. But she could have. One look at the man Jen had dubbed TDH, and Laura admitted the other woman had been right. He was tall—a few inches over six feet, she guessed, with long limbs and too-die-for green eyes. His hair was dark. So was he. She'd be willing to wager a week's salary that the deep golden tan he sported hadn't been courtesy of any tanning salon. She also doubted that those linebacker shoulders that filled out the expensive charcoal jacket so nicely were the result of a fancy personal trainer. A quick scan of slashing cheekbones, a strong jaw and a mouth curved into a wicked grin, and Laura had to agree with Jen's assessment. The man was flat-out gorgeous.

But then, so was her boss Nick. Fortunately, living in California where there were so many good-looking men, she had long ago developed an aversion, if not an immunity, to men with those movie-star looks.

"Here she is," Nick said as he hung up the phone and stood. Moving from behind his desk, he put an arm around Laura's shoulder and ushered her over to the hunk. "Josh, I'd like you to meet Laura Harte, not only the best assistant GM in the business, but the prettiest, too. Laura, meet Josh Logan, an old friend who's in town for a few days."

"Mr. Logan, it's a pleasure to meet you." Laura smiled and extended her hand. "And please, pay no attention to Nick. He considers it his duty to flatter every female who crosses his path."

"But in this case, I have to agree with him. You're even more lovely than he told me," he replied smoothly, a hint of the South in his voice as he took her hand. "And please, call me Josh."

Color warmed Laura's cheeks as much from the compliment as from the approval in his eyes, and not for the first time, Laura wished her skin weren't so fair. "Thank you," she murmured.

"I hope you don't mind if I call you Laura."

"No. Laura is fine." Keenly aware that he was still holding her hand, Laura withdrew it.

"Josh and I used to work together when we were in college," Nick explained as he led them to the grouping of couches and chairs that filled a section of the executive suite.

Laura opted for one of the overstuffed chairs positioned around the marble coffee table. "In Florida?" she asked, since she knew that's where Nick was from originally.

"Louisiana," Josh replied. "Nicky and I did a little of everything—bussed tables, parked cars, you name it. The hotel grunt work that no one else wanted to do."

Laura stiffened at the mention of Louisiana, her thoughts momentarily turning to the Jardine family. "Are you in the hotel business, too, Mr. Lo—"

"Josh," he corrected her, flashing her that smile again.

The full impact of that smile warmed her like a caress. Caught off guard by her response to him, Laura shook off thoughts of the Jardine family and told herself she'd need to concentrate if she were to hold her own against the likes of Josh Logan. "Are you in the hotel business...Josh?"

"In a manner of speaking. I deal primarily in acquisitions."

"Josh's family owns Logan Hotels," Nick informed her.

The words *Logan Hotels* and *acquisition* hit her like a slap of cold air. "I see," Laura managed to say despite the sudden knot in her stomach as she considered the purpose behind Josh Logan's visit. Larger than the Ambassador Grand Hotel that Nick operated, Logan Hotels was a major competitor known for its five-star properties throughout the country. The firm was also known for its rapid growth during the past decade by acquisition of competing luxury hotels.

"I'm afraid you don't see," Josh drawled, a hint of amusement in his voice. "At least not the right picture. Although the Ambassador Grand is a fabulous property, Logan Hotels isn't interested in buying it."

"Which is a good thing since it's not for sale," Nick added.

"Of course, there is that factor, too," Josh conceded, his lips curving into a grin that had Laura's stomach tightening again. "But the truth is, I'm not here on Logan Hotels business. This visit is strictly a personal one."

"Well, that's good news," Laura began, and could have kicked herself when Josh laughed aloud. "I'm sorry. I didn't mean that the way it sounded. I don't have anything against Logan Hotels."

"I'm glad to hear it," Josh told her.

Laura laughed. "It's true. I even stayed at your San Diego hotel a few years ago. It was lovely and fully deserving of its excellent reputation."

"But?" Nick coaxed.

"But I'd hate to see the Ambassador Grand sold."

"Because you like working for Nick?" Josh inquired.

"Yes. That's part of it. The other reason is the hotel itself. When new owners come in, there's a tendency to start making changes. I'd hate to see anything changed here. It's a beautiful property, so rich in history, and Nick has done such a wonderful job restoring it." Realizing how she must sound, Laura decided to change the subject. "Has Nick given you a tour of the hotel yet?"

"There wasn't time," Nick offered. "Josh and I had some other matters that we needed to discuss."

"Well, you're in for a treat," she told Josh.

"Sounds like it. Any chance I could convince you to give me a tour?"

Laura hesitated. "I…of course, I'd be happy to do it. But I'm sure Nick's looking forward to showing you around and using the opportunity for the two of you to visit a bit longer. Right, Nick?"

"Actually, Nick mentioned that he was going to be tied up all afternoon."

Laura cut a glance to her boss, caught the warning look he exchanged with Josh. She frowned. Was she imagining things? Was there some serious tension between the two men? "Nick, I can handle whatever you have scheduled for this afternoon if you like. That way you'll be free to show Josh around the hotel."

Nick paused. "Thanks, but I have a board meeting across town, and I'm afraid it's one that I have to attend personally."

"So what do you say, Laura? I'd really like to see the rest of the hotel."

"Well, if Nick is sure he doesn't mind," Laura began, confused by the undercurrents she was picking up in the room.

"It's all right, Laura. You go ahead, show Josh around," Nick finally said. He stood. "I'm afraid I need to get going if I'm going to make that board meeting on time."

"Of course," Laura replied as she rose. "I'll see you in the morning."

"Right," Nick said, his face somber. "But if you need me for anything…anything at all, you call me. Okay?"

"Sure," Laura said, puzzled by the remark.

"It was good seeing you again, Nick," Josh said,

extending his hand. "And thanks for the help. I owe you one."

"Just make sure I don't regret doing you a favor. I'd hate it if I'd allowed an old friendship to cause me to make a mistake."

He had made a mistake, Josh decided later that afternoon after Laura excused herself to respond to a page. Leaning against a column in the ornate lobby, he watched Laura cross the expanse to the front desk, where she began an exchange with a member of her staff and a middle-aged couple. Unable to hear the conversation, Josh's thoughts turned inward once more.

Yes, he had definitely made a mistake in the matter of Ms. Laura Harte. Of course, it wasn't the first mistake he'd made by any means, Josh conceded. A man didn't reach the age of thirty-three without making a mistake or two along the way. And while he was grateful he'd seldom made mistakes when it came to business decisions, he wished he could say the same when it came to his decisions concerning women.

Grimacing, Josh recalled some of his more serious errors in judgment when a female was involved. Among the first to come to mind had been shortly after his seventeenth birthday—when he'd wrapped his classic '65 Mustang around a telephone pole trying to impress Sarah Beth Whitney with his skill as a driver. Even now just the memory of wrecking that beautiful car made him wince. No question that had been a big mistake on his part—and a dumb one. So had the time he'd wasted a good bottle of Scotch getting sloshed after he'd been dumped by a woman. Puking his guts up for two days had been enough to cure his heartache. And as far as he was concerned, turning down the chance to do a horizontal tango with a future Miss Universe two years ago would always rank as a major flub.

Josh sighed. Experience should have made him a lot smarter and a hell of a lot more cautious when it came to dealing with females, he reasoned. Evidently, it hadn't. Otherwise, he would have run in the opposite direction the minute Olivia Jardine had outlined her wild scheme. But the crafty old gal had known just what bait to dangle in front of his nose to get him to agree to her plan—the Princess. She'd known he wouldn't refuse a chance to get the hotel back under the Logan banner where it belonged. It had all sounded so simple, and he'd had no doubt that he could pull it off.

Only he hadn't counted on Laura. And that's where he'd made a mistake—because Laura hadn't been at all what he'd expected. She'd surprised him. So had his response to her. Sure, he had known from her photo that he would find her appealing. With that mane of red hair, the pale blue eyes and a mouth made for sin, he'd anticipated the physical attraction. After all, he was a red-blooded male, and she was a beautiful woman. But he hadn't counted on the intelligence that shone in those blue eyes or the underlying strength in her grip when they'd shaken hands. And he hadn't been at all prepared for that fist-to-the-jaw punch of arousal he experienced each time he touched her. He certainly hadn't counted on being intrigued by Laura Harte.

But he was, Josh admitted, and he wasn't at all sure why. He encountered beautiful, smart women every day in his business and personal life. He'd lost count of the times his matchmaking mother and sisters had paraded beautiful, intelligent women in front of him at various social functions and dinner parties, hoping he'd be inspired to marry and settle down. None of those women had generated more than a second look on his part. Certainly none of those women had piqued his curiosity or challenged something in him as Laura had. He'd grabbed the ruse of having her show him the hotel because he'd wanted time to gauge her as an individual before jumping in with his reason for being there. But he hadn't expected to enjoy himself as he had. Continuing to watch her, he told himself there was no logical reason for him to find her so captivating.

Yet he did. Considering the role she played in his plans to reclaim the Princess, for him to become fascinated with Laura Harte was one mistake he couldn't afford to make. Not when so much was at stake.

A personal involvement with Laura wasn't an option, Josh reminded himself as she started across the lobby toward him. Still, there was no reason he couldn't enjoy the way she filled out that black dress or the natural sway of her hips as she walked or the sight of those mile-long legs in killer high heels. At the sudden image of those legs wrapped around his waist, Josh nearly groaned. Get a grip, Logan, he told himself, and jammed his fists into his pockets.

"I'm sorry. I didn't mean to keep you waiting," she said as she joined him.

"No problem," Josh replied. "Everything all right?"

"Yes. There was just a slight mix-up on a room reservation. The couple I was talking with are here for their anniversary, and when they made their reservation, they requested the same room they occupied on their wedding night. Unfortunately, the agent who took the reservation on the phone last month, and who happens to no longer be with the hotel, failed to make a notation of the request when he booked the reservation. And the particular room they'd wanted is already occupied.''

''I'm assuming from the smiles on their faces that you worked it out.''

''I guess you could say that. I upgraded them to a larger suite, ordered a bottle of champagne to be sent to their room with the hotel's compliments and issued them a voucher for a free weekend in the suite they originally wanted to be used at a future date.''

''Very smooth. And very smart.'' It was exactly what he would have done were he the general manager—keep the client happy, and make sure they want to come back.

''Thank you. All things considered, I thought it was the best way to handle it.''

''Absolutely. Customer goodwill is important. You've not only salvaged their weekend and ensured that they'll leave here happy, but that they'll come back to use that voucher when giving them a free room will have little impact on your profits. And since the room is free, I'm sure you've figured that they'll feel justified in spending more money in the hotel restaurant and gift shops.''

''Well, the thought did cross my mind,'' she said, grinning. And this time the smile curving her lips held none of the caution, none of the insipid politeness of her earlier smiles. This time the smile she gave him was genuine.

And the result was staggering. Desire tightened low in Josh's belly as he stared at her. He itched to fist his hands in that red-gold hair, to draw her close so he could breathe in that roses-and-sunshine scent of hers and then kiss that spot on her neck just below her ear.

Dropping his gaze to her mouth, he watched her smile fade, heard her quick intake of breath, and he knew she felt that heat shimmering between them, too. The realization sent need shuddering through him. He moved a step closer, wanting to explore the shape and taste of that tempting mouth. Instead, he settled for smoothing the stray curl that had tangled on her scarf.

Laura stepped back. She made a show of checking her watch. "I didn't realize how late it was. I guess the tour took longer than I thought it would. I'm afraid I tend to get caught up in the hotel's history and go on and on. You should have stopped me."

"Why? I enjoyed it."

"Thank you. But I'm sure you have other things you want to do during your stay. As for the hotel, I think you've seen just about everything there is now except for the kitchens. Do you want to see them?"

"Wouldn't miss it. I'd like a chance to compare the operation here with the one at our San Diego property."

"Then follow me."

As Josh followed Laura, he tried not to notice how her scent pulled at his senses, made him think of sultry southern nights and magnolia blossoms. He tried not to notice that her skin was the color of cream and looked as delicate as a rose petal. He tried not to notice that even with her lipstick worn away, her mouth was pink and lush and made for kissing.

She paused at the wide marble staircase that led to the mezzanine level. "Do you mind taking the stairs or would you prefer we take the elevator?"

"The stairs are fine," Josh managed to say, despite the resulting discomfort caused by his musings. Placing his hand at the center of Laura's back, he led her up the stairs where more polished marble floors, more glittering chandeliers and more urns of fresh flowers greeted them.

"Have you had a chance to visit the restaurant yet?" she asked as they crossed the spacious floor toward the restaurant.

"As a matter of fact, I haven't. Nick and I met outside the hotel for lunch."

"Well, you'll have to have at least one meal in the Redwood before you leave. The chef here is excellent. And the restaurant's won quite a number of awards for its food and service." She stopped a few feet from the restaurant's entrance, where from the looks of things business was brisk.

Noting her frown, he asked, "Something wrong?"

"No. Quite the contrary. It looks like a good night for the restaurant," she said, indicating the activity inside the restaurant and the line of people waiting at the door. "But I'm afraid with things this busy, the chef will have my head if I go traipsing through his kitchen with you in tow now."

"Since I'd hate to be responsible for you losing that pretty head of yours, what do you say we pass on the kitchen tour?"

"Sounds like a good idea to me," she said, smiling.

It was impossible for him not to return that smile. He swept his gaze toward the restaurant. "Think there's any chance I can still get a dinner reservation in there for tonight?"

"Well, seeing as how I happen to have an 'in' with the management, I think your chances are pretty good. Why don't we go find out?"

"Ms. Harte, how are you this evening?" the maître d' asked when they approached the restaurant's entrance. With his silver hair and refined demeanor the man reminded Josh of an English butler.

"I'm fine, Douglas. Looks like it's a busy night for you."

"Yes, it is," he said, a pleased expression on his face.

"Too busy to squeeze in another reservation?" Laura asked.

"For you? Of course not." The older man's eyes twinkled. He cut a glance at Josh and then back to Laura. "A table for two?"

"Yes," Josh answered quickly. He stuck out his hand. "Josh Logan, Douglas. I really appreciate this. After hearing Laura rave about the food, I have to admit that I'm not only anxious to sample it, I'm starving."

"It's my pleasure, sir. And I assure you, you won't be disappointed in the cuisine. If you'll just give me a moment, I'll see about a table for you."

After Douglas excused himself, Josh turned his attention back to Laura. "Thanks for using your influence," he told her.

"You're welcome. And since you're in good hands with Douglas, I'll leave you to enjoy your dinner. It was a pleasure meeting you, Josh."

Josh took the hand she offered, held it. "Do you have to rush off?" he asked. Besides the fact that he had yet to come clean about his reason for being there, he was also reluctant to have her leave.

"No. But I thought…I assumed you had plans for this evening."

"Nope," he assured her. "I asked for a table for two because I was hoping I could persuade you to stay and have dinner with me."

"That's very kind of you, but surely there's someone else—Nick or another friend or a business associate—that you'd rather have dinner with."

Josh shook his head. "Nick is going to be tied up all evening. That's why we visited earlier today, and I don't know anyone else in San Francisco. Besides, the least I can do is buy you dinner to thank you for answering all my questions and giving me a tour of the hotel."

She reclaimed her hand. "It's really not necessary. I love the Ambassador Grand, and I enjoyed showing her off to you."

Although the detective reports and his conversations with Nick hadn't given any indication that she was romantically involved with someone, it suddenly occurred to Josh that perhaps there was someone waiting for Laura. To his surprise, the notion that she might have a lover stirred something stormy inside him. Telling himself that his reaction was ridiculous, Josh pressed. "If you're refusing my invitation because there's someone waiting for you, you're welcome to ask him to join us."

"No. That's not it," she said. "I mean, there isn't anyone waiting. That is, I'm not involved with anyone at the moment."

Charmed by the sudden color tinging her cheeks, Josh told himself if he felt relieved by her answer it was because convincing her to accept Olivia's offer would be easier without a man in the picture. "Do you already have plans for this evening?"

"No," Laura answered, nerves dancing in those pale blue eyes. "It's just that…"

"It's just that Tuesday nights are when you wash your hair?"

Her lips twitched. "No."

Pleased that his attempt at humor had eased those nerves of a moment ago, he tried again. "Then tonight's when you swore to yourself that you'd clean the oven?"

"Hardly," Laura told him, and laughed aloud. "Besides the fact that I don't use the oven enough to get it dirty, it's self-cleaning."

"Then take pity on a lonely stranger. Don't force me to eat alone tonight. Say you'll have dinner with me."

She arched her brow. "You may be a stranger to San Francisco, Josh Logan, but somehow I doubt that you've ever been lonely a day in your life—unless it's by choice."

"Do I hear a compliment in there somewhere?" he asked, not at all surprised by her perception. She was right. There were actually a number of women in San Francisco he could call who would gladly join him for dinner and more. But none of those women were Laura Harte. And none of those women held the key to him regaining the Princess, he reminded himself.

Laura laughed again. "I have no intention of feeding your ego by pointing out your obvious attractions."

"Which are?"

Laura shook her head. "You're impossible."

"Have dinner with me, anyway," he said seriously. Because the urge to touch her was so strong, he reached out and curled a strand of her hair around his finger. "I'd really like a chance for us to get to know each other better."

She took a step back. "I don't think that's necessarily a good idea."

"Why?" When she didn't answer, he asked, "Is it because of Nick? You think he might object?"

"Nick has nothing to do with it," she told him.

"Then what's the problem?"

"I just don't think it's wise to mix business with pleasure."

"Then we won't mix them," Josh assured her. "Tonight will be strictly pleasure."

Five

"Is something wrong with your veal?" Laura asked, unnerved by Josh's steady gaze on her.

"The veal's excellent." As though to prove the point he took a bite, but his eyes never wavered from her face.

"Josh, you're staring," she accused, hoping the rebuke would diffuse the sexual tension that seemed to have escalated between them in the restaurant's cozy surroundings.

"I know," he admitted, and instead of being embarrassed to have been caught, he merely flashed her another of those killer smiles that had her stomach dipping and her heart beating just a little too fast. "I was remembering that old adage about the eyes being the mirror to a person's soul. Whoever came up with that particular phrase must have had you in mind, Laura Harte. You have the most incredible eyes—so expressive."

So much for dousing the sensual sparks, Laura thought. His answer and the way he was looking at her—like he was a big cat and she was a tempting bowl of cream—had her already fast pulse racing flat-out. She drew in a deep breath, trying to marshal her reaction to the man. "Thank you."

He chuckled. "See, that's what I mean. A moment

ago you were all business, and your eyes were an icy blue. But just now when I surprised you and you forgot to be Ms. Hotel Executive, the color of your eyes changed," he said, his voice dropping to a husky drawl. "Now they're a smoky blue—like the surf in St. Thomas at dawn."

"I think one of us has had too much wine," she said with a nonchalance she was far from feeling.

"Nope." As if to prove his point, Josh took another sip of the cabernet. "Just making an observation. Surely I'm not the first man to tell you that you have beautiful eyes."

"No," she murmured, but she couldn't remember any other man making her hot all over with just a look. "Thank you."

He nodded but continued to watch her over the rim of his glass. "I've embarrassed you."

"No, you haven't."

He grinned. "That's not what your eyes tell me. They truly are extraordinary, the most unique color. Just when I think I've nailed down the exact shade, they change again. But then, I guess you've heard that before, too."

"Actually, I haven't, and I suspect you know it," Laura said, determined not to let him fluster her. "You're very skilled at this."

"At what?"

"Flirting."

"Is that what you think I'm doing?" he asked, amusement in his voice.

"Isn't it?" she countered. "Those deep, soul-searching looks and all this talk about the color of my eyes when you and I both know that they're blue. Plain, ordinary blue."

Josh's lips curved again. This time slowly, seductively. He leaned forward slightly, which increased the feeling of intimacy between them. "Trust me, Laura. There's not a man alive who would look at you and ever see anything plain or ordinary about you."

Laura's pulse skittered. Her mouth suddenly dry, she reached for her wineglass, clutched it tightly and hoped he didn't notice the slight tremor in her fingers. She disliked the fact that she was nervous, Laura admitted as she sipped the expensive vintage. She dealt with lots of men in her line of work. Men never made her nervous. Josh didn't make her nervous. He certainly wasn't responsible for this light-headed feeling she had or for the butterflies buzzing in her stomach. As she studied him over the rim of her glass, she told herself the way she felt had nothing to do with Josh or the fact that he was handsome and charming, and she found him attractive. No, it wasn't Josh himself who was responsible for her feeling this way. It was the setting— the candlelight and romantic music. It was the fact that she was lonely and it had been well over a year since she'd been involved in a male-female relationship.

And she was lying through her teeth, Laura conceded. But only a first-rate **idiot** would buy the line he was feeding her. And she was no idiot. She'd met men like Josh Logan before—gorgeous, charming seducers out for a night or two of fun. And as interesting and attractive as she found Josh, a quick fling wasn't her style. Yet, sitting here with him now, she almost wished that it was. "You're a dangerous man, Josh Logan," she said, giving him her brightest smile. "I can only imagine the long trail of broken hearts you've left in your wake down South."

"Ouch," he said, slapping a hand against his heart.

"Those are some pretty sharp arrows you're slinging there, Ms. Harte. Do you always shoot a man when he pays you a compliment?"

"Is that what you were doing? Why, I could have sworn you were trying to seduce me."

She'd meant to make him laugh, had been sure he would find her comeback amusing. Yet the grin died on his lips. His eyes darkened, and she noted for the first time tiny flecks of gold in them. "Believe me, Laura, if I were trying to seduce you, you wouldn't have to wonder if that's what I was doing. You would know it."

Laura's breath stalled in her lungs. And despite her best efforts to prevent it, excitement shimmied down her spine.

"Are you finished, Ms. Harte?" the waiter asked, saving her from having to respond.

"Yes. I am. Thank you, Stewart."

Telling herself that she wasn't a coward for feeling grateful at the interruption, Laura used the opportunity to rein in her emotions. While Stewart cleared away the dishes and recited the dessert menu, Laura attempted to regain her perspective by reminding herself that Josh Logan was her boss's friend and a man whom she would probably never see again after tonight. Just because she'd been lonely since her mother's death was no reason to overreact to his innocent flirtation—a flirtation that was no doubt second nature to a man like him. Once the waiter retreated, they both said simultaneously, "I'm sorry."

She laughed.

So did Josh.

"Well, I'm glad we got that cleared up," she told him. "Thank you for what you said…about my eyes.

It was very sweet of you—which is what I should have said to begin with instead of accusing you of hitting on me. I was out of line and I really am sorry.''

"Since we're being honest, I suppose I should confess that you weren't totally off base,'' he replied, a wicked and totally unapologetic glint in his eyes. "Don't get me wrong, I meant what I said. You do have beautiful eyes.''

"But?''

"But I guess I was hitting on you. It wasn't a conscious thing on my part, but I was coming on to you all the same.''

"I understand,'' she said, disappointed because there was a part of her that had wanted to believe he'd been sincere in the things he'd said.

"Is that so?''

"Yes. I know it wasn't anything personal. It was instinctive—the 'you're a man, I'm a woman' thing.''

Josh frowned as he sat back in his chair and subjected her to one of those scrutinizing looks. "Tell me something, Laura. Do you have a poor opinion of the male population in general or is it just me in particular?''

She caught the edge in his voice, wondered how she had managed to put it there. "Neither.''

"And you, Ms. Harte, can't lie worth spit.''

"Now, just hang on a minute,'' Laura shot back, bristling at his reply.

"No, you hang on,'' he told her, and pinned her with a steely look. "What I was trying to say and have obviously done a damn poor job of it is that I'm attracted to you. You're a smart, interesting woman and I like the fact that you live and breathe this business like I do. I'm also fascinated by the fact that you look at an old hotel like this one and see more than just dollar signs or a lucrative investment. You see the beauty and history that gives the place its soul, that makes it unique. Add to that the fact that you're a beautiful, sexy woman, and I would have to be dead or have ice in my veins not to hit on you.''

His little speech took the wind right out of her sails. For a full five seconds Laura could do nothing more than stare at him. One thing she was sure of was that Josh Logan wasn't dead and never in a million years would she even think of suggesting he had ice in his veins. Quite to the contrary, Josh struck her as a man who would be passionate in all aspects of his life.

''Obviously, I've shocked you.''

The amusement in his voice nipped at her pride, making her feel like an awkward girl unused to going toe-to-toe with a man like him. Keeping her voice cool, she said, ''Not at all. I'm just not sure how to respond. I can't decide it you were apologizing to me just now or taking another stab at trying to seduce me.''

''Neither. I was simply stating the facts.''

''Thank you for clearing that up for me,'' she countered.

''Glad to do it. But there is one thing I think I should clarify.''

The gleam in his eyes, coupled with that handsome face, made her think of fallen angels. Still she asked, ''And just what would that be?''

''While I may have admitted that I was hitting on you a few minutes ago, I haven't tried to seduce you.''

Yet. The unspoken word hung between them like a live wire dangling in a storm, and Laura's already taut nerves grew even more tense. ''I didn't realize there was a difference.''

The smile he gave her was pure sin. "Believe me, there is. I'd be happy to explain it to you or even demonstrate, if you'd like."

"That's all right. I'll take your word for it," she said, deciding she'd be wise not to pursue the discussion. While she didn't consider herself a coward and had enjoyed the verbal volleying with him, she suspected Josh Logan was far better at this male-female thing than she was. So she held out her hand. "Truce?"

"Truce." But instead of shaking her hand as she'd intended, Josh kissed it. And Laura felt the touch of his lips all the way to her toes.

"It looks like dessert's arrived," she said, withdrawing her hand. And while the waiter prepared Bananas Foster table-side, Laura chattered about the restaurant's other sumptuous dessert offerings.

Once the flaming delicacy had been served and the waiter retreated, Laura decided she'd be wise to avoid any more of the sensual minefields they'd been stumbling across all evening by shifting to a safer topic. "Nick mentioned earlier that both your father and grandfather were hoteliers."

"That's right. Gramps was still in his twenties when he built his first hotel. By the time I was born, he owned more than a dozen."

"And now?" she asked before spooning up a taste of the ice cream.

"Now there are thirty-one hotels that bear the Logan Hotels banner."

"Very impressive," Laura said. "How does it feel to be part of a dynasty?"

He chuckled. "I'm not sure *dynasty* is the word I'd use to describe us Logans."

"I don't see why not. You and your family have been very successful in a business that's extremely competitive."

"True," he said as he shoveled up another spoon of ice cream coated with the thick brown-sugar sauce. "But it's hard thinking of Logan Hotels as a dynasty when I've been brought up to think of it as our little family business."

Laura arched a brow. "Somehow, I don't think thirty-one hotels classifies as anyone's little family business."

"Put like that, I guess it does sound silly. But it's what we do."

"And obviously you do it very well."

He shrugged. "Gramps was a good teacher. And my family's been lucky. We've gotten most of the hotels we've gone after, but we've also worked hard to make things happen."

"I imagine you have. Still, it must be nice…you and your family working together."

"It's both a blessing and a curse…."

While Josh spoke of the fun and the madness of working with his siblings and parents, Laura couldn't help but feel a twinge of envy. She thought of her own life, the closeness she'd shared with her mother, and considered the irony of the profession she'd chosen. Not for the first time since discovering the truth about her father, she wondered how her mother had felt about her decision to pursue a career in hotel management. Thoughts of her father invariably brought back the phone call from Olivia Jardine. Despite the older woman's insistence, her heritage wasn't in New Orleans. Why would she even want to claim the heritage of a man who had not only abandoned his pregnant lover, but had denied her as well?

"Is something wrong?"

Laura jerked her attention to Josh. "No. Not at all. I was just thinking about the dynamics of your family. How many of you Logans are there?"

"In my immediate family, there are five of us kids. There are also a half-dozen aunts and uncles and about twenty or so cousins."

For someone who'd had no one but her mother, it sounded like an army. "You have four brothers and sisters?"

"No brothers. Just sisters. Two older than me—Meredith and Rachel—and two who are younger—Hope and Faith. And they're all nosy, bossy and intent on driving their only brother crazy."

"Those are interesting descriptions of your sisters. Makes me wonder how they'd describe you."

"As their handsome, charming and perfect brother, of course."

Laura laughed at the outrageous claim.

"It's true," he assured her.

"Sure it is."

"And it's obvious that you didn't grow up in a house of pesky siblings."

"Afraid not. It was just me and my mother," Laura informed him, enjoying the easy banter between them. She sampled the banana swimming in the thick, rich sauce.

"You poor, deprived kid. You missed out on all the fun stuff like fighting for a shot at the bathroom, and when you get it, nearly getting choked to death on all the perfumes and girly lotions in the air. Or waiting your turn for the shower and discovering there's no hot water left.''

''You're right. I can't say I've had any of that fun.''

''And I don't suppose you know what it's like to find half of your shirts and shorts missing because the newest craze in female fashion is men's wear, do you?''

Grinning, Laura shook her head, both amused and intrigued by the images he was painting of his siblings. ''No, but my mom and I were the same size and she used to borrow my clothes sometimes. Does that count?''

''Not even close,'' he informed her. ''True sibling torture is to be a lowly red-shirted freshman on the football team and have the foxy senior-class cheerleader offer to drive you home after practice, and while the two of you are making out in her snazzy car in front of your house, your bratty little sisters are spying on you. Worse yet, they run inside and tattle on you to your parents.''

''You're making that up,'' Laura accused, unable to hold back her laughter.

He held up three fingers. ''Scout's honor. My sisters drove me crazy when we were kids, and now that we're adults, they take turns trying to drive me nuts.''

''But you love them,'' she said, hearing the affection in his voice, seeing it in his eyes.

He shrugged. ''What choice do I have? They're family. You have to love your family.''

Not always, Laura mused. She thought again of her father, of Andrew Jardine. For the first time since discovering the truth, she allowed herself to think of his children—her half brother and sisters. She couldn't help wondering what it would have been like if things had been different.

"What about you? What was it like for you growing up?" Josh asked.

Laura pulled her thoughts back to the present. "Compared to your childhood, mine was very quiet. My father…I never knew my father. It was just my mother and me."

"Nick told me she died recently and that the two of you were close."

"Yes. We were close. She was a wonderful woman—sort of a combination of mother, sister and best friend all rolled into one. She was so full of life. Always had a smile on her face. I don't think she ever met a stranger, or at least no one that stayed a stranger, for long. Everyone adored her."

"She sounds like a special lady."

"She was. And she didn't have it easy, raising me by herself. But she never complained, never once made me feel that I was a burden. I always felt loved, wanted. She was a very strong and brave woman."

"A lot like her daughter, I suspect."

Laura swallowed hard. "Thank you," she murmured, and stared down at her dessert.

"You still miss her a lot, don't you?"

"Yes," Laura admitted.

He tipped up her chin with his finger so that she met his eyes. "I'm sorry. I can't even begin to imagine how you must feel. As much as I complain about my family, I'd be lost without them."

Which described exactly how she'd felt during these past months—lost. But it wasn't just the physical absence of her mother. It was knowing that all those years she'd idolized a father who'd never existed, that she'd believed herself to be someone she wasn't. "I still have my friends. And, of course, there's Uncle Paul."

"Uncle Paul?"

"Well, he's not really my uncle. He's…he was my mother's attorney and oldest friend. I've known him all my life," she informed him. "He certainly treats me like family, though. He's always nagging at me to eat, to go out more, not to work too hard. Judging by the number of sons and nephews of associates that he's been introducing to me lately on one pretext or another, I think he's made it his mission to marry me off."

"Is that what you want? To get married and settle down?"

Something in Josh's tone had Laura look up from the spoon that she'd been licking. Excitement danced along her skin at the hunger in his eyes as he watched her. "I suppose so…someday. If the right man comes along."

"And what type of man is the right man?"

"He's someone li—" She'd been about to say, he was someone like her father had been. But her father hadn't been the man she'd believed him to be. He'd been an irresponsible coward and liar. "He's someone honest and trustworthy. Someone who lives up to his responsibilities, who does what's right regardless of the cost to him."

"Sounds like you're holding out for a hero," he said as he stole a spoonful of her Bananas Foster.

"I guess I am." She noted his empty dish as he swiped another bite of her dessert. "What about you?"

"Me?" He paused, his spoon already poised for another swoop of her ice cream. "I'm not holding out for a hero."

"Funny," she said, and tapped his spoon aside. His

expression fell as she zeroed in on the last of the dessert. So she divided the remaining bite in half. "I meant do you ever think about getting married and settling down?"

Polishing off the bite she'd left him, he grinned and said, "Not if I can help it."

"Josh, it really isn't necessary for you to walk me to my car," Laura said as they approached the bank of elevators that led to the parking garage.

"Sure it is." He pushed the button, signaling for the elevator. "It's late. The garage will be dark and you're alone."

"And your point is?"

"Besides the fact that it would be ungentlemanly of me not to accompany you, walking through a dark garage alone at night doesn't strike me as being particularly safe."

"Why? Because I'm a woman?"

"I didn't say that," he countered carefully, catching that slight edge in her voice and the defiant tilt of her chin.

"You didn't have to. Obviously you think that if some…some thug managed to get past the hotel's security—which is excellent, by the way—that I, being a mere woman, couldn't possibly handle the situation."

He was in stormy waters here, Josh told himself. Thanks to his sisters, he knew just how prickly a woman could get when she thought a man was being overprotective. "What I think is that any thug foolish enough to mistake you for a potential victim would end up getting his butt soundly kicked—by *you*."

"You're right. I would kick his butt," she told him, the militant gleam in her eyes vanishing.

"I'm sure you would."

"I'm glad you feel that way," Laura replied. "So why don't we just say goodbye now and you can go on back to your hotel room? I'll be just fine."

"I'm sure you will, but I won't." He hit the button for the elevator again, watched her wrinkle her brows. "In case you've forgotten, I'm from the South," he teased, exaggerating his drawl. "I've already gone against the code of the Southern gentleman by letting you convince me to just walk you to your car instead of seeing you home."

"There isn't any such code."

"Of course there is," Josh argued.

She eyed him skeptically. "Then how come I've never heard of it?"

"Because, my doubting Yankee, it's a secret code that only men from the South know about." The elevator dinged and the doors slid open. Josh gestured for her to precede him, then followed her inside. "What floor?"

"Five," she said. "Do you honestly expect me to believe that business about a secret code?"

He punched the number on the pad and the elevator doors slid shut, enclosing them in the small space. "Do you think I would make up such a thing?"

"What I think, Mr. Logan, is that you're very good at spinning tales and turning on that Southern charm to get your way."

Josh gave her a forlorn look. "There you go, slinging those arrows again."

When Laura burst into laughter, he couldn't help grinning in return. He liked the sound of her laughter, he realized. Almost as much as he liked the way her eyes sparkled and the way the dimple winked in her left cheek when she smiled. Suddenly itching to trace the tempting curve of her mouth with his finger, he shoved his hands into his pockets. The truth was there wasn't much about Laura Harte that he didn't like, Josh admitted, as he felt the sexual sparks that had been licking at him like flames all evening blaze into full-blown lust.

Lust he could handle, Josh told himself as the elevator continued its ascent. Back in New Orleans when he'd first seen Laura's picture, he'd anticipated the sexual chemistry. She was a beautiful woman, and he'd always had a healthy appreciation of women. Thanks to the dossier he'd read on her and what details Olivia had given him, his curiosity about the unknown Jardine heiress had been peaked long before he'd ever met her. So neither his attraction nor his curiosity about Laura had come as a surprise. What had been surprising was that he genuinely liked Laura Harte—not just the attractive package, but the woman herself. It was a complication that he hadn't counted on when he'd agreed to Olivia's plan. And it was the reason, he acknowledged silently, that all afternoon and evening he had put off telling Laura the real purpose of his visit—Olivia Jardine and the Princess.

Way to go, Logan. For a man who prided himself on never allowing personal feelings to blindside him in business, he had screwed up royally this time. He just hoped it wasn't too late to come clean with Laura and still salvage whatever was happening between them. The elevator stopped and he was grateful to be able to escape the intimacy of the confined space.

"Well, I guess this is it," Laura said as she turned to face him.

"Where are you parked?"

"On the other side of the garage. But you don't have to—"

"I thought we'd already discussed this," he said lightly. "Which direction?"

She shot him a sidelong glance. "Funny. I don't remember any discussion."

"Sure you do. You agreed I would walk you to your car and save myself from getting booted out of the Southern gentleman's union."

"There is no such union," she said, her lips twitching with laughter again.

"Are you willing to risk it and have my disgrace hanging over your head?"

"Whoever came up with the description of *charming* to describe Southern men forgot to mention that they were stubborn, too." She sighed. "Come on. My car's this way."

"Yes, ma'am," Josh said, and fell into step beside her. With his hand at her back, they started through the cavernous garage in the direction she'd indicated.

As they walked past row after row of cars of various makes and models, Josh was conscious of the shadows shifting along the garage's walls and the echo of Laura's heels as they clicked on the concrete flooring.

She stopped in front of a sleek blue convertible. "This is me," she said, and after unlocking the door with the remote on her key ring, she turned to him. "Thank you again for dinner."

"I'm the one who should be thanking you. I can't remember the last time I enjoyed an evening so much."

"Me, too," she murmured.

The lighting was poor, but bright enough for him to see the glint of silver in her blue eyes, the satin smoothness of her skin. Desire kicked him in the gut as he stared at her lush mouth. He wanted to sample that ripe mouth, had been eager to taste it all evening.

"It's getting late. I really should be going. So, I guess this is goodbye," she said, and extended her hand.

Josh looked at the hand she held out to him. The smart thing for him to do was to shake hands, make arrangements to see her in the morning so that he could tell her about Olivia and say good-night.

"Josh?"

To hell with being smart, he decided. Going with impulse, he pulled her to him. Against him. Into him. He heard the quick hitch of her breath, saw her eyes turn cloudy. And then he swooped down and took her mouth.

She tasted just the way he'd imagined—hot and sweet, soft and strong. She made some primitive sound low in her throat. Protest or plea, Josh wasn't sure which. He only knew that the desire for her that he'd managed to keep at simmer all afternoon and evening was now storming to a boiling point. And it showed no signs of slowing down.

Fusing his mouth to hers, he took.

So did she.

Tongues danced, mated. He filled himself with her scent, with her taste, with the explosion of her response. Still it wasn't enough. He wanted more. He tore his mouth free, speared his fingers into the fiery hair that framed her face. When her lashes fluttered and she stared up at him out of eyes that were the color of smoke, desire delivered another one-two punch to his system. He would have to pay for this lapse in reasoning later. Josh didn't have any doubt about that. But for now, for now he couldn't bring himself to care what retribution awaited him—not when the taste, the scent, the feel of Laura in his arms was a fire burning hot in his blood.

Using his teeth, he nipped at the soft skin of her lips, her jaw, her neck. He sloped his hands down her sides, shaped her waist, her hips. And when she arched her body, pressed herself against his arousal, Josh groaned.

"This is insane," she whispered, her hands racing over his shoulders, down his back, setting off new fires wherever she touched.

"Yes." It *was* insane. He knew mixing business and pleasure was asking for trouble. And considering the stakes, to do so now with Laura could prove disastrous. He didn't dare risk it. But oh how he wanted to. How he wished he could just say to hell with it and take what he wanted, what she was offering now.

"I should go," she murmured against his lips even as she wound her arms around his neck, drove her fingers through his hair.

"All right." He choked out the words and started to step back.

Laura yanked him by the hair and pulled his mouth back down to hers.

Hunger whipped through him lightning quick, driving every thought from his mind save one—Laura. He feasted on her mouth, groaned as her teeth scraped his lip. But her mouth wasn't enough. Not nearly enough. Breaking off the kiss, he captured her face between his palms. "I want you," he confessed. "I've wanted you from the minute I set eyes on you."

"I know. I know," she said, her breathing as ragged as his. "It's crazy. We hardly know each other."

"Doesn't matter." All that mattered was this. All that mattered was now. Blinded by need, he reached for the zipper at the back of her dress. And he froze at the grumble of a car's engine.

Sanity came slamming back to him in a rush as the headlights from an approaching car flashed on the wall behind them. Laura stiffened in his arms as the car turned off toward the exit lane and disappeared into the belly of the garage. When it was silent once more, Josh dragged in several breaths. He took a step back. "Laura, I—"

"Don't," she said, holding up a hand. She sucked in a few breaths of her own. "Whatever you do, don't you dare apologize."

"I have no intention of apologizing—especially since I'm not the least bit sorry."

"I…um, right. That's good, then. I guess."

Unexpectedly moved by the flush of pink to her cheeks and the distress swimming in her eyes, something inside of him shifted, softened. "Laura, it was only a kiss."

"I know that." She looked down at the ground as though it held all the answers to the mysteries of the universe. She looked everywhere and at everything except him.

He tipped her chin up so that he could see her eyes. "There's nothing to be embarrassed about. We're two healthy adults who are attracted to each other."

"I know. It's just that I'm not very good at this sort of thing."

"At kissing? You could have fooled me," he teased.

"That's not what I meant," she said, more color flooding her cheeks. "I meant that I don't usually end up crawling all over a man I've just met."

"That's good to hear, since I don't usually end up

necking in hotel parking lots with assistant general managers, either.''

She laughed as he'd hoped she would, then eased back a step. "I'd better go."

Josh stooped down, retrieved her keys where they had fallen just behind her foot. He held them out to her. But when she reached for the keys, he held on to them. He stared at her, wished that things could be different, that she wasn't Olivia Jardine's granddaughter and that his regaining ownership of the Princess was not tied to her.

"Josh? You're going to have to give me my keys. I need them to get home," she said, her voice light, teasing.

"I want to see you again. Will you meet me for breakfast in the morning? There's something I need to talk to you about."

The smile slipped from her lips as she reclaimed her keys. "Listen, Josh, there's no point in me denying that I'm attracted to you after what just happened. And I know Logan Hotels has a reputation of being a great firm to work for. But Nick Baldwin is not only my boss, he's my friend. I thought he was your friend, too," she said, her voice as cool as her eyes. "So if you want to see me again just so you can offer me a job, I can save us both some time and embarrassment and tell you right now that I'm not interested."

"Nick *is* my friend," he advised her, hurt that she would think he would stab his pal in the back by trying to steal his employee. "My wanting to see you isn't about business. It's personal."

"I—I'm sorry. It was foolish of me to jump to that conclusion. I had no right to assume—"

He cut off her apology with a quick, hard kiss. "You

had every right to jump to conclusions and assume just what you did. Now, is eight o'clock for breakfast too early?''

''No. But I have a meeting then. Could we make it for nine instead?''

''Nine o'clock is fine. I'll meet you in the hotel's dining room.''

''All right,'' she said.

After opening her car door for her, he waited until Laura had started the engine and strapped on her seat belt. Then he tapped on her window. Frowning, she eased down the car's window. ''Did you forget something?''

''Just this.'' Leaning through the window, he gave her a long, slow kiss. ''Good night.''

''Good night,'' she whispered.

For a long time after the taillights of the convertible had disappeared, Josh stood in the dimly lit garage and thought about the explosive kiss they'd shared. ''Dammit, Logan,'' he muttered as he stalked off toward the elevator. Laura Harte was forbidden fruit—Olivia Jardine's granddaughter and the key to his regaining the Princess. He had no business lusting after her because lust had a way of messing up a man's mind. So what if she kissed like a dream and just thinking about her had him rock-hard and aching? He'd get over it. No way did he intend to let a few hormones stand in the way of his plans. Laura Harte was a means to an end. Nothing more.

But later, much, much later, while he tossed and turned, unable to sleep, he kept remembering ghost-blue eyes dark with desire, the feel of satin-soft lips, the scent of flowers and sunshine.

Six

"Thanks to the tourist traffic generated by the wine crush in the Valley, our occupancy rate for October is running at ninety-five percent. That puts us up nearly ten percent over last year at this same time period."

Laura focused her attention on Tina Sawyer, the sharp brunette that she'd hired eight months ago as the hotel's director of marketing. The other woman had been doing a fabulous job, which was evident from her report to the department heads at the hotel's weekly meeting.

"Our holiday campaign blitz is already under way and the print ads are scheduled to start running on the first of November," Tina continued.

Try as she might, Laura found herself only half listening to Tina's report, her thoughts once again drifting to Josh. Despite a restless night in which she'd warned herself repeatedly not to read anything into that wild kiss that the two of them had shared, Laura hadn't been able to get him out of her mind.

"I want to see you again. It's personal."

A burst of longing arrowed through her as she recalled the husky tone of his voice, the hot gleam in his eyes. He'd looked at her as though he'd wanted to swallow her whole. Biting down on her lower lip, Laura acknowledged if only to herself that for one crazy moment last night she had wanted him. And what did that say about her? While she would like to believe it was the loneliness she'd felt these past months that had caused her to react so out of the norm, deep down inside she wasn't at all sure. She could imagine what her mother would have to say on the subject—no doubt something romantic about fate or destiny, Laura thought absently. A sharp pang hit her as reality came crashing back. She'd never know what her mother would have thought of Josh because her mother was dead. The jarring reminder sobered her. As Nick came to his feet, she realized she'd been in la-la land over Josh for most of the meeting. Silently, Laura promised herself to make up for the lapse in attention once Josh was gone.

"I think that about covers it for this morning, ladies and gentlemen. Thank you," Nick said from his position at the head of the conference room table. "Have a super day, and as always, if you have any problems, you know where my office is."

Amid the scrape of chairs and buzz of conversation, Laura stood and turned toward Tina, who was busy filing her notes away in a folder. "That was a good report, Tina. Very concise and informative. You're doing a great job."

"Thanks," the other woman said, a mile-wide smile on her face. "I just hope Mr. Baldwin is pleased."

"Mr. Baldwin is very pleased," Nick said as he joined them.

Tina blushed. "Thank you, sir. I just hope I can deliver for the holiday season."

"You will," Nick assured her.

Once the young woman had scurried off, Laura began gathering her own notes. "That was sweet of you," Laura told him.

"It's the truth. Tina's been a real asset to the Ambassador Grand and I have you to thank for finding her."

"Just doing my job." She took a quick peek at her watch. Ten minutes before nine. Enough time to check in at her office for messages and freshen her lipstick before going downstairs to meet Josh for breakfast. "Listen, I've got to run, but I want to hear all about last night's dinner reception later."

"Laura, wait," Nick called when she started to leave.

She paused, looked back at him. "Yes?"

"You got a second?"

"Actually, I'm supposed to meet someone in a few minutes," she said, for some reason reluctant to tell Nick that the person she was meeting was Josh.

"This won't take long. I have a meeting of my own to get to. But I wanted to make sure you're okay."

"I'm fine," Laura told him, puzzled by the remark.

He closed the door. "Would you like some coffee?" he asked as he picked up the carafe from the serving cart and filled a cup.

"No thanks."

"You sure?"

"Positive," Laura said, noting that Nick seemed in no hurry to get down to business—which was odd since Nick Baldwin was not a man to waste time. A demanding but fair boss, he was someone she not only respected, but considered a good friend as well. And something was troubling him. Guilt nipped at her conscience as she remembered picking up some strange undercurrents from Nick yesterday. Not only had she not made an effort to find out what was bothering Nick, she hadn't even given him a second thought, she admitted.

The realization shamed her. Determined to make amends, she decided meeting Josh would simply have to wait. Taking a seat at the table, she asked, "So how was last night?"

"Great. San Francisco's elite were all there in their finery, along with their checkbooks."

Laura grinned, knowing how much Nick would have preferred not to attend the fund-raiser. "It was for a good cause."

"That's what I tell myself every year," he said. "What about you? How did the tour with Josh go?"

"Fine," Laura said, feeling slightly uncomfortable because things between her and Josh hadn't remained all business.

"Douglas mentioned that the two of you had dinner in the restaurant last night."

"That's right," Laura replied, somewhat surprised. Not that it was a secret. It wasn't. But it seemed odd that the restaurant's maître d' would feel compelled to report her comings and goings to Nick. Unless, she amended, Nick had asked. "Is that a problem?"

"No. Why would it be?"

"It shouldn't. But since you mentioned it, I wondered if it was. I mean, I know Josh is a friend of yours and that he works for a competitor."

Nick chuckled. "Talk about understatement. Laura, Josh Logan doesn't work for a competitor. He *is* a competitor."

"I know, but—" Realization dawned. "Is that what's bothering you? Are you worried that Josh might have tried to hire me away from the Ambassador Grand?''

Nick's lips tipped into a smile. ''Friends or not, Josh knows that if he made any attempt to steal my very valuable assistant manager that I'd mess up that pretty face of his in a heartbeat.''

Laura laughed. ''Then I guess his face is safe. Because he didn't offer me a job.''

''And if he had, what would you have said?''

''I'd have turned him down.''

''That's good to hear.'' He took another sip of his coffee. ''So now that we have that out of the way, how did everything go with you and Josh?''

''If you mean the tour, it went fine. He was very impressed with the hotel.''

''Somehow I doubt it was the hotel that impressed him the most.''

Laura's cheeks heated, but she made no attempt to confirm or deny his statement. ''Anyway, after I showed him the hotel, we had a very pleasant dinner in the restaurant and then he went to his room and I went home.''

''So, did you two get a chance to talk?''

''Some,'' she replied, recalling how little talking they had done in the garage. ''Mostly we talked about the hotel industry and Josh told me about his family. Did you know that he has four sisters?''

''Yeah. Meredith, Rachel, Hope and Faith.''

''Talk about feeling foolish,'' she said, somewhat embarrassed by her gaff. ''Of course you know about his sisters. You're a friend of the family and probably know all of the Logans.''

''Not quite. The Logans are a pretty good-size family and I think they've gotten even bigger since I knew them. Besides, I wasn't exactly what you'd call a friend of the family. I was an employee who just happened to be friends with Josh.''

"Then you didn't know his family?''

"I met them all, but except for Josh, Faith was the only other Logan I spent much time around.''

"Faith?'' she repeated, recalling that there had been something in Nick's eyes yesterday when Josh had brought her name up.

"She's Josh's youngest sister. She used to help out at the hotel after school when I worked at Logan's in New Orleans. It was a long time ago and she was only a senior in high school then. I'd be surprised if she even remembered me.''

"Trust me, Nick. She'd remember you,'' Laura assured him, detecting what sounded suspiciously like yearning in Nick's voice as he spoke of Faith Logan.

He flashed her a smile. "Just because you find me unforgettable doesn't mean Faith did.''

Accustomed to their teasing banter, she said, "Lots of things are unforgettable, Mr. Baldwin, like the first wicked shot the doctor gave me or a trip to the dentist. Or that awful-tasting medicine—''

"I get the picture,'' Nick said dryly. "And since we're not going to discuss how unforgettable I am, let's talk about your dinner with Josh. Did you two discuss anything else? Or did Logan monopolize the entire evening talking about his family?''

"Not at all. I talked about my family, too—or at least about my mother and Uncle Paul. I told him about the accident.''

"Pretty rough, huh?''

She nodded. "Josh was very sympathetic.''

"That's good," Nick said, but a frown etched at the corners of his mouth.

Laura couldn't shake the feeling that something was still bothering Nick. "Nick, is everything all right?"

"Sure. What could be wrong?"

"Nothing I guess. You're not usually so interested in my dinner conversations."

Nick shrugged. "It's not every evening that you have dinner with an old friend of mine who also happens to be a competitor. I just wanted to make sure you were okay."

"I'm fine," she told him, but something about his answer and the concerned look in his eyes struck her as being off. "Nick, are you sure nothing's bothering you? You seem…worried."

"All hotel owners worry. It's a fact of life."

"If you say so," Laura replied, not entirely convinced he was being honest with her.

"I do." He looked at his watch, then pushed back his chair. "Look at the time. I didn't mean to keep you so long. And there are a couple of calls I need to make. I'll let you get going so you're not late for your meeting."

"Actually, it's not a business meeting. I'm joining Josh for breakfast."

Irritation flashed in Nick's eyes. "Logan's still here at the hotel?"

"As far as I know, he is. Why?"

"Because when I tried to reach him in his room earlier, I was told he'd already checked out. I didn't realize he was still here."

"He probably used the video checkout before going downstairs to the restaurant. That's where we're supposed to be meeting for breakfast. He said he had an early flight, so I imagine he'll be going straight to the airport from here. And speaking of the airport," she said, taking a look at her own watch, "I'd better get downstairs if we're going to have that breakfast before Josh leaves."

"I'm sure you're right." He walked over to the door and held it open for her. "Have a nice breakfast. I'll touch base with you later."

She paused, looked up at him. "I just realized that you said you'd tried to reach Josh this morning. Were you hoping to have breakfast with him yourself? If so, I'm sure you'd be welcome to join us."

"Thanks, but I've already eaten. And I was calling to follow up on something we'd discussed. I'll be in touch with him later."

"All right," she said, and smiled, reluctant to admit how pleased she was that Nick wouldn't be joining them. Hurrying down the corridor toward the elevator, Laura had just pushed the elevator call button when she realized she'd left her meeting notes in the conference room. "Darn it," she muttered, and retraced her path to the conference room to reclaim her file.

Poised to knock on the door, the sound of Nick's voice stopped her. Evidently he was on the telephone, she mused. Not wanting to disturb him, she slipped inside, intent on grabbing her file folder and leaving again. Nick stood in front of the sweep of windows, his back to her and his ear to the phone.

"Damn it, Logan! What in the hell kind of game are you playing?"

Laura froze. Uneasiness sprinted down her spine at the angriness in Nick's voice, the stiff line of his back. She should leave, not listen to another word, a voice whispered inside her head. Eavesdropping was never a good thing to do. Hadn't her mother told her that eavesdroppers invariably heard something that they were better off not hearing?

"So why haven't you told her yet? I thought you said that was the reason you came here in the first place."

She should go, Laura told herself. But some sixth sense paralyzed her. She didn't move. She barely breathed. All the while dread spread through her system as instinct told her that the "her" Nick had referred to was Laura herself.

Nick's free hand balled into a fist at his side, and Laura could all but feel the anger vibrating from him like waves. "So help me, Logan, you hurt Laura and I'll—"

She must have made some sound, Laura realized. Because suddenly Nick whipped around, swore when he spied her. "I've got to go." He slammed down the phone. "Laura…"

She took a step back, clutching the folder to her chest because she needed something to hold on to. A hundred unpleasant possibilities began spinning through her head. Nick was sick. He'd made plans to sell the hotel to Josh. And Josh had decided the new administration didn't need her. "What's going on, Nick? What is it Josh was supposed to tell me?"

He shoved a fist through his dark hair. "It's not as bad as it sounds."

"Why don't you let me be the judge of that," she suggested, amazed that she sounded so calm while inside she was churning. She closed the door and walked over to him. "Please. Whatever it is, tell me."

Laura almost felt sorry for him. The man looked as though he'd been sucker punched. But then, that's just how she felt. "I can't tell you because I don't know all of the details. You'll have to talk to Josh."

"I intend to. But first, I want you to tell me what you do know."

Josh spotted Laura the moment she entered the hotel's dining room. A vision of outraged femininity in a bold red suit with her blue eyes blazing fire, she swept past the maître d' and scanned the room. He swore when her eyes locked on him. He'd gambled and lost, he concluded grimly as she cut a path through the busy breakfast crowd and headed straight for him. Any foolish thoughts he'd been harboring of a personal relationship with her died a swift death. So did the faint glimmer of hope that Laura hadn't been the reason Nick had terminated their phone conversation so abruptly. Obviously, his friend had spilled his guts and she knew his reason for being in San Francisco. Not that he blamed Nick for telling her, Josh conceded. He didn't. Were the situation reversed, he'd probably have done the same thing. No. He didn't blame anyone for the mess he was in except himself.

And it was a mess. Judging by the look in her eyes, he was dead meat. Damn! If only he had gotten the business out of the way before things started heating up between them. There was no question that he should have said something to her about his reason for being in San Francisco before he'd kissed her. But then he hadn't been exactly thinking straight from the moment he'd set eyes on her. Nor had Olivia Jardine and the Princess Hotel been uppermost in his mind last night in the parking garage when she'd turned to fire in his arms. But no doubt hell would freeze over before she'd believe him.

So much for hindsight, he thought. It wasn't going to do him a lick of good now, he conceded as she stormed past a waiter and the guy nearly upended his tray of coffee to get out of her way. Smart fellow, Josh thought. Judging by the fierce expression on Laura's face, he was tempted to duck for cover himself.

Never one to take the coward's way out, Josh stood when she reached his table. "Good morning. I was beginning to worry you weren't going to be able to make it. I'm glad you did," he said, and gave her his friendliest smile. "You look wonderful."

"You can save the Southern charm and sexy grins, Logan. I know why you're here."

"For the same reason you are, I assume—breakfast." He pulled out her chair and wasn't surprised when she ignored the gesture and continued to stand.

"It isn't going to work."

"No? From the sights and smells that have been coming out of the kitchen, I was pretty sure breakfast would be every bit as good as last night's dinner."

"I'm not talking about breakfast and you know it."

The college-age waiter whose name tag read Pete stood uneasily to Laura's left. He cleared his throat. "Uh, Ms. Harte, is something wrong with your chair?"

"No." She practically growled the word, then immediately abandoned her stern expression when the waiter stumbled back a step, dropped his pad and pencil and began mumbling apologies. "It's all right, Pete. And the chair's fine," she said softly, and as though to prove it, she sat down.

Josh couldn't help feeling sorry for the kid as he resumed his own seat. "I think we'll need a few minutes, Pete. Why don't you just leave the menus and bring out another pot of coffee."

"Yes, sir."

From the way the young man hurried off, Josh suspected the fellow recognized trouble brewing when he saw it. He didn't blame the guy for wanting to escape. A person would have to be blind to miss the fact that Laura was spitting mad. Her body language alone broadcasted that fact. With her hands balled into fists, her chin jutted high and her back ramrod straight, she looked like an avenging goddess. Those blue eyes were shooting daggers of ice at him and that incredible mouth of hers was pulled into a forbidding frown. And damned if he didn't find himself captivated. So many layers to her, he thought, and he itched to explore them all. And judging by the scowl she directed at him, she'd rip him apart if he so much as tried.

"Wipe that smirk off your face, Logan. I have no intention of staying. The only reason I'm here at all is to tell you what a louse I think you are."

"Would you mind doing it while we eat? I'm starved," he said, deciding his only hope of salvaging the situation was to keep her talking.

Laura blinked. "You have got to be kidding," she shot back, her voice laced with disdain. "You actually expect me to have breakfast with you?"

"Aren't you hungry?" he asked, donning the calm demeanor he found effective when negotiating a multi-million-dollar hotel deal.

Her blue eyes snapped with fury and her never-still fingers strangled the napkin on the table in front of her. "I'd sooner eat with a snake!"

Josh checked the urge to wince and cast a bland smile to the interested party at the next table. Leaning forward, he said softly, "While I hate to put a damper on this interesting conversation we're having, you might want to lower your voice a bit. It seems we have an audience, and something tells me that's not going to sit very well with you.''

Laura whipped her gaze to her right and then to her left, where the occupants at both tables were openly watching and listening to them. Heat flooded her cheeks. Glaring at him, she said, ''As far as I'm concerned, this conversation is over.''

''Laura, wait.'' Josh placed his hand on her arm. ''Please, don't go yet. I'd like a chance to apologize and to explain.''

''I'm listening.''

Removing his hand from her arm, he said, ''I don't blame you for being upset with me. You have every right to be. I should have been up front with you and told you the reason I was here right from the start. You deserved to know the truth.''

''Yes, I did deserve the truth.''

Ignoring the reproach in her voice, he continued. ''And I'm sorry for not being completely honest with you. I regret that more than you can ever know—especially after last night.''

''It's done, Josh. It seems we both made a mistake.''

''Not all of it was a mistake. At least not for me. I enjoyed spending the evening with you, talking, getting to know you. Give me a chance to make things up to you. Have breakfast with me and let me tell you about your grandmother's proposition. Once we have that out of the way, I'll cancel my flight and then you and I—''

Her laughter cut him off. ''You have got to be kidding. Tell me, Logan, do you see the words *gullible fool* stamped across my forehead?''

Irritated that she'd dismissed his apology, he said, ''Obviously, you don't believe my apology is sincere.''

"Come on, Josh. I'm not a fool. You and I both know the reason you came on to me last night wasn't because you found me irresistible."

"Is that so? Then why don't you tell me what you think my reasons were," he said, his voice soft despite the temper sparking inside him.

"Because Olivia Jardine sent you. Evidently, she thought I'd be more receptive to her request if you delivered it for her in person."

Josh gritted his teeth, determined to keep a rein on his temper. "Think you've got it all figured out, do you?"

"Yes. The only thing that has me puzzled is why you agreed to go along with Olivia's plan. What was in it for you, Josh?"

The mark hit too close to home for comfort, and because it did, it infuriated Josh. Feeling the last threads of control on his temper shred, his voice took on a menacing growl as he said, "First off, no one sends me anywhere and no one tells me what to do. I decide for myself. While Olivia asked me to go to San Francisco to see you and plead her case, *I* was the one who made the decision to come. I've already admitted I was wrong not to tell you up front why I was here and apologized for it."

Never taking his eyes from her face, he continued, "As for my 'coming on to you,' as you phrased it so delightfully, my attraction to you was not part of some great plan your grandmother hatched so that I could persuade you to come to New Orleans. It didn't have a damn thing to do with Olivia Jardine or anyone else, but me. I kissed you last night because it's what *I* wanted to do. And God help me, despite the fact that you've insulted me by even suggesting otherwise, it's what I want to do again right now."

"You expect me to believe that?"

Her skepticism grated. "It's the truth. Spending the evening with you, kissing you, had nothing to do with business," he told her. "I'm attracted to you. And dammit. Whether you admit it or not, you're attracted to me."

She made a huffing sound. "Don't flatter yourself."

He leaned forward. "And don't lie to *yourself,*" he countered. "I was on the other side of that kiss last night, remember? And it wasn't all one-sided."

She met his gaze evenly, challengingly. "Maybe I did respond to you," she agreed haughtily. "But that was before I knew what a snake you are. Now that I do, you can be sure it won't happen again."

Her cool, dismissive response was like a match to dry tinder. Josh snagged her wrist, ran his thumb across it and smiled when her pulse quickened. "You wouldn't want to make a little wager on that, would you?"

She withdrew her hand. "Thanks, but I think I'll pass."

"What's the matter?" he taunted. "Afraid you might lose?"

"Hardly. I'm just not interested."

"No?" He slid his gaze down, lingered on her mouth for a moment before returning to her face. The desire he read in her eyes hit him like a fist. Suddenly he remembered how it had felt to kiss her last night. The texture of that generous mouth—soft, warm, like silk bathed in sunlight. And the way she'd tasted— hints of wine and the ice cream they'd consumed, mixed with a sweetness that was Laura's alone. "Sure I can't get you to reconsider that bet?"

"I'm positive. I never gamble."

"That's too bad," Josh said. "Because I can think of some very interesting stakes."

Seven

"**I**'m sure you can," Laura told him, flustered that he could make her feel so hot and needy with just a look. For one foolish moment, she'd almost believed him when he'd claimed his attraction to her had had nothing to do with Olivia Jardine. He'd seemed so sincere, his apology so genuine. Or maybe she'd simply wanted to believe him, she admitted. Because Josh had been right. She *was* attracted to him. And even now, while her blood ran hot with anger at his deception and knowing of his link to the Jardines, she was still drawn to him. The tug of awareness that had hummed between them throughout yesterday remained every bit as strong now in the clear light of day as it had last night in the dark garage.

She didn't like it. Worse, she didn't understand it. Josh Logan certainly was not the first man she'd ever been attracted to. There had been other men in her life—men she'd found equally attractive, men whose company she'd enjoyed, and one man in particular that she'd even been a little bit in love with. But none of those men had ever made her skin heat with just a look, her pulse race with only a smile, her heart ache at his touch.

Disturbed by his effect on her, she tried to make sense of the feelings he stirred inside her. She stared

across the table at him. The charcoal-gray suit he wore
fit as though it had been made for him. So did the deep
blue shirt and monochromatic tie. His skin was bronzed
from the sun, his hair as dark as midnight, his smile
bright and devilishly charming. He looked like what he
was—a man of wealth and privilege and power, a
power that had nothing to do with his money and everything to do with the man he was. Yet there was
something more—a pride and yearning that ran soul-
deep hidden behind his green eyes. And when he
trained those eyes on her, she sensed a hunger, a passion in him that went beyond anything physical. A need
that called out to her and touched something deep inside her heart.

Yet he'd deliberately deceived her, Laura reminded
herself. She'd fallen for his smooth, careless charm last
night. She refused to do so again. Despite his protests
and explanations, nothing could change the fact that
Josh had sought her out on behalf of Olivia Jardine.
But even without the deception between them, his connection to the Jardines made any relationship between
them impossible. His loyalty was to Olivia Jardine and
she wanted nothing to do with any member of the Jardine family. If nothing else, she owed her mother that.

Fury welled up inside her as she recalled her uncle
Paul recounting how her mother had returned from
New Orleans crushed and heartbroken. Laura couldn't
even begin to imagine how her mother must have felt—
alone and pregnant with no husband or family. No, she
would never forgive the Jardines and she would never
allow them into her life.

"Does your silence mean you're reconsidering that
wager?"

Laura shook off her dark musings and focused on

Josh instead. "Afraid not. You'll have to find someone else to play games with."

"What if you're the only one I want, Laura?"

His voice was rough, his eyes edgy with desire. And something in his tone, in the way he was looking at her, called to the emptiness that had filled her life these past months. Unnerved that he could exert such strong feelings in her, Laura averted her gaze. "Very smooth, Logan. But I'm not interested."

He placed his hand atop hers. "What would you say if I told you that I was interested in more than just games?"

She swallowed hard, a part of her wanting to believe he was serious while another part of her fearing that he was. Obviously she was susceptible to men with a hero's good looks and a misty Southern drawl, she decided. Hardening her resolve, she slipped her hand free. "As impossible as you might find it to believe, I really am not interested in you, Josh."

His lips twitched. Amusement danced in his eyes. "There's an easy way to test the truth in that statement," he countered, and slid his gaze to her mouth.

Laura's pulse jumped even as her temper flared at his arrogance. She was about to rip into him when Pete arrived at their table, all smiles, and brandishing a fresh pot of coffee. "Are you ready to order?" the young man asked, and started to fill her cup.

"Nothing for me," she said crossly, and waved off his offer of coffee.

"I'll take a refill," Josh told him, and held out his own cup. "And you can bring us two of the Grand's specials."

"One," Laura corrected him. "I'm not staying."

Pete looked from her to Josh and at Josh's nod, he

tucked his order pad into his apron slot. "One special coming up. I'll be back in a few minutes with your breakfast."

Once the waiter left, Josh sat back in his chair and sipped his coffee. A smile curved his lips as he said, "I believe we were considering a test to the accuracy of that last statement of yours."

"Wrong. You were looking for a way to salvage your bruised ego. Unfortunately, I don't have the time or inclination to indulge you." She pushed her chair back to stand. "Enjoy your breakfast, Josh. I have to get back to work."

Ever the gentleman, Josh came to his feet at once to assist her with her chair. "You surprise me, Laura," he said as she gathered her file folder. "I never would have pegged you as a coward."

Laura stiffened. Bristling at the remark, she hiked up her chin and met his gaze evenly. "I'm not a coward," she hurled back in response to his accusation.

"Then why are you running away?" he asked, invading her space with his wide shoulders and long limbs. "Why are you pretending that nothing's happening between us?"

"I am not running away. And there is nothing happening between us," she informed him.

"So how do you explain last night in the parking garage?"

"You mean that kiss?" she countered. "I hate to disappoint you, Logan, but you're not the first man that I've ever kissed. And I doubt that you'll be the last."

The amusement in his eyes faded and was replaced by something dark, threatening. When she started to glance away, he caught her chin, turned her face so that she was forced to look at him. His grip was gentle, barely more than the touch of his fingers. Yet she might as well have been caught in a vise because she could no more have looked away from him in that moment than she could have sprouted wings and flown. "Then maybe I should kiss you again to make sure you don't forget me."

The breath backed up in her lungs. For long seconds, the world around her seemed suspended. The murmur of voices ceased. The pianist playing a piece by Chopin stopped mid-note. The clink of china and crystal, the metallic tap of silverware and serving pieces, the chairs scraping against the floor all came to a halt. It was as though the world and everyone in it had stopped—except for her and Josh. Her heart beat frantically in her chest, urging her to go into Josh's arms, to offer him her mouth as she had last night, to find out if she had only imagined the power of his kiss, the rightness of being in his arms.

Some of what she was feeling must have shown in her face, because the hand holding her chin tightened. And his voice sounded as shaken as she felt as he whispered, "Laura."

The sound of glass shattering somewhere behind her brought the world crashing back into focus. Laura jumped and Josh released her at once. The sensual spell broken, she retreated a step, dragged in a breath and tried to regain her bearings. She registered the apology being made by the busboy to one of the diners a few feet away while he gathered up pieces of broken glass and china. What on earth had she been thinking? she chided herself silently. "I need to get back to work."

He wanted to argue. She could see it in his eyes and half expected him to challenge her again. Instead he stepped back and said, "I suppose it would be futile to

suggest that you stay a little longer and have breakfast.''

"Yes, it would. I need to get back to my desk."

"Nick certainly is lucky to have such a dedicated
employee. I hope he appreciates you."

She didn't miss the censure behind his words and
disliked it. "He does. Goodbye, Josh," she said, and
started to leave.

"Laura, there is just one more thing before you go
running back to your office."

Ignoring the jibe, she paused. "Yes?"

"We never did get around to discussing your grandmother and the reason she asked me to come see you.
If I were to come by your office in—" he glanced at
his watch "—say in an hour…do you think you could
spare me a few minutes?"

"There's really nothing to discuss," she said
quickly, now eager to escape. "I've already told Mrs.
Jardine that I'm not interested in pursuing any relationship with her or her family."

"She told me. But…" He paused, cut a glance to
the two women at the next table. "I don't know about
you, but I think we've provided enough entertainment
for the dining room troops this morning."

"I agree."

"Then the question is where do you want to finish
this discussion—here or in your office? Because I'm
not leaving until we do."

The steel in his voice was as hard as the look in his
eyes. He meant it. He wasn't going to leave her alone
until she at least listened to what he had to say. "All
right. In my office in thirty minutes."

Thirty minutes later Josh stood in Laura's office,
staring out of the window while he waited for her. He

shoved a hand through his hair, not sure who he was more annoyed with—Laura for refusing to admit that last night had meant something to her or with himself for pushing her as he had. He'd been brought up to respect women and to take a lady at her word. If she said she wasn't interested, then the subject was closed. While he might have tried using charm to persuade a woman to change her mind, he'd never in his life pressured a female. Yet, he'd been sorely tempted to snag Laura into his arms in front of God and everyone in that restaurant and kiss her senseless until she was clinging to him and sobbing his name.

And if he had, she'd have probably taken his head off. Josh couldn't help but grin at the thought. The lady was an interesting mix of contrasts. Perhaps that was part of the attraction. She was serious, practical to a fault and had a stubborn streak that was a mile wide. At the same time, she had the smile of a siren and skin as soft as silk. And remembering the hot arousal in her eyes when he'd touched her was driving him insane. How could a woman be so passionate and responsive, yet resistant at the same time?

"Laura, I was just going over—"

At the sound of Nick's voice, Josh whipped his gaze to the doorway, where Nick Baldwin had stopped mid-sentence upon spying him at the window. "Laura's not here."

"Yes, I see that." Nick shut the door behind him and strolled into the room. "I didn't realize you were still here, Logan. I was under the impression you were heading out of town this morning."

"I decided to delay my flight."

"Any particular reason?" Nick asked.

"Some unfinished business that needs taking care of."

"And I take it that unfinished business involves Laura."

Josh nearly smiled at the casual delivery of the remark. Neither Nick's tone nor his expression gave any indication of what his feelings were on the subject of Laura. But Josh knew from experience just how deceptive his old friend's politeness could be. In the year the two of them had worked the hotel bar, he'd witnessed Nick take down muscle-bound goons outweighing him by fifty pounds and do it without so much as raising his voice. Nick was as coolheaded and controlled as they came. It had been one of the things he'd always admired about him. Even as a twenty-two-year-old, Nick had been a master at keeping his emotions under wraps. A person never knew what was going on behind those cool hazel eyes of his. That talent had served him well on more than one occasion when tempers had run high both at the hotel bar and on the French Quarter streets. In the dozen years since then, Nick appeared to have become even more skilled at masking his thoughts. Fortunately, he knew Nick Baldwin well enough to recognize that the other man's question hadn't been prompted by idle curiosity. But then, Nick wasn't the only one who preferred keeping his own counsel. "That's right. It does concern Laura."

"Since you said this was business and not personal, I assume this involves her grandmother."

"I didn't realize she'd told you about our conversation."

"Actually, she didn't. I haven't seen Laura since earlier this morning. But if you met her for breakfast, you know that I'm the one who told her that you were here to see her on behalf of a relative of hers." He put down the report he'd been holding and sat on the edge of Laura's desk. "Of course, I didn't realize at that time that you hadn't gotten around to telling her your reason for being here."

Josh ignored the censure in Nick's voice. "The time never seemed right. I'd planned to tell her this morning over breakfast."

"But I beat you to it."

"It was my fault. I should have handled things differently."

"I won't argue with you on that point—especially since it turns out that she knew all about this mysterious grandmother. Laura said the woman had already contacted her and that she'd decided not to pursue the relationship. In fact, after my conversation with her this morning, I was under the impression that she'd planned to tell you the same thing."

"Like I said, we never got around to finishing our discussion. That's why I'm here." Josh glanced at his watch. "She was supposed to meet me here fifteen minutes ago."

"Evidently, she got tied up. Laura's very conscientious. She takes her responsibilities here at the hotel very seriously."

"I've noticed," Josh told him. "You're lucky to have her as an employee."

"I consider myself even more fortunate to have Laura as my friend. And because she is my friend, I wouldn't want to see her get hurt."

"Neither would I," Josh informed him.

Pushing away from the desk, Nick walked over to

the minibar at the counter. He held up the coffeepot.
"Coffee?"

"No thanks."

Nick poured himself a cup. Then he leaned against
the countertop, took a sip and smiled. "Not as good as
the stuff we use to drink down at the French Market
in New Orleans, but close."

Josh narrowed his eyes. "I assume that there's something more on your mind. So why don't you just cut
to the chase, and tell me what's bothering you."

"Actually, I'm not sure 'bothering' is the right word.
It's just ever since you showed up here a few days ago,
I've found myself thinking about the old days a lot.
You remember, back when you and I were just starting
out and I was still working for your dad in New Or-
leans."

"I remember. What about it?"

"I keep recalling what a tight-knit bunch you Logans were. For all the complaining you did about your
sisters and they did about you, all of you looked out
for one another."

Josh shrugged. "That's what families do."

"Not all families."

Josh paused as he remembered that Nick's family
situation had been a far cry from his own. Abandoned
by his mother when he was still a toddler, his father
drunk more often than he was sober. Nick had practically raised himself. While Josh had been playing football and dreaming of his first car, Nick had been throwing newspapers and hustling odd jobs to make ends
meet. That Nick had taken the lousy cards life had dealt
him and made a success of himself was one of the
reasons Josh had always respected him. It also brought
home to Josh just how lucky he had been to have a

loving family and a legacy like Logan Hotels. It was one of the reasons he had worked so hard to repay his family's faith in him by seeing that Logan Hotels continued to flourish and expand. And it was also one of the reasons that he had been so determined to make good on his promise to his grandfather by reclaiming the one prize that had eluded them all until now—the Royal Princess Hotel. Aware that Nick was watching him, Josh dragged his thoughts back to the present. "I heard about your father dying a while back. I'm sorry."

"He'd died inside a long time ago when my mother took off. The cancer just finished the job."

Josh thought of his own father and how devastating the loss would be if something were to happen to him. "Still, I don't imagine it was easy for you."

Nick shrugged. "I dealt with it. We were never close."

Because it was true and Josh felt both guilty and glad that his own relationship with his father remained a close one, he remained silent.

"But I didn't bring up your family's closeness in order to talk about the lack of unity in my own family. After our talk the other day, I couldn't help remembering how quick you were to warn me off your sister Faith when you found out she and I were seeing each other."

Josh frowned. "She was just a kid, barely out of high school. You were a lot older than her in years and experience."

"True. But I've always wondered if that riot act you read me that day was because of Faith's innocence or because I didn't quite fit the vision of the man you wanted to see your sister involved with."

"That's nothing but a crock and you know it. I ought

to knock your lights out for just suggesting I'm that kind of snob.''

"You're welcome to try."

"Don't tempt me," Josh countered, curling his hands into fists at his sides. "If you ask me, the only one of us who ever cared whether or not your blood was blue enough was you. I never treated you as anything other than my friend."

"You're right, and I apologize. You were a good friend to me at a time in my life when I didn't have the means to attract many friends."

"Forget it," Josh told him, disturbed by Nick's cynicism. "Besides, what does my having been a little overprotective of my sister have to do with anything?"

"You call threatening to tear my heart out and feed it to me a little overprotective?"

Embarrassed as he recalled attacking his friend, he said, "I was upset. Faith had been acting weird and she had that starry-eyed I'm-in-love look. When I overheard her telling her girlfriend that you were the guy she was in love with, I flipped out." Josh raked a hand through his hair as he recalled how worried he'd been for his baby sister. "Give me a break, Nick. You and I were best friends. Hell! We used to cruise the French Quarter together looking for chicks. I knew the type of women you kept company with. The same type of women we both kept company with—women who knew the score. Faith didn't. As it was, it took her a long time to get over you. If I hadn't put a stop to things when I did, she would have been hurting a lot worse. So if you're looking for an apology for what happened a dozen years ago, you're out of luck. I wasn't sorry then and I'm not sorry now. And if I had to do it over again, I would. There was no way I was going to stand by and see my sister get hurt by you or anyone else.''

"I understand. And I hope that you'll understand that there's no way I'm going to stand by and watch you hurt Laura.''

"It's not my intention to hurt her,'' Josh informed him. "But I hardly think you can compare my situation with Laura with what was going on between you and Faith.''

"Why not?''

"Because it's not the same. You were romancing Faith at a time when she was young and vulnerable.''

"And you've been charming Laura from the moment I introduced you. This morning, she was distracted and had that dreamy look in her eyes. She may not be as young as Faith was, but she's every bit as vulnerable. I'm not asking you to back off, Logan, I'm telling you to.''

"And if I don't?''

The smile Nick gave him was slow...chilling. "I haven't forgotten that you nearly broke my jaw when you found out about me and Faith. I let you get away with it because I felt that I deserved it. But that doesn't mean I wouldn't take advantage of the opportunity to even the score if you cross me on this.''

"Then it looks like you'll get the chance, because what's between me and Laura is none of your business and I have no intention of backing off.''

"Just remember that if you hurt her, I won't only threaten to rip out your heart and feed it to you, I'll do it.''

Laura stood in the doorway of her office, staring in disbelief at the two men snarling at each other like a couple of angry pups. Evidently the pair had been too busy sizing each other up to notice her, she concluded, because neither man had taken his eyes off the other.

"You're welcome to try, pal." Josh practically growled and motioned for Nick to come at him.

It was a wonder the air didn't sizzle from all that testosterone, Laura thought, irritated by the display of machismo. Stepping farther into the room, she said, "Does someone want to tell me what's going on here?"

Neither man said a word. And neither man so much as glanced in her direction. She was still edgy with nerves and temper from her earlier encounter with Josh; their silence was like a log being tossed on a fire. "Fine. Then let me remind both of you that this is *my* office and I'm going to be very unhappy if so much as a pencil gets broken. If you want to pound each other, go right ahead. But do it somewhere else or I'll call security."

When only silence followed and the two men continued to posture and glare at each other, Laura snatched up the phone and signaled the switchboard. "Hello, this is Ms. Harte. Could you please send up a couple of men from security to my office?"

Nick swore. "Dammit, Laura." He stormed over to the desk where she stood with the telephone receiver at her ear. Glaring at her, he said, "I *own* the hotel!"

"Hold off on sending up security—at least for the time being," she instructed the switchboard operator.

After she hung up the phone, Nick said, "I don't appreciate being threatened by an employee in my own hotel."

Folding her arms across her chest, Laura glared right back at him. "And I don't appreciate finding my boss and his supposedly good friend ready to tear each other apart in my office. Not everything in this office belongs to you, Nick Baldwin. Some of the things in here are mine. So if the two of you have a problem and want to beat each other senseless, go duke it out someplace else.''

Once she'd tossed out the reprimand, Laura held her breath. She'd always had a hair-trigger temper, and until recently she could have sworn she'd gotten a handle on it. Now she wasn't quite so sure. She stared at Nick's face, noted the tight lines of his mouth, the flush of red tinging his tanned cheeks. Perhaps taking the fellow who signed her paychecks to task in front of someone else wasn't the wisest thing she'd ever done, Laura decided, and waited for the fallout from her sharp tongue.

''You're right,'' Nick said. ''This isn't the time or place for this. I apologize.''

''So do I,'' Josh added, relaxing his fighting stance. He shifted his gaze to Laura. ''I've rescheduled my flight. If you have time, I'd like for us to finish our discussion.''

Laura tensed at the reminder of what they had been discussing. Her pride and her feelings still smarting from her earlier conversation with him, the last thing she wanted to do was face him again now—and to discuss Olivia Jardine.

''Laura?'' Josh asked. ''Is now a good time?''

When she hesitated, Nick took a step toward her. ''If you don't want to talk to Logan, you don't have to.''

Laura caught the protective note in Nick's voice, as well as the warning look in Josh's eyes. While she might have wished it was as simple as saying no, she knew that it wasn't simple at all. Even if Nick were to have Josh tossed from the premises, she would only be avoiding the inevitable. She didn't doubt for a minute that Josh would keep his word and refuse to give up until she heard him out.

"It's okay, Nick." She placed a hand on his arm, squeezed. "I'd just as soon get this over with now. Unless you needed to see me about something first?"

Nick looked from her to Josh and then back to her again. "It's nothing that can't wait. I left a report on your desk. Give me a call when you're free and we'll go over it."

"All right. I shouldn't be long."

"Logan," Nick said. "You might want to keep in mind what I told you."

"And you might want to keep in mind what happened the last time we disagreed about something."

Disturbed by the dangerous undercurrents between the two men, Laura slid her arm through Nick's and urged him toward the door. "I'll come by your office as soon as I finish up here."

Once Nick had left, Laura braced herself before she turned to face Josh. The tension in the room had been as thick as smoke when Nick and Josh had been facing off against each other, and Laura had been sure things couldn't possibly be any more strained. She'd been wrong. The air practically vibrated with the uneasy tension between them.

Drawing in a deep breath, she walked slowly over to the sitting area. "I still think this is a waste of time," Laura told him, doing her best to keep her voice even and businesslike. "I informed Mrs. Jardine when she phoned me that I didn't want to pursue any relationship between us. I haven't changed my mind.

"I have no interest in meeting her or any members of her family."

"They're your family, too," Josh advised her.

"Just because we share some DNA doesn't make them my family."

Josh's lips thinned. "That's a pretty cold way of looking at it."

"It's the truth."

"Listen, can we sit down and discuss this like two adults?"

Laura hesitated. She told herself it was a waste of time and emotional energy, and she admitted that the sting of learning the truth about Josh's interest in her had yet to dull. And the sooner she let him say his piece, the sooner he'd be out of her life. "All right," she said and motioned toward the pair of couches that had been grouped around a coffee table. She sat down on the nearest couch, expecting Josh to take the one opposite her. Instead he chose to sit next to her.

Her entire body tensed at his proximity. A part of her wanted to get up and move to another seat, while another part of her refused to show any such weakness. Still, she couldn't help but be aware of him—his size, his strength, his scent. When she'd selected the furniture for her office, she had purposely chosen the navy print couches and coffee table to add an air of comfort and ease to the surroundings. Yet seated here now, she was struck by the intimacy of her knees being just inches from Josh's and she dearly wished she had gone for something more formal.

"Relax. I'm not going to pounce on you. I just want to talk to you about your grandmother."

Doing her best to comply, she said, "I'm listening."

"First off, I want to apologize again for not telling

you right up front that Olivia asked me to come see you. Second, I want you to know that my attraction to you didn't...doesn't have anything to do with Olivia.''

Because a part of her still wanted to believe him, Laura cut him off. ''I don't want to rehash this, Josh, and I'm not interested in your apologies. You're the one who insisted on talking to me about Olivia Jardine. I suggest you do it or this conversation is over.''

Josh's mouth hardened. ''All right. If that's the way you want it.''

''It is.''

''Fine. I'm aware that you turned down your grandmother's offer for you to come visit her in New Orleans. Personally, I believe she should just wash her hands of you if that's the way you feel. But your ungracious attitude toward her doesn't seem to bother Olivia. And now that she knows you exist, she's determined to meet you. In fact, I think the only reason I'm the one sitting here and not Olivia is because ever since she turned eighty traveling has become more difficult for her.''

Laura tried to reconcile the image of an aging, fragile Olivia Jardine that Josh painted with the image of the coldhearted Olivia Jardine who had treated her mother so shabbily. Face-to-face, refusing the woman that Josh had just described to her would have been difficult, Laura conceded. Though she hated to admit it, she was the same softy she'd always been. With irritating frequency, she still fell for every sob story under the sun. And despite her training and the years she'd spent in management, she would rather face a root canal than to have to terminate an employee. ''Then I guess it's a good thing that she didn't make the trip and waste her time.''

"You're missing the point, Laura."

"Which is?"

"You and your grandmother have more in common than the color of your eyes. You're both as stubborn as a mule."

"Did I say you were charming?" Laura asked, but her voice lacked the bite of indignation because his remark about the color of her eyes had shaken her. Memories flooded her from her childhood. Her resemblance to her mother had been minimal and the comment she'd heard most often was about the unusual color of her eyes.

"I have my daddy's eyes."

How many times had she parroted those words, her only point of reference to their validity a few fading photographs of a man she'd never known? A fresh wave of pain hit her at the reminder of his betrayal. Swallowing past the sudden thickness in her throat, she straightened her shoulders and attempted to inject her voice with sarcasm as she said, "I obviously made a mistake. There's nothing the least bit charming about being compared to a mule."

"I'll be sure to remember that," Josh said, his lips curving up slightly. "But actually I wasn't trying to charm you. I was simply stating the facts, to try to make you see that your grandmother…Olivia," he corrected himself, evidently noting the familial reference bothered her. "Olivia wants to meet you. She's *determined* to meet you. And I have to warn you, she is one of the most tenacious persons—male or female—that I've ever known. When Olivia sets her mind on something, she doesn't know the meaning of *quit* and doesn't let anything or anyone get in her way. And right now, she's set her mind on meeting you."

"Then she has a real problem. Because I don't want to meet her and have no intention of doing so."

"Maybe this will make you reconsider." He reached inside his coat, retrieved an envelope from his pocket and offered it to her. "Olivia asked me to give it to you."

Laura clasped her hands together and made no attempt to take it.

Josh placed it on the table in front of her. "There's a note inside, along with a first-class, round-trip ticket from San Francisco to New Orleans for two weeks from next Friday with an open return date."

Not bothering to even look at the envelope, she said, "You can return it to Mrs. Jardine, and I'd appreciate it if you tell her, again, that I am not interested now nor will I ever be interested in meeting her or any of Andrew Jardine's children."

His expression stormy, Josh asked, "Aren't you at least going to read the note she sent?"

"No."

His green eyes cooled. "Considering that she's your grandmother and getting on in years, don't you think you're being a little tough on her?"

"She's a grandmother that I never even knew existed until a few months ago," Laura fired back.

"But now you do know that she exists. And she wants to meet you. How can you just turn your back on her? She's your flesh and blood, your family."

Laura bristled beneath the censure in his eyes, in his tone. "Juliet Harte is…was my family. Not the Jardines. They didn't want any part of my mother twenty-nine years ago. So I don't want any part of them now."

"So this is payback?" he countered, his voice sharp

with accusation. "You're punishing an old woman for something your father did nearly thirty years ago?"

"You don't know what happened."

"And you do?"

"I know enough," she snapped. More than she wanted to know, she conceded, recalling the clippings of her father. She thought of all the years he could have been a part of her life and had chosen not to be. When tears began to sting at the back of her eyes, Laura ruthlessly held them in check. She would not shed tears over a man who had cared so little for her and for the woman he'd claimed to love. "I know enough to be sure that I don't ever need or want any of the Jardines in my life."

"And what if they need you? What if your grandmother needs you?" he challenged. "Are you going to turn your back on her?"

"W-what are you talking about?"

"You're aware that your grandmother owns a couple of small luxury hotels in New Orleans?"

Laura nodded. What she hadn't figured out from the newspaper clippings, she had learned from her uncle Paul.

"One of those hotels—the Royal Princess—is in trouble. Serious trouble."

"What kind of trouble?" she asked warily.

"It's been losing money for quite some time. And now with so many new hotels going up and moving into the area, it's cutting deeper and deeper into the Princess's market share. As a result, the hotel is going under fast. I've told Olivia that she'd be better off cutting her losses and selling the place, but she refuses."

"Why?"

"Pride, I guess. Olivia's got enough of it to sink a ship."

Though her curiosity was peaked, Laura refused to allow herself to be drawn in any deeper. "Well, I'm sorry for her problems. But I don't see what any of it has to do with me."

"Haven't you figured it out yet? Olivia's thinks that you're the answer to her prayers. She's convinced herself that you're the one who can save the Princess for her."

Eight

"That's ridiculous," Laura insisted. She shot to her feet and began to pace.

"Tell it to your grandmother."

"But I...it's insane. She's never even met me."

"Doesn't matter," Josh informed her, and watched in fascination as the emotions played over her features. Shock. Uncertainty. Confusion. Despite her efforts to appear cool and unaffected, it was all there on her face, in her eyes. Just as the pain and longing had been there a few moments ago when she'd spoken of her mother. A complicated woman, he thought, not for the first time. Strong, yet vulnerable. Brave, yet fearful. He didn't doubt for a minute that Laura would fight and love wholeheartedly.

She whirled around, marched back to where he sat and pinned him with those flashing blue eyes. "What do you mean it doesn't matter?"

Comfortable and predictable, the lady was not. All that passion and temper wrapped in her sweet, sexy body could only spell trouble for a man, Josh told himself. A relationship with her would be messy. And he didn't like messy, had spent the better part of his thirty-three years avoiding complicated entanglements with women, he reminded himself. That he'd even considered becoming involved with her on a personal basis when he had so much at stake just proved how dangerous the lady was.

"Of course it matters," she snapped.

"Not to your grandmother. The fact that you're her granddaughter is apparently enough for Olivia."

"Well, it's absurd," Laura fired back. "She'll just have to find someone else to run her hotel. You're her friend," she told him, pointing a finger at him accusingly. "*You* find her someone else."

Faced with all that righteous indignation, Josh bit the inside of his cheek to hold back the grin that threatened. "Actually Olivia and I aren't exactly friends. We're more what you would call friendly adversaries."

The space between her brows squinched up as she considered his reply. "Then find your friendly adversary someone else to run her hotel."

"I've offered to and she turned me down flat."

"Then, try again. Find her a candidate with super management credentials that she can't turn down."

"You don't understand. I could tell Olivia that Donald Trump is willing to run the Princess for her and she'd tell him to take a hike."

"Maybe she doesn't like the Donald Trump type."

"Maybe she doesn't. I don't know. But what I do know is that I could parade the top ten hotel managers in the world in front of her and none of them would measure up because none of them have the one all-important qualification that she demands of a manager for the Princess."

She eyed him suspiciously. "Which is?"

He did allow himself to grin this time. "Jardine blood flowing through their veins."

"That's crazy."

"I agree. But that's how it is. And since you *do* have

Jardine blood, in Olivia's eyes that makes you perfect for the job."

"Wrong," Laura told him. "I am not perfect for the job. Because I don't *want* the job and I have no intention of accepting it."

"Are you going to turn down the inheritance, too?"

"What inheritance?"

"You really should read the letter." He motioned to the envelope still lying on the table that contained the airline tickets and the letter from her grandmother.

She shook her head, curled and uncurled her never-still fingers. "Just tell me," she said, her voice impatient, her face a shade paler. For the first time Josh noticed the shadows beneath her eyes.

"All right. Apparently after finding out about your existence, Olivia decided to amend her will. She's named you as one of her heirs."

"She can't do that."

"She can do it and she did," Josh informed her. "It's Olivia's money. She can do whatever she wants with it. And apparently what she wants is for you to share in her estate with the rest of your family."

"I don't want her money."

He'd seen snow with more color, Josh thought. Concerned, he went to the minibar, poured a glass of iced tea and returned to where Laura sat with her hands clenched tightly together in front of her. He shoved the glass into her hands. "Here, you look like you could use this."

She accepted the glass, drank deeply. "Thank you," she told him, and Josh noted that she clung to the sweating glass as though it were a lifeline.

"You might not want to be so hasty. Olivia Jardine is an extremely powerful and wealthy woman in New

Orleans. She owns two of the city's finest hotels and has quite a number of other lucrative investments. Even splitting the estate with your brother and sisters, you'd still stand to inherit millions.''

"I told you, I don't care about the money," she said, her voice more forceful this time. "I don't want anything from her or from any of the Jardines."

"What about your brother and sisters? Aren't you even the least bit curious about them?"

"No." She set down the glass and stood. "Now, if you'll excuse me, I need to go see Nick before my next appointment arrives."

Although Josh believed the appointment was pure fabrication, he didn't push it and allowed Laura to escort him out of the office.

"You can return this to Mrs. Jardine," she said, and held out the unopened envelope containing the tickets and Olivia's note.

"I gave Olivia my word I'd deliver that to you and I did. If you want it sent back, then you'll have to do it. But I think you owe it to yourself to at least read what she has to say."

Maybe his date canceling on him at the last minute was a good thing after all, Nick Baldwin told himself as he exited the elevator to the floor where the hotel's business offices were housed. He replayed in his head the phone conversation he'd had with his food and beverage manager that afternoon and couldn't deny the man wasn't the first one to complain to him about Laura during the past two weeks.

Entering the empty secretarial pool, he spied the beleaguered-looking woman exiting Laura's office, her arms loaded with files and papers. "I take it Simon

Legree is still in there?" he asked, motioning to Laura's office.

"Mr. Baldwin!" Wendy Temple, the newest addition to the clerical pool, practically jumped at his remark and sent the files in her arms tumbling.

"Here you go," Nick said, rescuing the files for her.

"I'm sorry, sir," she said, blushing to the roots of her pale blond hair. "I didn't know you were here."

"No problem." He placed the file folders on the desk. "Judging by the looks of this, you must be planning to spend the night."

"No, sir," she said, her cheeks pinkening again. "I'm just helping Ms. Harte."

"So the slave driver *is* still here, then."

"Sir?" she replied, her eyes wide and fixed on the black tie he wore with his tux.

"Sorry. Silly joke," he said with a smile, hoping to put the girl at ease. "I was referring to Laura. She in her office?"

"Yes, sir. She's dictating."

Which came as no surprise since Laura had been bombarding him and every department in the hotel with memos and analyses for nearly two weeks. It was a situation he'd put off addressing too long. But since his date for the evening had canceled on him now seemed as good a time as any to talk to Laura. However, having a heart-to-heart with the woman who was his friend, as well as his assistant manager, was something he preferred doing without an audience present. "Wendy, isn't it?"

"Yes, sir."

"It's kind of late for you to still be working. The clerical staff usually leaves at five and it's well past six o'clock."

"I realize that, sir. But Ms. Harte asked me to stay a little longer. She had some dictation she wanted me to get out. And I didn't mind. She's been extremely busy," the girl said politely.

"Then Ms. Harte and the Ambassador Grand are very lucky to have someone like you working here. And while I'm sure Ms. Harte appreciates your dedication, as I do, it's the Ambassador Grand's policy not to intrude on its employees' personal lives. I think you've worked hard enough for one day. Why don't you clock out and head for home? You can finish up those reports for Ms. Harte tomorrow."

She hesitated, bit her lip. "Ms. Harte said she wanted these typed before tomorrow morning's meeting."

"Wendy, you do know that I own this hotel, don't you?"

"Yes, sir."

He gave her another smile, hoping to ease some of the nerves the girl seemed to be plagued with. "Then that makes me the boss, doesn't it?"

"Yes, sir."

"And as the boss, I'm telling you that it's okay to call it a day."

"But Ms. Harte—"

"—works for me," he told her, and couldn't help thinking that he sometimes wondered if Laura realized that fact. "Don't worry. I'll square things with Laura. You go on home."

"Thank you, sir," she murmured. And within moments, she'd closed up her desk and retrieved her purse and coat. After bidding him good-night, she disappeared into the corridor toward the elevators.

Nick rapped on the door and marched into Laura's office without waiting for an answer.

She held up her hand, cutting off his greeting, then lifted one finger, indicating that she needed a moment. She continued dictating into a handset, "After reviewing the food costs for last month..."

Nick folded his arms across his chest and waited. She was a picture of efficiency seated behind the desk with files and reports lined up in neat stacks before her. Several flame-colored strands had escaped the tame-looking twist she'd pulled her hair into and fell in wisps about her face and neck. Her skin looked pale against the vibrant blue suit she wore, but it was the shadows beneath her eyes that worried him. He hadn't pressed her following Josh's departure ten days ago. He'd taken Laura at her word when she'd said that she was okay and didn't want to discuss it. And although he'd been tempted to track down Logan and tear into him for upsetting Laura, he'd respected her wishes and had left it alone. Still, he suspected Laura's determination to work herself to the brink of exhaustion wasn't solely due to the discovery of an unknown grandmother. Looking at her now, he wondered if perhaps he had made a mistake by waiting as long as he had.

"Please copy Mr. Baldwin on this memo and include copies of the cost of goods reports. Also, put a copy of the memo and the attachments in my weekly meeting file. Thank you." She returned the handset to the dictation machine and sat back in her chair. "Sorry to keep you waiting, but I wanted to get that dictated while my thoughts were still fresh."

"No problem," he said as he dropped down into the chair across from her.

"So what are you doing here? I thought you were

taking the lovely Ms. Jenkins to the mayor's fund-raiser this evening.''

''Samantha canceled.''

Laura arched her brow, but her only comment was ''Hmm.''

''You want to translate that for me?''

She smiled, but it lacked any real sparkle—which was a pity, Nick thought, because Laura had one of those wonderful smiles that was lit from within. He'd often attributed her success in placating even the most ornery of hotel guests to that smile. ''I'm just surprised that she'd cancel. That's all.''

Nick made a snorting sound. ''Spill it, Harte. You know you're dying to.''

''Well, since you insist. I'm surprised Samantha would pass up the chance to parade around in public attached to your arm.''

Nick laughed. ''You make her sound like some sort of appendage.''

''I think she'd like to be a permanent one. I got the distinct impression the last time she and I ran into each other at one of the hotel functions that she had every intention of staking a claim on you—one that came with the title Mrs.''

''Looks like you were wrong because she's on her way to France to shoot a commercial for some designer. Apparently the model originally scheduled fell and broke her leg skiing.''

''Lucky Samantha to be able to slip right in and fill the job,'' Laura replied.

''Yeah, that's what she said. It was a great break…no pun intended…for her career.'' And a lucky break for him personally, Nick thought, if Laura had been right about Samantha's interest in a more permanent relationship.

"You don't look very disappointed."

"I'm not," he told her. Quite the contrary, he felt relieved when she'd canceled the date even though he'd been dressed and on his way to pick her up. Which said a lot considering the fact that he'd been dating the lingerie model for the past two months. Of course, it didn't help that since Josh's appearance two weeks ago, he'd found himself thinking of a dark-haired brunette with innocent green eyes. Disturbed that Faith Logan had managed to steal into his thoughts again, he shoved the memory aside and focused on Laura. "But I didn't come here to discuss my love life," he told Laura.

"That's good. Because I don't have time to give you a lecture about dating women whose bra size is higher than their IQ."

"Ouch!"

Laura laughed. "Seriously, Nick, unless you've got something that's really pressing, I need to get back to the occupancy projections."

"Actually, I came by to send you home."

"Quit joking. I told you I'm busy and I really do have a ton of work to do."

Nick stood. "I'm not joking, Laura. It's long past quitting time and I want you to go home."

"But—"

"No buts. The occupancy projections and budget analyses or whatever it is can wait," he insisted. "You've been working too hard and I know you haven't had a day off in over two weeks. Do us both a favor and go home. Kick back and try to relax for a few days."

"A few days?" she all but squawked. "I can't possibly take off time now. We're about to launch the holiday promotions."

"We can launch it without you. Go home, Laura. I don't want to see that pretty face of yours in this office or anywhere in this hotel again before Monday."

"Monday! Are you insane? Today's only Thursday. I can't possibly take off three full days."

"You can if I say you can. In case you've forgotten, I *am* your boss," he told her. Coming around the desk, he pulled her to her feet. "And the boss is telling you to take some time off."

"But I don't want any time off," she argued, and dug in her heels when he attempted to usher her toward the door. "Nick, this is ridiculous. I don't need any time off."

"Take it, anyway. If not for you, then do it for the rest of the staff."

She sucked in a sharp breath. "Have they…has the staff been complaining about me?"

He sighed and regretted causing that stricken look in her eyes. "They're concerned about you. So am I. You've been pushing everyone from the clerical staff to the busboys relentlessly for the past two weeks. And you've been pushing yourself hardest of all. The staff needs a break, Laura. And so do you."

"I don't know what to say. I didn't realize…"

"It's all right. It's not the end of the world. Even when you're being a tyrant, you're the nicest assistant GM in the business." He sighed. "I know all about burying yourself in work when things aren't going the way you'd like in your personal life. I should have said something instead of keeping quiet and waiting for you to work through whatever's been bothering you."

"I have worked through it. Nothing's bothering me."

He shook his head. "You and I both know that's not true." Removing her coat from the coatrack, he held it out for her.

Laura shrugged into the navy trench and belted it at the waist. He handed her her purse and briefcase. Shooting him a mutinous look, she asked, "Just what is it you're hoping to accomplish by banishing me from my office for three days?"

He pulled the lapels of her coat together and stared into her eyes. "I'm not banishing you, sunshine. Just asking you to take a breather. You've been hit with a lot these past few months. Your injuries from the accident, your mother's death and the discovery of an unknown grandmother." Nick purposely didn't mention Josh and whatever it was that had happened between them. "All I'm asking is that you take a few days, try to sort through your feelings. Figure out who Laura Harte is and what she really wants to do with the rest of her life."

She'd begun to think that even three years wouldn't be enough time for her to figure out who she was, Laura conceded as she tore off a strip of packing tape and sealed another cardboard box filled with her mother's books. Nick had been right. She had needed time to think. She felt confused and unsure of herself. All her life she had been so self-assured because she'd known who she was—the much-loved daughter of Juliet and Richard Harte. Having part of her identity stripped away had left her reeling, she admitted. Even throwing herself into work hadn't eased the uncertainty inside of her.

Irritated by such emotional weakness, Laura shook off her sad thoughts. What she needed to do was focus on her goals, Laura told herself as she rolled her shoulders to relieve the kinks from all the bending and packing. Maybe she wasn't as sure of herself as she had been before the rug had been ripped from beneath her feet, but she'd always been a goal-setter and it was time she refocused on what she wanted.

And the best time to start was now—by listing those things that she did want. She wanted to be appointed as the general manager for the Ambassador Grand or another hotel similar to it. She wanted to forget that the last few months had ever happened. More important, she wanted to forget that her father wasn't the hero she'd believed him to be but a liar and a cheat who'd gotten her mother pregnant and abandoned her. She wanted to forget the name Jardine all together. She wanted to forget that she had a grandmother and three half siblings down in New Orleans. And most of all, she wanted to forget she'd ever been foolish enough to be charmed by the likes of Josh Logan.

Blast him, she thought, ripping off another length of tape and slapping it at the seams of the box. It had been more than two weeks since her encounter with Josh Logan and she didn't want to think about him. As it was, he'd been the main reason she'd worked so fiendishly these past couple of weeks. She'd wanted to hit her bed at night too tired to think about him, about Olivia Jardine and her family, about the woman's outrageous offer, about the letter that still remained unopened in her handbag. A lot of good it had done. Thanks to Josh Logan and Olivia Jardine, she'd been banished from the job she loved, and regardless of how tired she was, she hadn't been able to escape the dreams. Annoying dreams of the way Josh had looked at her with those hot green eyes. Dreams of how it had felt to be in his arms, to have his mouth hot and hungry on hers.

And then there had been the disturbing dreams—old fantasy dreams from her childhood—dreams in which her father would walk through the door of their house and tell her and her mother that the navy had made a mistake. He wasn't dead. He was alive and he'd come home to his two girls. And then he would swing her up into his arms and dance her around the room. She hadn't had that silly dream since she'd been eight years old. It didn't take a genius to figure out why it had resurfaced now. Nor to figure out why she'd awakened the past week with her face wet with tears.

"And you're never going to finish unless you get moving," she told herself. After marking the carton's contents for donation to the local library, she added it to the small mountain of boxes lining the wall in her mother's den. Looking around, she stared at the results of her work from the past two days and was pleased with her progress. She had put a major dent into the job of closing up the house and disposing of its contents. With the exception of a few items that she intended to keep for herself, most of the furnishings had been earmarked for donation to local charities or to be given to close friends of her mother. The only task that still remained was packing up and sorting through the items in her mother's bedroom.

She had saved that room for last, knowing it would be the most difficult. While her mother's imprint was evident throughout the small ranch-style house that had been Laura's home growing up, it was in Juliet Harte's bedroom that Laura felt her mother's presence the strongest. Returning to the bedroom now, she paused in the doorway.

Emotion choked her. The room looked as though her mother had just stepped out of it only a moment ago, Laura thought, noting the cheerful curtains, the climbing rose pattern on the bedspread, the book on the nightstand with her mother's reading glasses beside it. Moving into the room, Laura picked up the book, smiled as she noted it was Sandra Brown's latest thriller. Her mother always had been a fan of Sandra Brown, she thought as she retrieved the glasses and returned them to their case. She placed both the book and the glasses in the box of things that she wanted to keep. Taking a deep breath, she turned toward the closet. It was time to get to work.

She worked nonstop for the next two hours—neatly packing away clothing, shoes and accessories from her mother's closet. Perfumes and unopened bath talc from her dressing table found their way into another box. She began emptying the chest of drawers, putting sweaters and slacks into another box marked for donation. In the last drawer, she came to an assortment of items that had apparently been her mother's treasures. Among them was a red sweater wrapped in tissue, a twin to the one she had owned as a toddler. Laura recalled the photo that had sat in the den of the two of them dressed in those matching sweaters one Christmas.

Lost in the past, Laura continued to unearth the mementoes that her mother had obviously cherished. Tears sprang to her eyes as she flipped through photos and keepsakes that marked happy moments in her mother's life. When she came to the red velvet box, she opened it. There was a jumble of different items, but it was the packet of letters tied with a faded pink ribbon that drew her. Removing them from the box, Laura sat back on her heels with the letters in her lap. She thumbed through them, noted the military post office box return address and paused. There were at least a dozen of them, she guessed. And she knew that they were from her father. While one part of her rejected him and didn't want to know anything more about him, another part wanted to know everything. The part of her that still ached for the father she'd loved and lost won out. With hands that had suddenly gone damp, she removed the tissue-thin sheet from the first letter. For a moment, she stared at the bold, firm scrawl and envisioned the handsome navy pilot in the photograph writing it to her mother. Bracing herself, Laura read.

My darling Juliet,
Your letter arrived this morning and I've read it and reread it so often that I think I can recite every word. As I sit here in my quarters awaiting orders and thinking of you, for once I actually feel grateful for this nightmare of a war, because were it not for the war, I never would have found you

I love you, my Juliet. It is the memories of you and the times we've shared together that sustain me now in this country so torn apart by the ugliness of war and despair. Knowing that I'll soon be returning to you is what gets me through each day.

Always, always you are with me, my darling. In my thoughts. In my heart. Please don't worry about me. Knowing that you'll be there waiting for me when I return is all the incentive I need to keep myself safe. Soon, we'll be together again.

> All my love,
> Drew

Laura's throat tightened. She told herself she had no right to read the letters. It was obvious they were meant only for her mother's eyes. Yet, how could she not read them? She so wanted to understand, to forgive her mother for the lie, so she picked up the next one and the next.

By the time she reached the bottom of the stack of letters, Laura's eyes burned with tears. Unlike the other letters that bore a military postmark, this one had been postmarked from New Orleans. Laura withdrew the elegant cream stationery with the raised gold crest of a royal crown. Engraved in the same rich gold was The Royal Princess Hotel—Where Our Guests Are Treated Like Royalty.

A chill went through her as she noted the date of the letter and realized that it had been written while she'd been no more than a tiny seed in her mother's womb. With her heart in her throat, she began to read.

My darling, Juliet,
I'm so sorry I missed your call this evening. Although the housekeeper said you left no message, I knew it was you. I hate that we've had to keep our love a secret this way when what I truly want is to shout from the top of the hotel's roof that I love you.

I miss you terribly, love. The two weeks since leaving you have felt like two years, and were it not for my mother's health, I would already be on a plane for San Diego and returning to you. But I cannot abandon my responsibilities here. Even though mother seems to grow stronger each day and there appears to be no permanent damage, the stroke has left her weakened. She has always been such a strong woman that I must admit I was shaken to see her this way. I'm optimistic about her recovery since speaking to the doctors, but I'm concerned about the stress she is under. She worries incessantly about the hotel and the renovation it's undergoing. I seem to spend half of my time at the hospital reassuring her that the hotel can function without her at the helm and the rest of my time trying to make good on that promise.

Unfortunately, I fear my responsibilities to my mother and to the hotel will keep me here for the foreseeable future even though my heart is with you. I love you so much, Juliet. As you would expect, Adrienne has been to the hospital several times to see my mother, but I've avoided spending any time alone with her and continue to make excuses for not seeing her. I've felt terribly guilty for not telling her the truth—that I want to end our engagement because it's you I love and you that I want to marry.

While I know we agreed I would wait until after my mother was fully recovered before telling her about us, I'm afraid last night after Adrienne's visit I broke that promise. I told my mother about you, my darling, and how very much I love you. As I predicted, Mother was not pleased when I told her that I plan to end my engagement to Adrienne so that you and I can marry. I tried to explain to her that going through with the marriage to

Adrienne when it is you that I love would be unfair to everyone. While I do dislike hurting Adrienne, I see no other solution. I cannot marry her—not when it is you that I love.

Although Mother is not happy about my decision, I do believe she has accepted it. I had hoped to speak to Adrienne right away, but Mother has asked that I wait until after she has been released from the hospital at the end of the week. She's also asked that you come to New Orleans so that she can meet you. Will you come, my love? I know I am asking a great deal of you, but I believe in my heart that once Mother meets you, she cannot help but love you as I do and any reservations she may have about us marrying will be put to rest.

Please, my darling, say you'll come. Call me after you receive this letter and I will arrange to have airline tickets sent to you. And remember, my darling, I love you.

All my love,
Drew

Enthralled by the drama of her parents' long-ago love, Laura came to the end of the letter and reached for the next one. Her fingers met empty space. Looking down at the box where she'd found the letters, she sighed as she realized there weren't any more letters from her father.

She blew out a breath, deeply moved by the glimpse into her parents' love affair. She carefully retied the stack of letters with the ribbon and set them aside. Then she began to sift through the remaining items in the box—a wilted rose wrapped in tissue, a matchbook from a dinner club in San Diego, a theater playbill of a production she'd never heard of, a strip of photos taken in one of those boxes they used to have at carnivals. They were shots of her mother and Drew Jardine laughing and kissing for the camera.

She traced the edges of the photos with her fingertip. They looked so young, so happy and in love, she thought, swallowing past the sudden thickness in her throat. What had happened? she wondered. She knew from her uncle Paul that her mother had gone to New Orleans, but she'd returned alone. Why? Had Olivia rejected her? Had Drew Jardine been too weak to go against his mother's wishes? How could the man who had written such beautiful, loving letters turn his back on the woman he claimed to love and his own child?

Did the answers even matter now? Not really, she told herself as she put the photo strip aside. It was in the past, and since she had no intention of ever claiming the Jardine family's heritage as her own, perhaps it was best to leave the past buried. Instead she would embrace the memories of all the happy times with her mother.

Thinking of her mother, missing her, Laura retrieved the last item from the velvet box—a slim white missal that must have belonged to her mother as a young girl. She smoothed her fingers over the cross on the leather cover, then opened the book. Tears filled her eyes again as she saw her mother's name written neatly on the title page. She closed the prayer book and started to return it to the box when she spied the edge of a note sticking from between the pages. Curious, Laura removed the single, folded sheet of paper.

It was a note, she realized, her heart pounding as she recognized the Princess Hotel stationery. But instead of

Drew Jardine's bold script, the note had been typed and there was no signature at the bottom. Frowning, Laura scanned the short message.

Dear Juliet,
I am sorry that things did not turn out for you as you had hoped. I realize you have been hurt, and for that I am also sorry. But we have all suffered for the mistakes that were made. I hope you can understand that there was no other choice that could be made. Family honor and responsibility must come first, before all else—even love.
    Enclosed is a cashier's check in the amount of $50,000. While this money cannot make up for the pain you have suffered, it will enable you to take care of your problem and perhaps to begin a new life.

Reeling from the cold formality of the note, Laura shot her gaze to the date on the letterhead. She sucked in a breath. It was dated three months after that last letter from Drew Jardine, asking her mother to come to New Orleans. And she realized that the "problem" that needed taking care of had been her.

Her stomach pitched as she reread the note once more. She thought of her mother receiving this cold missive, reading it, having her dreams and hopes shattered. Laura ached for her mother as she realized how deeply those words must have cut, of how frightened she must have been—alone with no family and pregnant with the child of a man who'd betrayed her.

And as she thought of her mother, a white-hot fury enveloped Laura. Who had sent the vicious note? Drew Jardine himself? His mother? His fiancée? Suddenly all the other unanswered questions that she'd tried to convince herself no longer mattered burned inside her, added fuel to her anger.

Shoving to her feet, Laura rushed into the kitchen where she had left her purse on the countertop. She yanked open the black leather tote and pulled out the letter from Olivia Jardine. She stared at her name, written in neat letters across the front of the envelope, and tore it open.

She didn't even bother glancing at the airline tickets, simply tossed them onto the counter beside her purse and unfolded the cream stationery bearing the now-familiar gold crest. Quickly she scanned the brief message written in the same precise script and the implicit summons in the invitation for her to come to New Orleans to meet her family.

Reaching for the phone, she dialed Nick's home number and left a message for him to call her. Then she picked up the business card that had been enclosed with the note and punched in the office number for Olivia Jardine.

Nine

"What went wrong?" Olivia demanded to know as she stared at Josh across the desk in the library of the Jardine mansion.

"As I already explained to you when I called from San Francisco, nothing went wrong," Josh said, striving for patience. After spending the better part of two weeks shuttling between Logan's West Coast and East Coast hotels, he'd finally made it back to New Orleans on a red-eye last night. But instead of sleeping for the next twenty-four hours straight as he'd planned, he'd been hit with a room shortage crisis caused by a faulty boiler unit in the New Orleans hotel. As a result, he'd spent the entire day finding accommodations in the sold-out city for the hotel's displaced guests. The urgent summons from Olivia to meet her at the mansion tonight had been the final send-off to a killer day.

She smacked the bottom of her cane against the Aubusson rug. "Of course something went wrong. My granddaughter's still not here, is she?"

"No, she's not."

"And according to you, she's not coming."

"That's correct."

"Then something went wrong. No one in their right mind would turn down what I offered the girl."

"Laura did," Josh pointed out.

"Then—I repeat—something went wrong. Now tell me what happened."

Josh sighed. Had he honestly thought the lengthy phone conversation he'd squeezed in despite his frantic schedule would satisfy Olivia? He should have known better. "There's not a lot more that I can add to what I told you when I phoned from San Francisco. She simply wasn't interested in your offer."

"It was your job to convince her. That's why I sent you," she countered.

"No," Josh corrected her, an edge of steel in his voice as he met Olivia's eyes. "It was not my job to convince her. I agreed to meet with her on your behalf and try to get her to consider your offer."

"And?"

"And I did just that, but she made it clear that she wasn't interested." He didn't bother telling her that the lady had tossed both the offer and his apology for the way he'd handled things right back in his face.

"Did you tell her about the inheritance?" Olivia asked, pinning him with those pale blue eyes so like Laura's.

"Yes."

"Well, out with it, Joshua. What did the girl say?"

"The *girl* couldn't have cared less." He just wished he could say the same. He enjoyed women. The way they looked. The way the smelled. The way their thought processes worked. He'd enjoyed the company of quite a few women and had been shot down a time or two. But he'd never been a man to brood over a woman. Yet he had been brooding for the past two weeks over Laura Harte. It irked him that he hadn't been able to get her out of his head. How on earth had she managed to get under his skin so quickly?

"Then she's either very foolish or stubborn," Olivia said. When he didn't comment she said, "Tell me about her."

Josh jerked his thoughts back to Olivia, who was eyeing him over the rim of the glass of sherry. "The detective report was pretty thorough and, from what I observed, accurate."

She set down her glass with a decisive thud. "Don't be obtuse, boy. I want to know what she's like, what your impressions of her are."

Josh chose his words carefully, telling himself he needed to be objective and not let his personal feelings toward Laura color his assessment. "She's sharp. She knows her job and is good at it. She's also organized and very good with people," he began. "She's dedicated and loyal. The people she works with seem to respect her. My friend Nick Baldwin who owns the Ambassador Grand where she works thinks she's the best thing since sliced bread. He really sang her praises."

Olivia narrowed her eyes, frowned. "This friend Nick of yours, is he involved with the girl?"

"No," Josh said quickly, recalling that he'd wondered the same thing himself at first.

"You sound very sure. But from the photographs, she appears to be a very attractive young woman."

"She is attractive," Josh conceded, thinking Laura was far prettier in person than in the grainy photos. "But from the vibes I was picking up, there's nothing romantic about the relationship. He cares about Laura and is protective of her, but from what he said, and I believe him, his feelings for Laura are as a good friend and a boss for a first-rate employee. I'm sure Nick sees

Laura's potential and it's the reason he hired her in the first place.''

"Meaning?"

"Rumor has it that Nick's got his eye on buying a hotel down South. If he's successful, my guess is he'll appoint Laura as the GM of the Ambassador Grand to free himself up for the new venture.''

"And do you think it would be a smart move on his part? Appointing Laura as a GM?''

"I think she could probably handle it and just about anything else that was thrown at her. The lady's tougher than she looks,'' he said, remembering that steel will of hers.

"Hmm. Attractive, smart, tough and loyal. She almost sounds like a saint.''

"Hardly,'' Josh said, making a face. "She's got a quick temper to go with that red hair of hers and she's as stubborn as a mule.''

"Did you like her?''

"Yes,'' Josh admitted. "I liked her.'' More than he should have. More than he wanted to.

"And how did she feel about you?''

Josh shrugged. "But I suspect you wouldn't find my name on her list of favorite people.'' Irritated by the fact that he hadn't been able to quite dismiss Laura from his mind while she had obviously dismissed him from hers, Josh put down his untouched brandy and stood.

"Did you two have a problem?''

Josh didn't quite trust the glimmer in Olivia's eyes. "Nothing important,'' he said, and told himself that was the truth. A few kisses hardly classified as a romance. "She wasn't pleased that I didn't tell her right away about my connection to you.''

"Any particular reason you waited?"

"It seemed like a good idea at the time. Obviously, it wasn't—at least not in Laura's estimation." Edgy and eager to put any thought of Laura out of his mind, Josh stood. "It's getting late. I really need to be going."

Olivia nodded. "Thank you for coming by, Joshua. And thank you for going to see Laura."

Josh walked around the desk, kissed her cheek. "I'm sorry, Duchess."

"Save your apologies," she said with a wave of her hand, but her words lacked their usual bite.

Some of the starch seemed to go out of her spine. When she leaned her head back against the chair and closed her eyes, Josh frowned. Suddenly Olivia looked all of her eighty-one years. It worried him. Olivia Jardine had been such a formidable adversary for so long, that seeing her vulnerable like this disturbed him. Unable to leave, he stooped down, bringing himself to her eye level. He caught her hand, squeezed it. "I'm sorry I let you down, Duchess."

She opened her eyes, stared at him. "You didn't let me down, Joshua. I'm just tired."

"And disappointed?"

"Yes. I was so sure that Laura would be the answer to my problems at the Princess."

"There's always Katie," he said, referring to one of her granddaughters. "You know she'd jump at the chance to take over the Princess."

Olivia shook her head. "Katherine has the Regent to run. And even though she's doing an excellent job, she's not suited to a hotel like the Princess. No, the Princess needs someone who understands and appreciates an older hotel and the nuances of operating it,

Katherine's talents are put to better use at a bigger, more modern hotel like the Regent.''

Josh had to agree with Olivia's assessment. While he had no doubt Katie would do a good job at the Princess, she would find the intricacies of running the smaller, older hotel maddening. "What about Ali?" he offered, referring to Katie's twin. "She's great with people and she wouldn't hesitate to step in if you asked her."

"I would never ask it of her. You and I both know Alison would find the responsibility crushing—especially since the divorce. That Derek Dawson really did a number on her."

"Speaking of Dawson, any word on what's happening with him?"

"Not since he received the blackmail money he demanded in the settlement in order not to fight Alison for custody of Victoria. It's been six months since he's even been to see his daughter."

Josh clenched his fists as he thought of the slick-talking con man who had wormed his way into the Jardine family's operations by marrying a young, naive Ali. "They're both better off without him."

"I agree. It's bad enough the louse cleaned Alison out financially, but he's done far worse damage to her self-esteem." Olivia sighed. "She's doing better. I think filling in for the pastry chef at the Regent has been good for her. From what I gather the hotel staff adore her and the hotel guests rave about her pastries."

Josh smiled as he thought of Alison Jardine. What the woman was able to do with a few eggs, flour and sugar was a sin. "She does have a gift when it comes to cooking."

"One that was wasted on Dawson, I can assure you."

Josh didn't doubt that it was true. Alison Jardine's youth, sweet disposition and wealth had made her an easy target for that social-climbing swine Derek Dawson. Instead of taking pride in his wife's talents, he'd made her the victim of his verbal cruelties and criticism. The fact that Ali's situation so closely resembled his sister Faith's own failed marriage only added to Josh's dislike of Dawson.

"And aside from the fact that she lacks the experience, Alison has enough on her plate to deal with right now." She paused, looked up at him. "Do you think it would do any good for you to talk to Laura again?"

Josh remembered the look on Laura's face and the conviction in her voice when she'd dismissed him. "No. I could ask her again, but I honestly don't think she'll change her mind. I'm afraid you're going to have to scratch her off your list as a possible replacement."

"You're probably right."

Hearing the defeat in her voice only added to his guilt for handling things with Laura as he had. "Of course, you do know that if you want me to take the Princess off your hands, all you've got to do is say the word and I'll buy her," Josh teased, hoping to lighten her spirits.

As he had hoped, the light of battle came back into her eyes. "Not while I'm still breathing," she told him.

"Which is going to be for a long, long time to come because you're so crabby," he said with a grin.

"That right. Now, get out of here." She shooed him away. "And for heaven's sake go home and get some sleep. You look like hell."

Josh was about to shoot her a comeback when a tap

at the library door was followed by Alfred, the butler, saying, "Excuse me, Mrs. Jardine. I know you said you didn't want to be disturbed, but there's a Ms. Laura Harte on the phone who insists on speaking with you. Should I tell her you'll call her back?"

"No, Alfred. I'll take it. Thank you."

When Alfred retreated, Olivia's gaze shot to Josh's and there was no mistaking the gleam in her eyes as she said, "Well, Joshua, perhaps you were more convincing than you thought."

"Laura, are you sure going to New Orleans like this is the right thing to do?" her uncle Paul asked as he waited in line with her at the check-in counter of the airport.

"Not too long ago you were the one who said that I owed it to myself to meet with Drew Jardine's family."

"I know," he admitted. Worry lines bracketed his mouth and eyes. "But perhaps I was wrong. Maybe you were right to leave things alone."

"I was dead set against the idea at first," she admitted. "But I've had time to think about it, to get used to the idea, and I've changed my mind. It doesn't mean I want a relationship with Olivia Jardine or anyone else in the family, but I want to meet them. Maybe once I do, I'll be able to come to terms with mother lying to me all those years and put it behind me." She saw no point in telling her uncle about the letters and the note she'd found or her real purpose in going to New Orleans. If she did, he would try his best to convince her to let the past stay buried.

"I suppose you're right," he conceded. "I guess I

Metsy Hingle

just didn't envision you taking a leave of absence from the hotel and going so quickly."

"I explained why," she reminded him, giving him a reassuring smile as they inched up in the line to the ticket counter. "It works out better for me to go now while there's a lull at the hotel."

"I know. It's just that the more I think about it, the more reservations I have. I mean, after all, Drew is dead."

"What about Olivia Jardine?"

"I know she's your grandmother," he told her. "And while I only met her a few times, she never struck me as the nurturing type. She was totally different from your mother. I remember thinking before Juliet went to New Orleans to meet her that the two of them wouldn't do well together."

"Didn't my mother ever say anything about what happened when she went to New Orleans?"

He shook his head. "I'm sorry."

She patted his arm. "It's all right. I imagine I'll know more about the Jardine family soon enough."

He closed his hand over hers. "I hope you won't be disappointed, Laura. Be careful of Olivia. She's a very shrewd and demanding woman."

"What about her daughter-in-law? Drew's wife? What is she like?"

"I only met her once—when she and Drew became engaged. I recall her having impeccable taste in clothes, the type of woman who would never have a hair out of place or her lipstick smudged and who would know exactly which fork to use at a fancy soiree. I imagine she made an ideal wife for someone like Drew, who moved about in high-powered business and social circles."

"She doesn't sound anything at all like my mother," Laura said. Adrienne Jardine sounded prim, proper and positively dull, Laura thought.

Uncle Paul's lips twitched at the corners. "She wasn't. I think it was the fact that Juliet was so different from Adrienne that attracted Drew to her in the first place."

But apparently when it came time to marry, Drew Jardine had played it safe and married the more suitable Adrienne, Laura surmised, unable to hold back a stab of bitterness.

"I imagine meeting her won't be easy for you."

Laura shrugged. "I'm probably more anxious about meeting her children. It's hard to get used to the idea of having three half siblings after being an only child all these years."

Her uncle's expression grew fierce. "I can't see any good coming out of this, Laura. I wish you wouldn't put yourself through this. It's not too late to change your mind."

"Please try to understand, Uncle Paul. I have to do this. And try not to worry. I know what I'm doing. I can handle it," she assured him. And she would, Laura told herself silently. Because beneath the anger and resentment at being the child Drew Jardine had chosen not to acknowledge, she felt a burning curiosity to know more about his other children. But even greater was the burning need for answers. What had happened in New Orleans nearly thirty years ago? And who had sent her mother that note with the check, suggesting that she have an abortion?

"Good morning," the ticket agent said as Laura's turn came at the counter.

Conversation between her and her uncle ceased as

Laura returned the agent's greeting. She gave him the ticket she had purchased, feeling a strong sense of satisfaction at her decision not to use the ticket purchased by Olivia Jardine. She produced her ID and answered his questions about her luggage.

"Here's your ticket and boarding pass, Ms. Harte. We have you with two bags checked through to New Orleans' Moisant airport," the airline agent confirmed. He handed her the items and returned her driver's license. "You can proceed to gate B-6. The flight will be boarding in ten minutes."

"Thank you." Picking up her carry-on tote, Laura walked in silence with her uncle to the security checkpoint. "I guess I'd better be going. Goodbye, Uncle Paul."

"Goodbye, honey. I'm going to miss you." Her uncle hugged her close and she breathed in the familiar scents of tobacco and peppermint.

"I'm going to miss you, too. But it's only for three weeks. I'll be back before you know it."

He kissed her head. "You're right, of course. Have a safe trip. And remember, I love you."

"I love you, too."

He took a step back, but kept a gentle hold on her shoulders for a long moment and simply looked at her. "If things don't work out or you change your mind, I want you to promise me that you'll catch the very next plane and come home."

"I promise." At his solemn expression, Laura cupped his cheek. "Try not to worry, Uncle Paul. I know what I'm doing. I'm going to be just fine."

But she didn't feel fine, Laura thought, as she stared out the window of the plane and watched the city of

San Francisco disappear from view. In fact, she thought as she leaned her head back against her seat and closed her eyes, she was beginning to wonder if her decision to go to New Orleans had been an error in judgment, after all.

Her palms grew damp as she recalled her brief conversation with Olivia Jardine. The woman hadn't sounded any warmer during this second exchange than she had the first time. While she had been prepared to be grilled as to why she'd changed her mind, the questions never came. It had been quite civil, an exchange of information, nothing more. There had been no weeping, no pleasantries, nothing at all personal, and the call had ended with Olivia insisting she would have someone meet Laura at the airport.

Hardly the conversation Laura would have expected to take place between a grandmother who'd been seeking a relationship with her long-lost granddaughter. But then, maybe Olivia Jardine didn't really see her as a granddaughter. So why had the woman added her name as a beneficiary in her will?

It was one of many questions that she hoped to find answers to during her stay in New Orleans. *And what about Josh Logan?* Laura dismissed the nagging voice and refused to allow herself to think of him. She cringed just remembering her stupidity where he was concerned. They were not each other's type. She'd known it and ignored it, anyway. And had paid the price of humiliation. Josh Logan was one mistake she had no intention of repeating. With any luck, she'd breeze into New Orleans and out again without ever crossing his path.

Suddenly tired, Laura stifled a yawn. Giving in to the need, she closed her eyes. She'd been running on

nerves fueled by anger since finding that long-ago note
to her mother. Restricted as she was in the airplane
seat, the past week of sleep-shortened nights caught up
with her and she drifted to sleep.

When Laura opened her eyes again, the flight attendant was announcing the plane's descent into the New
Orleans area. Sitting up in her seat, Laura stared out
the window as the city came into view. And as the
plane drew closer, the nerves came back in a rush and
she was already regretting her decision to come. When
the wheels of the plane touched down for landing, her
stomach was in a knot. And as the plane taxied to a
stop and the seat belt sign went out, she knew it was
too late. There was no going back.

Ten

Laura exited the plane at the airport terminal and paused to scan the people there to meet the arriving passengers. Ignoring the obvious reunions of families and loved ones, she narrowed her search to those persons holding up signs bearing the name of the party they were there to greet. Quickly she skimmed the placards, but none of them bore the name "Harte" or "Laura" or even "Jardine" on it.

She should have gone with her initial plan and insisted on taking a taxi, Laura told herself, wishing she had refused Olivia Jardine's offer to have someone meet her flight. Shifting her tote from one hand to the other, she moved out of the path of the passengers exiting the plane and swept her gaze over the area again. She zipped past two marines, an elderly couple surrounded by a flock of people and the stewardess talking to a tall, dark-haired man. Laura stopped and doubled back. Frowning, she stared at the back of the man who was busy chatting up the lithesome flight attendant. There was something familiar about him, she thought—the cocky stance, the fit of the jacket across his shoulders, the midnight hair that looked as though a woman's fingers had been run through it.

When the brunette leaned closer, whispered something in his ear and tucked a slip of paper in his coat pocket, he tipped back his head and laughed. And Laura froze, suddenly realizing why he seemed familiar.

It was Josh Logan.

For the space of a heartbeat, Laura considered turning around and getting back on the plane. Just as quickly, she rejected the idea and berated herself for being such a coward. After all, the man meant nothing to her, she reminded herself. So they'd spent a few days together, shared a few kisses. It was no big deal. The only reason the brief association had made an impact on her at all was because he'd caught her at a time when she was feeling particularly lonely and vulnerable.

And if her pulse had skipped a few beats just now, it was only because she was anxious about her impending meeting with Olivia Jardine. Nothing more. Chances are he wouldn't even remember her, she told herself. Which was a relief since she would just as soon forget she'd ever met him.

What if he was the person sent to meet her?

She immediately dismissed the notion. Josh had made it plain that he'd come to see her in San Francisco as a favor to Olivia. He was far too important of a man to be playing chauffeur. He'd told her he traveled a great deal and this was the city's major airport. He was probably here because he was on his way out of town. Relieved by that conclusion, she reminded herself that New Orleans was a big city and Josh was a busy man. The chances that their paths would have any reason to cross during her brief stay were slim.

And since he was obviously busy with the brunette, she would save them both the awkwardness of running into each other now by leaving before he spotted her.

Abandoning any attempt to locate the Jardines' driver, she decided to find a taxi instead. But first, she needed to claim her luggage. She located the sign to the baggage claims area and started in the direction the arrows pointed when Josh turned around and saw her.

"Laura!"

Her pulse jumped as he waved and smiled, heading toward her. Disgusted by the fact that just seeing him again had her heart racing, Laura clutched the tote in her hand even tighter.

"For a minute there, I thought I'd missed you. I'm glad I didn't," he said in that slow, sexy drawl she'd found so charming a few weeks ago. "Not only would I have been very disappointed, but your grandmother would have probably had my head on a platter."

"My…Mrs. Jardine sent *you* to pick me up?"

"She *asked* me to meet you. She thought you might feel more comfortable seeing a familiar face." He reached for her bag.

"She shouldn't have imposed. I could have taken a taxi," she said, clutching her bag tightly.

"It was no imposition. And I wanted to come. I wasn't happy with the way I handled things between us in San Francisco. I was hoping I'd have a chance to make it up to you and set things right. Now that you're here, maybe I'll get that chance."

Feeling her pulse dance under the heat of his gaze, she averted her eyes and steeled herself against the spell he wove so easily. She didn't doubt the man could seduce the skin off of a snake with all that Southern charm and those sexy smiles of his. But she had no intention of being charmed a second time. "That really isn't necessary. Besides, I'll only be here for a few weeks and I expect I'll be busy. And I imagine, so will you.''

''Then we'll both have to make time, won't we?''

''I wouldn't count on it.''

He remained silent, but from the gleam in his eyes, Laura realized he'd taken her response as a challenge. Silently she cursed her sharp tongue and was so busy trying to curb her reaction to the man that she failed to understand his pointed look at her carry-on bag.

''Um, Laura, while I'm all for equal rights and a woman being independent, I think I should point out that you are in the South now,'' he told her.

''I'm aware of that,'' she said, puzzled.

''Then I hope you're not going to make me arm-wrestle you for the right to carry that bag for you.''

Laura glanced down at the tote bag she still had in a death grip, then shot her gaze back to Josh's face. She flushed at the laughter brimming in his green eyes. Relinquishing the tote to him, she murmured, ''Thank you.''

He nodded. ''My pleasure. And before we go claim the rest of your luggage and head for your grand-mother's, allow me to be the first person to welcome you to New Orleans.'' Setting her bag on the floor, he took her hand in his.

And before she could recover from the jolt of his touch, he leaned in to kiss her. Suddenly realizing his intent, Laura turned her face and his lips brushed her cheek instead of her mouth. She'd barely recovered her breath at the close call when he lifted his head and stepped back.

''I'm really glad you're here,'' he said. He picked up her bag and flashed her another one of those toe-curling smiles. ''Now, what do you say we go rescue

your luggage and I'll take you to meet your grandmother.''

Josh tried to keep the conversation light and the
sleek black Mercedes within the speed limit as he
moved in and out of the late-afternoon traffic. ''Feel
free to change the CD if you'd like to listen to something besides jazz,'' he told her. ''There are some other
CDs in the console.''

''Thanks,'' she said.

She immediately began flipping through the CDs
with the same nervous energy that she seemed to do
with everything. She was like a fire, Josh thought,
bright, hot and guaranteed to burn.

''How about this one?'' she asked, holding up a col-
lection of classic rock hits.

''Good choice,'' he told her, and popped in the new
CD.

For the next ten minutes a series of foot-stomping
hits of the late fifties filled the car. As he exited Interstate 10 and headed for the city's uptown area, the fast-
paced tunes gave way to the slow beat of ''You've Lost
That Loving Feeling'' by the Righteous Brothers.

He turned onto St. Charles Avenue, once the site of
the city's premiere residences, and where the real estate
alone now equaled a king's ransom. More modest
homes gave way to stately mansions that had once been
part of large plantations. A streetcar ringing its bell ran
down the center of the divided boulevard as it made
its way toward the business district. Josh continued
traveling in the other direction, moving deeper into the
residential section. Noting Laura's gaze on one of the
more striking Greek Revival-style homes when they
stopped at a red light, he said, ''Pretty, isn't it?''

"It's beautiful. They all are."

Josh chuckled. "Wait until you see your grandmother's house—Jardine House. It's a real showplace."

At the mention of the Jardine name, Laura stiffened. Josh could have kicked himself for being the one to cause her to tense up again. And despite his stories and anecdotes about the various places they passed, she grew more uptight with each passing minute.

"Try to relax," he urged her.

"I am relaxed."

"That why you're trying to strangle the strap of your purse?" he asked.

Her fingers stilled, then relaxed the hold on the thin black strap of the bag in her lap. "So, I'm a little nervous."

She was more than nervous, Josh realized. Laura was scared. And the realization had every protective instinct inside him kicking in. It also blew any hopes he'd had of keeping things simple between them. He'd always been a sucker for a lady in distress. The fact that he was also attracted to this particular distressed lady only made things that much more complicated. "I'd say you're entitled to feel a little anxious. I can't imagine it's been easy finding out you have a family you never knew existed."

"No, it hasn't been easy."

The pain in that simple statement was like a fist around his heart and made him wish Andrew Jardine was still alive so he could have a go at the man. To discover that the father she'd always believed had died before her birth had actually been alive all along, raising a family that never included her had to be difficult for her. It made him want to stop the car, pull her over into his lap and hold her. He settled for reaching across the console and taking her hand in his. Her gaze shot up to his face, and when she started to pull away, he squeezed her fingers but didn't release her.

She tugged again, but he made no attempt to relinquish his hold. She shot him a withering look. "I'd like my hand back," she said, her voice sharp as a knife.

Preferring the fire in those eyes to the pain and stress that had been there a moment ago, Josh brought her fingers to his lips and pressed a kiss to them before letting her go.

She crossed her arms and looked straight ahead. "How much farther?" she demanded.

"About ten minutes," he told her, and waited for the light to change at the intersection. The nerves were back, he noted, and this urge he had to protect her kicked in again. So did the desire he'd been doing his best to ignore since seeing her again in the airport.

Must be some weak gene in the male species of the Logan family, he told himself. One that specifically applied to Logan men tangling with Jardine women. If he needed any proof, he had only to look at his own family history. After all, it had been his grandfather falling for Olivia Jardine that led to the infamous bet that cost the family the Princess Hotel. And it was his vow to reclaim the Princess Hotel that had managed to get him ensnared in this game Olivia had set into motion with Laura. His grandfather had evidently passed along his gambling gene as well, Josh decided. Because despite every instinct that told him to fold his hand and walk away from Laura and Olivia's schemes before it was too late, he knew that he wasn't going to do it. He wanted them both—the Princess *and* Laura Harte.

When he turned onto the street that led to the Jardine mansion, she began to fidget with her purse. "Quit worrying. The French settlers left the guillotines in France before coming to Louisiana."

"I'm not worried," she insisted, and remained still for all of ten seconds.

"If it makes you feel any better, I'm betting that the Duchess is just as anxious as you are."

"The Duchess?"

"Your grandmother," he explained.

"That's what you call her?"

"Much to her dissatisfaction, I'm afraid. She hates the nickname and tears a strip off me every time I use it."

"So why do you? Call her Duchess, I mean."

Josh shrugged. "I've known her since I was a kid and it's how I've always thought of her."

"Why?"

He thought about it a moment, wondered how to explain. "Olivia Jardine's not a very big woman, but she has this tremendous presence about her. It's an air of dignity, I guess you'd call it, that's always made me think of monarchs and peasants. With Olivia being the monarch and me as the peasant, of course."

"Somehow, I don't see you filling the role of peasant very well."

Josh laughed. "That's good, since I'd much rather be the king."

"Well, at least you have one of the qualifications of a king down pat."

"You think so?"

"Oh, definitely," Laura told him.

The smile she gave him was deceptively sweet, he

thought. Still he said, "I'm almost afraid to ask, but which one?"

"Arrogance."

Laura was still laughing at having scored one off of Josh when he pulled the Mercedes to a stop in front of a home surrounded by an intricately carved wrought-iron gate. Suddenly, the laughter died in her throat as she realized she was there—Jardine House—the home where her father had lived with his other children.

Josh identified himself into a security speaker box and the gates swung open. He drove down a long driveway beneath an archway formed by the branches of the huge oak trees that stood like sentries on either side of the road. The dwindling afternoon sunlight peeked through the heavy Spanish moss that draped the tree branches. As the house came into view, Laura sucked in a breath. The place looked as though it had come straight out of the pages of a *Town & Country* or *Southern Living* magazine. A magnificent plantation-style home with imposing white columns and galleries, it was nestled amid more towering oaks that Laura was sure had to be at least a century old. She spotted several magnolia trees, their leaves a deep velvety green, dotting the nearby landscape.

"This is it," Josh said after stopping the car and shutting off the engine. Still staring at the imposing home, she hadn't even unbuckled her seat belt when Josh was opening her door.

Exiting the car, Laura continued to stare at the house. She'd worked in more than one beautiful hotel, had visited her share of impressive homes and rubbed elbows with the wealthy often in her job. But her exposure to the world of the rich and glamorous was far removed from the world in which she actually lived. Her mother's income as a nurse and her own working at the hotel had enabled them to live a full but modest lifestyle. Never in her dreams could she imagine growing up in a home like this.

"What do you think?"

"It's beautiful," she told him honestly.

"But imposing," he said, taking her arm and leading her up the stairs.

She had to agree with him, she thought as she caught the sweet scent of jasmine in the air. The size of the house alone would be imposing. And from what Josh had told her, only four members of the Jardine family lived here.

"I've always thought this was a great place for parties, but I'd never want to live here."

Surprised, since she suspected the Logans' holdings were substantial, she tipped her gaze toward him. "Then the Logan homestead isn't similar?"

He laughed. "Hardly. I grew up in a two-story Acadian with four bedrooms and two baths. The only reason I got my own room was because I was the only guy in the house besides my dad. With five of us kids, you could forget ever finding the house quiet or yourself alone. But in this place," he said, indicating the Jardine mansion, "a person could get lost and it would take someone a week to find you."

Laura chuckled. "I doubt it's that bad."

"Maybe not. But given a choice, I'll take crowded and comfortable over elegance and grandeur any day."

Once again Laura found herself agreeing with Josh. While he rang the doorbell, she was struck by the sudden realization that this could very well have been her home. Had things turned out differently between Drew

Jardine and her mother, she might have grown up living here. For the life of her, she couldn't see herself here. And she couldn't even imagine her mother being happy in this place.

The front door opened and revealed a tall gentleman in formal butler's attire. "Good afternoon, Mr. Josh. Miss," he said, bowing his head.

"Hello, Alfred. This is Ms. Harte. Laura, this is Alfred Bennett. He's the person responsible for keeping this museum in such tip-top shape."

"How do you do, miss?" he said, and bowed his head again politely. "Welcome to Jardine House."

Laura was instantly charmed by the soft-spoken man with twinkling dark eyes and whose balding head was striking against the tufts of snow-white hair just above his ears. "Thank you, Alfred. It's a pleasure to meet you."

"Alfred won't admit it, but rumor has it that he's been here at Jardine House since it was built."

Alfred smiled, revealing a mouth filled with gleaming white teeth. "Pay him no mind, Miss Laura. Mr. Josh has been making his little jokes since he was in short pants. We just ignore him."

Laura smiled. "It sounds like good advice. Thank you."

"My pleasure, ma'am." Alfred stepped back and waited for them to enter. "Mrs. Jardine is on the telephone. She's asked that you wait for her in the library. If you'll follow me, I'll take you there now."

With Josh at her side, Laura followed the butler down the ornate entry hall and tried to ignore the nerves in her stomach by focusing on her surroundings. She noted the high ceilings, the crystal chandelier and gilt-edged mirrors, the paintings that she suspected were originals and not reproductions. Beautiful though the house was, Josh had been right. It reminded her more of a museum than someone's home.

Alfred opened the doors to a large, lovely room that smelled of lemon oil, books and flowers. "Mrs. Jardine will be with you shortly."

"Thank you, Alfred," Josh said before the butler exited the room, closing the door quietly behind him.

Everything about the place shouted wealth, class, privilege, Laura thought. And she could no more imagine her mother living here than she could imagine Josh Logan as a monk or herself as an heiress. That last thought had her nerves kicking in again.

Unable to keep still, Laura stepped farther into the room. She noted that the antique desk, which rested atop an Aubusson rug, was free of any clutter. Neatly arranged books filled the shelves, which stretched from floor to ceiling. A beautiful arrangement of fresh flowers filled a cut-crystal vase on a polished table surrounded by comfortable-looking chairs. The heavy damask drapes of rich burgundy had been pulled back to reveal a garden lush with blooms and greenery. Drawn to the freedom beyond the windows, she walked across the room and stared out into the fading daylight. But not even the beauty of the gardens could stop her thoughts from turning to her impending meeting with Olivia Jardine.

"While you're waiting for Olivia, I'm going to run out to the car and get your bags to save Alfred the trouble."

"Wait," Laura said, whipping around and moving toward him before she could stop herself. Suddenly panicked at the thought of being alone with the woman she'd come here to face, she gripped the sleeve of his jacket. "Would you...could you stay?"

"Sure," he said, covering her hand with his own. "I'll get the bags later."

Embarrassed and disturbed by the quickening of her pulse at his touch, Laura started to tell him never mind when the door to the library opened. She tensed. And as though he sensed her uneasiness, Josh gave her fingers a quick squeeze before releasing them, but he remained at her side.

Olivia Jardine was not what she'd expected. The woman with the cool, Southern voice that she'd spoken to on the telephone hadn't fit any of the preconceived notions she'd associated with the term *grandmother*. So it came as no surprise to discover that Olivia Jardine did not resemble the stereotypical sweet, little, gray-haired lady image. Despite the cane she leaned on, she stood tall, proud and elegant in the solid black dress. Matching pearls at her ears and neck were her only adornment. Her silver hair had been swept up, away from a face that showed far fewer lines than she'd have expected for a woman who had already passed eighty. Except for the faint rose lipstick she wore, the only relief from the stark black and silver was the pale blue of her eyes. It was the fire and energy in those eyes now trained on her that gave Laura pause.

"Hello, Duchess," Josh said, breaking the silence.

"Don't call me by that insipid name," Olivia commanded and shot Josh a look that Laura thought would make most people cringe.

Unfazed, Josh walked over and kissed the woman's cheek. "Alfred, why don't you give me that?" Josh suggested, and Laura noted the butler had entered and stood waiting with a wheelchair.

"I told you to leave that thing in the other room. I don't need it," Olivia snapped.

Laura shifted her gaze back to the older woman. She recognized the stubborn pride burning in Olivia Jardine's eyes and realized she had been determined not to show any weakness. Laura couldn't help but feel a grudging admiration because she, too, could understand the need to appear strong.

"Mrs. Jardine, you know that Dr. Guillory said you're to stay off that ankle," Alfred reminded her.

"And James Guillory is a fussy old man who's trying to justify those exorbitant fees he's been charging me. Take that thing out of here and dump it in the trash. I'm not going to use it."

"Hang on a second, Alfred," Josh said when the butler started to leave. Rubbing his jaw, Josh made a show of walking around the wheelchair, checking out the controls. "I tell you what, Duchess. If you really are going to toss the thing, would you mind if I take it?"

Olivia narrowed her eyes. "And what do you want with it?"

Josh grinned. "With a few adjustments, I think I can soup this baby up and turn it into a racing chair. My nephew Scotty and I will have a ball racing it down my folks' street at Thanksgiving."

Olivia's mouth pulled into a thin line. "Alfred, take that thing away from this young fool before he figures out a way to use it to break both his own neck and his nephew's."

"But if you're going to throw it out," Josh started to argue.

"I'm not throwing it out! Alfred, put the chair over there at the end of the table for me, please."

"Yes, ma'am."

As Olivia followed Alfred to the table, Josh winked at Laura. "And don't think I'm too old and feeble to see through you, Joshua Logan," Olivia told him as she sat down in the chair. She rested the cane beside her. "I simply don't want to deal with your foolishness right now. I want to meet my granddaughter. Introduce us." With Josh's hand at her back, she walked toward the other woman.

"Olivia Jardine, I'd like to present Laura Harte, your granddaughter." In the same formal manner and serious tone, Josh continued, "Laura Harte, I'd like you to meet Olivia Jardine, your grandmother."

Laura said nothing. She simply met the older woman's stare. "Come closer, girl," Olivia commanded. "Let me get a better look at you."

Laura tipped up her chin, and keeping her back ramrod straight, she walked over until she stood within a few feet. Olivia remained silent for a long time, seemingly taking her time to study her features one by one. It was an unsettling experience and did nothing to ease the knot in Laura's stomach. Yet she refused to be the first to look away or speak.

"You have the look of your mother about the mouth and nose, but the resemblance is only minor. There's no mistaking the fact that you're a Jardine with those eyes and your coloring," Olivia told her.

A burst of anger at the cool assessment quickly doused any nervousness she'd been experiencing and also loosened her tongue. "Most people think I resemble my mother," Laura countered, knowing even as she said the words that they weren't true. Her resemblance to her mother had been faint at best. It had been one of the things that she had always regretted—not simply because her mother had been a beautiful woman, but because she'd longed to see a marked resemblance between them as so many of her friends did between themselves and their parents. That she could look at Olivia Jardine and immediately recognize that resemblance irritated Laura. Especially now when Olivia's mentioning of her mother had Laura envisioning a young, pregnant Juliet Harte facing a younger, stronger version of this stern woman. With her sweet and gentle nature, her mother would have been no match for Olivia Jardine. And it made Laura all the more determined to discover the truth about what happened twenty-nine years ago.

Olivia arched her brow imperiously. "Then I'd say the people in California must have a problem with their eyes. It's clear that you're a Jardine."

"My name is Harte."

"Changing it to Jardine shouldn't be difficult. I'll put my attorney to work on it first thing tomorrow."

"Mrs. Jardine—"

"You may call me Grandmother. Now that I'm aware of your existence, I fully intend to acknowledge you as my granddaughter."

"Mrs. Jardine," Laura repeated pointedly, refusing to accord this woman a title that implied any familial or emotional attachment. "Just because we happen to share a biological tie doesn't mean we're family."

Olivia struck the end of her cane on the floor. Her eyes sparked at the slight as she said, "We most certainly are family. I'm your grandmother."

"Be that as it may, I have neither the desire nor any intention of changing my name to Jardine."

In the shocked silence that followed, Laura was sure she could have heard a pin drop—and probably would have were it not for the anger pulsing through her that had her heart pounding like a drum in her chest.

"I see Joshua didn't exaggerate. He said you had a quick temper, but he failed to mention you also have a sharp tongue."

"For which I have no intention of apologizing," Laura told her.

"I didn't expect you would," Olivia said evenly. "And while I don't appreciate your impertinence, I am pleased to see that you have a backbone. I was worried you might not since your mother was such a timid creature."

"Don't you dare say a word against my mother," Laura fired back, taking a step closer, curling her hands into fists. Josh caught her arm, kept her from snarling in the old woman's face. "My mother was a kind, brave and wonderful woman. And I won't stand for you or anyone else speaking ill of her."

"I'm sure Olivia didn't mean any offense. Did you, Duchess?"

"Of course I didn't mean to offend her," Olivia said impatiently. "I was merely stating the truth."

Josh tightened his hold on her arm. "Uh, Duchess, you might want to refrain from making any further remarks about Laura's mother."

"Very well. If that's what you wish, Laura, I won't mention Juliet again," Olivia offered.

But before Laura could respond, the door to the library opened and a maid entered the room, bearing a tray laden with tea.

"There you are, Jane." Olivia waved her into the room. "I was beginning to think you'd gotten lost. Just leave the tray on the table and then you may go. Please see to it that the Rose Room is ready for Laura and tell Cook I'd like dinner served at half past seven.''

Laura was about to tell Olivia that she'd changed her mind about staying at the house and would go to a hotel instead when Olivia turned to Josh and said, ''You will stay and join us for dinner this evening, won't you, Joshua?''

''Actually, I hadn't planned to.''

''Laura, would you serve the tea, please?''

Although it was disguised as a question, Olivia Jardine had left little room for any refusal on her part, Laura noted. Evidently, the other woman didn't even consider that her request might be turned down because she'd already turned her attention back to Josh.

''I would appreciate it if you would stay,'' Olivia told him. ''And I'm sure Katherine, Alison and Mitchell would love to see you again.''

''Then you've talked to Katie?'' Josh asked, and Laura didn't miss the warmth in his voice as he spoke of Katie Jardine.

''Of course I've talked to Katherine. I make it a practice to talk to all of the members of my family,'' Olivia informed him.

''You know that's not what I meant,'' Josh countered.

''One sugar, no milk,'' Olivia told Laura, and after thanking her, she took the cup of tea Laura offered.

''Duchess, quit stalling. Did you or did you not tell them about Laura?'' Josh demanded.

''If you're asking did I tell them that Laura would be our guest for the next three weeks, the answer is no. I intend to inform them tonight over dinner.''

Laura nearly dropped the silver teapot as she jerked

her gaze to Olivia's face. ''You mean they don't even know that I'm here?''

''My dear child, except for me, no one in the Jardine family even knows you exist.''

Eleven

"**Y**ou can't be serious," Laura replied, her voice as shocked as her expression. "If this is your idea of a joke—"

"My dear, I *never* joke," said Olivia.

"But why would you even consider doing such a thing? Springing me on your family without...without any warning? It's...it's cruel."

"She's right, Duchess. This is *not* a good idea." Josh echoed Laura's sentiments. He'd assumed that Olivia had told her grandchildren about Laura by now. Discovering that she hadn't and that she had planned to present Laura to them without any warning disturbed and disappointed him. He'd expected better of Olivia Jardine. Surely the woman realized how much Mitch, Katie and Alison had adored their father. For them to learn that the man had fathered another child who was their half sibling would be devastating for all of them— but especially for Katie. Because, of the three Jardine children, it was Katie who had been closest to her father. She'd idolized the man. "Think of what a shock this will be for them. You can't just spring Laura on them like this without any warning."

"I don't need you to tell me how to deal with my family."

"I was offering you advice…as a friend and some-one who cares about you."

"I don't recall asking you for advice," Olivia in-formed him.

"But—"

"Enough," she countered, cutting him off. "I know what I'm doing."

"Do you?"

"Yes," she replied firmly.

But Josh wasn't at all sure that Olivia did understand what a serious mistake she was making. Her need to control he understood. But this went beyond that. Was it possible that the woman who had proved a smart and formidable business opponent to three generations of Logans could be so blind to the repercussions her ac-tions would cause? Despite her no-nonsense, crusty ex-terior, he believed that Olivia loved her family. But there was no question in his mind that someone would be hurt by this. "For your own sake, Duchess, I'm asking you to reconsider. I don't think you realize just how much is at stake here."

"You should know better than to underestimate me, Joshua Logan. Unlike your grandfather I don't ever wager more than I can afford to lose."

Josh narrowed his eyes at the word *wager*. "I wasn't talking about money."

"Neither was I," Olivia told him.

But Josh couldn't shake the feeling that they were talking about a great deal more than the fallout that would be caused by Laura's appearance. He also couldn't shake the feeling that he'd just been issued a warning.

"I'm a careful gambler." She tipped her head, eyed him closely. "What about you, Joshua? Are you a reckless gambler like your grandfather? Or do you have the good sense to play it safe?''

"I play to win."

"I take it that means you'd risk more than you should."

"It means what I risk depends on how badly I want the prize," he told her.

"And if the prize was something that you wanted more than anything else in the world, but the odds were stacked against you, would you still take the wager? Would you gamble it all to win what you wanted?"

Josh knew for certain now that they were no longer speaking of just any wager—but of *the* wager—the one he and Olivia had made a month ago, the wager he had been cursing himself for making ever since he'd laid eyes on Laura. He'd written off hope that he would ever see Laura again after botching things as he had in San Francisco. Yet here she was in New Orleans, in Olivia Jardine's home. And if Laura were to stay, if she were to take over operation of the Princess and turn it around, he would have a shot at reclaiming the hotel and making good on that long-ago promise to his grandfather.

"What would you do, Joshua? Even knowing how much it might cost you were you to lose, would you still gamble for a chance to claim the prize you want so badly?"

No wonder the woman had given his grandfather fits, Josh thought. How had she figured out that he wanted both Laura and the Princess when he'd barely known it himself before now?

"Would you risk it?" she asked, hammering him to answer the question.

Perhaps he could have turned his back on Laura or

the hotel. But the chance to have them both? No. It was a gamble he wouldn't walk away from and a risk that he knew he would take regardless of the odds. "Yes. I'd risk it."

She shook her head. "The apple truly doesn't fall far from the tree. It appears I was right. You're every bit as reckless as your grandfather was."

"But unlike my grandfather, I'm not blinded by love. Make no mistake, Duchess, I intend to do everything within my power to change the odds in my favor and I intend to come out the winner."

"Excuse me," Laura said, her voice dripping with disdain as she looked from him to Olivia. "I'm not sure what's going on here, and to be perfectly frank, I don't care about any stupid bet between the two of you. What I do care about and what I resent is that you've obviously mapped out some sort of agenda in which you plan to use me to...to ambush your own grandchildren. Well, I won't have it."

"It appears you've inherited your mother's dramatic streak," Olivia replied, her tone dismissive.

"You leave my mother out of this," Laura shot back.

"Very well. But I suggest you calm yourself, child. I have no intention of 'ambushing' my grandchildren, as you put it. I've merely chosen not to inform them about you before now. I assure you I have my reasons."

"What possible reasons could you have for being so heartless?" Laura demanded.

Olivia's eyes hardened. "My reasons are my own and not your concern."

"It is my concern when you're trying to use me to further your own agenda. I don't like being treated like a fool, Mrs. Jardine. I have no intention of being used. By you or by anyone else,'' Laura told her. In a gesture eerily similar to Olivia's, she hiked up her chin and turned to Josh. "Since my bags are still in your car, would you be kind enough to take me to a hotel?"

"Don't be absurd, girl. You're staying here. This is your home."

"This is not my home," Laura replied icily. "My home is in San Francisco—where I'll be returning just as soon as I can book another flight."

"You'll do no such thing," Olivia commanded. "You agreed to stay here for three weeks."

"I've changed my mind," she informed Olivia before turning back to him. "Will you give me a lift to a hotel or should I call a taxi?"

"I'll take you," Josh said without hesitation, knowing that his response would irritate Olivia and probably skewer any hopes he had of buying the Princess. But his own sense of honor would allow him to do nothing else. "We'd better go before the others arrive."

Yet even as he uttered the words, the door to the library burst open and in rushed Katie Jardine. "Josh, you dog," she squealed as she raced into the room and launched herself at him. "What are you doing here? I thought you were still on the West Coast buying up hotels and breaking some poor foolish female's heart."

"Hello, brat," he said, catching her in his arms.

"When did you get back? And why didn't you tell me you were going to be here? Did Grandmother ask you to stay for dinner? It doesn't matter. You *have* to stay. I want to hear about your trip and there's an idea I want to run by you. What do you think of—"

"Stop," Josh protested even as he laughed at the woman who'd been his friend for ages and who had draped herself over him as though he were a comfortable, old couch. In typical Katie Jardine fashion, the woman knew only one speed—fast. "Take a deep breath and give me a minute to catch up. My head's still spinning."

"Honestly, Katherine, is that any way to enter a room? And quit strangling Joshua," Olivia chided. "Where are your manners?"

Josh bit back a grin as Katie rolled her eyes before releasing him and turning to face her grandmother. "Sorry, Grandmother," Katie said in a voice that didn't sound the least bit contrite. "I saw Josh's car out front, and when Alfred said he was here, I didn't stop to think before I came rushing in."

"That much is obvious," Olivia replied. "Perhaps if you conducted yourself like a lady, you would have noticed that we have a visitor before you embarrassed everyone with your lack of decorum."

Katie jerked her gaze to her grandmother's left, spied Laura and winced. "Oops!"

"If that's your idea of an apology, Katherine Elizabeth," Olivia began, her voice as cool and disapproving as her eyes, "I can see that I was correct in my initial assessment that that ridiculous finishing school your mother insisted you and your sister attend was a waste of time and money."

"Now she tells me," Katie muttered. "I never did want to go to that dumb school."

Josh smothered a chuckle, remembering all too well the fun he'd had teasing a thirteen-year-old Katie about the prim charm school she'd been forced to attend and had hated.

Olivia rapped the floor with her cane. "Speak up,

Katherine. You know I detest it when you mumble. Now, what did you say?"

"Sorry, Grandmother. I said I didn't realize we had company," Katie replied, and shot Josh a withering glance when he snickered. Smiling, she started toward Laura with her hand extended. "Hi, I'm Katie Jardine and I hope you'll accept my apology. I'm not usually quite so rude."

Laura's hesitation was as brief as her handshake. "Laura Harte. And no apology is necessary."

"Hear that, Grandmother?"

"Impertinence is not attractive, Katherine."

"Yes, ma'am," Katie said demurely, but her eyes were filled with sass. "So Laura," Katie said. "Are you a friend of Josh's?"

"I...well..."

Josh felt that kick to his ribs again at the combination of shock and stress swimming in Laura's eyes. He was also worried about Katie. "Actually, Laura and I met a couple of weeks ago when I was in San Francisco," Josh offered.

"Really?" Katie countered. Her blue eyes, a shade deeper than Laura's pale ones, twinkled with speculation.

"Yes," Laura answered, her discomfort evident.

"Laura arrived this afternoon," Josh explained.

Katie arched her brow in a manner very similar to her grandmother's. "Well, you certainly picked a good time to visit. November in New Orleans is usually very pleasant. Not too hot, not too cold. Will you be staying long?"

"No. As a matter of fact, I was about to leave when you came in."

"Oh, that's too bad. I hoped we'd have a chance to

visit. Maybe I'll see you again before you return to San Francisco.''

"I don't think so. I'll be leaving first thing in the morning.''

Katie squinched her brows together. "But I thought you just arrived.''

"I did, but I can't stay. Please forgive me, but I really do need to go.'' The look she tossed Josh's way was laced with panic. "If you'd like to stay and visit, I can take a taxi.''

"I said I'd take you,'' Josh reminded her before turning his attention back to a confused-looking Katie. "I'll give you a call later,'' he told his friend, then met Olivia's furious gaze. "Duchess, thanks for the invitation, but I'm afraid I'll have to pass on dinner. I hope you'll forgive me.''

"I will not forgive you, nor will I excuse your behavior,'' Olivia fired back.

"I regret that,'' Josh told her, and meant it. With his hand at Laura's back, he started toward the door, wanting to get out of the place before things got any worse.

"Laura, I demand you stop this foolishness this instant and come back here!''

"Grandmother?'' Katie called out, surprise in her voice.

Olivia slapped her cane on the table. "I'm warning you, Laura, do not make the mistake of walking out of here.''

Laura's back stiffened beneath his palm and she halted in the middle of the room. Every instinct inside him said to drag her across the room and out of the house before everything blew up around them. But Laura was already turning around to face Olivia. Anger practically shimmered from her in waves.

"Duchess, don't do this," Josh cautioned.

Olivia ignored him and kept her attention focused on Laura. "If you walk out on me now, I swear you'll regret it."

"The only thing I regret is that I was foolish enough to come here in the first place. I wish I'd never heard the name Jardine and that I'd never set eyes on you. Rest assured, it's a mistake I won't make again," Laura told her.

"How dare you speak to me in such a manner," Olivia hissed, her pale skin flushed with temper, her blue eyes icy cold. "How dare you treat me with such disrespect?"

"You don't deserve my respect," Laura informed her.

"Now, hang on a minute," Katie told Laura, jumping into the fray. "I don't care if you are Josh's flavor of the month, where do you get off talking to my grandmother that way?"

"Stay out of this, Katie," Josh warned.

"I will not stay out of it. Your bimbo here just insulted my grandmother," she said, her voice snide, her expression scornful. "And unless she wants me to rip that red hair of hers out by the roots, she'd better apologize."

"Let's go," Josh urged Laura, all but dragging her toward the door.

"I'm warning you, Laura, do not leave this room," Olivia chimed in.

Katie narrowed her gaze and stared at her grandmother. "She just insulted you and you want her to stay?"

"Hey, what's wrong? Why are you shouting?" Alison asked as she entered the room and hurried to her twin's side. Identical in looks, the two women were opposites in temperament and demeanor. Where Katie was quick to anger, Alison wasn't easy to rile and generally played peacemaker.

"Nothing's wrong," Josh said, and wondered if things could get any worse.

"You sure about that?" Mitch Jardine asked as he entered the room and joined the party. After kissing his grandmother's cheek, he held out his hand to Josh. "Didn't realize you were going to be here, Logan," he said, flashing him an easy smile. "Why don't you introduce me to your pretty friend and then you can tell me what all the yelling is about?"

Josh sighed. Things had definitely gone from bad to worse, he thought. "Laura Harte, Mitch Jardine and his sister Alison." As Josh made the introductions, he was aware all the while of the tension in Laura and the seething anger in Katie.

"If you're finished playing social director, I'd like an answer to my question," Katie informed him.

"What question?" Alison asked.

"Where Josh's girlfriend here gets off insulting our grandmother?" Katie charged.

"It's between me and Mrs. Jardine," Laura said evenly. "It doesn't concern you."

"The hell it doesn't," Katie shot back.

"That's enough, Katherine," Olivia chided.

Katie whirled around to face her grandmother. "You're defending her?"

"You don't understand," Olivia said patiently.

"Then explain it to me." When Olivia remained silent, Katie sliced her attention back to Laura. "You want to tell me what's going on here?" When Laura, too, remained silent, she shifted her gaze to Josh. "All right, Josh, since no one's talking, why don't you tell us what's going on here?''

"Josh?" Alison said his name softly, expectantly.

"Leave it alone, Ali. I promise I'll explain things later."

"You'll explain things now," Katie insisted.

"Maybe it would be best if you did as she asked," Mitch suggested. He moved to stand beside his sisters and Josh couldn't help but note the united front the three presented.

"It's not my place. You'll have to ask your grandmother."

"Grandmother?" Mitch addressed the older woman.

Olivia remained silent for several heartbeats, her gaze fixed on Laura, and Josh thought she wasn't going to answer her grandson. Then she shifted her gaze from Laura to Mitch. "I made a remark that offended Laura, and when she wanted to leave, I upset her even more by insisting that she stay here instead of going to a hotel."

"But why would you insist she stay here?" Alison asked.

"Because this is her home now."

"This is *not* my home," Laura informed her.

"That's where you're wrong, my dear girl. This most certainly is your home. Just as it's been home to all the Jardines for nearly two centuries."

Mitch's deep blue eyes shifted to Laura, narrowed as he watched her. "Are you a distant relative?" he asked Laura.

"The girl's not a distant relative, Mitchell," Olivia answered. "She's your sister."

She was having a nightmare, Laura told herself. And any minute now she was going to wake up and find it was all a terrible dream. But at the sound of Josh swearing beside her, Katie's scream of denial and Alison's shocked gasp, Laura knew it was no nightmare— at least not the kind that she could awaken from and dismiss.

"It isn't true," Katie protested.

"I assure you, Katherine, it is the truth. Laura is your father's daughter, and therefore, she's your sister."

Katie spun around, shoved her red-gold hair from her face and pinned Laura with dark blue eyes. "It's a lie."

"Katie, calm down," Josh soothed.

The swift stab of envy she experienced at the sight of Josh's arm slipping around Katie's waist and pulling her close surprised Laura. To feel the least bit jealous over Josh Logan was absurd, Laura assured herself. After all, hadn't the man already proved himself to be an opportunistic snake? So what if he was gorgeous and the chemistry between them was fire hot? She'd never allowed chemistry to override logic in the past. She certainly wasn't about to start doing so now.

"I think you owe us an explanation," Mitch told Laura. "Why should we believe that you're our sister?"

"Because she is," Olivia answered. "I've already had it verified. Laura is your father's daughter. But even without confirmation, you only have to look at her to see she's a Jardine."

Alison took a step toward Laura and made a careful study of her face and features. And as she studied her, Laura studied the other young woman. Alison's hair, like her twin's, was lighter in color, closer to a strawberry blond than Laura's own auburn. And her eyes were a deep, intense shade of blue. All those years of looking at others and never finding anyone whose features or coloring resembled her own, and now she was surrounded by people who all bore a sharp resemblance to the face she saw each morning in the mirror.

Alison's eyes widened. "Grandmother's right. She does have Daddy's eyes…Grandmother's eyes."

"Lots of people have blue eyes," Katie argued. "I don't know what kind of game you're playing or what kind of story you cooked up to get my grandmother to believe you're our sister, but I don't believe you for a second."

"Believe what you want," Laura countered. "Trust me, I'm no more eager to claim you as my sister than you are to claim me. I never should have come here."

"Then why did you?" Katie asked.

"Because I sent for her," Olivia replied, and saved Laura from having to answer.

What would she have said, anyway? Laura wondered. That she'd come here because she'd wanted to find answers to the questions that had been plaguing her since finding that letter among her mother's things? That she'd wanted to find out what had caused her mother to walk away from a man she supposedly loved nearly thirty years ago. That she'd wanted to find out who had tried to pay her mother to get rid of her. That she'd wanted to find out if her uncle Paul had been right, that her father hadn't known of her existence, or if he had known and chosen to ignore her.

"But why, Grandmother?" Katie countered. "You must know that she's lying. Everyone knows Daddy adored Mother and never even looked at another woman."

"Katherine, your father was my only child, and as

much as I loved him even I knew that Andrew was no saint. He had a rebellious streak in him just as you do—especially when he was a young man. He didn't always do the right thing. Before he married your mother and while he was in the navy stationed in California, he met Laura's mother. They had a...a liaison. Laura is the result of their affair.''

The result that someone had wanted destroyed, Laura thought with bitterness. But who? she wondered. Olivia Jardine? Surely the woman would have wanted to avoid the scandal. Or maybe Andrew Jardine's wife Adrienne had wanted Laura and her mother out of the picture. Or perhaps it had been her father himself.

''If all this is true, then why are we just hearing about it now?'' Mitch asked.

''Because I only learned of Laura's existence myself a couple of months ago when her mother died.''

''Which is also when Laura learned the truth about her father's identity,'' Josh explained as he moved to Laura's side. Not for the life of her would Laura admit that facing the three Jardine siblings had made her feel more alone than ever before, or that Josh standing beside her helped to ease her discomfort.

''Just how do you fit into this picture, Logan?'' Mitch asked.

''Your grandmother asked me to go see Laura for her.''

Hurt flashed in Mitch's eyes for a moment before he banked it. ''You asked Josh instead of your own flesh and blood?''

Olivia's expression softened. ''I wasn't sure how you'd take the news,'' she explained. ''Laura had turned down my requests to come to New Orleans, so I asked Joshua to go convince her to come.''

Katie made a snorting sound. "Evidently she didn't need much convincing. I wonder what made you change your mind—learning about the Jardine money or Josh's skill in bed?"

Laura's temper spiked, and were it not for Josh's restraining hand on her shoulder, she would have been in the other woman's face. Instead she settled for attacking with words. "Maybe your decisions are made based on money and sex, but mine aren't."

"Why you—"

"You're out of line, Katie," Josh objected, his body suddenly tense, his anger at the insult almost palatable. "None of this is Laura's fault," he defended. "Learning the truth about her father was as much a shock to her as it has been for you."

"He's right," Mitch told his sister, and Laura took some satisfaction in seeing shame color Katie's cheeks. "As Josh said, this has been a shock—for all of us." He turned those deep blue eyes on Laura and gave her a half smile. "It's not every day I discover that instead of being outnumbered by two sisters, that I'm actually outnumbered by three. I hope you'll accept my apology."

Laura swallowed hard. "Of course," she managed to get out past a throat that had suddenly gone tight with emotion—emotion that she did not want to feel.

"I'm sorry, too," Alison said. Stepping forward, she caught Laura's fingers in her hands and squeezed them. Her lips curved into a grin that shone in her eyes. "I hope we can start over. I kind of like the idea of having another sister."

"This is all very touching," Katie said, her mouth pulled into a frown. "But aren't all of you forgetting something?"

"What?" Alison asked.

"Mother," Katie supplied. "Who's going to tell her?"

"I'll tell her," Mitch offered.

"No, I will speak with Adrienne," Olivia told them. "She's my son's widow and my daughter-in-law."

"And she's my mother," Mitch argued.

"What difference does it make who tells her?" Katie lashed out. "How do you think she's going feel when she hears the news about Daddy's bastard child?"

"Katherine!"

"It's all right, Mrs. Jardine," Laura said as she met Katie's hostile gaze. Josh squeezed her shoulder, and whether she'd imagined the compassion in his touch or not, it enabled her to continue. "I understand how Katie feels. But the next time she wants to sling those arrows my way I think she needs to consider the fact that I'm not the only target she's hitting."

Katie eyed her warily. "What's that supposed to mean?"

"It means that the only reason I am a bastard is because your father made me one."

Twelve

"That's enough," Olivia informed them. "I will not tolerate such talk in this house. Laura is your father's daughter and my granddaughter and I'll not have any member of this family treat her otherwise."

Katie watched as her grandmother, looking every bit like the duchess Josh called her, moved over to the bell pull and rang for the butler. Simmering with resentment and hurt, Katie stared at Laura Harte. Reluctantly she admitted that she saw the resemblance. As much as she wanted to believe her grandmother, Josh, Mitch and even her twin had been duped by the young woman, she couldn't deny the fact that Laura had her father's eyes. *Her* father.

And Laura's father, too. The admission ripped at her heart, made her ache inside as nothing ever had before except her father's death. Learning her father had betrayed her mother hurt all the more because she'd believed her father had been too honorable to ever stray. Certainly the man she'd loved and tried so hard to please growing up had been too honorable not to own up to his mistakes.

Unless he hadn't known.

Laura's mother hadn't told him, she decided. It was the only explanation. From what her grandmother had said, Laura had been conceived before her parents' marriage. If her father had known about Laura's existence, he would have acknowledged her. Despite what Laura thought, the one at blame here wasn't her father—it was Laura's mother.

"You rang for me, Mrs. Jardine?" Alfred said from the doorway, jarring Katie's attention from her musings.

"Yes. Would you have Miss Harte's bags moved from Mr. Logan's car into the rose guest room. Ask Mrs. Baxter if it's possible to delay dinner for an hour and then send Ellen up to my rooms with my medication. I'll give myself the injection," she said, referring to the insulin shots she had been administering to herself for the past two years.

"I told you, I'm not staying," Laura said, a trace of panic in her eyes that didn't reach her voice.

"That will be all, Alfred," she dismissed the butler. "Of course you're staying. You agreed to a three-week visit, and as I told you, this is your home now and we're your family. Now, if you'll excuse me, Adrienne should be home shortly and I need to speak with her. I'll see all of you at dinner. And, Joshua, I hope you'll change your mind and join us."

"Wait," Laura cried out to her grandmother's retreating back. "I'm not staying. This isn't my home and you're not my family."

"But, Laura, we *are* your family," Alison pointed out, drawing Laura's focus back to them. "And since this was our father's home, that makes it your home, too."

Not for the first time Katie marveled at the difference between her and her twin. Evidently when the egg from which they'd come had split in two, Alison had been the one who'd gotten all the sweetness, patience and goodness there was. Because as Josh had often pointed out, she was not only foul-tempered, but impatient and distrusting to boot.

"I...thank you, Alison. That's very kind of you. But I don't belong here. My home is in San Francisco and I'm going back as soon as I can get a flight out. In the meantime, I'll just stay in a hotel."

"Good luck trying to find a room," Katie chimed in. "November's a huge convention month in New Orleans. Every hotel room within a hundred-mile radius has been booked for the past six months. I should know, I've been turning down reservations requests for weeks."

"Katie's right," Josh told her. "And I'm afraid getting a flight out of here isn't going to be a picnic, either. At least not right away. Since you've already taken the time off from your job, why don't you just stay? Give me a chance to show you the city?"

"Please, Laura. Say you'll stay...at least for a little while," Alison pleaded. "You're my sister and I'd like the chance to get to know you and for you to meet my daughter."

Katie's lips twitched as she watched Laura squirm. She knew exactly how it felt to be on the receiving end of that sweet, pleading gaze of her sister's. Besides, it had been a long time since Ali had genuinely seemed excited about something. If the prospect of having Laura Harte stay and play big sister for a few weeks would make Ali happy, then she would simply have to deal with it, Katie told herself. "You might as well save yourself the trouble of arguing and give in," she told Laura, not because she was eager to welcome Laura into the fold, but because it was what Ali wanted. After the heartache that louse Dawson had put her sister through, she'd walk through fire if it meant putting a smile in her eyes again. "Ali's like a bulldog when she gets an idea in her head. She doesn't know the meaning of the word *no*."

"There's nothing wrong with being tenacious," Laura advised her, and from the redhead's expression, Katie realized she was defending Ali. Since she'd been her twin's champion her entire life, Katie wasn't at all sure how she felt about Laura's sudden protectiveness toward her sister.

"Well, what do you know?" Mitch said. "It appears Laura's stubborn, too. Not that that should come as a surprise since you, my dear sister Katie, are one of the most stubborn people on the face of the earth."

"Sounds to me like the pot's calling the kettle black," Katie told him.

"While you children squabble among yourselves, I think I'll go give Alfred a hand," Josh said.

"Josh, wait," Laura called out. "I'm sorry, Alison, but I really can't stay."

"Please," Alison implored. "Stay."

"But you don't know anything about me."

"I know that you're my sister, my father's daughter. I don't need to know more than that," Alison insisted. "But I'd like the chance to get to know you. Please, Laura, say you'll stay."

"All right. I'll stay...for now."

More than an hour after dismissing the maid and assuring the woman that she could unpack her own things, Laura stared at the two suitcases she had yet to touch. Except for kicking off her heels, she'd done nothing but replay over and over the scene downstairs with the Jardines—and she was still no closer to deciding what she was going to do.

Should she stay and try to find the answers she came here in search of? Or should she leave now before things became even more complicated?

And they were becoming complicated, Laura admitted. She'd expected to battle wills with Olivia Jardine and it had come as no surprise when they did. But she hadn't expected, nor had she liked, that jolt of recognition that shot through her when she'd met her three half siblings. Evidently, Katie hadn't liked it any more than she had and made no attempt to disguise her dislike. Which was fine with her, Laura conceded, because she didn't like Katie Jardine, either. Mitchell was another kettle of fish altogether. He wasn't an easy man to read. He was quieter, more serious than his sister, and Laura sensed a wariness in him where she was concerned. She understood that wariness, even respected it. Just as she admired his protectiveness toward his siblings. And as much as she might have liked having a brother, she was smart enough not to fool herself by thinking Mitchell would see her as his long-lost sister.

But it was Alison Jardine who troubled her. She hadn't counted on Alison. Or more precisely, she hadn't counted on liking Alison and having her emotions stirred by the gentleness of a sister she'd been so sure she would never want to claim.

Restless and confused, Laura prowled about the huge guest room, her bare feet sinking into the plush white carpet. Shutting off her thoughts, she concentrated on the room instead. It was beautiful, she admitted. Feminine, elegant, inviting. A room straight out of a dream. Wandering over to the four-poster bed, she ran her fingertips along the edge of the damask duvet in a soothing foam green and noted the big, fluffy pillows in shades of ivory and rose that were piled against the headboard. With one end of the duvet turned down, the bed looked soft and inviting and served as a reminder of how poorly she'd slept the previous night.

But sleep was a luxury she could ill afford at the moment, Laura reminded herself. Sighing, she turned away from the bed and moved toward the blaze in the old-fashioned fireplace. Flames licked at the logs, taking the edge off the chill in the air and giving the room a soft, cozy glow. The silk wall covering with its climbing rose pattern seemed to shimmer beneath the spray of light from the crystal lamps on the bedside tables. The Queen Anne desk had been buffed and polished so that Laura could almost see the fragrant white roses reflected in the gleaming finish. Another vase of rose blossoms graced the small table that had been grouped with a love seat and two chairs in coordinating damask and silk. Thick books about Louisiana history and gardens rested atop the tables. Moving about the room, she skimmed her fingertips across the spines of what appeared to be first editions tucked onto the bookshelf and paused to study an alabaster figurine. The room Olivia had assigned to her was every bit as lovely and elegant as the rest of the house, Laura thought. It was a house made for a princess. Or rather two princesses and a prince, she amended, thinking of the three Jardine siblings.

What would it have been like for her to be a child here growing up?

The question came out of nowhere, catching her off guard. And with it came other questions. *Had Drew Jardine known her mother was pregnant? Had Olivia?*

Why had her mother returned to California? Why had she kept the truth about her father from her all these years? Or had her father known and chosen to ignore her?

"Laura?"

Laura started and spun around at the tap on the door. "Yes?"

"It's Alison. Can I come in?"

"Yes, of course."

The door opened and Alison came in holding a dark-haired, blue-eyed beauty by the hand. "This is my daughter Tori," Alison said. "Say hello to your aunt Laura, sweetheart."

"'Lo, Aunt Lawwa."

Laura brought her hand to her throat in an effort to ease the sudden lump that had formed at the little girl's greeting. "Hello, Tori," she finally managed to say, and stooped down to bring herself to the child's eye level. "That's a very pretty dress you're wearing."

"It's pink," Tori explained. "And I a princess."

"Well you certainly look like a princess," Laura told her.

"And I pretty."

"Tori," Alison admonished. "Proper young ladies don't go around making statements like that."

"Why? Uncle Josh says I pretty."

"And your uncle Josh is right," Laura replied with a smile as she stood. "You are very pretty."

"Thank you," Alison said as she stroked her daughter's dark curls.

Laura didn't miss the pride gleaming in the younger woman's eyes as she stared at her daughter. Nor could Laura ignore the flush of pleasure that went through her at the realization that this exquisite child was actually her niece. "She really is lovely. I feel sorry for you when she hits her teens. She's going to steal a lot of male hearts."

Alison laughed and rolled her eyes. "She's been stealing them since they wheeled us out of the delivery room at the hospital—starting with the doctor who delivered her. Of course Mitch and Josh are no help. Those two are putty in her hands."

"I can see why," Laura said as Tori squinched up her little pug nose and sniffed at the roses on the table. "I can't imagine anyone being able to resist her. I bet she's got her daddy wrapped around her little finger." The moment the words were out, the smile on Alison's lips died and Laura could have bit off her tongue.

"Tori's father is very busy. He doesn't have much time for children."

"Alison, that was thoughtless of me," Laura said and tentatively touched the other woman's hand. "I'm sorry. Josh told me you were divorced and I should have remembered. I simply didn't think before I opened my big mouth."

"Please don't worry about it. It's all right." She looked over at Laura's suitcases. "I see you haven't unpacked yet. Would you like me to send Ellen upstairs to help you?"

Recognizing the change of subject for what it was, Laura said, "No. I can manage."

"In that case, Tori and I will get out of your way." Alison scooped up her daughter.

"But you don't have to go," Laura told her, reluctant to see them leave when she knew that she had upset Alison.

"Actually we do. It's time for this little princess to go to bed. Say good-night to your aunt Laura."

"'Night, Aunt Lawwa,'' Tori said, and offered her mouth for a kiss.

That fist around Laura's heart tightened again as she pressed her lips against Tori's rosebud mouth. "Good night, sweetie."

When Alison hesitated at the door, Laura asked, "Is something wrong?"

"No. It's just that…my mother will be joining us for dinner."

Laura sank down on the bed. "Does she know about me yet?"

Alison nodded. "I saw Grandmother and her go into the library. I imagine she's been told by now."

Laura wondered how the other woman would take the news that her husband's love child was a guest in her home. "Maybe I shouldn't stay, after all."

"Oh, no," Alison told her. "I didn't tell you because I wanted you to go. I just thought I should warn you. I'm not sure how my mother will take the news. She was devoted to my…to our father. I hope you won't be offended if she's…distant."

"I won't be." In fact, she could understand if Adrienne Jardine demanded that she be shown the door.

Alison whooshed out a breath. "I knew you'd understand. Now, we'll get out of your way, but you'll need to hurry. We usually meet in the parlor for drinks before dinner. Since that's only about thirty minutes from now, you might want to wait until later to unpack and just freshen up so you can go downstairs. Grandmother doesn't like to be kept waiting."

"I'll remember that," Laura assured her, and wondered just what the great Olivia Jardine would do if she didn't come down at all.

As though Alison had read her thoughts, she said,

"Try not to judge us too harshly, Laura. Grandmother's not really the dragon she pretends to be and Katie isn't nearly as bad-tempered as she may have come across this afternoon."

"They could have fooled me," Laura informed her.

"It's been an emotional day for all of us—including you. But I really am glad that you're here. And I know I can count on you not to disappoint me by locking yourself up in this room and refusing to come downstairs to dinner, can't I?"

Laura narrowed her eyes. "Did anyone ever tell you that you're a sneaky one, Alison Jardine?"

"Mitch and Katie do all the time," she said unabashedly as she opened the door. "But I prefer to think of myself as clever. Promise I'll see you downstairs?"

"I promise," Laura assured her, but already she was regretting that promise.

Josh exited the bathroom where he'd gone to freshen up and spied Laura standing outside the closed parlor. Even with the thick walls and closed doors, there was no mistaking the sound of raised female voices coming from inside the room. Moving up behind her, Josh whispered, "It's not polite to eavesdrop."

Following a muffled shriek, she whirled around and leveled him with pale blue eyes snapping with temper. "What is it with you, always sneaking up on me? Do you have any idea how dangerous that could be?"

"No, but I suppose you're going to tell me," he said, and earned a scowl.

"Suppose I'd had a gun? I could have shot you."

"Do you?" he asked, noting that she'd changed from the bold red suit to a sweater dress in an arresting shade of burnt orange that hugged her curves like a lover.

She looked at him as if he were insane. "Do I what?"

"Have a gun hidden somewhere under that dress."

Glaring at him, she made a frustrated sound that was a cross between a growl and a scream.

And for some crazy reason he found even Laura's anger arousing. Man, he had it bad, Josh admitted, catching her scent of flowers and sunshine. He wanted to tuck the strand of hair behind her ear, press his mouth to the curve of her neck and breathe in her scent, her taste. He moved a step closer, allowed himself to trace the gold-and-sapphire pin at her collar. "Nice brooch," he murmured as his finger brushed her collarbone.

She slapped his hand away. "You have this annoying habit of always touching me, Logan."

He shrugged. "What can I say? There's Italian on my mother's side. We Logans are a demonstrative bunch. Touching comes naturally to us. But you'll find that out for yourself when you meet them."

"You're beginning to worry me, Logan. Why on earth would you think I'm going to meet your family?"

"Because I told them you would."

She looked at him as though he'd lost his mind, and Josh wondered if perhaps he had. "Then you can tell them you made a mistake. I'm beginning to think you're delusional."

Maybe he was delusional. How else could he explain his fascination with Laura? The woman was prickly, hot-tempered and would probably drown before she'd ever admit that she might need help. Yet he'd been fascinated by her from the start. He liked her quick mind, her courage and the vulnerability that she masked behind that smart mouth of hers. Remembering the feel and taste of her hot, urgent mouth made it impossible for him to forget her. He knew because he'd tried repeatedly since leaving her in San Francisco.

And he'd failed miserably.

He was through with beating his head against the wall over Laura Harte. The only way he was going to get her out of his system was to take the sexual tango they'd begun in San Francisco to the conclusion they both wanted. And if it dovetailed with his plans to reclaim the Princess, all the better. "My parents are really nice people. There's no reason for you to be nervous about meeting them."

"Josh, listen to me. I am not nervous about meeting your parents because I am not going to meet them."

"Sure you are." There was something to be said for patience and persistence, he thought, undaunted by Laura's sounds of exasperation. "I told them I'd bring you by the hotel sometime tomorrow."

"Why on earth would you tell them that?" she demanded.

"Because they asked to meet you."

"But—"

"Shh. Hear that?"

She narrowed her eyes, squinched her brows. "What?"

"Silence. I think Katie's finished—at least for the moment. We'd better go inside while things are quiet."

"Katie?" Laura repeated. "But I thought…"

"That it was her mother?"

Laura nodded.

He shook his head. "Not likely," Josh told her as he thought of Adrienne Jardine. An attractive, stylish blonde, Olivia's daughter-in-law always looked as though she'd stepped right from the pages of the latest fashion magazine. And she exuded about as much warmth as a mannequin. "I've known the Jardine family all my life and I've never once seen Adrienne lose her temper. No way would you ever catch her doing something as unladylike as shouting. My sister Hope swears the woman wakes up with every hair in place, her makeup perfectly applied and a strand of pearls around her neck. The lady gives new meaning to the term *cool and controlled*. Unlike her daughter." Even as a young man, he'd often had trouble reconciling the notion of a cold fish like Adrienne creating a child with Katie's fire—especially since Andrew Jardine had always struck him as a man who only went through the motions of enjoying life. Now that he'd learned about Laura's mother, he wondered if she had been the reason Andrew had often appeared sad.

"But I heard two women arguing," Laura pointed out.

"Sure," he said, tucking the observation aside to ponder on later. "That was Katie and the Duchess. The two of them have been known to go at it every now and again."

"But I would have thought…I mean, Olivia's her grandmother."

He didn't bother pointing out that Olivia was her grandmother as well. Somehow, he didn't think she'd appreciate the reminder. "And they adore each other. That doesn't mean they don't have their share of squabbles. The two of them are a lot alike. They've got quick tempers and are very passionate about how they feel. Just like you." And before she could protest, he dropped a quick kiss on her lips and opened the door.

All eyes immediately turned in their direction. Keeping his hand splayed at the center of Laura's back, he urged her inside the room. Beneath his palm he could feel the tension in her body, but she kept her head lifted high and walked into the room as proudly as a queen about to inspect her court.

"Laura." Alison came over to greet them and Josh could have kissed Katie's twin for that welcoming smile she gave Laura when she reached for her hand. "Come. I want you to meet my mother."

Josh leaned close and whispered, "Go on. If the ice lady tries to bite, you can always whip out the gun you're hiding under that dress and use it on her."

"You're a dead man, Logan," she muttered before she allowed Alison to lead her over to Adrienne, who stood beside Mitchell looking cool and elegant.

"Mother, I'd like you to meet Laura Harte," Alison began. "Laura, this is my mother, Adrienne Jardine."

"Mrs. Jardine," Laura replied, and after a pleading look from Alison, she held out her hand.

Adrienne made no attempt to take the hand offered. She simply stared at Laura. And for the first time ever, Josh thought he saw real emotion flicker in those icy green eyes before her lashes swept down.

Laura's hand fell to her side, clenched into a fist.

"Mother, are you all right?" Mitchell asked, concern in his voice as he moved closer to the petite blonde.

"Yes darling. I'm fine." When Adrienne opened her eyes, the cool remoteness Josh had come to associate with the woman was back. "You'll have to forgive me," she said politely. "Although Olivia told me about you, I didn't want to believe her."

"What?" Laura replied, a hint of challenge in her voice, in the stiff line of her spine. "That I existed?"

"In part. I could accept that you're Juliet's daughter. I just didn't want to believe that you were Drew's daughter, too."

Thirteen

"I should think the fact that she's Andrew's daughter is obvious," Olivia replied.

"It's not obvious to me," Katie objected. "I still say we should have a DNA test done."

Laura bristled at Katie's suggestion, but knew that if she were in the other woman's shoes, she would demand the same thing. But before she could offer to have the test done, Olivia jumped in. "Be still, Katherine."

"Why should I? Just because she comes waltzing in here, claiming Daddy's her father doesn't mean that she is. I can't believe you're willing to just take her word for it. You should be demanding proof that she's who she claims she is," Katie countered.

"Believe me, I'd like nothing better than to find out that I'm not Andrew Jardine's daughter," Laura told Katie. In fact, she wished she'd never learned the truth and could go back to being Richard Harte's daughter. But there was no going back, and she had come here for a reason, Laura reminded herself. "And for your information, it was your grandmother who contacted me—not the other way around. As for your demanding that I undergo a DNA test, I'll be happy to do so. I have nothing to hide."

"There will be no test," Olivia informed them. "I

have all the proof I need. Laura is Andrew's daughter and my granddaughter. And I won't tolerate anyone saying otherwise.''

''But—''

''Your grandmother is right,'' Adrienne told her daughter, dabbing at her eyes with a lace handkerchief even though Laura could see no evidence of tears. ''I know how much you loved your father. How close the two of you were. You never could abide anyone saying a word against him.''

''Mother, don't,'' Katie cautioned.

''I'm sorry, darling. But it needs to be said. Your father was a good man, but he wasn't perfect. He was simply a man. And like most men, he had his faults, his weaknesses. Laura's mother was one of those weaknesses. He told me about her, and I forgave him. I'd hoped that you and your sister and brother would never know. But I see now it can't be helped. What your grandmother told you is true. Your father did have an affair with Laura's mother, and evidently Laura is the result of that affair. As much as it pains me to admit it, Laura is Drew's daughter.''

Even without Adrienne's speech and Katie's defiant expression, Laura picked up the stormy undercurrents between mother and daughter, and wondered at the source of animosity between the pair. Recalling her own close relationship with her mother, she couldn't help feeling a little sorry for Katie.

''And that makes Laura our sister,'' Alison reminded them, putting another dent in the heart Laura had been so determined to protect.

''So she is,'' Adrienne conceded. ''Which means now she's also one of your father's heirs, as well as Olivia's.'' She turned her cool gaze on Laura. ''But then, I'm sure you've already thought of that, haven't you, Laura dear?''

Laura's back went up at the implication, but she met the other woman's gaze evenly. "Actually, I hadn't given it any thought since I didn't come here with the intention of demanding an inheritance.''

"Then why did you come?" Adrienne asked.

"She came because I needed her help. Laura's going to take over the operation of the Princess," Olivia informed them.

Katie looked as though she'd been slapped. "You would actually turn over the Princess to *her*—to an outsider—when I told you that I wanted to run it?"

"Katherine, we've already been over this. You have your hands full at the Regent.''

"I told you that I could run both hotels, and I can," she insisted.

Olivia shook her head. "You and I both know that the strain of operating both hotels would be too much—even for you. No, Katherine. My decision stands. You belong at the Regent. That's where your heart is.''

"And you think her heart will be in saving the Princess?" Katie fired back.

"She's right, Olivia. Think about what's at stake," Adrienne reasoned. "For all intents and purposes Laura is a stranger. And despite the fact that the hotel may have been losing money recently, it's still a valuable piece of property. Why, my friend Eugenia says she could get you a fortune for the place even with the negative cash flow. But if you turn it over to someone who doesn't know what they're doing, it'll drive the value right into the ground.''

"Your concern over my financial well-being is heartwarming, Adrienne."

"It's you I'm concerned about," Adrienne told her. "You gave us all a scare when you had that heart attack earlier this year. All this stress over the Princess isn't good for your health. You'd be better off just selling the place."

"I have no intention of selling the Princess, not now...not ever."

Adrienne sighed. "If you won't sell it, the least you can do is appoint Katie or Alison to take over its operation."

"I've already explained my reasons for not appointing Katherine as the general manager, and we both know hotel management is not where Alison's interests lie. Now, I've heard enough on the subject. I've made my decision. Laura is going to be the new general manager of the Princess."

"What could she possibly know about running a hotel like the Princess?" Adrienne argued.

"Actually, I know quite a lot about running a small luxury hotel," Laura informed the other woman. "You see, hotel management is what I majored in at school and I've been working in hotels in various positions since I was sixteen years old."

"Laura is the assistant general manager at the Ambassador Grand in San Francisco," Josh advised.

"Which is where I'll be returning when I leave here," Laura added for everyone's benefit, but especially Olivia's. She met the older woman's pale blue gaze and once again experienced the eerie sensation that she was looking at a reflection of herself fifty years into the future. "I made it clear before I agreed to come here that I wasn't interested in your offer to manage the hotel. Nor am I interested in any possible inheritance.''

''Then why did you come?'' Mitchell asked.

Laura looked at the tall, sandy-haired man, noted his protective stance toward his mother and sisters and his wary regard of her. He was her brother, too, she thought, and the realization sent an unexpected pang of regret through her. She immediately snuffed out the unexpected sentiment, blaming her emotional reaction on her earlier encounter with Alison. ''I came because I have several questions that I'm hoping to get answers to.''

Olivia narrowed her eyes. ''What questions?''

''For starters, I'd like to know about my mother's visit here twenty-nine years ago.''

''I'm afraid you're mistaken,'' Adrienne advised her, her voice calm, sure. ''Your mother never came to New Orleans. After Andrew was discharged from the navy and returned home, she did call and speak with him. But once Andrew explained that the relationship was over, she left him alone. She certainly did not come here to get him to change his mind.''

Though it cost her not to lash out at the woman's ugly insinuations, Laura managed to keep a rein on her temper. ''I'm sorry, but you're wrong,'' she said evenly. Even though she didn't care for Adrienne Jardine or her cool smugness, Laura couldn't bring herself to tell the woman in front of her children that Andrew had planned to break his engagement and marry her mother instead. What she wanted to know, what she needed to know, was what had happened that caused her mother to go back to San Diego, quit her job and move to San Francisco instead of returning here to marry the man she loved. "My mother did come here at Andrew Jardine's request."

"I'm sure this is difficult for you to accept, but you *are* mistaken," Adrienne told her. "There was no reason for Andrew to ask Juliet to come here. He loved me, and we were engaged to be married. Your mother was simply a warm respite for a lonely sailor. Once he was home, he realized his mistake and ended things with her. He never saw her again."

"He did see her at least one more time—when she came to New Orleans. If you don't believe me, ask Mrs. Jardine."

Adrienne looked at her mother-in-law. "Olivia?"

"This is not the appropriate time for this discussion," Olivia replied.

"But—"

"We'll discuss this later, Adrienne." In a dismissive gesture that prevented further discussion, she stood. "Come, let's go into dinner."

If the tension-filled atmosphere around the dining room table didn't give a man indigestion, nothing would, Josh decided as he took another bite of the succulent-tasting fish. Tuning out Adrienne's story about some new art find, he was once again struck by the differences between family dinners in the Logan household and this one at the Jardines. He couldn't remember the last time his mother had used Dresden china and Lalique crystal for a meal that wasn't part of a holiday or birthday celebration. He certainly couldn't remember ever sitting at a dinner table that, for the most part, was silent. If anything, he usually had to work to get in a word or two when one of his sisters or his parents stopped to take a bite of food.

Were it not for Adrienne's chatter, he suspected he would be able to hear the wax of the candles melt. Given Katie's usually sharp wit and even sharper tongue, it made her unnatural silence as she sat beside him all the more pronounced. Glancing around the table at the other members of the Jardine family, he noted Mitch's guarded expression as he feigned interest in Adrienne's recounting of some social event. Even Alison, always the quiet and gentle twin who played peacemaker among her siblings and their demanding grandmother, didn't quite pull off her show of attention to what her mother was saying. And the Duchess— bless her soul—she didn't even pretend to listen to her daughter-in-law. No, instead she appeared to be taking measure of her family members—particularly of Laura.

Not that he blamed Olivia, he had difficulty not watching Laura himself. *How had a woman that he'd known for only a matter of weeks managed to tie him up in knots so completely? Why was it that despite the fact he'd known the other people at this table most of his life that it was Laura he was most keenly aware of?*

He didn't need to look across the table at Laura's plate to know that she had barely touched the meal. To the others she probably seemed quiet, maybe even a bit reserved. But he sensed her wariness, the tension that shimmered from her like waves. He couldn't even imagine how she must feel—like a stranger among members of her own family. Yet that's exactly what she was. A stranger in a family in which she wasn't exactly welcomed and might even be viewed as a threat.

Recalling her reaction to Katie's hostility and Adrienne's innuendos, he had to admit that Laura had handled herself well. Which shouldn't have surprised him. Laura was far too smart not to have anticipated that her arrival would generate some animosity. Yet, she had chosen to come, anyway. And he, for one, was glad that she had come—despite the dent to his ego. While he would have liked to think seeing him again had weighed into her decision to make the trip, it had been all too apparent from her earlier conversation with Adrienne that it hadn't. For that matter, neither had the lure of running the Princess. Obviously Laura had an agenda of her own. He just wished he knew what was on that agenda and how it would impact his deal with Olivia to reclaim the Princess.

"Did I mention that I saw Regina de la Barre at the opera guild luncheon today?" Adrienne asked, breaking into his thoughts with the question. But before he or anyone else could respond, she continued. "She announced that she and Roger are hosting a Mardi Gras extravaganza at their mansion this year, where they plan to introduce another visiting artist to the city," she informed them. "You remember the de la Barre family, don't you, Olivia?"

"I know the name," Olivia responded, making no attempt to hide her disinterest.

"Then you'll recall they were instrumental in bringing attention to a number of prominent artists whose works focused on New Orleans last year. It appears their annual Mardi Gras party is becoming quite the hot ticket. And I understand it has proved to be very lucrative for their Royal Street gallery," she offered conspiratorially. "Perhaps you'll feel well enough to attend with us this year," Adrienne suggested to Olivia.

"Whether I'm well or not, the last place you'll find

me is at some society party. Honestly, Adrienne, don't
you think I have more important things to do with my
time than to sip watered-down drinks and nibble on
crackers at the de la Barres'?''

"Really now, Olivia. The de la Barres are lovely
people and very influential in New Orleans."

"That doesn't mean they aren't boring. I'm sure no
one else at this table is any more interested in hearing
about them and their parties than I am."

"I see," Adrienne replied, her tone polite, her spine
poker stiff. "Then I hope everyone will forgive me if
I bored you. I was simply trying to make conversation."

He'd never particularly cared for Adrienne Jardine,
Josh admitted. Her cool demeanor with her children
and her social-climbing tendencies had turned him off
long ago. Yet, he couldn't help but feel sympathy for
her now. Having a woman like Olivia for a mother-in-
law all these years could not have been easy, he reasoned. "Actually, Adrienne, I found the information
about the de la Barres' party quite interesting," Josh
said, and earned a reproachful look from Olivia.

"Thank you, Josh," Adrienne replied. "But I'm
afraid Olivia is right. Sometimes I tend to forget that
not everyone shares my passion for the arts."

"True. But I'd say everyone here has a passion for
what works when it comes to business. I'd heard the
de la Barres' sales at their gallery had nearly doubled
this past year too—and most of it was attributed to out-
of-town buyers who'd either attended or heard about
their party. I, for one, appreciated confirmation of the
rumor. It sounds to me as though the parties have
proven to be a great way for them to advertise. And I
suspect it probably cost them a lot less than it would

have if they'd taken out an ad in the trade publications. If you ask me, it sounds like they've found a smart, inexpensive way to increase their business.''

''Maybe we should try something similar to get the occupancy rates up at our hotels,'' Katie suggested.

Olivia frowned. ''From the reports I've seen, the occupancy rates at the Regent are running at all-time-high levels.''

''True. The hotel is doing well. But I was thinking of the Princess,'' Katie explained.

''Maybe you could host a masquerade ball at the hotel,'' Laura offered and from her expression Josh suspected she hadn't meant to voice her thoughts.

''We used to,'' Adrienne informed her. ''But Olivia discontinued the balls years ago.''

''But it's not a bad idea,'' Mitch added. ''Maybe it's time to reconsider. Those masquerade balls at the Princess were real attention-getters when it came to the media. People spent months planning what costumes they were going to wear. And every time I turned around at the hotel or here, there was a reporter or a photographer in my face. Even after the ball was over, there were articles and photos popping up about the hotel and our family for months. To this day, I've never forgotten the one party that I attended.''

''At least *you* got to attend one,'' Katie pointed out, her mouth forming a pout that reminded Josh of what a competitive brat she'd been as a kid. ''Alison and I never got to attend any.''

''That's because the two of you were still kids,'' Mitch goaded.

Katie rolled her eyes. ''Like two years made you all grown up.''

''If these masquerade balls were so much fun and

good for business, why did you stop hosting them in the first place?'' Laura asked, drawing all eyes to her again and rendering an uneasy silence at the table.

''The masquerade ball was your father's baby,'' Josh explained when no one responded to her question. ''I'm afraid once Andrew passed away, the annual ball stopped, too.''

''I'm sorry. I didn't realize,'' Laura said.

Eager to ease the tension, Josh said, ''You know, Duchess, Laura might be on to something. Mardi Gras is only a few months away. Maybe you should consider resurrecting the masquerade ball at the Princess this year. The free press it would generate for the hotel might prove useful.''

Alison clasped her hands together. ''What a wonderful idea!'' She cast a pleading look toward her grandmother. ''What do think, Grandmother? Can we host the masquerade ball this year?''

''I'm not sure that would be wise,'' Olivia countered. ''You have no idea what an undertaking it would be to orchestrate such an affair. I don't even have the energy to run the Princess any longer. I certainly couldn't take on a party like this.''

''You wouldn't have to. We would do it. Mitch, Ali and I. And mother,'' Katie argued.

''And where would you find the time? You've got your hands full at the Regent. Mitchell has his business to run. Alison has Tori to attend to and your mother is sitting on the board of no less than twelve different organizations—all of which require her time and attention for their fund-raising projects.'' Olivia shook her head. ''No, I'm afraid it's out of the question.''

''Your grandmother's right,'' Adrienne told her.

"I'm overcommitted as it is and no one else really has the time it would take to do this properly."

"I could do it," Alison offered. "I've been thinking about enrolling Tori in a Mother's Day Out program a few times a week so that she has a chance to play with other children. So I'll have a few mornings free every week."

"You'll need more than a couple of mornings a week to plan a masquerade ball," Olivia advised her.

"I'm very good at organizing things, and I'm not exactly a stranger when it comes to planning the ball. Remember, I was the one who used to help Daddy out with some of the little details," Alison reminded them. "And I'm sure Laura wouldn't mind helping me. Would you, Laura?"

"Me?" Laura all but squeaked in reply. "I don't know anything about masquerade balls."

"What's there to know? It's just a big party. Josh said you were the assistant general manager at a luxury hotel back in San Francisco, so I figure you've planned at least one or two big parties as a part of your job."

"That's true, but—"

"Then planning the ball should be a cinch. Just think of it as a big party—only instead of fancy dresses and tuxedos, the guests will be wearing costumes and masks."

"But I'll be returning to San Francisco soon."

"So, help me while you're here," Alison reasoned. "And then you can come back in February for the ball."

"An excellent idea, Alison," Olivia said. "We'll hold the ball the week before Mardi Gras the way we used to do, and of course, Laura will be here."

"Then it's settled," Alison insisted, gripping

Laura's hand. "Please say you'll come back for the ball and that you'll help me pull everything together?"

"Ali, I'm not sure that's a good idea. I don't even know how long I'll be here, let alone whether or not I'll be coming back in a few months," Laura hedged.

"But you'll stay for now, won't you?"

"If Laura's so anxious to return to California, then let her go. You don't need her," Katie informed her twin. "I'll help you."

Josh bit the inside of his cheek to keep from grinning. In the short time he'd known Laura Harte, he had no doubt that Katie's dismissal of her was the one thing guaranteed to make the redhead dig in her heels and stay.

"Since I've already scheduled to take the time off, I don't see any reason why I shouldn't stay," Laura said. She tossed Katie a defiant look before returning her attention to Alison. "All right, Ali. For the next three weeks, I'm at your disposal. Just tell me what needs to be done and I'll help you in any way that I can."

"Thanks. I knew I could count on you. Both of you," Alison told her sisters. "I'll take whatever help I can get. You, too, Mitch, if you can spare the time."

"I'll make time," Mitch told his sister.

"Oh, this is going to be so much fun. I just know it will. If only Daddy could be here to see it all come together."

"Yes. I bet he would have gotten a kick out of us doing this," Katie added.

"I think he'd have been proud to know his children were carrying on his tradition of the masquerade ball," Josh told them.

"So do I," Mitch replied. "I'd almost forgotten how

much he loved the Mardi Gras season. It was his favorite time of year,'' he continued, a sad smile curving his lips.

''I think the marching bands were his favorites—especially the military drill teams. He always liked watching them,'' Katie reminded them.

''And the parades. He adored the parades, hardly ever missed them. He was always right out in the front, screaming for beads and trinkets like a kid,'' Alison explained. ''Katie, remember how he used to take turns putting us up on his shoulders so the riders on the floats could see us over the crowds and throw to us?''

''I remember.''

''Remember the year he caught us those stuffed pink squirrels?'' Alison asked.

Katie laughed. ''How could I forget? They were the ugliest things I'd ever seen.''

''They were not,'' Alison challenged.

''No? Then how come you had nightmares about pink fuzzy creatures hiding under your bed at night for a week?''

Alison giggled. ''All right. They *were* ugly. But Daddy was so proud he'd caught them for us.'' Her smile dimmed. ''He was such a great dad. I wish you could have known him, Laura. I think you would have liked him.''

Laura said nothing, but Josh didn't miss that momentary flicker of pain in her eyes before she schooled her expression.

''Everyone liked Andrew,'' Adrienne added, apparently indifferent to Laura's feelings. ''He was a wonderful father. And he absolutely adored his girls.''

''I'm afraid I'll have to take your word for it,'' Laura said softly, her pale blue eyes as frosty as her voice.

"Adrienne!" Olivia exploded.

"Mother," Alison admonished simultaneously.

"What?" Adrienne responded, then as realization dawned, her cheeks flamed and she jerked her gaze to Laura. "Oh, my," she whispered. "I'm sorry, Laura. I never meant to imply...I simply wasn't thinking about you and your...situation."

"Perhaps you should start thinking about it," Olivia informed her daughter-in-law, the steel in her voice matching the hard look in her eyes.

"I'm sure Mother meant no insult," Mitch intervened.

"Mitchell's right, of course," Adrienne conceded. "I meant no offense. My apologies if I've upset you."

"Why should I be upset? After all, I never knew him," Laura said. Tossing her napkin down beside her plate, she stood. "But I'm pleased to hear that Andrew Jardine was a good father—at least to those children he didn't desert."

Fourteen

"Where do you get off making accusations against my father?" Katie demanded, following the shocked silence.

"It wasn't an accusation. It was a statement. And since he's my father, too, I think I have every right," Laura said calmly, but Alison didn't miss the slight tremor in the fist she held clutched at her side. "Now, if you'll excuse me. It's been a long day and I'd like to call it a night." Without waiting for a reply, she turned and exited the room.

"If she thinks she can bad-mouth Daddy and then just waltz out of here, she'd better think again," Katie all but snarled as she scraped back her chair and started to go after Laura.

Josh caught her arm. "Let it go, Katie."

"Who are you to tell me what to do?" Katie exploded, anger and betrayal chasing across her face.

"I'm your friend," Josh said quietly. "And I don't want that nasty temper of yours to cause you to do or say something you'll regret."

Katie jerked her arm free. "The only thing I regret is that *she* ever came here in the first place."

"You're not being fair," Josh told her. "Laura was upset. Tonight can't have been easy for her."

"And you think it was easy for me? For my mother? For any of us?" she fired back.

"No. But you do have the advantage of having one another. Laura doesn't have anyone," he reasoned.

"Josh is right," Alison said, trying to soothe her twin's pain. "As much of a shock as this has been for us, it has to be even more difficult for Laura. I mean, at least we had both Daddy and Mother growing up."

"Why are you defending her?" Katie demanded. "You're my sister, my twin."

"And Laura's *our* sister. I don't believe for a minute that Daddy deserted her and her mother. I'm sorry," Alison said to her mother, knowing that Laura's existence had to be painful for her too. "I can't help but think that if Daddy had known about Laura that he would have made sure she was a part of our lives. He would have wanted us to accept her."

"I'm sure you're right, darling. As you've pointed out, Laura's your half sister, so I have no choice but to accept her. But you'll forgive me if I don't feel a need to welcome her with open arms."

"There's no need to blame the girl, Adrienne," Olivia said from her seat at the head of the table. "After all, none of this is her fault."

"You're right, Olivia. She's not the one to blame for this unholy mess. Your son is for betraying me in the first place. Now, if you'll excuse me, I seem to have lost my appetite."

A hushed silence fell over the room following their mother's departure. Alison looked around the table, where the serving pieces and sterling silverware gleamed against the antique lace tablecloth. The crystal glasses filled with wine sat untouched beside plates of mouth-watering trout amandine and fettuccine that had scarcely been tasted. The praline torte she'd prepared for dessert and had looked forward to serving earlier remained on the sideboard. There was something impossibly sad about the abandoned meal, Alison decided.

But there was nothing sad about the vibes she was picking up from her twin. Always attuned to Katie, she didn't have to look across the table where her sister sat mangling her napkin to know that Katie was worried over the confrontation between Mitch and their grandmother. But unlike her, Katie had never been one to stew in silence— Perhaps if she had been more like her sister, Derek would never have flaunted his infidelities as he had. He certainly wouldn't have been able to brazenly hold up her and her family for a small fortune as he had in the divorce. But then, as Derek had reminded her so often, she lacked her sister's passion.

The tension before Laura and her mother's departures had been ripe, Alison admitted. But now, between the anger emanating from Katie and the hostile glare Mitch was directing toward their grandmother, the tension was even worse. It felt as though a rope had been stretched across the room dividing them and it had been pulled so thin, so tight, that it was in danger of snapping in two.

"If there's something you want to say to me, Mitchell," their grandmother began, evidently not missing his angry stance, "I suggest you go ahead and say it."

"Perhaps I should leave," Josh suggested, and started to rise.

"Why bother?" Mitch asked in a voice so calm and so cold it gave Alison goose bumps. "Since my grandmother has seen fit to include you in tonight's little family drama, I don't see why you should miss out on the rest of the performance.''

Alison swallowed. She rubbed her hands up and down her arms to ward off a chill that had nothing to do with the weather. Never before could she recall her older brother looking quite so forbidding, so deadly. Suddenly fearful of what would follow, she attempted to diffuse the situation by saying, ''You know, Mitch, Mother seemed pretty upset when she left. Maybe you and I should go see if she's okay.''

''You go ahead. I'll join you in a minute,'' Mitch replied, his eyes never straying from their grandmother's face. ''Since everyone in this family, including me, has always tried so hard to comply with Grandmother's wishes, I wouldn't want to disappoint her now by not doing as she asked.''

Olivia made a dismissive sound. ''Considering the fact that you insisted on opening that security business four years ago instead of taking over management of the Princess as I'd intended for you to do, I doubt seriously that you're worried about disappointing me, Mitchell.''

''If you truly believe that, Grandmother, then you don't know me at all. But that's another matter all together.''

''You're talking nonsense. Something's obviously bothering you. And since I don't have the time or the inclination to sit here playing word games with you, I suggest you tell me what it is.''

''All right, Grandmother. I will.''

Mitch steepled his fingers and remained silent a moment as though choosing his words carefully.

''From the time I was a boy, I accepted the fact that you were different from other grandmothers. I learned not to expect baked cookies or kisses and hugs from you when I got a bump or a bruise. I learned not to expect you to tell me bedtime stories or play games with me the way the grandmothers of my friends did with them. I also learned not to expect you to shower me with affection and praise. And the truth is, most of the time I didn't mind it. I used to tell myself that I was actually luckier than my friends because when you did spend time with me, you treated me like an equal, not a child. You taught me about the hotel business, about how to deal with people, about my responsibilities to my family and the people who worked for us. You taught me about having goals and the importance of striving to reach those goals. You taught me about the importance of doing what was right, what was honorable.''

Alison pressed a hand to her chest, to ease the ache in her heart as she listened to her brother describe the relationship they had all shared with their grandmother. Olivia hadn't been the cookies-and-hot-chocolate type of grandmother who cuddled and indulged her grandchildren. While growing up, she'd often thought of her grandmother as a drill sergeant—someone who demanded their best, insisted they learn everything there was to know about running the hotels and do a good job.

"You and I have never been close. I know that's largely my fault. I let you down when I didn't follow the path you wanted me to and take over management of the Princess.''

"Honestly, Mitchell, I don't know why—''

"Please, Grandmother," he said, holding up his hand. "Allow me to finish.''

"Very well.''

"Despite the fact that we're not close I do love you. And I've always admired and respected you. Until tonight. Tonight for the first time, I'm ashamed to have you as my grandmother," Mitch said, his voice soft, making the impact of his words all the more powerful.

Alison sucked in a breath, held it, as she watched her grandmother and waited for the older woman to tear into Mitch. But to her surprise, her grandmother said nothing. She simply sat there at the head of the table in silence. And though her posture remained ramrod straight, her head tipped up proudly and her expression autocratic, Alison glimpsed a vulnerability in her eyes that hadn't been there a few moments ago.

"I don't know what happened between my father and Laura's mother," Mitch continued. "And even if I did, I'm not sure I would be able to understand or forgive him for being so careless with other people's lives. But at this point, whether or not I understand and forgive him doesn't really matter. What does matter is that *you* could have made my father's less-than-noble actions much easier for everyone to accept. *You* could have spared everyone in this house a great deal of pain and embarrassment tonight if you'd simply told us what you were planning. Instead you chose to surprise us with the news that Laura is our father's daughter and then shock us by announcing that you were appointing her as GM of the Princess. Why, Grandmother? Did you do it to keep us on our toes? Or was it so you could manipulate us, play us against one another, so that you would get what you wanted?"

When she said nothing, Mitch continued, "I think your plan has backfired, Grandmother, because I don't think Laura is going to accept your offer. And I prom-

ise you I'll do everything in my power to convince
Katie and Alison not to take the job, either.''

"Are you finished?" Olivia asked, her voice even,
her expression inscrutable. Yet Alison believed her
brother was right. Their grandmother had tried to retain
control and erred in the process.

"Not quite," Mitch replied. "First I want to make
sure that you realize just how much damage you did
here tonight. Not only did you upset Laura, but you
showed absolutely no consideration whatsoever for my
mother. She's been your daughter-in-law for nearly
thirty years and she's the mother of your grandchildren.
Yet you deliberately embarrassed and hurt her tonight
by presenting her with the news of her husband's betrayal without even a second thought.''

"Are you through cataloging my sins?" Olivia
asked.

"No. There's one more. You risked my and my sisters' memories of our father, a father that we loved
very much, by playing your manipulative games," he
said, his voice sharp. "Don't you think we deserved to
be told about Laura and given time to come to terms
with the fact that she's our sister before you sprang her
on us the way you did?"

"I don't owe you or anyone else an explanation for
my actions," Olivia told him, her pale blue eyes swimming with anger, with hurt.

"It's just as well because nothing you could say
would excuse what you did here tonight."

Olivia gripped her cane, slapped the handle against
the table. "You dare to speak to me this way? To judge
me?"

"I'm not judging you, Grandmother," Mitch replied.
"I'm telling you that what you did was wrong. You

have no right to sacrifice people's feelings in order to satisfy this...this obsession you have to save the Princess."

"You sit there so smug in your indignation, so sure that you're right to condemn me for my actions," Olivia told him, her voice reflecting the fire and conviction burning in her eyes. "When you know nothing of my feelings, of all that I've had to sacrifice."

Transfixed, Alison couldn't take her eyes off her grandmother. She'd witnessed her grandmother angry before. She'd even seen her in deep despair when her only son had died. But never before could she recall seeing Olivia in quite this way—her eyes blazing with passion, that same passion that she'd often glimpsed in her twin and today in Laura. She'd always known her grandmother had loved the Princess Hotel. As its owner, it had been a viable part of who she was. But until now she'd always attributed her grandmother's attachment to the old hotel to the fact that it was the anchor in the family's holdings. Now for the first time, Alison wondered if perhaps she had been wrong. Had there been another reason behind her grandmother's obsession with the Princess?

"I wonder how much comfort that righteous indignation of yours would be if I decided to cut you out of my will," Olivia threatened.

"Go ahead," Mitch told her. "The hotels and the money have always meant more to you than they do to me."

"You expect me to believe that you don't care if I cut you from my will?"

Mitch shrugged. "Believe what you want. But the truth is, I never cared about the inheritance. Money isn't what I wanted from you."

"What did you want?"

"Your approval. For you to be proud of me. To love me." A fleeting smile crossed his lips. "But then I guess I was expecting too much, wasn't I?" Shoving back his chair, Mitch stood. "If you'll excuse me, I think I'll go see how my mother is."

"Mitchell, wait," Olivia said, her voice breaking. "Mitchell! Come back here at once. I haven't finished."

But Mitch didn't slow his stride. He didn't look back, either. He simply kept moving until he'd disappeared from the dining room. "I'll go talk to him," Alison offered.

"No. No, I'll go," Olivia said quietly. She stood, her movements slower than they had been, the fire of a moment ago gone. "I'm the one who's hurt and disappointed him. It's up to me to make things right between us again."

Laura bolted upright in bed late the next morning. Disoriented, she looked around at the strange surroundings for a moment before she remembered she was in New Orleans at the Jardine estate. Thoughts of the Jardine family and last night's events came back to her in a rush. Biting back a groan, she sank against the pillows and closed her eyes. Her less-than-pleasant encounters with Olivia, Katie and Adrienne Jardine had taken a toll on her system. Adding the time difference to the mix, it was no wonder she'd tossed and turned until the wee hours of the morning. Now as a result, she'd slept long past her usual waking time. And as much as she'd like to, she couldn't just hide out here forever—not if she intended to confront Olivia and demand answers about her mother's visit.

With that thought in mind, she stifled a yawn and kicked off the covers. She had just slipped on her robe when a tap sounded at the door. "Just a minute," she called out, belting her robe as she walked over to open the door.

"Good morning, Miss Harte," the maid greeted her, while holding a tray laden with the most delicious scents. "Miss Olivia said I should bring you up a tray since you missed breakfast this morning."

"That was very kind of her. Ellen, isn't it?" Laura asked as she stepped back for the young woman to enter.

"Yes, ma'am," the dark-haired woman replied. She moved over to the table and set down the tray. Once she had done so, she crossed the room to the windows, pulled open the drapes and sent sunshine spilling into the room.

"This looks wonderful," Laura told her as she began uncovering dishes filled with fresh fruits, scrambled eggs and sausages. She unwrapped a basket and found it filled with warm croissants, buttered toast, cinnamon rolls and hot, flaky biscuits. Her mouth watering, she broke off a piece of biscuit, popped it between her lips and moaned as it practically melted in her mouth.

Ellen poured her a half cup of coffee and without asking topped it off with warm milk. "Here you go, ma'am. Café au lait. There's sugar and sweetener if you need it."

"This is fine," she said, taking the cup the other woman offered. She took a sip, closed her eyes and savored the taste.

"Will you need anything else, Miss Harte?"

"Just a small army to help me eat all of this food. This is way too much. I'll never be able to eat half of it," Laura complained even as she began slathering butter on another piece of biscuit. Suddenly ravenous, she blamed her appetite on the fact that she'd been too upset to eat dinner the previous evening.

The dimple in Ellen's cheek winked at her remark. "Mrs. Jardine wasn't sure what you liked. So she said to send you an assortment. Just eat what you want."

"Thank you. And thank Mrs. Jardine for me. I had intended to come downstairs before breakfast. But I'm afraid I overslept. It was very kind of her to send up the tray."

"I'll tell her, miss. You can just leave the tray on the table there when you finish. I'll come back up later to clear it away," Ellen offered. "In the meantime, if you need anything else, there's an intercom button on your phone. Just buzz Mrs. McNalty and tell her."

"I'll do that," Laura said before taking another taste of the wonderful coffee. It was a good thing her visit here was going to be a brief one, Laura told herself as she tucked one foot beneath her and began to sample the eggs and sausage. Otherwise, she could get all too used to meals like this one.

"Your father was a good man, a good son and a good father," Olivia told her when Laura joined her and began expressing her displeasure at how things had gone the previous evening with Katie.

"Then why did he desert my mother? Why did he desert me?" Laura asked, hating the slight hitch in her voice.

"Andrew didn't desert Juliet or you. Your mother's the one who deserted him. Not only did she break his heart, she left without seeing fit to tell him that she was pregnant and he was going to be a father."

There was such conviction in Olivia's voice, Laura almost believed her. Almost, until she remembered the note addressed to her mother with the check to take care of her problem. Fury washed over her as she realized that while her mother had been alone and pregnant, Andrew Jardine had been enjoying a society wedding. And while her mother had been giving birth to his illegitimate daughter, Andrew had been celebrating the impending birth of his legitimate son. "I don't believe you. My mother was in love with him. She planned to marry him. She would never have walked away from him without good reason."

"Well that's exactly what she did," Olivia fired back. "I knew Juliet was wrong for my son the moment I met her and she proved me right. She left him like a thief in the night without a word. He nearly went insane when he couldn't find her. Had it not been for Adrienne, I don't know what he would have done. As it was, even with his marriage to Adrienne and his children, he was never quite the same again."

"You didn't like her, did you?" Laura asked. All too easily she could envision her sweet-natured mother having to deal with a formidable woman like Olivia Jardine.

"No, I didn't," Olivia informed her. "Juliet would not have made a suitable wife for Andrew."

"Unlike Adrienne."

"That's right. Adrienne is a vain, self-absorbed woman, but she loved my son and she was a good wife to him."

"You mean she was the type of wife you wanted for him," Laura replied, thinking of the letters her father had written to her mother and his stress over Olivia's objections. Whatever had happened, she was convinced that at one time Andrew Jardine had loved her mother.

"That's right. Andrew and Adrienne were a good match. They had similar backgrounds, interests. They suited each other, and until he met your mother, Andrew thought so, too."

"My mother coming here must have put a real kink in your plans."

Something flickered in Olivia's eyes a moment. *Guilt?* Laura wondered, but it was gone so quickly, she feared she had imagined it.

"If you're implying that I forced Andrew to end his relationship with your mother and marry Adrienne, you're wrong. He was not someone who could be forced to do anything he didn't want to do. Andrew was headstrong—a trait no doubt that you inherited from him."

Laura's stomach dipped. She'd already discovered she had Andrew Jardine's eyes. Or rather that he'd had his mother's eyes and he had passed them on to her. Even without anyone commenting on that fact, she could see it for herself in the pictures of him and each time she looked at Olivia or the twins. To learn that she shared an aspect of the man's personality as well made it all the more difficult for her not to think of him as her father. And she didn't want to think of Andrew Jardine in that way. She wanted no connection to him, to Olivia, or to this family.

"Despite all my objections and my threats, Andrew was determined to marry Juliet. Had she not left him, I have no doubt that he would have."

"Then why did she leave?" Laura countered.

"At the time, I had assumed it was because she cared for Andrew, and realized how ill-prepared she was to be a wife to a man with his position, his responsibilities. I thought her disappearing as she did was an act of selflessness on her part.''

Laura tipped her head to the side, studied Olivia. "And now, I take it your opinion of her has changed?"

Olivia pushed aside her teacup and met Laura's gaze evenly. "Now I wonder if Juliet loved Andrew at all. Because if she had, she would never have kept you a secret from him."

"Maybe she felt she didn't have a choice," Laura offered, thinking again of that note and remembering all that her uncle Paul had told her.

"We all have choices, and your mother chose not to tell Andrew about you. As a result her silence not only stole from him a chance to know his daughter, but she stole from you the chance to know your father and your family. What she did was selfish and inexcusable.''

"It was not," Laura defended hotly, confused by Olivia's outrage and guilty because a part of her felt anger toward her mother for taking the money and keeping silent. She'd wanted desperately to blame Andrew or Olivia for sending the note and money to her mother. Yet now, listening to Olivia, she wasn't at all sure she could. Fisting her hands in her lap, she said, "You have no right to judge her. You don't know why she made the decisions she did.''

Olivia sighed and some of the spark seemed to go out of her. "You're right. I have no right to judge your mother or anyone else—a fact that has been pointed out to me recently. I don't know why Juliet kept silent, and neither do you. And since we don't, I suggest that we put it behind us and try to deal with the present.'' She paused as though measuring her words. "Regardless of the circumstances of your birth, you're still my granddaughter and I would like you to be a part of this family.''

''I'm not sure that's possible,'' Laura told her honestly.

''I realize that's how you feel and I'm trying to understand it. But I want you to realize that I'm an old woman who's had a granddaughter for the past twenty-eight years that I didn't know existed.''

Laura unclenched her hands, smoothed her palms on the legs of her slacks. ''As you pointed out, we can't go back and undo the past. We may be related, but we're strangers.''

''We don't have to remain strangers. You did agree to a three-week visit,'' she reminded her.

''I only agreed to come to find answers.'' And she was slowly coming to the conclusion that those answers might very well remain lost to her forever.

''I realize that. But there's no reason you can't stay and use those three weeks to get to know your family, to learn about your heritage.''

Laura narrowed her eyes, not at all sure she trusted this amenable side of Olivia. ''If you're thinking you'll get me to change my mind about staying on and managing the Princess Hotel, I can tell you right now that I won't.''

Olivia's lips curved in the closest thing Laura had seen to a smile since meeting her. ''Joshua said that you weren't a woman who could be bullied.''

''He was right,'' Laura told her, and did her best to ignore the flutter in her pulse at just the mention of Josh's name.

''Hmm. Then I suppose he was also right in telling me that I'd made a mistake yesterday when I tried to bulldoze you into committing to taking over management of the hotel.''

Her throat suddenly dry at the thought of Josh knowing her so well, Laura nodded.

''Well, I guess I shouldn't feel quite so miffed at him for insisting that I promise not to bring up the subject of you running the Princess again during your visit.''

Olivia dangling the manager's position at the Princess had been a complication and a temptation she hadn't wanted. If Josh was the one responsible for Olivia abandoning the subject, she should be grateful to him. And she would thank him personally—just as soon as she had successfully snuffed out her ridiculous attraction to the man.

Olivia looked at her watch. ''He was supposed to be here by now. I wonder what's keeping him.''

''Him?'' Laura blinked and firmly slammed the door to thoughts about Josh. ''I didn't realize you were expecting someone,'' she began, and started to rise.

''I'm not expecting anyone. But *you* are expecting Josh,'' Olivia said, frowning. ''And as usual, the blasted boy is late.''

''Taking my name in vain again, Duchess?'' the blasted boy replied in that whiskey-roughened voice, sending a shiver of awareness skipping along Laura's nerve endings.

''It's about time you got here,'' Olivia informed him, but the scowl on her face didn't quite match the pleasure in her eyes.

''Sorry. I got tied up at the office.'' He kissed Olivia's cheek. Then he turned, winked at Laura and gave her a full-powered grin. ''But now that I'm here, I'm all Laura's for the next four days.''

Images of that kiss they'd shared, the feel of being in his arms, having his mouth hot and hard on hers flooded Laura's brain. Her throat went bone-dry. She swallowed hard against the memories, reminded herself what a mistake she'd be making to travel that path with this man again. "I beg your pardon," she finally managed to get out, but the words held none of the disinterest she'd hoped to convey.

"No need to beg, darling," he said as his gaze made a lazy cruise over her, starting at her eyes, moving down her body and returning to linger on her mouth. "I told you. I'm all yours."

Laura hadn't thought it was possible, but somehow the man managed to kick up the voltage on that smile. Despite her efforts not to respond, her foolish pulse skittered like a long-tailed cat in a room full of rocking chairs. She swallowed. "All mine for what?"

"You didn't tell her, Duchess?" he said dryly.

"Tell me what?" Laura asked.

"That I've asked Joshua to show you around the city," Olivia responded before turning that stern blue gaze on him. "I was waiting for you to arrive before making the...suggestion to Laura."

Somehow, Laura doubted that Olivia made suggestions. More than likely she would have given orders. But she'd give the woman the benefit of the doubt, she decided. "That's very thoughtful of you," she told Olivia. And with an aloofness she was far from feeling, she told Josh, "I appreciate the offer. But I'm sure you have more important things to do than play tour guide for me."

"That depends on what you consider important," he said as he started toward her. "At the moment, right at the top of my list is showing you New Orleans."

He stopped in front of her, and before she realized his intent, Josh caught her hands and tugged her to her feet. "Ready?"

Ready? She could hardly breathe for the spurt of lust that shot through her at his touch. She moistened her lips with her tongue and looked away from those compelling green eyes, trying to clear her senses. Pulling her hands free, she took a step back and her knees came up against the seat of the chair.

He steadied her. "You all right?"

"I'm fine," she lied while she made an attempt to marshal her thoughts. "And I don't need you to give me a city tour. If I want one, I'll hire a guide."

"Now, why would you want to do that?" he began while tucking her arm in his. He tipped his head in Olivia's direction and turned them toward the door. "When you can have a real native like me show you all the city's secrets and sins, not to mention the best places to eat and listen to music?"

When they reached the door, Laura dug in her heels. "Haven't you been listening? I don't want a city tour."

"I'm afraid neither one of us has a choice. I'm under strict orders from the Duchess on this one."

"Strict orders on what?" she asked.

He gave her that slow, sexy grin again. "Why, Laura darling, I'm supposed to see to it that you fall in love with New Orleans."

Fifteen

She might as well give up, Laura decided more than a week later while she sat at one of the outdoor tables at the Café du Monde, sipping her coffee and watching the activity surrounding Jackson Square. She had never intended to fall in love with New Orleans. In fact, she'd been bound and determined not to like the place, the people or anything at all about it.

And she'd failed.

At some point between the time she'd reluctantly taken that carriage ride with Josh through the French Quarter streets that first afternoon and hearing the bells of the cathedral ringing while she watched the sun come up over the Mississippi River this morning, she had fallen completely under the city's magical spell. She loved New Orleans, she admitted. She loved the charm of its French Quarter with the balconies and hidden courtyards, the musicians and tap dancers on nearly every corner. She loved the odd mix of artists with their paints and casels around Jackson Square, who dispensed philosophy, dished up the latest gossip and provided Chinese horoscopes freely to customers and onlookers while they painted.

She loved the spicy foods, the quaint neighborhood delis and the elegant mansions lining St. Charles Avenue that reminded her of Tara, the plantation home in the movie *Gone With the Wind*. She even loved the folklore and superstitions, the ancient tearooms and voodoo shops where she'd been advised she could get a gris-gris should she ever need one.

She'd even begun to love the humid climate—although it made it impossible for her to wear her hair in its sleek style, it did wonderful things for her skin. But above all, she loved the people in New Orleans with their friendly smiles and their distinctly Southern accents—which seemed to be an odd mix of Southern drawl and New York Yankee. Never before had she encountered people who were so quick with hugs and kisses and who seemed to believe it was their sworn duty to feed every stranger that passed their doorstep.

"Ya want some more coffee, hon?" the waitress asked.

"No, this is fine. But could I get a go cup?"

After Laura had transferred the contents of her mug into the foam cup, she dropped a few ones on the table. She stood up to leave, then hesitated. Reaching for a paper napkin, she unfolded it and wrapped the remains of her beignets—the delicious deep-fried doughnuts covered in powdered sugar to which she'd quickly become addicted. She stuffed the wrapped pieces of beignet in the pocket of her jacket, picked up her coffee and headed out onto the street toward Jackson Square.

"Morning, ma'am," one of the carriage drivers said, tipping his hat to her as she walked past him. "How's about a carriage ride for you with me and old Bessie this morning?"

"No thanks," Laura told the driver, and opening the black iron gates, she entered Jackson Square. Recalling the brief history lesson Josh had given to her that first day, she knew that the fences and gardens had been installed by the Baroness Pontalba. Originally a drill field constructed in the 1720s and called the Place d'Armes, it had been renamed for Andrew Jackson, the hero of the 1815 Battle of New Orleans and for whom the statue of the general on his steed had been placed at the square's center. Laura smiled as she remembered Josh telling her about the continuing battle the city faced with the pigeons that flocked to the statue.

But it was the feathered creatures she'd come to see. As usual, the pigeons weren't the least bit intimidated by a human wandering through the gardens. In fact, more often than not, she found herself sidestepping them. Finishing the last of her coffee, she dropped the empty cup into one of the disposal cans and reached into her pocket for the beignets. "Okay, fellows, how about a treat?"

Within moments, the cooing pigeons had flocked to the section where she'd scattered bits of leftover doughnuts for them. Laughing, she tossed out the last of the beignets and dusted her hands. "Sorry, guys, that's it," she told the pigeons, who continued to check the grass and walkways for more of the treat.

A riverboat horn sounded, and Laura lifted her head to gaze out toward the Mississippi. For some reason the river had her thinking of San Francisco and that in less than two weeks she would be leaving here to return home.

Funny, she thought, as she tucked her hands into her pockets and headed toward the river, she had been so eager to leave here and return home when she'd first arrived. But now the thought of returning held little appeal. Yet, as much as she loved New Orleans, it didn't seem like home, either.

Retracing her path past the café and tourist shops,

Laura climbed the stairs of the Moonwalk and followed the path that overlooked the Mississippi River. She leaned against the iron rails, no doubt installed to keep tourists from tumbling down onto the rocks of the levee and into the river, and watched a paddle wheeler chug by. The wind whipped at her hair, and though the sun had been up for several hours, the chill in the air had Laura snuggling into her jacket and grateful that she'd worn jeans.

Determined to ignore the cold, Laura continued to follow the paddleboat's progress despite the fact that bigger boats, cruise ships and barges added to the river's traffic. She liked the idea of the old-fashioned paddle wheeler still operating amid the more modern vessels. Probably for the same reason she liked the older one-of-a-kind hotels still holding their own against the big chains that commanded most of the market, she decided.

Enjoying the game she'd devised, Laura remained oblivious to the tourists and locals who joined her at the rail and walked past while she managed to keep track of the smaller boat.

"Excuse me, miss." A woman with a delightful British accent approached her with a dapper-looking gentleman in tweed. "But I was wondering if you might direct us to the French Market? We were told it's not very far."

Amused to find herself able to help them, Laura said, "It's not far at all. You're only a few blocks away." After giving the couple directions, Laura turned back to her study of the river. But the paddle wheeler was gone. In just those few minutes, she had lost sight of the vessel, she realized.

Just as in the space of little more than a week, she

had lost sight of her own reasons for coming to New Orleans—to find out what had happened to make her mother leave twenty-nine years ago and who had paid her to end her pregnancy. When she'd agreed to come to New Orleans, she had been so sure the blame lay with Drew Jardine himself or his mother. But after her conversations with Olivia, in which the lady had been quite frank about her disapproval of Juliet as a potential wife for Drew Jardine, it seemed out of character for the other woman to deny having a hand in her mother's leaving.

Laura brushed a strand of hair from her face and continued to stare out at the river, her thoughts filled with the past. Although the hurt and anger since learning the truth about her father had eased somewhat, it was still there, like a splinter imbedded in a finger—something she could put out of her thoughts for long periods of time, only to suddenly be hit with a sharp reminder that the splinter was still there. It would have been easier for her to accept if she'd been able to lay the blame at Drew Jardine's feet and make him the focus of her anger, she conceded. But each time she tried, she thought of the letters he'd written to her mother. The tone had been tender and filled with longing. He'd sounded like a man desperately in love and torn between his love and his sense of duty. The image of the man that had emerged from listening to Josh, Olivia, his children and the servants was that of a man who was sensitive, honorable and devoted to his family. It didn't fit with a man who would coldly turn away his pregnant lover and pay her to abort their child.

Olivia had claimed that Drew hadn't known that her mother had been pregnant. And though she hated to admit it, Laura believed Olivia. Any notion she had harbored that Adrienne had been the culprit behind her mother's departure and the money fizzled that first evening when she'd witnessed the other woman's shattered expression upon learning that Juliet had been in New Orleans.

"So who does that leave?" she muttered in frustration, burrowing deeper into her jacket as the wind began to kick up and send water splashing against the wall of rocks. It didn't leave anyone, she realized. Which could only mean that someone had lied.

But who? Who had written her mother that note and sent her fifty thousand dollars to abort her child and begin a new life?

She didn't know the answers. Worse, she was beginning to believe she might never find them. *And if she didn't learn the truth?*

She'd simply have to find a way to put it behind her and go on with her life. And she would. She wasn't the same person she'd been when she'd arrived in New Orleans. She had turned a corner, Laura realized. She'd recognized as much a few days ago and could feel it in her bones. A part of it had been because of Alison. She couldn't help liking the younger woman and felt the beginning of a bond forming between them. The idea of having Alison as a sister warmed her, made her feel less alone.

Katie was another matter. She didn't like the hot-tempered woman and for the life of her she couldn't understand how identical twins could be so different. As for Mitch, she felt none of the mutual animosity for him that she shared with Katie and none of the burgeoning affection she felt for Alison. She'd been left with the distinct impression that she was like a new cat brought into a house with a dog, and the two of them seemed to be circling each other, deciding whether they would be friends or foes.

And then there was Josh. After that fiasco between them in San Francisco, she'd equated her attraction to him to the mumps—a disease she'd had once and now that she had, she was forever immune. Only she hadn't been immune to him as she'd hoped. In fact, during the past week, she'd gone through an extreme range of emotions where the man was concerned. Charmed by him one moment, furious with him the next. And always, always the attraction was there. The quickening of her pulse when he smiled at her. That hot need tightening low in her belly when he touched her. That foolish whisper in her head that kept saying, why not?

Laura whooshed out a breath and stared at the cloud her breath had become in the cold, damp air before disappearing. It reminded her of how she felt since finding out about her parents, Laura thought. She felt like that wisp of breath, without a clear shape or direction. She felt lost, Laura admitted, no longer sure of who she was. And she had a sick, sick feeling in her heart that without those answers she just might never be able to find herself again.

Josh found her at the Moonwalk, leaning on the railing overlooking the levee and the river. The November sun had ducked behind a cluster of clouds, taking with it the sunshine's warmth. A strong wind had kicked up, causing the moist air coming across the Mississippi and slapping against the rocks to feel a good ten degrees below the fifty-degree temperatures the weatherman had reported on the morning news. Those few tourists and locals who'd come to enjoy the river view had already begun to scurry back down to the street, no doubt in search of some place to get warm and to find something hot to drink.

That is, everyone except Laura.

He'd spotted her the moment he'd climbed the stairs to the Moonwalk. She was a tall, slender figure dressed in jeans and a navy leather jacket with her face turned into the wind, her dark red hair whipping about her face and shoulders. Leaning on the railing and staring out at the river, she didn't seem to take any notice of the fact that everyone else had left or of his approach. From her profile, she appeared to be lost in thought. And judging by the droop of her shoulders and the sad look on her face, her thoughts weren't happy ones.

A warmth and tenderness unfurled inside Josh as he watched Laura. Despite his best efforts and repeated self-lectures on all the reasons a relationship between the two of them could never work, he hadn't been able to quell his attraction to her or the feelings she stirred inside him. And while she'd done a much better job of masking the sexual pull between them than he had, he'd known she'd felt that pull just as sharply as him. That's why last night while he'd been lying in bed thinking of her, wanting her, remembering the taste of her that had lingered on his lips long after that brief kiss he'd surprised them both with, he'd made up his mind to stop fighting.

Laura was going to be here for less than two weeks. They'd wasted more than a week already dancing around what was happening between them. He was through with the denials. He didn't intend to waste any more time. He fully intended to enjoy every single one of those days that remained before she returned to San Francisco. Hopefully, they would enjoy them together.

Who knows, he thought as he began to walk along

the Moonwalk toward her, she might even decide to stay in New Orleans. And perhaps she would even agree to Olivia's request to run the Princess. If she did, he thought as he closed the distance between them, he might not only succeed in getting the woman he wanted, but at reclaiming the Princess, too.

Joining her at the railing he whispered, "Penny for your thoughts."

"Josh." She said his name in a hushed whisper as she jerked her gaze to him. "What are you doing here?"

"Looking for you."

"Me?" she replied. "But why? Is something wrong?"

"No. I just wanted to see you." Tucking the wind-ravaged hair behind her ears, he caught the lapels of her jacket and pulled her closer. "And I wanted to do this," he said, and covered her mouth with his. Josh felt the shock go through Laura as he kissed wind-chilled lips. And for a moment when she remained stiff in his arms, her hands fisted against his chest, he thought she might reject him. Then her lips softened, parted and she opened her mouth to him.

Cautioning himself to go slower, he took the kiss a shade deeper. It was like popping the cork on a bottle of champagne and sending bubbles shooting to the surface. The taste of her exploded through him, filled his senses, and shot all thoughts of moving slowly straight to hell.

Josh tore his mouth free. Burying his face in her hair, he dragged the cold air into his lungs in an effort to douse the desire for her that was threatening to consume him. As though she'd sensed his withdrawal, her palms flattened against his chest and she eased back a fraction. Then she surprised him by touching his jaw and turning his face so that he was once again staring into those luminous blue eyes. Her cheeks were flushed, her mouth moist and pink, and it took everything in him not to kiss her again. When she lowered her gaze to his mouth, need shuddered through him. He squeezed his eyes shut.

"Josh?"

At the sound of his name, he clenched his fists to keep from reaching for her again.

Then Laura was the one taking the lapels of his jacket and pulling his mouth back to hers. When her tongue swept inside and tangled with his, the desire that he'd struggled so hard to keep leashed, ripped free. Groaning, he speared his fingers into her hair and plundered that soft mouth.

He took. So did she. And within seconds what was meant to be a gentle kiss, a kiss of promise, had quickly turned into a kiss of hunger and demand.

The hell with slow, Josh thought, his body on fire for her. Knowing he'd never make it back to his house, he wondered if they could make it to his car. When she nipped his lip with her teeth, his brain shut down and he decided they wouldn't even make it off the Moonwalk.

Finally the persistent tooting of a foghorn from the river, followed by a round of cheers and whistles, penetrated his senses. Josh ended the kiss. With his arms wrapped around Laura to shield her and her head pressed against his chest, he looked out at the river where one of the city's riverboat casinos, filled with lively patrons waving at them from aboard the deck, cruised on by.

When Laura lifted her head, her cheeks were flushed

and her mouth bare and frowning. "I'm not sure what happened just now."

She looked so confused and adorable, Josh couldn't help it. He grinned. "I'd be happy to show you again."

She narrowed her eyes. "I don't think that would be wise."

"Maybe not wise," he said, thinking of how close he'd come to giving that cruising casino boat a great deal more than a few steamy kisses to gawk at. "But it sure would be fun."

"At the moment 'fun' isn't at the top of my agenda," she told him.

"Fun belongs on everyone's agenda. Want to know what else is on mine?"

"Not particularly," she informed him, and attempted to put him at arm's length.

Unfortunately for Laura and lucky for him, he had nearly a hundred pounds on her and her muscles were far too puny to budge him. "At the moment all I'm really interested in is getting out of this cold. I'm freezing."

He grinned. "I know some surefire ways to help warm you up."

"I bet you do. But unless you back off," she said sweetly, too sweetly, as she lifted her leg and sent her knee sliding up between his thighs, "you're going to discover that I know some surefire ways to cause big guys like you a lot of pain."

No fool to the dangers of a female knee, Josh dropped his arms and took a step back. She brushed past him at a quick clip and headed for the stairs that led to the street. Josh followed. And when she set off toward the French Market, he shifted to the street side and adjusted his gait to match hers. "Something tells me you don't want to talk about what happened just now up on the Moonwalk.''

"You're right. I don't want to talk about it. We kissed. And we shouldn't have. End of story.''

Not the end, he thought, but the beginning. Laura just had to get used to the idea. "You mind telling me where we're going in such a hurry?''

Laura stopped at the street corner, waited for the light to change to green. "I'm going to the parking lot to get the car Mrs. Jardine loaned me and then I'm going back to her house.''

"Great,'' Josh replied. "That's where I'm going too. We can go together.''

"Isn't there a hotel somewhere that you need to go buy?''

They stepped off the curb together. "Nope. I try to stick close to home during the holidays and save any traveling I need to do until after the first of the year.''

Laura frowned. "This Thursday is Thanksgiving. I'd almost forgotten.''

Suddenly Josh wanted to kick himself for not realizing talk of the impending holidays would remind Laura of past holidays. "I'm sorry. I wasn't thinking. I guess you're not particularly looking forward to the holidays this year. I mean, this first year without your mom. It's going to be tough on you.''

"I hadn't really given it a lot of thought. But you're probably right. It is going to be rough. Mom was really crazy about Christmas. And for her, the season began with Thanksgiving,'' she told him, and this time, she didn't seem to notice when he reached for her hand, entwined it with his as they walked. "She'd spend days cooking the Thanksgiving meal and always made way too much food for just the two of us. We'd end up eating leftovers for at least a week." A tremulous smile touched her lips and Josh had to strain to catch the words.

"Sounds like my house—except for the leftovers. With five kids, food had a way of disappearing fast."

Laura slanted him a glance. "I bet. It must have been nice growing up with a big family."

"It had its moments. It still does. With the nieces and nephews as well, it's usually chaos," Josh told her, and couldn't help but smile as he thought of his family's holiday celebrations. "The truth is I love watching my nieces and nephews make my sisters jump through hoops."

Laura arched her brow. "And something tells me they get lots of encouragement from their uncle Josh."

He flashed her a grin. "It's payback for what they put me through as a kid."

She laughed as he'd hoped she would. "Your poor sisters. It's a wonder they don't kill you."

"That's why they're not allowed near the carving knives. The only one I have to worry about is my sister Rachel. She's not married and doesn't have any little monsters yet. But since she's a cop, she carries a gun. She's picked up some new self-defense moves that cause as much damage as that one of yours with the knee."

"Hmm. She sounds like a lady I'd like to meet," Laura said, laughter in her voice.

"That's a great idea," Josh told her. "I don't know why I didn't think of it myself."

Laura frowned. "Think of what?"

"Having you come with me to Thanksgiving at my parents' house so that you can meet my family."

"Josh, I was only kidding," she informed him.

He stopped in the middle of the sidewalk, turned her to face him. "I'm not. Come with me, Laura. I know my parents would love to meet you. And so would my sisters."

Laura pulled her hands free, tucked them into her pockets. "Your family doesn't know a thing about me, Josh. I couldn't possibly go."

"They know I've been seeing you."

"And do they know that I'm Andrew Jardine's bastard daughter?"

Anger slammed through him hard and fast at the slight to herself. He grabbed her by the lapels of her jacket again and hauled her close so that her face was mere inches from him. "They know you're Andrew Jardine's daughter," he told her, making no attempt to keep the heat from his voice. "My parents taught us to believe that a child is a gift—regardless of whether it was planned or not. The only one you shame by using such ugly words to describe yourself is you, Laura Harte. Personally, I'm damned grateful to Drew Jardine and your mother for creating you. And you should be, too."

"You're right," she told him, her words barely a whisper. "I'm sorry. It's just that sometimes it's so hard to accept. Ever since I learned the truth, it's been as though I've lost my identity, a part of who I am. And I hate it. I hate not feeling sure of myself, not knowing who I am."

At the sight of tears swimming in her eyes, Josh felt as though he'd been kicked in the gut. He hugged her to him, held her close and stroked her hair. "I know who you are. You're Laura Harte, a beautiful, intelligent woman that I'd like very much to have join me for Thanksgiving dinner.'' He eased her away from him so that he could see her face. ''Will you come?''

''I... All right. But I'll need to speak with Olivia. I don't know if she has anything planned or not.''

''Josh wants to take you home to meet his family?'' Katie remarked later that afternoon when Laura mentioned the invitation.

''I'm sure he was just being kind,'' Laura told the other woman, and gave Tori a push on the backyard swing.

''Right,'' Katie shot back, making no attempt to hide her skepticism. She nudged Laura aside and gave her niece a little push. ''Josh is always kind—especially when it comes to a pretty woman.''

''Cut it out, Katie,'' Alison told her twin as she watched her two sisters vying for their niece's attention. Of course, her darling daughter was loving having two aunts to shower her with attention. Laura promptly nudged Katie aside and took her turn at giving Tori a push on the swing.

''Come on, Ali,'' Katie countered. ''When you and I were teenagers, we both took bets on which little blond debutante Josh was going to fall in love with each year.''

''You make Josh sound like a womanizer, and he's not. Trust me, I know the difference.'' And she did since she'd been married to one, Alison thought. ''Besides, that was ten years ago. We were kids then.''

''You're right,'' Katie conceded, regret in her eyes that Alison knew was meant for having dredged up bad memories. Her entire family knew what a louse Derek had been. She just hadn't realized that they had known all along about his unfaithfulness. ''Josh really is a great guy. I was just surprised he invited Laura for Thanksgiving dinner. That's all.''

"Why?" Laura asked.

Katie shrugged and gave Tori another push on the swing. "I've known Josh all my life and I can't ever remember him asking a woman to go with him to a family dinner.''

"As I said, I'm sure he was just being kind," Laura replied. "He and I are friends.''

"I'll say. That kiss I saw him give you last night on the porch looked *very* friendly to me.''

Color shot into Laura's cheeks. "Is that how you get your kicks, Katherine? Spying on people?''

Before Katie could tear into Laura, Alison stepped between them. "That's enough for today, angel," she said, and halted the swing's motion. She swept a protesting Tori up into her arms. "If you've got your heart set on joining the Logans, I'm sure Grandmother will be all right with it.''

"Maybe it isn't such a good idea, after all," Laura said. "I wouldn't want his family or anyone else to get the wrong idea.''

"Trust me, Laura. The one thing I've learned is that people will believe whatever it is they want to believe whether you give them any reason to or not.'' Even after more than a year, Alison still wanted to cringe every time she thought about the field day the gossip-mongers had had following her divorce. Derek had done an excellent job of portraying her as a spoiled rich girl who hadn't been prepared to be a wife and mother. And he'd successfully bedded a string of her sorority sisters who had been all too eager to believe the lying snake. With Tori in her arms, she climbed the stairs to the gazebo and sat down on the old-fashioned glider swing. Pushing off with her right foot, she set them to swaying.

Katie took the seat on the matching glider across from her, while Laura stood at the gazebo entrance. "I say, do what you want, and to hell with what people say or think."

"Watch your language," Alison chided, but she was pleased to see her two sisters were no longer spitting at each other like cats. Somehow Katie and Laura had made it past the animosity. And while they were still wary of each other, Alison recognized the fact that the three of them had begun to form a bond. It was a bond she was grateful for and would like the chance to see grow stronger.

"What about you, Ali? How do you feel about me going?" Laura asked, eyeing her with Tori, who was beginning to doze on her lap, then glancing at Katie, on the opposite glider. Laura opted for one of the single seats positioned on the wall between the two gliders. "I keep getting this feeling that you're disappointed. Would you rather I pass on the invitation to spend the holiday with Josh and his family?"

Alison smiled. "You're very perceptive," she told her sister. She'd suspected from the start that Josh's interest in Laura was personal and went beyond him fulfilling her grandmother's request to show Laura around town. And the truth was she was glad for Josh's interest in Laura. She'd even hoped that the romance between them would blossom and Laura would decide to stay in New Orleans. "I am a little disappointed," she admitted. "Since this will be our first Thanksgiving as sisters, I'd hoped we could spend it together as a family."

And her new sister needed her family, Alison realized. It was as plain as day that Laura was still feeling confused. What she needed was time for her hurts to heal and a chance to come to terms with the fact that they were a family—and what better place to do it than with them? Laura needed her family now, even if Laura herself didn't realize it yet. Comes from being a mother, she thought smugly as she adjusted her sleeping daughter on her lap and stroked the little angel's head.

"I hadn't thought…" Laura began. "I mean, you've been wonderful, Ali. But I guess I never thought about our situation and the holidays as you had. Of course I'll tell Josh I won't be able to come."

"Oh, for Pete's sake, Ali. You've got her tripping over herself with guilt." Katie cut a glance at Laura. "Listen, if you want to go to the Logans for Thanksgiving, then go. We'll be just fine."

"Perhaps I should remind you now, sister dear, that Grandmother's given Alfred and the rest of the staff the day off to be with their own families and that I'm the one who'll be cooking the holiday meal."

Katie smiled. "I know. I can hardly wait for your oyster dressing."

"Then you won't mind helping to make it," Alison replied.

Katie narrowed her eyes. "What are you talking about?"

"Did you forget that I've been filling in for your pastry chef at the Regent for the past month? That means I haven't had much time to prepare for the holiday meals this year. I was going to ask Laura to help me with it. But of course, with her at the Logans, I guess I'll have to draft you."

Beneath her scowl, Katie had gone pale. "You know that kitchens and I are a terrible combination."

"True. But I don't have any other choice. I can't possibly do it all myself. So I guess you'll have to learn."

"Get Mother and Mitch to help you."

Alison smiled, enjoying the fact that the mere thought of cooking a meal could strike the fear of God into her oh-so-competent and fearless sister. "Mitch is under the gun to complete a security proposal for the new convention center. And you know as well as I do that Mother hasn't even been inside the kitchen since she went through that maternal phase when we were six. As you'll recall, the cook quit and Mother nearly burned down the place trying to bake biscuits. Grandmother not only had to completely remodel, but she had to swear Mother wouldn't come within ten feet of the kitchen again before the cook would agree to come back."

"God, she really was awful at the cooking thing, wasn't she?" Katie asked, chuckling.

"The worst," Alison agreed.

"Did she really burn down the kitchen?" Laura asked.

"Yes," Katie responded, her eyes filled with laughter. "The fire department sent three trucks out. I can still see Mother's face when she looked at that pan of charred biscuits. She was so crushed, I didn't have the heart to tell her how much we all hated the things and that Mitch had taken the ones left over from the day before and used them as a doorstop in his room."

"You're making that up," Laura accused, laughing.

"It's true. A cook our mother is not," Ali confessed,

enjoying the light moment with her sisters. "What about your mother, Laura? What was she like?"

"She didn't cook anything nearly as good as you do, but she wasn't as bad as your mom. She did know how to do the basics. At least the basics important to a growing kid—macaroni and cheese, pizza and hamburgers. And oatmeal raisin cookies. We always made those together." While the smile remained on Laura's lips, there was a sadness in her eyes. "Sometimes Uncle Paul—he was a friend of my...of your dad's," she corrected herself. "Sometimes he would join us for special occasions. But most of the time it was just me and my mom. She was so much fun. We used to do a lot of things together before...before she died."

"Grandmother said she was killed in a car accident," Katie commented.

"Three months ago. She was going with me to an awards banquet to celebrate my promotion to assistant general manager," Laura explained, her voice growing softer. "I'd gone to pick her up and was driving back to the city. It was raining really hard that night and the roads were slick. A truck jumped the median and hit us head-on. Mom hadn't buckled her seat belt because she didn't want to wrinkle her dress and she was thrown from the car. She died there on the road in my arms."

"I'm sorry," Katie told her.

"I know you're still not comfortable at the idea of us being sisters," Alison began. "But we are sisters. Right now we may only be related by blood because of our father. But I'm hoping with time, you'll feel the connection goes deeper. I'd like us to be sisters in our hearts. I know it's what Daddy would have wanted."

"I can't promise anything, Ali."

"I understand," Alison told her. She'd have to be satisfied with the progress they'd made and hope that time would take care of the rest.

"So what are we going to do about this Thanksgiving dinner?" Katie demanded.

"We're going to cook it," Alison informed her.

"Well since you've pointed out the fact that we're sisters, I don't see why I have to slave away in the kitchen with you and she doesn't," Katie said, jerking her head in Laura's direction.

Alison sent Katie a grateful look. She knew her twin was extending the olive branch to Laura, and that she'd done it for Alison's sake. "So what do you suggest?"

"I suggest that Laura send Josh her regrets. And she and I will both help you with the meal."

"I'm great at tasting cookie dough," Laura offered.

"Fat chance," Katie told her. "How are you at chopping onions and washing dishes?"

"Probably as good at it as you are, Katherine."

"I know where to put the soap in the dishwasher," Katie said with a grin.

"That's too bad," Alison told them. "Because Grandmother's china and crystal have to be washed by hand."

Sixteen

He must have been out of his mind to insist that Laura come by his folks' home for dessert, Josh decided, watching three of his sisters sizing Laura up for the title of Mrs. Josh Logan. He supposed he should be grateful that Rachel had been called into duty by her police captain just after lunch; otherwise, she'd be right in there with the rest of them.

Josh bit back a groan of frustration. It was his own fault, he supposed, for not anticipating his meddlesome siblings would jump to the conclusion—that his bringing Laura over to meet his family meant that he was entertaining the idea of marriage.

He wasn't.

And even if he could understand how they might make such an erroneous assumption, given the last time he'd brought a girl home to meet his family he'd been a sophomore in college, that still didn't justify the three of them sitting there, grinning at him like cats who'd just been given a big bowl of cream.

"Oh, look, Laura. Tommy likes your hair." His sister Hope beamed as his newest nephew who was all of eight months grabbed a fistful of Laura's red hair and attempted to eat it.

"Looks to me like he's hungry," Josh grumbled while Laura made cooing noise and removed the strands from the baby's fist. "Maybe his mommy should go feed him."

"I fed him while you went to pick up Laura. He's good for at least another two hours," Hope informed him. Smiling, she turned her attention back to Laura. "So tell me, Laura, how do you feel about large families?"

"Well, I, um…I imagine they're very nice."

"Then you plan on having several children?" his oldest sister Meredith asked none too subtly.

"Actually, I hadn't given it a lot of thought," Laura told her. "But I would hope that if I were to become a mother that I'd be able to have at least two. That way they would have each other for company as children and then later when…when I was no longer around, they wouldn't be alone."

As she had been, Josh thought, wishing once again he could ease that loneliness inside her. It had been part of the reason he'd asked her to join his family for Thanksgiving dinner, he admitted. But his motives hadn't been all self-serving, he conceded. He'd asked Laura to come because he'd wanted to be with her, to share some of the special warmth that came from being a family. But from what he'd observed when he'd gone to pick her up at the Jardines' house this afternoon, it appeared Laura and her siblings were beginning to bridge the differences between them and form a family.

"Are you going to be my aunt?" Megan, his sister Faith's six-year-old, asked.

"Megan, you know we don't ask grown-ups personal questions like that," Faith chided her daughter gently. She picked up the tiny blond moppet and held her on her lap. "I'm sorry if she embarrassed you,

Laura. I don't know where she could have gotten such an idea.''

"I heard Aunt Meredith telling Grandma that Uncle Josh was going to marry Laura," Megan replied innocently. "And if he marries her, then she would be my aunt, wouldn't she?"

"That's right, sweetheart," Faith said, her cheeks red. "Whomever Uncle Josh marries will be your aunt."

"And it would be nice if everyone would allow Uncle Josh to decide to do the asking," he replied, and was pleased to see that at least his sister Faith had the grace to lower her head in embarrassment. Which was more than he could say about his other siblings.

"Here we are," his mother, Jenna Logan, said as she returned to the dining room carrying a tray with the Italian cream cake that Alison had insisted on sending over. She set the tray on the table and tucked a stray hair back into place that had no doubt come loose while his father had helped her with the coffee.

"And here's the coffee," Thomas Logan announced as he followed his wife into the room, bearing a tray filled with steaming cups.

"It was so sweet of Alison to send over the cake," his mother commented.

"I keep telling Olivia that girl should open a restaurant. No one bakes like your sister Alison," his father told Laura as he swiped a fingertip through the frosting on one of the slices of cake and earned himself a smack on the hand from his wife.

"You're right, Mr. Logan," Laura replied, and Josh released the breath he hadn't realized he'd been holding. "Ali is a genius in the kitchen. It's a good thing

I'm going back to San Francisco at the end of next week. Otherwise, my waistline might never recover.''

The mention of her leaving hit Josh like a blow. Somehow the idea of Laura being thousands of miles away left him feeling hollow inside—which made absolutely no sense, Josh told himself.

"That's right," Jenna Logan said as she passed a slice of cake to Laura. "Josh mentioned that you've been working as an assistant GM at a hotel in San Francisco. Josh has been wanting us to acquire a hotel out there. But so far, he hasn't found the right property."

"Oh, I've found the right property. The Ambassador Grand where Laura works. It would fit right into our system, but Nick wouldn't even discuss it."

Faith's head shot up. "Nick?"

Josh looked at his baby sister, thought of the lousy time she'd had of things this past year after divorcing that scuzzball husband of hers. The last thing he wanted to do was mention Baldwin and bring back memories of another painful romance for her.

"Nick Baldwin," Laura said, taking the option of whether to say anything to her out of his hands.

"You work for Nick Baldwin?" Faith asked, the slightest tremor in her voice.

"That's right. He owns the Ambassador Grand. He's been a terrific boss and a wonderful friend." She paused as though she, too, had sensed something in Faith's expression. "I understand that you know him. He mentioned working with Josh and you at one of your family's hotels."

"That's right. I think he did work at Logan's New Orleans for a while," Faith said offhandedly.

But his sister's sudden concentration on clearing

away the cake crumbs that had fallen from Megan's plate onto the table didn't match her seeming disinterest. Interesting, Josh thought, remembering Nick's reaction when he'd mentioned Faith had been as off-kilter as his younger sister's was now. Testing a theory, he said, "Come on, Faith, I'm the old guy here. Don't tell me you've forgotten that Nick's the one who trained you on the front desk during your first summer stint."

"You're right," she said. "He and I worked together that first summer before my freshman year in college. He was a good teacher."

"And a hard worker," Thomas Logan added. "The boy had all the makings of a fine hotelier. Smart and lots of ambition. I would have loved to have been able to keep him. I even offered him an assistant manager job at one of the Logan properties when he gave me his resignation. Turned me down flat, said he didn't want to work for other people. He wanted to work for himself. I'm not surprised to hear he's doing well. He was determined to recoup his father's losses. I'm glad he did. You be sure to give him my regards when you get back to San Francisco."

"I'll do that," Laura said. "I'm sure he'll be glad to know that you remember him."

At the mention of Laura leaving, Josh felt that one-two kick to his gut again. He didn't want her to go. The realization surprised him—especially since he'd resigned himself more than a week ago to the fact that this scheme of Olivia's wasn't going to work. Laura would be returning to San Francisco, and his bargain to reclaim the Princess simply wasn't going to happen.

Josh frowned as he thought of his grandfather and the promise he'd made to him all those years ago—to return the Princess under the Logan banner. For some reason, he found the prospect of not making good on that long-ago promise far less disturbing than the prospect of Laura flying back to San Francisco and out of his life.

"It sounds to me like Joshua has given you quite an extensive tour of the city," Olivia commented over breakfast a few mornings later after hearing Laura's response to Mitch's question about which places she'd visited since her arrival.

"He has," Laura replied, still guarded with Olivia even after living under her roof for nearly three weeks. "It was very kind of you to suggest he show me around. Thank you."

Olivia inclined her head regally like the duchess that Josh often called her. "I must admit that when I made the suggestion, I had no idea Joshua would occupy so much of your time."

Laura caught the note of disapproval in the older woman's tone, and her back stiffened. "I hadn't realized how I spent my time was a problem."

"I'm sure Grandmother didn't mean to imply that it was," Alison offered, once again playing peacemaker.

Olivia frowned. "I don't need you to explain what I meant, Alison. I'm quite capable of doing it for myself. As it is, I think my comment was straightforward. Joshua has been taking up a great deal of Laura's time."

"Funny you should mention that, Grandmother," Katie offered, shifting her gaze so that Laura caught the gleam of humor in her eyes. "I was commenting to Laura just a few days ago how much time she and

Josh have been spending together. I'm not sure I've ever seen Josh quite so attentive.''

Laura shot Katie a quelling glance. "And as I told you, Josh and I are friends. He's been very kind to me and has generously given up a lot of his own time to show me around New Orleans.''

Katie grinned at Laura over the rim of her coffee cup. "Somehow I get the feeling that good old Josh hasn't found squiring you around a real hardship.''

"Of course it hasn't been a hardship," Olivia added, obviously having no inkling of what they were talking about. "I'm just surprised the boy has found that many museums and landmarks to show you.''

Laura flushed, knowing that what Olivia said was true. "There's a great deal more to see in New Orleans than just the museums and landmarks," Laura offered.

"Like what?" Katie asked, all innocence.

"Like the French Quarter. The architecture and history there alone would take weeks to fully explore. And there's the river, the bayous and plantations.''

"Has Josh introduced you to any nighttime activities yet?" Katie asked.

"He's taken me to a few of the clubs to hear the music," Laura replied through gritted teeth, knowing full well the little witch hadn't been referring to the music for which the city was so popular. She also knew that Katie wasn't totally off base. Despite her own denials and excuses, there was more than friendship between her and Josh. In fact, she was very much afraid they were already well past friendship and in serious danger of becoming lovers.

Which would be a terrible mistake, she reasoned. Not just for her, but for Josh, too. It would be unfair to both of them for her to let things progress any further between them—especially since she'd be returning to San Francisco soon. But oh how she wanted to, Laura admitted. Every time she was with him and they shared one of those scorching kisses, she was finding it more and more difficult not to rip off the man's clothes and demand he make love to her. Dear God, what was happening to her? she wondered on a shuddering breath. Here she was sitting at a breakfast table and thinking about sex. It was the city's sultry atmosphere, Laura told herself. That's all. Once she was safely back in San Francisco, she'd forget all about Josh Logan and how his kisses made her blood heat and her body weak.

"Laura?"

Laura jerked her thoughts back to the present at the sound of Mitch's voice. "I'm sorry, did you say something?"

He gave her a puzzled look. "I said that from your reaction it sounds like you like New Orleans."

"Oh, I do. I love it," she told him honestly. "It's a fabulous place. There's so much more here than I'd ever imagined. It's a fascinating city."

"You sound like a walking advertisement for the tourist commission," Mitch said, chuckling. Laura couldn't help feeling pleased that Mitch's attitude appeared to have warmed toward her. "Maybe Katie should introduce you to her contacts there. They could use you."

"Maybe I should," Katie replied. "Seeing as how Laura's fallen so hard. For the city," she added when Laura glared at her.

Olivia made a huffing sound. "It sounds to me like Joshua has wasted a great deal of time showing you tourist traps when he should have been showing you our hotels."

"Actually, I have seen them. We drove by them and Josh pointed them out to me."

"What do you mean the boy drove you by them? He should have taken you inside, made sure you were given a tour and introduced to the employees. He knew I wanted you to see the Princess. What on earth was that boy thinking? Pointing out the hotels to you as though you were some stranger with no interest in them whatsoever?"

A collective hush fell around the table after Olivia's outburst. Although she had held to her bargain with Josh not to pressure Laura about the job at the Princess, apparently Olivia hadn't forgotten about it. In fact, she apparently had expected Josh to help. That he hadn't warmed Laura's heart. "The truth is, 'the boy' did offer. But I declined. As I've said, I'm not interested in staying in New Orleans or in running your hotel."

"But they're a part of your heritage, you should—"

"Grandmother, I think Laura's made her feelings clear on the subject. Perhaps you should drop it," Mitch said quietly, firmly, earning him her gratitude. And for a moment she allowed herself to imagine he'd done so to defend her because she was his sister. Which was an absurd idea, Laura reasoned. He might have jumped to Katie or Ali's defense, but not hers. He didn't think of her as his sister, she told herself.

Dismissing her foolish notion, she waited for Olivia to tear into her grandson. But to her surprise, Olivia remained silent. Laura looked from one to the other, wondered as she had at Thanksgiving what had transpired between the pair. On the few occasions she'd seen Mitch during her visit, she had sensed a change in the relationship between grandmother and grandson and wondered at it. She also wondered what caused the older woman to heed Mitch's advice. Whatever the reason, she was grateful.

"Since Grandmother wants you to see the hotels, why don't you meet me for lunch at the Princess today," Alison suggested. "I'm supposed to go over some of the details for the masquerade ball with the catering department this morning, but I'll be finished by eleven-thirty. You could meet me there, I'll give you a tour of the hotel and then we can have lunch."

"All right."

Great," Alison said. "There's this terrific little costume shop just a few blocks from the hotel that has the most gorgeous period ball gowns. After lunch we can go pick out what we're going to wear to the ball."

"I'll take you up on the tour and the lunch, but I think I'll pass on the costumes. I'm not sure I'll be able to come back for it," Laura explained.

"Of course you'll come back for it," Olivia argued. "The Jardines are hosting it. It would be rude of you not to be there to greet the family's guests."

Laura started to correct her, tell her she wasn't a Jardine, but decided it wasn't worth arguing about. Besides, for her to disclaim herself as a member of the family would only hurt Ali. Although she hadn't planned it, she had begun to accept the sweet-natured Alison as her sister and was glad of the connection.

"Please, Laura. Say you'll come," Alison pleaded.

"I'll try. That's the best I can do for now. I need to talk with my boss see if I can get away. But I'll go and look at costumes with you."

"Fair enough," Alison said before she slid a glance to her twin. "What about you, Katie? Can you get away and join us?"

"My schedule's too tight. There's no way I can get

to the Princess for lunch and keep my meetings.'' She paused, tapped a finger to her lips. Suddenly her face brightened. ''I have a better idea. Laura, why don't you come by the Regent and let me give you a tour. Then when Ali finishes her business, she can meet us there and we'll have lunch together. Afterward the two of you can go to the Princess. Ali can give you a tour, and then you can go shopping. How does that sound?''

''It sounds great to me,'' Ali replied.

''Laura, what about you?'' Katie asked. ''You up for a tour of the Regent and lunch with the two of us?''

''I'd like that,'' Laura said, both surprised and pleased by Katie's offer.

''Then it's a date,'' Alison said with a smile. ''What about the shopping, Katie? Is there any way you could break away and join us for that too?''

''Absolutely not,'' Katie told her. ''My feet haven't recovered from the last time you convinced me to hit the shops with you. Be forewarned, Laura, wear comfortable shoes. Our sister here is a champion shopper.''

''But I thought we were just going to buy a costume,'' Laura said in confusion.

''Oh, you'll buy a costume, all right. But once you have the outfit, you're going to need the right shoes and the right purse and the right jewelry and all the other accessories that go with it.'' Katie shuddered. ''No thanks. You two can have fun without me.''

''You're going to need a costume, too,'' Ali pointed out to Katie.

''And since you're the one with all the fashion sense, you can pick something out for me,'' Katie replied with a grin.

''You might not like what I choose,'' Ali warned her.

"I'll love what you choose. You have excellent taste when it comes to clothes, and I don't have any. Whatever you decide will be fine with me. Besides, that's the beauty of being a twin. I don't have to worry about shopping for clothes because whatever looks good on you will look good on me, too," Katie said proudly.

"Excuse me, it's time for my medication," Olivia said. "No, no. Don't get up. You children finish your breakfast. I'll see you this evening." She stood, paused and looked over at Laura. "Laura, I'll be anxious to hear what you think of the Princess."

"Why don't I walk with you, Grandmother," Mitch said. "I need to be going."

"Me, too," Alison said. "I need to get Tori off to school. I'll see you both at noon."

"It's a date," Laura said, and debated whether to finish her own breakfast or leave. She'd spent very little time alone in Katie's company and wasn't sure she wanted to spend any now—especially while she was irked by Katie's imposing manner with Ali.

As though she could read her thoughts, Katie looked up from the toast she was buttering and asked, "Something bothering you?"

"As a matter of fact, there is. You have no right to treat Ali as though she's your...your servant. You have her filling in at the hotel when you lose a pastry chef. You encourage Olivia to dump the masquerade ball plans on her, and then you expect her to do your shopping. Well, if you need a personal shopper, hire one."

"My, my. Ruffled your feathers a bit, didn't I?" Katie countered, licking bits of butter and crumbs from her fingers. "That's not the first time I've seen you jump to her defense. I'm glad to know you care about her."

"Of course I care about her. She's my...she's my sister. And I don't like to see you take advantage of her."

"She's my sister, too, and I'd sooner slit my own throat than take advantage of her or let anyone hurt her again," Katie told her. "Don't get me wrong. I do detest shopping, and Ali loves it, so that works out just fine for both of us. If I came on a bit high-handed it's because Ali needs to feel she's needed."

Stunned by the revelation, Laura sat back, stared at Katie. "Of course she's needed. Besides the fact that she's Tori's mother, all anyone has to do is spend ten minutes in this house to know that Ali's the one who keeps it and this family together."

"You know that. And I know that. But Ali can't see it," Katie explained. "Ali's not like us, Laura. I guess I take after Grandmother more than I care to admit. I accused her of being obsessed with the Princess, but I was the same way about the Regent. I always knew that I would run it when I grew up. Mitch was more like our father. He knew pretty quickly that he wasn't interested in the hotel business, and after a brief stint in the navy, he came home and opened the security business."

"And Ali wanted a home and family," Laura said, surmising that was the reason she had married so young.

Katie nodded. "The problem was she married a real SOB who was more interested in her position as Olivia Jardine's granddaughter and one of her heirs than he was in Ali. She's rid of him now, but it cost her plenty—emotionally and financially," Katie said, her eyes hard, flat. "The money doesn't matter, but what he did to Ali's self-esteem does."

"And it's the reason you keep giving her so many projects to handle," Laura concluded.

"Bingo."

Embarrassed, Laura said, "I feel like an idiot. I guess I owe you an apology. I'm sorry."

"Nearly choked on it, didn't you?" Katie responded, laughing.

"I don't like to be wrong about someone, and I'd made up my mind not to like you."

"Then we have that in common since I'm not sure if I like you, either," Katie told her. "But since it's important to Ali, I'm willing to give it a try."

"So am I."

Katie glanced at her watch, yelped and jumped out of her chair. "I'm late. I need to get out of here. I'll see you at eleven-thirty at the Regent?"

"I'll be there."

"The hotel's lovely, and business appears to be good," Laura told Katie as the two of them sipped iced tea and waited for Alison to arrive.

"Business *is* good," Katie informed her. "Between the new hotels going up and the empty buildings being converted into hotels, the market here is a lot tougher than it used to be. Since the Regent's a small hotel, staying competitive with rates and services isn't easy."

"I'm aware of the difficulties in operating a small hotel," Laura told her. "You might recall, I'm the assistant manager of one back in San Francisco."

"Then you'll appreciate the fact that I work my fanny off and my staff's fannies off, too, to make it happen. One of the reasons our occupancy rate remains high is because I make sure we get our share of the market."

Everything the other woman said was true. She knew firsthand the drawbacks to being a small, luxury hotel in a business world fueled by high expectations at lower prices. But Katie was looking so darned smug, Laura couldn't keep from saying, "I guess modesty is another one of those virtues you didn't learn in finishing school."

"Oh, drop the snippy tone," Katie told her as she added another lemon to her tea and tasted it again. "You're impressed, and we both know it."

"I suppose you're a mind reader, too?"

Katie grinned. "Don't have to be. I saw you watching me deal with that testy mother-of-the groom. Admit it. You were impressed."

"All right," Laura conceded, a smile curving her own lips. "I was impressed with how you handled her. I still can't believe the woman actually expected you and the hotel to accept responsibility for her son running off with one of the waiters who served at his rehearsal dinner."

"It was obvious the woman was taking a lot of heat because she booked the rehearsal dinner here in the first place. Probably the bride and her family were threatening a lawsuit of their own against her."

"I'm sure you're right. Still, your offer to add a statement to your press release on the matter, absolving her of any responsibility in the mess, was truly inspired."

Katie laughed. "You're right. It was. She certainly backed off quickly, didn't she?"

"Yes, she did."

Once they recovered from their mutual fits of laughter, Katie said, "I'm glad we did this, Laura. I've liked getting to spend some time with you."

"You needn't sound so surprised," Laura told her.

"Oh, but I am surprised," Katie advised her, her eyes gleaming with amusement. "In case you hadn't noticed, I haven't been at all thrilled to find out we're sisters."

"I haven't exactly been overjoyed by the prospect myself. I'm still not sure how I feel about it," Laura told her honestly. "I grew up loving my father—or at least the image of the man in the picture frame I was told was my father. I believed all my mother's stories about how kind and wonderful he was, how much they had loved each other. And even though I'd never met him, I missed him. Lots of times when I was faced with a problem or a decision, I'd try to figure it out by thinking what he would have wanted me to do." Her throat tight with emotion, Laura swallowed hard and eased out a breath before continuing. "Finding out the truth…that he was alive all those years, married, living here, raising you and Ali and Mitch…it's been hard to accept. Sometimes I feel so hurt, so angry—at him, at my mother, even at you because he *was* your father, and he was never mine."

"I'm sorry," Katie told her. "I can't say I know how you feel or how I would feel if I were in your place, because I don't. I do know that our father was a kind and honorable man. He wasn't the type of man who would cheat on his wife. I know because I saw the way women looked at him, and he never looked back." Katie paused. "This is hard for me to admit—especially to you—but my parents' marriage wasn't the happy, blissful one that my mother thinks it was."

"What do you mean?"

"Thanksgiving Day when you went by the Logans' for dessert, did you notice how Mr. and Mrs. Logan were? I'm talking about the way they would give each other little pecks on the cheek for no reason or the way Mr. Logan would reach for his wife's hand and give it a little squeeze when they were next to each other.''

She had noticed the affection between the senior Logans, Laura admitted silently. She'd noticed it and had been warmed by it. "You mean like those little 'I love you' looks they send each other across the table?''

"Exactly," Katie replied. "You only have to see them together to know that the romance is still very much alive in their marriage—even after five kids and more than thirty-five years of marriage.''

"So what's your point?''

"The point is, my parents didn't share that. I don't mean that they didn't love each other. I know they did. But it was more like a love between two friends than between a husband and wife. What I'm saying is, I don't think there was ever any passion between them, and I think maybe it was because Daddy never stopped loving your mother.''

"There's no way you can know that. There's no way any of us will ever know," Laura protested, even though it eased the ache in her heart somewhat to think that her father had truly loved her mother, after all.

"You're right," Katie said, pushing her tea aside. "But I do know that if my father had known about you, he would never have kept you a secret. He loved us kids, and he made sure we knew we were the most important thing in the world to him. Even my mother would tell you that. You're his daughter, Laura. And regardless of what happened between him and your mother, he would have loved you and wanted you. I know that in my heart. There's no way he would ever have denied you or allowed your mother or anyone else to keep you from him."

Confused by the feelings stirring inside her, Laura refused to meet Katie's eyes, sure she would see the tears burning at the back of her own. Instead she looked at her watch and frowned. "Ali should have been here twenty minutes ago. Do you think something's wrong?"

Katie frowned. "It's not like her to be late."

"Maybe you should call her cell phone, and find out where she is?"

"That's if she remembered to bring the thing with her. She thinks it's a toy for Tori," Katie grumbled, and punched out the number from her own cell phone. "She's not answering. I'll give the hotel a call and see if she's still there."

"So what's the story?" Laura asked, when Katie ended the call a moment later.

"Tori had a tummy ache, and Ali went to pick her up at school. It's nothing serious, apparently, but she can't make lunch."

"Oh," Laura said, somewhat disappointed because she enjoyed Ali's company. That didn't surprise her. It was impossible not to enjoy Ali since she made everyone feel so welcome. The fact that she had enjoyed Katie's company is what surprised her.

"So, since we've managed to spend nearly an hour with each other without drawing blood, do you think we should risk trying to have a meal together without Ali playing referee?" Katie asked.

"Since I haven't felt the lash of that acid tongue of yours in the past hour, something tells me I'd be pushing my luck if I said yes," Laura replied dryly, and bit back a grin at the scowl on Katie's face. "But since I am starving, and I keep seeing and smelling the most delicious things coming out of that kitchen, I'm willing to risk it if you are.''

"How could I refuse such a gracious invitation?" Katie replied.

Laura grinned and flipped open her own menu. Her eyes widened as she read the prices. "And they say the prices in California are high."

Katie grinned right back at her. "Don't worry, sister dear. If you don't have enough cash on you, we take credit cards.''

"Oh, but I wasn't worried about me being able to afford these prices. I was worried about you."

"Me?"

"Uh-huh," Laura murmured as she skimmed the menu and tried to decide between the shrimp scampi and the crab cakes. "You invited me, remember? That means you're buying."

Seventeen

"Ms. Jardine, I'm sorry to disturb you," the maître d' said. "But there's an urgent call for you. Do you want to take it here or in your office?"

"I'll take it here, Raul," Katie said, immediately concerned that something had happened to her grandmother. "This is Katherine Jardine," she said when she was handed the phone.

"Miss Jardine, this is Seymour Winston at the Princess. I'm sorry to bother you, but you said to call you instead of your grandmother if I had any problems."

"That's all right, Seymour," Katie replied, wondering what was the newest catastrophe the front desk manager who'd been serving as acting GM decided he couldn't handle. "You told the operator it was urgent," she reminded him.

"Yes. Yes, it is. There's been a…an incident. And I really think you should be the one to deal with the authorities and the press."

Katie's blood turned to ice. "What's happened?"

"There was a fire in the Anastasia Suite," he began, referring to one of the hotel's most requested and expensive suite of rooms. "No one was hurt, but the guests occupying the suite suffered quite a bit of damage to their things. They were very expensive things, Miss Jardine," he added.

"Seymour, please…just get to the bottom line. How bad is it?"

"Very. The firemen got the fire under control fairly quick, but the water damage has put the entire floor out of commission. We have no rooms for the guests who've been displaced, plus we have the heart surgeons conventioneers arriving tomorrow and a wedding party and reception this weekend, and we have no place to put them. And then somehow the press found out…"

Things could be worse, Katie told herself, as Winston cataloged the mountain of problems she would somehow have to solve. At least no one had been hurt, and the hotel hadn't burned to the ground, she thought. "Seymour, just hang tight. I'll get back to you."

"But, Miss Jardine," he objected. "What should I tell the reporters?"

"Tell them 'no comment' and refer them to me," she said, and promptly ended the call. Katie leaned her head back against the chair and closed her eyes.

What was she going to do? The Regent could probably handle a few displaced guests tonight, and maybe send some to the Logans' hotel, if pressed. But what about the new arrivals and the wedding reception Winston said was scheduled there for the weekend? And how was she going to keep this from her grandmother? If she were to find out, her grandmother would ignore the doctor's orders and be back at the Princess in a heartbeat.

She couldn't let that happen, couldn't risk her grandmother having another heart attack. She would have to find a way to handle it. But how? How?

"What's wrong?" Laura asked.

Only vaguely aware of Laura sitting there, Katie opened her eyes. She dragged a hand through her hair and gave herself another moment to try to engineer a way that she could take control of management at the Princess and still retain control at the Regent. And somehow solve all the daily headaches and problems of both hotels and keep her sanity.

"For Pete's sake, Katie, what is it?"

Pulling herself from the haze of panic, Katie took a deep breath. She could handle it, she told herself. She *would* handle it, she corrected herself. She'd start by canceling her meeting with the tourist commission, and then she would go to the Princess and assess the damage herself. Then she'd figure out what to do.

"Dammit, Katherine Elizabeth, you're scaring me. Tell me what's wrong!"

The anger in Laura's voice finally penetrated. Katie gave herself a mental shake and focused on the other woman. "I'm sorry. I'm going to have to renege on lunch. There's been a fire at the Princess and there's some serious water damage. Apparently there's a lobby full of press, police and angry guests. I need to get over there and see what I can do to salvage the mess before Grandmother gets wind of it."

"But what about the GM?"

"The acting GM is a desk clerk that I convinced Grandmother could handle the job on a temporary basis to keep her from going back to run things herself. Unfortunately, Seymour Winston panics when he runs low on hand towels for the bathrooms. He can't handle this. If anything, he'll make the situation worse."

"But I thought you had some big presentation you were making this afternoon."

"I do...or I did. With the tourist commission. It took me months to set it up," Katie said, sighing with regret. She motioned the waiter for a check. "But I don't have any choice. No one else on my staff can make the presentation, and I can't be in two places at once. I'll have to cancel it."

"No, you don't," Laura told her. "I'll go to the Princess for you."

In the act of signing the restaurant ticket, Katie paused, looked up at Laura. "I can't ask you to do that."

"You didn't ask. I volunteered," Laura informed her. "Go wow them with your presentation. I'll handle things for you at the Princess."

"If I were a sweet, generous person like Ali, I'd tell you that you don't know what you're getting into and would refuse to let you walk into that mess."

"But we both that know you're not a sweet, generous person like Ali," Laura tossed back with a smile.

"No, I'm not," Katie answered with a smile of her own. "So I'm going to take you up on your offer. I'll call Winston and tell him my older sister's on the way." The words were out before she could take them back, and Katie braced herself, unsure of how Laura would react.

"You do that," Laura told her, with only the slightest of pauses before her smile widened. "Just remember, you owe me."

Katie owed her. Big time, Laura decided as she hung up the phone in the executive office of the Princess. Exhausted but satisfied that she'd been able to handle all the major crises that had cropped up as a result of the hotel fire, she leaned back in the chair and put her aching feet up on top of the desk. Sighing, she closed her eyes and ordered herself to relax.

Despite the fatigue, she was charged, Laura admitted. It had been an exhilarating experience to jump into the frenzy of running a hotel again—especially knowing that here at the Princess, unlike at the Ambassador Grand, she was the one holding the reins, calling the shots. It had been a somewhat frightening, but heady experience, she realized. And she couldn't help but feel pleased with herself for having met the challenge. Wait until she told Josh, she thought, only to remember he was out of town for the day. She missed him. Missed seeing him, talking to him, kissing him, she admitted. She should be alarmed by the realization and the fact that Josh was the first person she wanted to call and tell about her day. The man was occupying her thoughts entirely too much. It was good that he was away, she reasoned. She needed some time, some distance from him. She'd be leaving soon. It was best that she begin making the break now.

"Well if that isn't a pretty sight."

Laura's pulse jumped at that slow, sexy drawl. So much for making that break, she thought. Not even bothering to open her eyes, she smiled and said, "Hello, Logan."

"Hello, Laura darling."

Then his mouth was brushing against hers. Slowly. Softly. Gently. A moan slipped past her lips before she could catch it. When his tongue traced the seam of her lips, desire pooled low in her belly, exploded through her system, making her blood heat, her heart race. How she wanted this man, she thought. Giving up the battle, she slid her arms around his neck and opened to him.

His kiss was hot, hard, ravenous.

"Damn," he muttered as he tore his mouth free. "I'm sorry. I never meant to attack you."

"You didn't." She stood, reached for his hands and placed them on her breasts. His eyes went hot and sent another burst of lust sluicing through her veins. "I want you, Josh."

He swore. "Are you deliberately trying to kill me?" he demanded, his voice ragged, his expression feral.

Laura tugged on his tie, brought his mouth down until it was only a breath from her own and whispered, "No. But I might kill you if you insist on talking instead of making love to me."

Josh grabbed her by the shoulders, hauled her up and kissed her again. This time there was nothing tame or gentle about the kiss. It was savage, ruthless, thrilling. And she nearly whimpered when he set her from him and dragged in a deep breath.

Having a little trouble getting her own breath back as she dealt with the tight ball of need fisted in her stomach, she asked, "What's wrong? I thought this is what you wanted, too."

"Of course I want you, you idiot," he said, turning those hot, hungry eyes on her.

"Then why...why did you stop?"

"Because I don't think your grandmother would appreciate it if she came in here and found me making love to her granddaughter on top of her desk."

"What?" she squealed, realizing now that she hadn't even asked him how he'd known where to find her.

"As it is, I don't know how I'm going to be able to conduct a conversation with the woman when all I can think about is getting you out of that prissy little suit and naked."

Laura swallowed. Hoping distance would help, she took a step back, felt the edge of the chair hit her legs and sank into the seat. She looked at the desk, felt the spurt of need hit her again. Looking away quickly, she tried to get her brain functioning again by replaying the other half of Josh's statement—Olivia was coming here. "But Olivia can't come here," she told him, recalling Katie's concern for the older woman's health if she found out what had happened at the hotel. "You have to call the house and tell her not to come."

"I'm afraid you're too late, dear. I'm already here," Olivia said from the doorway.

Despite the cane, there seemed to be a lightness to her step, and there was no question about the gleam in her eyes. "I, um, I wasn't expecting you," Laura said. Realizing she was sitting at Olivia's desk, she shot to her feet.

"Oh, sit down," Olivia insisted. She tilted her head, studied her. "You look good sitting there. Well, except for your jacket. You might want to adjust your buttons."

Flushing, Laura immediately straightened her clothes. Worried, she asked, "Does Katie know you're here?"

"Since I didn't feel the need to obtain Katherine's approval to visit my own hotel, I doubt it. But I imagine she'll find out soon enough." She handed Josh a handkerchief. "You might want to wipe that lipstick from your mouth."

At any other time, the sight of Josh's reddening cheeks would have been amusing, Laura thought. But not now. Not when all she could think about was getting Olivia out of the hotel before she found out about the problems at the Princess. "I was just about to leave. Would you like me to give you a ride home?"

"Oh, do stop fretting, child. Alfred's waiting downstairs for me with the Rolls. He'll take me home when I'm ready." She took a seat across the desk from Laura.

"Was there something you wanted to see me about?" Laura asked.

"Why to thank you, of course."

"You know then...about the fire?" Laura asked.

Olivia laughed, and Laura realized it was the first time she'd heard the sound. "You don't honestly believe I'd let your sister convince me to turn over the Princess to that spineless creature Winston, do you? I only agreed so Katherine would stop worrying."

"But how? How did you know?"

"You forget, Laura dear, I've run this hotel for more than fifty years. And as difficult as you may find it to believe, I've endeared myself to a number of the employees. Their first loyalty, particularly among those who've been here for a while, is to me."

"In other words, you have a spy," Laura finished.

"Several," Olivia said proudly. "And it did my heart good to find out I'd been right about you. Didn't I tell you she was the right one to take the reins of the Princess, Joshua?"

"Yes, Duchess, you did."

"Now, hang on a minute. Just because I stepped in and helped out today doesn't mean I've changed my mind about working for you. I already have a job in San Francisco that I like very much," she reminded Olivia. "Why would I want to give it up?"

"For the challenge, and the satisfaction. You and I both know you're ready to run a hotel on your own, Laura, not just fill in when the real manager's off duty. Here, at the Princess, you'll be in charge. You'll run the show. And you'll have the satisfaction of knowing you made it all work."

"Or the misery of knowing I've failed," Laura pointed out.

"You won't."

"You don't know that," Laura argued. She wasn't considering this, she told herself. She couldn't possibly consider it. "There's no way you can be sure I won't fail."

"I *am* sure. But since you're worried, I can have Joshua work with you on a consultant basis."

Laura's gaze shot to Josh, who remained silent, his expression inscrutable. "No, it's out of the question. My life is in San Francisco."

"This is where you belong. This is your heritage," Olivia told her firmly. "Are you going to pass up an opportunity like this because you're afraid?"

Laura's chin came up. "I'm not afraid."

"Prove it. Agree to stay on a trial basis. See if you have what it takes to turn the Princess around. If after the trial period you've succeeded, I'll sign you to a ten-year contract at a very generous salary."

"And if I'm not successful?" Laura asked.

"Another position will be found for you within one of the family's businesses. If it doesn't suit you, I'll see that you're given excellent references to seek employment elsewhere. Either way, after functioning as the general manager of a hotel like the Princess, you won't need to beg anyone for a job. Quite the contrary, you'll have any number of firms knocking on your door."

Laura knew Olivia spoke the truth. Her value would go up substantially with management of the Princess added to her résumé. Still, she hesitated. "How long would this trial period have to be?"

"A year."

"I couldn't possibly commit to that long," Laura told her. "Four months."

"Eight months," Olivia fired back.

"Six months, and Josh comes on board as a consultant."

"Done."

Her momentary sense of victory at getting Olivia to agree to a six-month trial period dimmed as she noted the triumphant look in the other woman's eyes. Suddenly Laura had a sinking feeling that she had just been outmaneuvered by a master.

"I'll be going now," Olivia said, and stood. "Joshua, could you walk me out to the car? I'd like to have a word with you."

"Well, my boy, it looks like our plan is coming together," Olivia told him as she waved the elevator operator away and the two of them stepped into the car alone.

"What plan?" Josh asked, still shocked that Laura had agreed to take the job. She'd been so set against it that he'd written off the chance that she would accept Olivia's offer. Instead, he'd spent a good portion of the day looking into possibilities that would make a long-distance relationship more viable.

"Why, our little wager," she informed him. "At the end of six months if you and Laura turn the Princess around, I'll sign the hotel over to whichever one of you wins the high-card draw. Just as I promised."

"Duchess, I have no intention of holding you to that," he told her. Especially not now, not when things had become more personal between him and Laura. "I dismissed the whole idea the first day Laura arrived and turned you down. As far as I'm concerned, you don't owe me anything other than my standard consulting fee for any help I give Laura."

The elevator came to a stop, and just before the doors slid open, she told him, "We made a bargain, and I intend to keep my end of it. The wager stands."

When she stepped out into the lobby, Josh followed. "Then why didn't you tell Laura what was at stake?"

"The girl has enough pressure. If she knew that ownership of the Princess was at stake, it would only add to her stress."

The doorman held open the door, and the two of them walked out into the cold, damp night air. When Alfred opened the door of the Rolls for Olivia, Josh stepped in front of her. "Not so fast, Duchess. I'm not buying it. You don't even believe in stress. So what's the real reason you don't want Laura to know what you're planning?"

She waved Alfred away. Despite the cane and the silver hair that bore witness to the fact that the woman was past eighty, there was a fire in those pale blue eyes as she stared up at him. "I don't want Laura to know yet because I'm worried Adrienne will see my actions as a slap in the face."

"Adrienne?" Josh repeated.

"Yes. She's been acting strange ever since Laura arrived, and though she hasn't said anything, I know it bothers her that Laura is becoming closer to her sisters and Mitchell. She knows I want Laura to take over the Princess, so even if she doesn't approve, she'll accept it." Olivia sighed. "I'm not at all sure how she'll react when she finds out my plan for Laura...or for you to be given the hotel."

"She'll probably be worried about how it will affect her own children's inheritance," Josh reasoned. "And I can't say I'd blame her."

Olivia shook her head. "I've provided for the others in my will fairly. No, I don't think it's the money that's bothering Adrienne. It's something else. Something to do with Andrew, and the fact that Juliet is Laura's mother. Whatever it is, I need time to find out so that I can prepare Adrienne."

Offering a silent regret to his grandfather, Josh said,

"Then why don't we forget about the wager, Duchess? When we revisit the situation in six months, if Laura's successful, you can sign the hotel over to her, and I'll offer to buy it."

"I would think you'd take this chance to make good on your promise to Simon."

"Granddad told you about that?" Josh asked in astonishment.

"Simon and I were close," she said quietly. "He loved you a great deal."

"And I loved him," Josh told her, surprised at the rush of emotion speaking of his grandfather brought back.

"Before he passed away, he told me that one day the Logan banner would fly over the Princess again. He said you'd promised him it would, and he believed you."

"I meant to keep my promise," Josh told her, and feeling like the thirteen-year-old boy he'd been when he'd made the boast to his grandfather, he said, "I can still keep my promise to Granddad if you'll sell the hotel to me. I'll give you whatever you want, Duchess. Just name your price."

Olivia shook her head. "There is no price. If you want to keep your promise to Simon, you'll have to win the Princess from Laura—just as I won it from him."

A gust of wind whipped down the street, and Olivia pulled her coat tightly about her. "You'd better go," Josh told her, and helped her into the car.

He stepped back from the curb, when the window slid down. "I want your word, Joshua. This stays between you and me until I can sort through things with Adrienne."

"All right. But then you need to tell Laura. Because if you don't, I will."

Eighteen

"Hello, sunshine."

"Nick! What a surprise," Laura said three weeks later. Putting aside the room reports she'd been reviewing, she sat back in the chair at her desk. Instead of signing the vouchers on her desk, she decided to forget multitasking and enjoy the luxury of doing absolutely nothing for a moment but talking to her old friend on the phone. "It's so good to hear from you. How are things going? Is the new assistant GM working out all right? What about Jen, did she have her baby yet?"

Nick chuckled. "I see becoming a GM hasn't changed you. You're still moving at the speed of light."

"I'm sorry. I guess I have been moving at a quick pace lately."

"In answer to your questions, things are great. While Abby isn't you, she's working out, and I'm sure she's going to do just fine. And Jen had her baby yesterday. A boy. Nine pounds and six ounces, and they've named him Michael James."

"What a lovely name. I'll have to send her a note and gift. Thank you for letting me know."

"She told me to be sure and let you know that it was a baby boy, after all."

"She swore it would be," Laura replied. Suddenly

her eyes misted as she listened to Nick's voice, thought of him, her friends back in San Francisco.

As though he'd detected her melancholy, he asked, "Laura, are you all right?"

"Yes. Yes, I'm fine," she said as she dabbed at her eyes with a tissue. "I'm just missing you and everyone there."

"You can always come back," he teased.

"Yes, I know. You made that clear, and I appreciate it. I'm also grateful to you for understanding. I know I left you in a bind, resigning the way I did. I just never expected…I never thought I'd want to stay."

"Hey, no feeling guilty. We discussed this, remember? You made the right decision. I would have done the same thing if I'd been in your shoes. So tell me, how are you holding up, Miss General Manager?"

"Pretty good actually," she told him. "I've been putting in some long days, but things are coming together. The hotel staff has been great. And Katie and Ali, my…my sisters," she qualified after a brief hesitation, realizing that she had begun to think of them as her sisters, which was something she never would have thought possible two months ago. "My sisters have been a godsend. Working with Josh has been wonderful, even invigorating. He knows so much about hotel operations and has such a fresh approach to management problems."

"Logan always was sharp," he said, but Laura thought she detected concern in his voice. "I'm surprised he agreed to work as a consultant, considering he's in the same business and you're working for a competitor."

"His family and the Jardines are good friends, sort

of friendly rivals. I'm sure he only agreed to take the job as a favor to Olivia Jardine.''

"Somehow I doubt that was Josh's primary motivation. He made no secret of his attraction to you when he came to San Francisco. The man's no fool, sunshine. He knows working as a consultant at that hotel gives him more access to you.''

"Maybe," she said, unable to help being pleased at the thought that she had played into Josh's decision. "Whatever his reasons, Josh has been a good friend to me.'' And she was beginning to worry that her feelings for him were moving beyond friendship. In fact, had it not been for the fact that she'd been working practically around the clock, she suspected they would already be lovers. All those long, drugging kisses, the innocent brush of fingertips, the caress of a cheek, those steamy looks he sent her across a meeting room table were slowly driving her insane.

"Did you hear me, Laura?"

"I'm sorry," she said, embarrassed to have been caught daydreaming about having sex with Josh. "What was that?"

"I said I ran into Paul yesterday."

At the mention of her uncle's name, guilt niggled at her. He hadn't been happy at her decision to remain in New Orleans, and she suspected the reason she hadn't heard from him was because he was upset with her. "How is he?"

"All right, I guess. Maybe a little sad. I suspect he misses you like everyone else. He said he hadn't talked to you for a while. You might want to give him a call."

"I'll do that. Thanks for letting me know."

"Anytime," Nick told her. "Well, I know you're busy, and I don't want to keep you. But I had a free moment and wanted to call and wish you a Merry Christmas. I love you and miss you, sunshine. Remember to take care of yourself.''

"I will. I love and miss you, too, Nick. Merry Christmas.''

As she hung up the phone, Laura glanced up and her heart stuttered at the sight of Josh in the doorway. He was dressed all in black—black sweater, black jeans and black boots—but it was the thunderous expression on his face, the dangerous gleam in those green eyes, that gave her pause. "Hi, I didn't realize you were here," she said, doing her best to sound nonchalant.

"Obviously.''

Laura hiked up her chin at his tone. "What's that supposed to mean?''

"It means I don't like coming here to surprise you by suggesting we spend the evening together and finding you on the phone telling another man that you love him.'' He marched over to the front of her desk, slapped his palms on the surface. "And I especially don't like it when you've never once said those words to me.''

"That was Nick," she explained, stunned by his anger.

"I know damn well who it was. And I still don't like it.''

Outraged at his high-handed manner, Laura fired back, "That's tough. Just because we've been out a few times and shared a few kisses doesn't mean I owe you any explanations. Now, if you'll excuse me, I have work to do.'' Dismissing him, she picked up the room report and made a determined point of focusing on it.

She didn't even hear him move. Lightning fast, he'd spun the chair about so that she faced him and planted a hand on either side of her, caging her between the chair and him. "We've been on a few dates, shared a few kisses," he mimicked, his face so close that she could see the rim of black around those angry green eyes. "Are you going to sit there and tell me that that's all there is between us?"

Laura swallowed, tried to hear above the pounding of her heart. "It's true."

"Liar," he growled.

The denial died on her lips and her fast-beating heart jumped in her chest as he swooped down and took her mouth. He possessed her mouth, Laura thought, for there was no other word to describe the thrill that shot through her as his mouth demanded, tempted, seduced.

The taste of him was dark. Dangerous. Potent.

And she couldn't get enough.

Her blood heated, sending liquid fire spilling through her veins as the taste of him curled through her system. Desire clawing at her, she fisted her hands in all that rich black hair and deepened the kiss. This time she took. And Josh gave. She possessed. Josh surrendered. Arching her back, Laura pressed her breasts against his chest, wanting him to feel the frantic rhythm of her heartbeat, the burning need inside her for him. So lost in the feel and taste of him, Laura couldn't keep the sound of protest from escaping her lips when he lifted his head.

"Look at me, Laura," he commanded, his voice rough, edgy.

Opening her eyes, she looked at his face, saw the anger and the hurt that glittered in his eyes. "You still want to claim there's nothing between us? That I have no right to be angry? That I have no right to object to you telling another man that you love him when it's me who makes you tremble? When it's me who makes your heart race?''

Her fury at his possessive manner had faltered beneath the onslaught of his kiss. But it was the hurt behind his words, in his voice, that vanquished the last of her temper. ''It was only Nick, Josh. He's my friend.''

''And what am I, Laura?''

''You're my friend. A very special friend,'' she told him.

''And if I want more?'' he asked, sliding his hand into her hair and tilting her head so that she could see nothing but him. He kissed her softly, sweetly.

''D-define *more*,'' she managed to say as the heat began to build in her again.

''What if I want a relationship?'' he asked against her lips while he began easing open the buttons of her blouse, replacing his fingers with his mouth as he bared her flesh. ''What if I want to be your lover?''

''Yes,'' she told him as the desire sprinted through her. ''Yes, I want you,'' she told him, and streaked her hands down his shoulders, his arms, to the waist of his pants. Now that she'd made the decision, she was eager to see him naked, to taste and touch all those hard, taut muscles. When she reached for the buckle of his belt, Josh caught her hands.

''Laura, darling, you've got to slow down,'' he told her, his voice ragged. ''Otherwise, you're going to find yourself naked and stretched out on that desk.''

When she looked at the desk in question, Josh groaned and grabbed her by the arm. ''I'll be damned if the first time I make love to you I'm going to do it on a desk with cleaning staff roaming the halls. Let's go.''

"Where are we going?" she asked as he thrust her bag at her and grabbed her coat from the hook on the door.

He pulled the coat around her, kissed her hard. "My place, where there's a bed—if I can manage to make it out of the garage without hauling you into the back seat first."

They made it to his place. Barely. Somehow Josh managed the short drive from the hotel to his house and got them inside the front door despite the hunger for Laura that threatened to consume him.

"Where's the bedroom?" she asked, and sent desire spiking to a new level.

He spun her around, pressed her against the door and satisfied some of the raw need inside him by savaging her mouth with another kiss. Though it cost him, he released her long enough to get her out of her coat.

"I want you," she told him, and fused her mouth to his once more.

For the space of a heartbeat, when her hands streaked up under his sweater and tried to rip the shirt from his skin, Josh considered forgetting about the bed and making do with the floor. Instead, he pulled his mouth free, scooped her into his arms and charged up the stairs.

He stumbled into the room, placed her on the edge of the bed and made himself release her. Telling himself he needed to slow down or he'd cheat them both by not taking the time to savor each moment, he dragged in a steadying breath. When she reached for him again, he caught her hands. "Darling, you're in the South now," he told her as he brought those slim, soft fingers to his mouth and kissed them. "Down here we try to take things slower. It's more enjoyable that way," he told her, and releasing her hands, he dropped down before her and took off first one pretty high heel...and then the other.

He slid his hands up her ankles, her calves, every inch of those long, silk-covered legs, and felt each tremble, each quiver go through her at his touch. An image of those legs wrapped around him while he was buried inside her heat flashed through his mind, and sent that ball of lust shooting straight to Josh's loins. Beating back the urge to rush, he took his time sliding his palms up higher beneath her skirt, over her hips to the waistband of her panty hose. He pulled the hose down slowly, kissing each inch of that satin skin as he exposed it.

By the time he'd removed her skirt and peeled off her blouse, he was sweating bullets despite the chill in the room. Still he refused to hurry. To do so would be a sin. He wanted to savor each sigh, each moan that came from her incredible mouth. He wanted to savor each quiver, each shudder that sweet, slim body made. "You're so beautiful," he said at the sight of her in the two scraps of lace.

When he unhooked her bra and filled his palms with her breasts, she whimpered. He took her into his mouth, circled one rosy nipple with his tongue while he massaged the other with his thumb.

"Josh, please," she cried out, arching against him. "I can't stand this."

But she did stand it. So did he when she yanked off his sweater, wrestled the buttons open on his shirt and pressed her hot mouth to his skin. She tore at his belt, fumbled with his zipper, and he shucked off his jeans and briefs. When she reached for him, closed her fist around him, his vision blurred.

He swore, "Dammit, Laura! Wait!"

"I can't wait. I won't wait."

"Yes, you can. You will."

And he made them both wait because he wanted to bind her to him, to possess her, to make her his as no one else ever had, as no one else ever would again. And it was that need to make her his alone that had him hanging on to his control.

Easing one knee between her thighs, he cupped her. She lifted her hips, pressing herself against his hand. He eased one finger inside her and then another, and felt her muscles contract around him. Then he began to move inside her, and within moments she exploded and cried out his name.

He took her up again, watched those beautiful blue eyes register shock as pleasure vibrated through her, through him. And when she was moaning, gasping, cursing him, and he could wait no longer, he reached for the packet of protection he'd had the good sense to remember. He ripped it open with his teeth, sheathed himself. "Open your eyes, Laura. I want to see your eyes, I want you to see mine when I come inside you."

When her lashes fluttered and she was looking at his face, he entered her in one swift stroke. He sucked in a breath, bit off a moan and willed himself not to move yet. She was so tight, so hot, so wet. And she fit him like a glove.

With a control he didn't know he possessed, he began to move inside her slowly. In and out, nearly withdrawing each time before entering her again, each stroke a little harder, a little deeper, a little faster until he was sure he would die from the pleasure.

"Josh!" She screamed his name, dug her fingers into his flesh. "I can't..."

"Yes, you can, darling. You can," he urged her, taking her up again, and again, drinking the cries of pleasure from her lips.

And when he could wait no longer, he surged into her one last time, and in a cry of triumph, he followed her over that cliff.

He didn't want to move, wasn't all that sure he could, Josh admitted. With Laura beneath him all soft and silky and warm, her arms and legs still tangled with his, he couldn't imagine a nicer way to end a day. Or to begin one. Aware of his heavy weight pressing into her, he rolled over onto his back, and brought that long, trim body of hers sprawling across him.

He stroked her head, ran his hand down her back and felt her tremble beneath his touch. And although he'd have sworn he was wasted, incapable of recovering so quickly, desire licked through him, and he felt the distinctive stirring begin again in his loins.

He made love with her again. And this time he allowed her to set the pace. With the edge off his hunger and hers, he encouraged her to take her time, to go more slowly. And when she would have hurried him, hurried them both to completion, he gentled her as though she were a champion racehorse at the starting gate.

Instead, he took his time and showed her the pleasures of not rushing, of going slow, by exploring each curve, each dip, each line of her body. He showed her the pleasure that could be found in savoring each sigh, each gasp, each moan that came from her lips.

And when she lowered herself onto him, sheathed him once more in her heat, he gripped her hips and gave over the control to her. He allowed Laura to show him the excitement that could be found in not waiting, the thrill of flying at breakneck speed, and the glory of flying blindly into the storm.

Laura found him in the den—barefoot, bare-chested and wearing the same black jeans she remembered trying to rip from his body a few hours ago—crouched before the hearth. As he added more wood to the fire, muscles rippled across his shoulders and back, sparking memories of the feel of those muscles beneath her palm, the heat of his skin. He set a match to the kindling. The tiny light sparked, burst into flame and began licking at the logs. And as the scent of seasoned oak and fire curled in the air, Laura could feel desire curling inside her again.

As though he sensed her presence, Josh looked up and smiled. "Hi."

"Hi," she said, wrapping the robe she'd found in his bathroom around her. "I hope you don't mind. I had trouble finding some of my things and thought I'd locate them before getting dressed."

"I don't mind at all. It looks good on you," he told her. He moved toward her, caught the belt of the robe. "But I think I prefer you wearing nothing at all."

Laura flushed at his frankness, felt the quick spurt of desire kick through her at the heated look in his eyes. Feeling awkward, she took a step back and swallowed while she tried to steady her thoughts. "I... um...what happened..." She whooshed out another breath. "I don't want you to think I usually just hop into bed with someone I've only known for a short time. I mean, what I'm trying to say is I'm not casual about sex."

"Laura..." He said her name patiently and tipped her chin up. "I never thought you were. Neither am I." He smiled at her, and Laura's knees went weak. "This doesn't have to be awkward, darling. We're lovers. You and I have been heading down this road from the first day we met. In fact, I've been heading down it a bit longer than you since I knew that I wanted you the moment Olivia showed me your picture and asked me to go see you in San Francisco."

"Is that why you came?"

"It's one of the reasons. But if you're asking if I went there planning for us to become lovers, the answer is no. I didn't plan it, but it's what I wanted. And I've known since that day I picked you up at the airport in New Orleans that it was only a matter of time before we did become lovers."

"I see," she said, not sure whether to be pleased or insulted. "You were very sure of yourself. And me."

"Darling, I wasn't sure at all. I didn't want to want you. And I knew you didn't want to want me. But we did, and we do. Deal with it. And while you're dealing with the fact that we're lovers, you might also want to deal with the fact that I have no intention of sharing you with Nick Baldwin or anyone else as long as we're involved."

"All right," she said. "For the record, Nick and I are just friends. He and I...the two of us were never lovers. We never had an affair."

"I'm glad to hear that. But you and I aren't having an affair, either. I told you earlier, I want a relationship with you—in and out of bed—in and out of the office. I care about you. In fact, I think I'm falling in love with you."

A spurt of fear kicked through her. "Josh, I don't

know what to say. I'm flattered, even tempted. But my life is all mixed up right now. I came here searching for answers…searching for a part of myself that I felt I'd lost. I never planned on accepting Olivia's offer, or falling into bed with you. I'm still not sure I made the right decision about either of those things.''

"And do you always have to be sure of everything? Do you always have to know how something is going to end?''

"Usually," she said. "It's safer that way. I don't like surprises.''

"Sometimes surprises can be fun. Like my falling for you. That was a fun surprise. You're really not my type, you know. But for some reason, I'm nuts about you. The way you look, the way you taste," he murmured, and proved it by sampling her lips. When he reached for her hand, urged her down to the rug with him, the haze of desire began clouding her brain again.

"The way you feel. I love the way you feel," he whispered against her mouth as he untied the sash of the robe and opened her to him. He shrugged out of his jeans, moved between her thighs and slid into her. "And I love the way you make me feel whole when I'm inside you."

When Laura came awake again, the fire was still burning in the hearth, casting the room in a soft, warm glow. Sitting up, she looked around the cozy den that she had paid little notice when she'd first arrived. She noted a pair of comfy-looking couches each with a brightly colored afghan draped over the back, two over-stuffed chairs, a wood-and-glass coffee table with a scattering of books atop it. Bookcases lined with books took up an entire wall. Framed photos of members of his family were crammed atop tables, the mantel and every available space.

And then she spied the Christmas tree—a huge blue spruce with its lush bluish green branches covered in white lights and ornaments and an angel perched at the top that stretched up toward the vaulted ceiling. Beneath the tree were dozens of brightly wrapped packages trimmed with ribbon.

Unable to resist, Laura padded over to the tree. She stroked her finger over an ornament in the shape of a star, delighted in the shimmer as it swung on the branch. When she tipped a small gold bell on one of the branches and heard the musical tingle, she smiled.

"Do you like my tree?" Josh asked as he came up behind her carrying a tray with cups of hot chocolate and a bowl of marshmallows and two skewers.

"It's lovely," she said as she looked at the contents of his tray and arched her brow.

"I thought we might roast a few marshmallows to go with the hot chocolate," he told her as he set the tray on the table. "But first, I want to give you your present."

"My present?"

"Your Christmas present," he told her, and stooped down to retrieve a package wrapped in gold foil with a red ribbon from beneath the tree. "I know it's early. But I wasn't sure we'd have much time alone together between your family and mine, so I thought I'd give it to you now. It was the other reason I came to the hotel looking for you tonight."

Laura took the box, simply stared at it a moment, at the tag that read To Laura From Josh. "You didn't have to get me a gift."

"I know that. I wanted to. Go ahead, open it."

She'd never been one of those people who could patiently remove the ribbon and paper from a present. She wasn't patient now. Excited, she yanked off the beautiful bow and tore away the gold paper. She lifted off the top and peeled back layers of tissue to reveal a beautiful jeweled egg. It reminded her of the famous Fabergé eggs, set with diamond- and emerald- and ruby-colored stones. Taking care, she lifted it from its bed of tissue and held it up against the lights of the Christmas tree. "Josh, it's beautiful," she whispered.

"There's a little catch here," he showed her, pressing a small lever. "You open the egg, and there's a surprise."

She did as he'd instructed, and when she lifted the top of the egg, a haunting melody began to play and two ice skaters at the center of the egg began to dance. "It's a music box," she whispered.

"It's playing 'Lara's Theme.' I know the spelling is different, but I saw it and thought of you. I hope you like it."

"Like it? I love it," she said, tears filling her eyes. And if she wasn't very, very careful she was going to find herself believing Josh. Believing that they really could have a future together. Believing that she really could have a life and family here.

Nineteen

Laura awoke Christmas morning to the feel of tiny hands tugging away her covers and disturbing a delicious dream where she'd been alone in a meadow, making love with Josh.

When she reached to pull the covers over her again and try to catch the dream before it faded, she heard, "Aunt Lawwa. Wake up." And off went the covers again.

Groggy, she struggled to sit up. "Tori? What is it, honey?" she asked her niece, who had climbed up into the bed with her.

"Need to wake up," Tori insisted again. "C'mon."

Laura glanced at her clock, saw that it wasn't yet seven. "But honey, it's early. And it's Saturday."

"It's Christmas," Tori informed her. "Santa Claus came and bringed us bunches of stuff. C'mon."

"Okay, angel, I'm coming. But could Aunt Laura go to the potty first?" she asked, and sprinted for the bathroom.

She'd barely exited the bathroom when Tori grabbed her hand, and Laura allowed herself to be dragged down the stairs.

Laughing, for the next two hours she found herself caught up in the swirl of Christmas seen through the eyes of a child. Even Adrienne's cool disapproval of her arriving downstairs in her robe and slippers had failed to dim her spirits. Laura excused herself just long enough to get dressed and returned to enjoy the rest of the morning. She shared in Tori's delight as she uncovered each special treasure left by Santa.

When Ali asked her to join them for Christmas Mass, Laura had gone with the family. Discovering that the Jardines were Catholic hadn't come as a surprise to her, because although her mother had been of another faith, she had baptized and raised Laura Catholic. Laura remembered asking her why, and she'd accepted her mother's explanation that her father was Catholic, and it would have been what he wanted.

During the mass, she thought of all that had happened. Sometime during the months since her mother's death and now, the anger and hurt she'd felt toward her mother for deceiving her had passed. She'd never found the answers she'd hope to find in New Orleans, and had resigned herself she probably never would. She still didn't understand or condone what her mother had done, but she had forgiven her, Laura realized.

Her eyes misted as she listened to the priest give his sermon about the birth of the Christ child in the manger. She thought of her mother, of how much she must have suffered and sacrificed for her. *I miss you, Mom, and I love you.* Laura prayed in silence.

She missed her mother. There was no way she would ever celebrate this particular holiday and not miss her mother. But the grief now wasn't quite as sharp. She could think of past Christmases without unleashing a flood of pain, Laura realized as they left church to return to the house.

During the drive, she thought of her uncle Paul and felt a prickle of guilt. Had she been wrong not to honor his request and fly home to San Francisco to spend the holiday with him? she wondered. She had cited work and time as an excuse, but Laura knew that wasn't entirely true. She could have found a way to make the trip, if she had wanted to do so, she admitted. But she hadn't gone because she had wanted to be here. In New Orleans. She had wanted to spend Christmas with Josh. And, she admitted, she had wanted to spend it with her family. Because she had begun to think of them as her family, Laura realized. Ali, Katie, Mitch. Perhaps it was the holiday season, but she'd even felt a softening toward Olivia.

The car had barely stopped in the drive before Tori was scrambling to get free of her seat belt. When Laura exited the car, she reached for her hand. "C'mon, Aunt Lawwa. Play tea wif me."

There was no way Laura could resist. She settled down in the living room with Tori and entered her make-believe world. "Oh, thank you." Laura played along and pretended to drink tea from the cup that Tori had served her. "It's delicious. Could I have some more?"

Beaming, Tori refilled her cup.

"Grammaw, want more tea?" Tori asked Olivia.

"Why, I'd love some, dear," Olivia said, and had Tori grinning in delight as she played the game.

"Hey, what about me?" Katie asked as she came bustling into the room, her arms laden with packages.

"It's about time you got here," Ali told her twin as she promptly began relieving her sister of her packages. "I've been waiting for you to get here so we can give Laura her gift."

Ali dragged a large brightly wrapped box from beneath the tree and handed it to Laura. "This is from me and Katie. Hurry up, open it. I can't wait to see what you think.''

Knowing what wonderful taste Ali had, Laura was eager to open it too. But first she said, ''Tori, why don't you come help me open this big box?''

Tori didn't need further coaxing. Between the two of them they sent ribbon and paper and tissue flying. When Laura shoved away the piles of tissue, she sucked in a breath. It was a dress. Or rather an exquisite replica of a gown worn by a Spanish *señorita.* Made of scarlet satin and black lace, the skirt was full, the bodice cut low.

''There's more,'' Ali told her, and Laura dug through more tissue and found the black lace mantilla.

''Ali…Katie…I don't know what to say.''

''You might try 'thank you,''' Katie said saucily. ''You do realize it's your costume for the masquerade ball.''

''Yes,'' Laura replied. Somehow she'd never gotten around to finding a costume. While she'd told herself it was a question of time, Laura suspected she'd delayed finding a gown because she hadn't been at all sure she would still be here by the time Mardi Gras came around.

''When Katherine and Alison told me what they'd planned to give you, I thought you might like to have this,'' Olivia said, and handed her a slim, wrapped box.

Laura took the package, and after tearing away the paper, she opened the box. Nestled on a bed of crushed velvet was an ivory cameo brooch attached to a black satin ribbon. ''It's lovely,'' Laura said. She traced the delicate carving of a woman's face, struck by its beauty and familiarity. Then it hit her. ''It looks like you,'' she told Olivia.

She nodded. "I was a Spanish *señorita* at my first masquerade ball in a costume very similar to yours. Someone very dear to me had the cameo made especially for me. He gave it to me as a gift to wear with my costume that night. I only wore it that one time."

And she'd been in love with the man who'd given her the brooch, Laura surmised, sensing a sadness, a loneliness in the older woman as she stared at the cameo, ran her fingertip over the carving. She tried to imagine Olivia as a young woman in love and attending her first ball. Surprisingly, she could, and in that moment Olivia seemed far less the formidable dragon she'd believed her to be all these months and simply a woman who had loved and lost. What had happened to the man who'd given her the brooch? Laura wondered, but suspected if she asked, Olivia wouldn't give her the answer. "Perhaps you should keep it," Laura suggested.

"No," Olivia dropped her hand. "It's yours now. Whether you choose to wear it or not is your decision."

"I'll be honored to wear it. Thank you."

Returning the cameo to its velvet box, Laura couldn't help but think of Josh and wonder if she would be left with sad memories when their time together ended. For it would end, Laura conceded. She'd known that from the start. She'd accepted Olivia's challenge, told herself she'd do her best for the six months, and then she'd be on her way. And while the financial situation at the Princess had improved, it was still operating in the red. With only four months of her trial period left, it would be difficult at best to bring the operation into the black on time. Even if she did, she'd never intended to stay.

"May I see it?" Adrienne asked.

Pulled from her somber musings, Laura handed Adrienne the brooch. While Adrienne studied the piece, Laura studied her. As always, the other woman was dressed stylishly in a festive green suit with diamonds and emeralds at her ears. Her makeup was perfect, and not a single blond hair was out of place. And the woman left Laura absolutely cold. Not that she could blame her. If anything, Adrienne's cool civility toward her when their paths crossed was admirable. And except for the night of her arrival, she'd never again heard the other woman voice any objections to her presence. But Laura didn't kid herself that Adrienne Jardine merely tolerated her and would have preferred it that Laura not stay. She also suspected that she hadn't approved of Laura's growing relationship with her children.

"How sweet," Adrienne said, handing the brooch back to her. "I suppose you'll be attending the masquerade ball, then?"

Until now, Laura hadn't been at all sure that she would. But with the gift of the dress from her sisters, Olivia's brooch and the distinct impression that Adrienne would prefer that she not attend, Laura couldn't resist. "I wouldn't miss it."

"Speaking of the ball," Ali said as she extricated herself from Tori. "I'll be sending out the invitations next week. Laura, is there anyone back in San Francisco that you'd like to invite?"

"As a matter of fact, there is," Laura replied, thinking of Uncle Paul and Nick.

"Fine. Just get me the names and addresses, and I'll put them on the list."

Two months. They had been lovers for two months now, Josh mused, and still he found her fascinating and himself thinking of her all the time. Amused at himself, he stood in the doorway of Laura's office and watched her forehead crease as she read the report in front of her. Her lips pulled into a frown, and she snatched up a pencil, made some notation, then went back to poring over the papers as though they held the secrets to life itself.

She was incredible. Or maybe he was just a lovesick idiot because he actually liked watching that analytical brain of hers at work. There was something incredibly sexy about the way she gave those reports her complete focus, he thought with a smile. And it amazed him that he could find himself as mesmerized by the sight of Laura tallying up numbers as he had at having her naked in his bed only a few hours ago. At the admission, he scrubbed a hand down his face.

Damn, you've got it bad, Logan, he told himself. Wouldn't his sisters find it a hoot? He'd managed to go fall in love with a woman who not only wouldn't admit to being in love with him, but she had convinced herself that their relationship was only temporary. Oh, she'd managed to dodge the issue neatly whenever he'd brought up the subject. She refused to ever spend an entire night with him, always insisted on returning to her grandmother's before dawn. She'd shot down his suggestion she get her own place because she didn't want to commit to a lease when she was still working on a trial basis at the Princess.

Josh scowled. Did she think he was blind to the fact that she saw their relationship as temporary, too? A stopover to coincide with her trial period at the Princess. Did she honestly think that regardless of what happened at the Princess three months from now when her trial period was over that he would just let her pack up her bags, leave the city and him? If she did, Ms. Laura Harte was sadly mistaken. But then she didn't know about the determination of the Logan clan. He wanted her, and he'd be damned if he wouldn't have her.

Clamping down on the emotions stirring in him, he reminded himself about the importance of timing. And now was not the time to tell the woman she was going to marry him. She'd find out soon enough. Right now, he had to break the news that he wouldn't be able to see her for the next two weeks.

He tapped on the door. "Morning," he said as he strolled into the office and over to her and kissed her hard on the mouth.

"Josh." His name came out as part gasp, part whisper. The huskiness in her voice and that glazed look in her eyes had his body growing hard, a reminder to him of how lonely the nights would be without her these next two weeks. "Is it time for the meeting already?"

"Not yet," he told her, and deciding to steal another taste of her to tide him over, he sieved his fingers in her hair, held her head and kissed her again. This time softly, tenderly. When he lifted his head, he regretted even more that he'd committed to handling the negotiations on the Logan Hotels acquisition in London.

"I was just going over the financial reports before we meet with Olivia. Did you want to see them?"

"In a minute. I came by early because I wanted to tell you that I'm going out of town for the next couple of weeks. We're at a critical point in negotiations for a hotel in London, and since I'm the one who put the deal together initially, I have to be there for it."

"Of course. I understand," she told him. "I'm surprised you haven't been out of town more as it is. You told me at Thanksgiving that after the first of the year, you'd be traveling a lot.''

Leaning against the edge of the desk, he took her hand in his and stroked her palm with his thumb. ''I should have been, but since I'd much rather be here with you, I've made a point of delegating and rearranging my schedule so I wouldn't have to be away more than a day at a time. Unfortunately, I can't do that with this one.'' Tugging on her fingers, he pulled her to stand between the vee of his thighs. ''Will you miss me while I'm gone?''

''Yes,'' she whispered, cupping his cheek. ''I'll miss you.''

He kissed her palm as it slid along his jawline, looked up into her eyes. ''Enough to stay with me tonight?''

''I…Josh, you know I can't. What would I say to Olivia? To Ali or her mother?'' she asked, already withdrawing emotionally even though he still held her hand.

''You might try telling them the truth.''

She pulled her hand free, temper and fear swimming in her eyes. ''What? That they shouldn't expect to see me in the morning because I'll be spending the night with my lover?''

''Well, at least that's part of the truth,'' he told her, unable to keep the bitterness from his voice.

''What's that supposed to mean?''

''It means, my sweet little cynic, that whether you choose to acknowledge it or not, we're involved in a serious relationship with each other.''

That stubborn chin of hers jerked up. ''That's what I said, didn't I?''

"No, you said that we were lovers. But for you the word implies our relationship is only a physical one. Well, darling, it's not. I'm in love with you," he shouted the words at her. "And if you'd take those blinders off, you might realize that you're in love with me, too."

Her face paled, and damn if she didn't look terrified, he thought. Regretting his loss of patience, he reached for her. "Laura—"

She stepped back. "Oh, no, you don't. I'm not going to let you push me on this, Josh. Just because the sex between us is good doesn't mean—"

Temper had him seeing red, and before he could stop himself, Josh grabbed her by the wrist. "Don't," he said, unable to keep the threat from his voice. "Don't insult me or yourself by cheapening what we have."

And because he didn't quite trust himself, he released her and stepped back. "Give Olivia my apologies, but I think I'll skip the meeting and see if I can't get an earlier flight to London."

"Josh, wait," she called after him when he started out the door.

He turned around to look at her, refusing to allow himself to be moved by her distress. "Yes?"

"You said you'd be gone for two weeks. The masquerade ball is only twelve days away. Will you...will you be back in time for it?"

Because he was hurting, and she was the cause, he said, "I don't see that it should matter to you. After all, I'm only the guy you occasionally sleep with. I'm sure you can find a replacement easily enough." And then he turned and walked out the door before he made an even bigger fool of himself by staying.

* * *

He wasn't coming.

Laura felt the sting of tears behind her mask as she finally admitted the truth. Josh had been gone for nearly two weeks now. When the first week had gone by and he hadn't called her, she'd thrown herself into work, done her best not to think about him and had managed not to pick up the phone. By the middle of the second week, she'd swallowed her pride, called his office and left him a message. That had been two days ago. And he hadn't returned her call.

"Champagne, miss?"

"No, thank you," Laura told the waiter, and continued to wander about the grand ballroom, feigning interest in the elaborate and often outrageous costumes the guests wore. Alight with music and laughter, the ball was no doubt a success, she surmised. Thanks to Ali's efforts.

Her sister had done an incredible job, Laura thought with pride, as she considered the work that had gone into transforming the hotel's ballroom into what now resembled a royal palace's garden. Faux pillars of gold with guards stood at the entranceway. Tiny white lights had been strung through trees moved inside to add to the outdoor effect. A ceiling the color of midnight dotted with shimmering stars completed the feeling of nighttime in the garden. Flowers were everywhere—roses, azaleas, exotic lilies. Fountains flowed with champagne. Ice sculptures in the shape of swans glistened atop a mock pond with floating blossoms made of spun sugar. Waiters dressed like royal guards stood at carving stations serving prime rib and pork, while others manned tables with choices of succulent shrimp, marinated crab legs and salmon. Still two more stations boasted an array of Ali's mouth-watering pastries.

Despite the masks, she recognized several of the guests as local politicians, prominent citizens and members of the press. Her sisters looked fabulous in their matching southern belle outfits, and Olivia very much resembled the formidable Catherine the Great, whose costume she'd chosen. Mitch looked quite dashing in his pirate disguise, and Adrienne was difficult to ignore as an elegant Madame Pompadour. It seemed half the city of New Orleans had turned out for the masquerade ball. So had the members of the Logan family. Everyone had come except Josh.

"Say, why the long face, sunshine?"

Shaking off her melancholy, Laura smiled at Nick, who'd chosen to come as a Confederate soldier. "Just a little tired," she told him. "It's been a long day and an even longer night. Did I tell you how glad I am that you came?"

"Several times. Seriously, it was kind of you to invite me, Laura. I'm glad I came. It's been good to see you again. And it gave me a chance to catch up with old friends I hadn't seen in a long, long time."

"Friends like Faith Logan?" she asked, having noticed the two of them dancing together earlier.

He narrowed his eyes. "You can forget playing matchmaker, Ms. Harte. That horse race ended a long time ago, and I lost. Now, why don't you come with me to try some of the fabulous-looking desserts."

"I'll be happy to, Mr. Baldwin, since my sister Ali happens to be the chef."

"You're kidding? She's not only beautiful, but she can cook, too? Point her out to me, and I'll propose marriage right now."

Laughing, Laura tucked her arm in his and allowed him to walk with her around the room. "You're good for me, Nick. I didn't realize how much I'd missed seeing a familiar face from home.''

"Your uncle Paul couldn't make it, I take it?"

"No. He said he was too busy," she said, saddened by the distance between her and her uncle that she suspected had nothing to do with miles, and everything to do with her staying in New Orleans. "It's funny, but since he was the one who had initially encouraged me to meet my father's family, I thought he'd be more accepting of my decision to stay on for a while. Instead, it's just the opposite. I think he's hurt and even angry and sees my being here as a rejection."

"Maybe he didn't anticipate you wanting to stay and make it your home."

"But it's not my home," she told him, surprised that he thought it was. "My trial period at the Princess will be ending soon, and then I'll be coming home to San Francisco. My roots are there. It's where I belong."

Nick stopped, waved off a waiter and asked, "Are you sure, Laura? As much as I'd love to have you back, from what I've seen, you have roots here. You have a family that obviously cares about you. And that old adage about home being where the heart is...maybe you should give it some thought. Ask yourself where your heart is." He kissed her cheek. "I need to go, I have a meeting in the morning, and then I'll be leaving on an afternoon flight. Thanks again for inviting me."

After she bid him goodbye, Laura pretended to sip champagne and considered what Nick had said. As she did so, she couldn't stop her head from filling once more with thoughts of Josh, the things he'd said to her before he'd left, how angry he'd been. And as though she'd conjured him up in her mind, she glanced over at the doorway, where a man stood watching her. He was dressed all in black from his boots to the cape that hung over one shoulder. A strip of black cloth with slits for his eyes had been fashioned into a mask and tied at the back of his head. A dangerous-looking sword of silver hung at his side.

Her heart hammered triple time as she watched him cut a path through the crowd toward her. She stared at his mouth; surely she'd know Josh's mouth, she thought, but hesitated at the sight of the black mustache that covered his upper lip. By the time he reached her, Laura's throat had gone dry.

"Good evening, *señorita*," he said in an accented voice as he bowed and kissed her hand. "May I have this dance?"

Unable to speak, she nodded. And then he swept her into his arms. He danced her about the room while the band played a slow melody and sang a tale of love and loss, made all the more haunting by the accompaniment of violins. She stared at his face, sure that only Josh had eyes that color green. But he said nothing as he glided her about the floor, moving their bodies as one in time to the music.

When his gaze moved from her eyes to her mouth, her pulse jumped. As though he sensed her reaction, he pulled her closer. Her body responded instinctively, fitting to him intimately in the dance with music as she did with him in the dance of love. And by the time he waltzed her out into the real garden in the crisp night air and moonlight, her head was spinning and her heart was pounding.

"Laura." Her name sounded like a prayer on his lips. When he kissed her, she nearly wept with joy. Wrapping her arms around him, she gloried in the feel of his mouth, the taste of him, the heat of his passion as he made love to her with his mouth. When he ended the kiss much, much too soon, Laura heard a whimper, and realized it had come from her.

"Oh Josh, I've missed you so much. I tried to call, but—"

"Laura, are you out here?"

Recognizing Mitch's voice, she considered not answering for a moment, then thought better of it. "I'm here, Mitch," she called out, reluctantly leaving Josh's arms.

"Hi, I've been looking for you," he told Laura. "Is that you, Logan?"

"Sure is. Hi, Mitch," Josh said, extending his hand.

"We'd heard you were out of town and wouldn't be back for the ball," Mitch said, and Laura could have sworn the stern look he sent Josh had been a warning.

"Just got back less than an hour ago. I stopped home long enough to change into my costume and came here."

"Did you need me for something, Mitch?" Laura asked, picking up strong undercurrents laced with testosterone between the two men.

"I was hoping I could steal you for a dance."

His request surprised and pleased her. In the months since her arrival their relationship had grown warmer, closer. Mitch seeking her out for a dance somehow strengthened the tenuous bonds they'd been forming as siblings. "I'd like that," she said. "If you'll excuse me, Josh."

When Mitch danced her out onto the floor, she sensed there was something he wanted to tell her. So she asked. "Mitch, I think it's sweet of you to ask me to dance, but I have this feeling that's not why you came looking for me. Am I wrong?"

"No," he told her. "I saw Logan waltz you out there, and I didn't think it was a good idea."

Laura stopped dancing in the middle of the floor to look at him. "Mitchell Jardine, are you by any chance trying to play big brother?"

Grinning, he swung her into the dance again. "And what if I am?"

Laura felt a warm glow in her heart. "In case you forgot, I'm older than you."

"Yeah, but I'm bigger. So that qualifies me as a big brother. And part of the job description in the big brother's rule book is to watch out for little sisters when they're being circled by a wolf."

Laura laughed. She couldn't help it. "You think Josh is a wolf?"

"I think Josh Logan is a great guy. Don't get me wrong. We're friends. Katie, Ali and Grandmother think the world of him. And so do I."

"But…" Laura prompted.

"But whether he intends to or not, Josh is bad news when it comes to women. He's a heartbreaker. I'm not saying it's all his fault. It isn't. Women just get stupid where he's concerned and end up getting hurt." He paused and gave her a somber look. "You're my sister, Laura. I'd hate to see you get hurt."

The song ended, and moved beyond words, Laura stood up on her toes and kissed Mitch's cheek. "Thank you," she murmured, her voice thick with emotion. She swallowed hard and tried again. "I always wished I'd had a big brother when I was growing up. You can't know how happy I am to find out that I have one now, and that he's you."

"I'm glad, too," he told her.

She touched his cheek. "Thank you for caring

enough to warn me off Josh. But you don't have to worry. While I do admit I have feelings for him, I'm not wearing rose-colored glasses. I know what I'm doing.''

"All right. But promise you'll be careful. Because I'd hate to have to mess up Josh's pretty face and have my sisters and grandmother all mad at me."

She held up three fingers. "I promise."

"Okay. Go have yourself a good time. I'm going to check on the security."

"Is there a problem?" she asked.

"No. But there are enough diamonds and jewels in this place tonight to stock Tiffany's and Harry Winston's. We took out an extra policy for the evening and I have extra guards on hand undercover, but if a clever thief decided to hit the hotel, he'd hit the jackpot."

I have a brother.

As incredible as it seemed, at twenty-eight, she finally had a brother. A brother, she thought again, her heart full as she watched Mitch stride away. She had a brother. Wrapping her newfound joy close to her, she spun around and went in search of Josh to share the news.

Twenty

She was being seduced.

She wouldn't have thought it possible, had considered herself too practical to be seduced. Yet that's what was happening, Laura realized. Josh was seducing her. He had begun the seduction at the masquerade ball with that first dance, followed by that bone-melting kiss in the garden. After she'd returned to him in the garden following her conversation with Mitch, he'd swept her indoors amid the throng of people when all she'd wanted was to be alone with him, to rip off his clothes, to lose herself in his arms.

But the sly, sly man had insisted they stay at the ball. She had guests, he'd told her. Her grandmother would be disappointed, he'd said. So they'd stayed. And stayed.

And he'd spent the better part of three hours seducing her. He'd done it with all those seemingly innocent brushing of fingers, a gentle touch at her elbow, a lingering hand at her back. With those heated glances while they were in a conversation with her family. With those whispered promises in her ear of what he intended to do to her later just as a reporter approached. With those slow spins around the ballroom floor, his body moving in rhythm with hers, conducting a mating ritual under the guise of a dance.

By the time the last waltz ended and he'd driven them back to his house, she was vibrating with need like the plucked string of a harp. Once they were inside and Josh had closed the door, Laura grabbed the sword and cloak from his hands and tossed them to the floor. "God, I thought we'd never be alone," she told him, not bothering to hide the desperation in her voice.

"Laura darling—"

She launched herself at him, cutting off his words with a kiss. A thrill of pleasure sprinted up her spine as a moan slipped from his shocked lips. She ran her hands over his body. He was hard and hot, just as she remembered. Already she could see them together, their sweat-slicked bodies locked in an embrace. His mouth feasting on her breasts. His shaft—smooth as satin and hard as steel—buried deep inside her.

Josh pulled his mouth free, panted. "Laura, we—"

Impatient, she backed him up against the door and aimed for his mouth again. She kissed him, tried to tell him with her lips what she seemed unable to put into words. That he was important to her. So important that he scared her silly. That she was sorry they had fought, sorry that she'd hurt him, hurt herself. That she'd missed him more than she'd ever be able to put into words.

So she told him with her mouth. Of how she wanted to hold him close, to have him hold her. Of how she wanted to drink him in and have him fill her, as only he could fill her, until all those empty spaces inside her were healed. And she wanted it all now—fast, furious, wild.

Swearing at her, at himself, his eyes went hot and black, adding to her excitement and the explosive need. And when she kissed him again, he ravaged her mouth with his tongue and teeth until they were both trembling. When she attacked the buttons at the front of his shirt, Josh pulled his mouth free. He caught her frantic fingers and, gasping, he said, "Laura, wait!"

"I don't want to wait," she told him while she struggled to break free so she could return to the task of getting him naked. "I've waited all night," she complained, and had the satisfaction of hearing him groan when she nipped at his jaw. His grip loosened on her fingers for a second, and sensing her advantage, she dove lower in search of his zipper.

"Dammit, Laura! Hang on a minute—"

She brushed his bulging manhood with impatient fingers, and Josh swore again. Then he swooped down and savaged her mouth with his. When he abruptly ended the kiss a few moments later and held her away from him, he was panting. So was she.

After a moment, when she could speak again, she said, "I know what you're going to say. You're going to say we should talk."

"It seems like a good idea, don't you think?"

"Yes. No," she said, feeling frustrated and confused. "I don't want to talk, Josh. Talking just gets things mixed up between us, and you'll be angry with me again. I know that you think you love me..."

"I do love you," he corrected her.

"And I have feelings for you, Josh. Strong feelings. Feelings that I've never had for anyone else ever. You're...important to me."

"But..."

"But I didn't plan on you coming into my life. I didn't plan on so many things that have happened since I came here. I came here to find a part of myself that

I'd lost. How can I make promises to you when I still haven't kept the one to myself?"

"So what do you suggest we do?" he asked.

"Can't it be enough for now to know that it's you I want to be with? Only you."

"It's enough," he told her as he scooped her up into his arms and started toward the stairs. "For now. It's enough for now."

"For now," she repeated as he brought her to the bed and sent her heart and body spinning as he began to undress her.

When she eagerly reached for the snap at his slacks, he caught her fingers, kissed them. "Laura darling, I'm going to teach you the pleasures of going slow and easy."

True to his word, he taught her the pleasures of going slow, of going easy. And in what could have been hours or perhaps only moments later, she climaxed in an explosion of white light and searing heat.

Josh might have shown her the pleasures of doing some things slow, Laura thought with a smile as she zipped down the sidewalk after her meeting downtown. Walking, however, wasn't one of them. As she raced down the block, she caught sight of a row of azalea bushes bursting with bright pink and rose-colored blooms. Struck by their beauty, Laura sighed as she passed them and made a determined effort to slow her pace. Instead of dashing across the street when the pedestrian crossing light flashed yellow, she stopped at the corner and tipped her face up toward the April morning sunshine.

There was only one problem when a sprinter like herself decided to take a stroll, Laura decided ten minutes later as she glanced at her watch and rushed into the hotel. Her day had been scheduled at a sprinter's pace and didn't allow for ten extra minutes to stop and smell the roses.

Damn! She hated being late. Racing to the elevator banks, she punched the button. The display panel revealed all four cars were near the top floors. Tapping her foot impatiently, she watched the panel of lights indicating the elevators' slow descents and took another peek at her watch. Two minutes. She had two minutes to make it upstairs to the boardroom before the monthly financial meeting with Olivia and Josh was supposed to begin.

When the panel indicated that the nearest elevator had stopped on the tenth floor, Laura blew out a breath and resigned herself to the fact that she would be late. It wasn't the end of the world if she were a few minutes late, she told herself. But she couldn't help feel that by doing so, she was at a disadvantage, which she didn't like when it came to Olivia, she admitted. Despite the fact that she'd been living under the other woman's roof for more than five months, Olivia remained a stranger to her. She knew the distance between them was due in large measure to herself, Laura conceded. Olivia had made several attempts to forge a relationship with her—first with the cameo brooch and again at the masquerade ball. Yet each time Laura had felt a stirring of sentiment toward the older woman, images of that cruel note to her mother with a check flashed into her mind, and she'd instinctively pulled back. She'd told herself to let it go, had tried to let it go. But she simply couldn't.

The elevator bell sounded, breaking into Laura's thoughts. Now was not the time to be thinking of this, she reasoned while she waited for the doors to open and the passengers to begin to exit. What she needed now was to focus on her meeting. Despite Mardi Gras and the influx of spring conventions, the hotel had still operated at a loss. But the losses were smaller, and if she hit the numbers in her business plan for May she just might turn that red to black on the next month's financials. She wanted to hit the numbers for May. Part of it was her own pride in her abilities, she admitted. And part of it was to prove to Olivia that she could. The realization surprised her—especially since she still wasn't at all sure what she would do after next month.

Should she go home to San Francisco?

Her ties and her life were in San Francisco. It was where she belonged, she told herself. Then she thought of her sisters and Mitch and little Tori. Already she ached at the thought of leaving them. But there were telephones and airplanes, and they could visit one another.

And what about Josh?

Since his return from London, he'd honored her request and hadn't pressed her for an answer. But he would expect one soon. And he would deserve one. The idea of leaving him sent panic swimming in her blood. If only she didn't feel so confused.

"Morning, Miss Harte."

Laura yanked her gaze to Cliff Sabrion, the elevator operator who stood holding the door open for her. She smiled as he tipped the brim of the red-and-black hat that matched his uniform. Of average height and thinly built with skin darkened and lined as much by the hot Louisiana sun as from age, the joke among the staff was that Cliff had been here since the hotel had been built. "'Morning, Cliff. How are you this morning?"

"I'm just fine, miss. You going up?"

"Yes, I am. To the executive offices. And could you please use the express button? I'm running late for a meeting," she said.

"Yes, ma'am," he said.

When she stepped inside the car, she was surprised to see the petite woman seated on the stool that Cliff usually kept near the control panel. Dressed in a rose floral print, she held her purse and white gloves in her lap and an old-fashioned pillbox hat sat perched atop snow-white curls. The term "dressed in Sunday best" came to mind. "Hello," she said to the woman. "I'm Laura Harte."

"I'm Elizabeth Sabrion," she said with a friendly smile. "Clifford's wife."

"Today is my and Elizabeth's fifty-first wedding anniversary. We usually spend the day together, but since I was scheduled to work we thought it would be okay if she just rode up and down with me." He paused. "I hope you don't mind."

"Of course I don't mind," Laura said, moved by the couple's devotion to each other. "But you should have said something to Seymour and had him rearrange your schedule."

"Elizabeth and I don't mind. It seemed kind of fitting that we'd spend the day here seeing's how I fell in love with her the first time I saw her right here on this elevator. Kissed her here for the first time, too," he told her with a wink.

"Clifford," Elizabeth admonished. "I'm sure Miss Harte isn't interested in hearing about that."

"Oh, but I am," Laura told her, delighted by the story of their romance. "You were a guest at the hotel?"

"Oh, no, miss. I was a maid. It was my first day and I'd been assigned to take care of the rooms on the ninth floor. Back then there were only two elevators and no one told me that the one without an operator was the service elevator and that was the one I was supposed to use. So I just marched into the passenger elevator with my linen cart and told Clifford I needed the ninth floor." She blushed. "And Clifford, the naughty thing, he told me he'd come back to get me when I was ready to go down."

"Knew the minute I set eyes on her that she was the girl I was going to marry."

"What a lovely story. Thank you for telling me." When the elevator stopped at her floor, Laura thought of Olivia and Josh waiting. Then she thought of this man and woman so devoted to each other still after more than fifty years. Surely love like that deserved recognition. She glanced at her watch, frowned. Oh, what the heck. She was late already, she told herself. What difference would another few minutes make. "Cliff, can you set this car to stay here for a minute? I want you and Elizabeth to come with me to my office. I want to give you a little anniversary gift on behalf of the hotel."

"It's all taken care of," she told the couple five minutes later, and felt an enormous satisfaction. "Cliff, as of two minutes ago you are officially off duty and given today as a paid holiday. If you'll check at registration, you'll be given the keys to the honeymoon suite for tonight. You also have dinner reservations in the dining room at half past six." Knowing she was grinning like an idiot, Laura said, "Happy anniversary."

"Miss Harte, I don't know what to say—"

"Never in all my years did I think that we would ever spend the night in such a fancy hotel, and to stay at the Princess," Elizabeth gushed.

"It's my pleasure and the hotel's."

Elizabeth's eyes filled, and Laura wasn't at all surprised when the tiny woman gave her a hug. "Oh, what a sweet girl you are. Just like your mother. Your father would have been so proud of you."

Laura went still at the woman's words. "I..." She drew away, tried to catch her breath. "H-how would you know my mother?"

"Well, I didn't really know her. Just talked to her when I came up to clean her room for those few days she stayed here."

Laura felt the color drain from her face. Her hands trembling, she reached blindly for a chair, afraid if she didn't sit down, she would fall.

"Miss Harte? Are you all right? If I said something to upset you—"

"No, no," Laura said, barely managing to get the words out. "Please. You just took me by surprise. That's all." She sucked in a calming breath, tried to get her brain to function.

"Elizabeth didn't mean no harm, Miss Harte. And I apologize if she spoke out of turn," Clifford told her as he came to stand by his wife. He placed an arm around her shoulders. "But seeing's how Mrs. Jardine told the staff that you were her granddaughter, I didn't think there was any harm in telling Elizabeth."

"Of course there was no harm, Cliff. Please forgive me. As I said, Elizabeth mentioning my mother surprised me. When I first arrived I'd asked, but no one seemed to remember her. I can't imagine how you could remember her, Elizabeth. She was only here for a few days, and that was twenty-nine years ago.''

"Oh, I can explain that,'' Cliff offered. "Elizabeth here has one of those photocopy memories.''

"Photographic memories,'' Elizabeth corrected him. "And I can speak for myself, Clifford Sabrion.''

"Then you really do remember her?'' Laura asked, feeling both excitement and fear at the prospect. "Her name was Juliet Harte—no, she would have been Juliet Henderson back them.''

"I remember her. Pretty thing. Tall, but on the thin side. With hazel eyes and dark hair and the smile of an angel. I'd have remembered her, anyway, because she was very sweet to me. She talked to me like I was a real person, didn't just give orders or look through me the way some folks do. If you know what I mean?''

Laura nodded.

"But the other reason I remember her is because Mr. Andrew made such a fuss that everything be just perfect for her. He wanted to be sure she liked her room, that she had everything she needed. He gave me instructions to put a red rose on her pillow every night. Mr. Andrew was crushed when she up and left like she did.''

Laura's heart ached, and for the first time since learning the identity of her father, she felt a stirring of affection for him. "Do you...do you know why she left?''

"She never said. I knew she'd come here to meet Mr. Andrew's momma. I could tell she was scared and nervous. I mean, everyone knew Mr. Andrew was engaged to Miss Adrienne back then, and that Mrs. Jardine wanted that match.'' Elizabeth's expression softened as she seemed to lose herself in the past. "But sometimes our hearts tell us differently. And it was clear as glass that Mr. Andrew was in love with your momma and that she was in love with him. All a body had to do was see the way they looked at each other. She seemed like a brave little thing to me. I was real surprised when I came into her room that night and she told me she had to leave.''

''Did she say anything else? Did she say why she had to go?''

Elizabeth paused as though thinking. ''No. It was late, nearly ten o'clock, and I'd come into her suite to turn down the bed and put the rose on her pillow like Mr. Andrew wanted. And there she was. Her eyes all puffy, and her crying something fierce. She was trying to shut her suitcase and couldn't seem to see past all those tears that she had a shoe poking out the side.

''So I got a wet facecloth from the bathroom and poured her a glass of water to drink. Then I sat her down, wiped her face and told her to drink the water, and I'd take care of the suitcase.''

''What happened then?'' Laura asked.

''When she calmed down, she asked if I could get her a cab. Said she had to go to the airport. She was going home. And she gave me a letter and asked me to give it to Mr. Andrew for her when he came to the hotel in the morning.''

''But she didn't say why she was leaving?''

''No. She said something about the importance of family and honoring responsibility.''

Frustrated and disappointed, Laura asked, ''Did she see or talk to anyone else before she left?''

''I can't say for sure,'' she said and averted her gaze.

''Elizabeth, please. It's very important to me that I

know. I...did someone else besides my father come to see my mother while she was here?''

Cliff placed a hand on his wife's shoulder. "Tell her, Lizzie.''

"Mrs. Jardine was here about nine o'clock that evening. The only reason I know is because that's when I'd normally turn down the bed and leave the rose. I thought your momma was out, so I let myself into the room. But the moment I came in, I could hear them in the living room. Mrs. Jardine was with her.''

"What did she say?'' Laura asked.

"I'm sorry. But I didn't stay. I backed out as quiet as I could. Then I waited around in the employee kitchen, and when I saw Mrs. Jardine leave, I went back upstairs.''

"Thank you,'' Laura told her. "Thank you both,'' she said.

After the couple left, Laura sat in her office, her blood chilling and a fury burning in her heart. She wasn't sure how long she sat there. She only knew in that moment that she hated Olivia Jardine.

When the intercom buzzed, an icy calm had settled over her. "Laura Harte.''

"Laura? It's Josh. Olivia and I are waiting in the boardroom to start the meeting. Are you going to join us?''

"I'm on my way.''

"Is everything okay?'' he asked, as though he'd sensed something wrong.

"Everything is fine.''

Everything wasn't fine, Josh decided as he sat at the meeting table with Laura and Olivia. He couldn't put his finger on it. Laura said all the right things. She was well prepared as always for the meeting, and she handled Olivia's questions like the pro that she was. But those pale blue eyes of hers that he'd seen filled with excitement, with fury, with passion, were flat now. Void of emotion. And there was a rigid calmness about her demeanor, a steel-hard control, that bordered on cold. Something was seriously wrong. And the realization had a knot the size of Texas fisting in his gut.

"I'm impressed with the improvement to the bottom line," Olivia told them as she sat at the head of the table in the hotel's boardroom with the monthly financial reports in front of her. "There's no question that in the five months since Laura took over the hotel's management and you came on as a consultant, Joshua, that there's been a marked improvement to the bottom line each month."

"But it doesn't reach your expectations," Laura added, her voice as flat as her eyes.

Olivia frowned. "No. I wouldn't say that. But in lieu of our agreement, I had hoped that by now the hotel would be showing a profit—however small."

"Duchess, we both knew going into this that six months wasn't nearly long enough to reverse the downward spiral the hotel was in. A situation that took years to create," Josh argued. In fact, he felt it had been just shy of miraculous that Laura, with some assistance from him, had been able to cut the hotel's losses so significantly given the current market. The wager he'd made with Olivia no longer mattered to him, Josh conceded. What did matter was that Laura might actually leave at the end of the six months if she didn't attain her goals. Could that be what was bothering her now? he wondered. "I think under the circumstances Laura has done a remarkable job."

"I agree with you, Joshua. And as you'll recall, I did suggest a one-year trial when we made this arrangement."

"But you'll recall that *I* insisted on only six months," Laura pointed out. "I'm aware of the terms of our agreement, Olivia. And I intend to honor them—whatever the outcome."

Olivia placed the report she'd been referring to in the folder on the table in front of her and sat back in her chair. "As Joshua pointed out, six months isn't a very long time. If you'd like more time, I'd be willing to extend the terms of our initial agreement."

"No, thank you. I stand by the six months deadline I set."

"Then you think you'll be able to make that turn-around date?" Olivia asked, her eyes sharpening. "You actually believe you can close out May in the black?"

"I believe there's a very good chance we will. From the number of nights already on the books, it appears our Jazz Fest promotion is successful. So is our push for visiting parents for the university graduates next month. I think if we're able to meet the numbers in our budget for those periods and keep the operating costs in line, we may show a profit for the month."

"Excellent," Olivia said, and gave them a rare smile.

"If, however, we don't hit the projections and the financials reflect a loss for the month, then you'll have my resignation."

Josh narrowed his eyes, tried to read what was beneath this too calm, too cool demeanor. For the first time since he'd met Laura, he felt as though there was a wall between them—one that he simply couldn't scale. The thought disturbed him, as much as it annoyed him.

"Yes, well then. I think perhaps that's a discussion we should save until next month and only if it's warranted." Olivia stood, made her way to the door. She paused, and as though she, too, sensed something off, she said, "Laura, we haven't seen much of you at the house lately. It appears that we're already in bed when you get home in the evenings and you leave most mornings without breakfast."

"I've been very busy lately."

"I see," Olivia replied. "Will we see you at home this evening for dinner?"

"I suspect you won't. I expect to be busy."

"What Laura means is that she's here from dawn to dusk working, and I've been occupying her evenings," Josh explained, seeing no reason not to state outright what anyone could see except Laura herself. And since he didn't trust Laura not to use that paperweight she was holding on to and also because he needed to touch her to shake this uneasy feeling he had, he caught her hand. Her fingers were ice cold, which did nothing to reassure him. Removing the paperweight from her hand, he set it down and brought both her hands to his lips. He kissed them while he stared at her, searching her eyes. The emptiness he read there sent ice flooding through his blood. Wanting desperately to see some life in her—even if it was anger, he said, "I hope you don't mind, Duchess. But I've fallen in love with your granddaughter."

Laura made an angry hissing sound, and fire leapt into her eyes as she attempted to tear her fists free. No doubt she wanted to use them on him, he thought, refusing to release her as relief flooded through him.

God, help him. He had to be a head case because he'd rather have Laura spitting mad at him any day than to have her staring at him with those cold, emotionless eyes.

"I hadn't realized your...friendship had progressed that far," Olivia addressed him.

"It hasn't," Laura fired back.

"It has," Josh assured Olivia, and when Laura opened her mouth to protest again, he pressed a quick, hard kiss to her lips.

"And exactly what do you intend to do about it?" Olivia asked.

"I'm working on it," he told her with a wink.

"Well, since Laura herself has chosen not to discuss the situation with me," she told him, her voice filled with censure and, he thought, possibly hurt, "I hope you'll keep me informed."

"You can count on it."

The moment Olivia exited, he released Laura's hands.

"Why, of all the arrogant, high-handed, chauvinistic things to do," she ranted.

Choosing to let her get some of it out of her system before trying to reason with her, Josh walked over to the bar. Since it was too early for a stiff drink—even though he suspected he'd need one after laying the facts out for Laura—he poured himself a glass of water instead. And he waited.

"How dare you tell her you're in love with me?" Laura demanded.

"Because I am in love with you," Josh told her, his own temper beginning to fray. He slapped his glass down onto the counter untouched. "I haven't made a secret about it. I told you at the start that I had feelings for you. That I thought I was falling in love with you.''

''And I care about you. You know I do.''

''You're in love with me. You're just too stubborn, blind or afraid to see it,'' he countered.

''Even if I wanted it to be true, it could never work. Don't you see? You have roots here. Your life is here. Your family is here. Mine aren't.''

''Your family *is* here, Laura. And you could have a life here with me, with your family, if you wanted to. I want you to stay. So does Olivia. Why do you think she offered to extend that contract?''

She whirled on him. ''I don't care why she offered to extend it. I'm not taking it. I could never stay here.''

The words were like a kick in the stomach. They left him reeling. Furious, anger riding him like a beast, he marched over to her and grabbed her by the arms. ''What do you mean you could never stay here?''

''I...I can't.''

''Why not?'' When she didn't answer, he gripped her harder. ''Why not?''

''It doesn't matter.''

''The hell it doesn't,'' he fired back. ''I want an answer, Laura. You owe me an answer. Why couldn't you stay here?''

''Because Olivia Jardine is the one responsible for me not having a father,'' she cried out, tears streaking down her cheeks. ''I found out today that she's the one who sent my mother away. She had to be the one who sent the letter.''

''Laura, you're not making sense. What letter?''

''The letter I found in my mother's things.'' She swiped at her eyes. ''The one that said she was giving my mother fifty thousand dollars to get rid of me.''

"What?" Josh said, stunned by her accusation. "Laura, you must be mistaken."

"No, I'm not. The letter was addressed to my mother, and it was written on the Princess Hotel's stationery. It said...it said the money was to take care of my mother's little problem. To take care of me," she told him. "She paid my mother to take care of her son's mistake, to have me destroyed."

"Where did you find this letter? When?"

"I found it back home...when I was packing my mother's things."

"You found it what, six, seven months ago? You've been carrying this around inside you all these months, and you never mentioned it to me?"

"Why should I tell you? It didn't concern you. It had nothing to do with you."

Her answer left him feeling as though he'd been cold-cocked. Josh released her at once. "You didn't think it concerned me? I tell you I love you, that I think I want a life with you. And you didn't think I'd want to know that this has been eating at you? Hurting you?"

"It wasn't your problem. It *isn't* your problem," she amended. "It's mine. And I'll deal with it. It doesn't concern you."

"Forgive me. You're right," he told her politely, coldly, while he grappled with the white-hot pain of the blow she'd delivered to him. "As you've pointed out, it doesn't concern me. And since it's obvious that we're not on the same page in what either of us wants and needs in a relationship, I think this is as good a time as any to call it quits."

"Josh, wait!"

"No, Laura. I've waited long enough," he said, and walked out of the door.

Twenty-one

"Good afternoon, Miss Laura," a surprised Alfred greeted her as she stumbled into the house in the middle of the afternoon. In a daze of pain and grief, she brushed past the butler without a word.

"Miss Laura, are you all right?"

She kept moving, headed up the stairs. She had to get to her room, to be alone. She had to lick her wounds in private, try to stem this ache in her heart. With tears burning her eyes, she managed to navigate the stairs. Once inside her room, she threw herself onto the bed and began to sob. Deep, heart-wrenching sobs for Olivia's betrayal—her grandmother, the woman that she only now realized she had begun to care about.

Laura cried. For herself. For her mother and the father she'd never known. And she cried most of all for the sorry mess she had made of things with Josh. What was she going to do? She'd never seen him so angry. And that cool, polite way that he had looked through her, dismissed her and walked out. "Oh, God," she sobbed. It hurt. It hurt so much.

And that's how Katie found her—curled up in a ball on her bed, her arms wrapped around herself, her clothes and face a mess. She couldn't even bring herself to care. And the best response she could come up with in answer to Katie's demand to know what was wrong was "Just go away, and leave me alone."

"The hell I will! Dammit, Laura, I don't have time for this," Katie railed at her. "I left the head of a movie production team sitting in my office, about to sign a contract for catering and rooms for a crew of fifty for a month, when Alfred called and said something had happened to you. So you damned well better stop that blubbering and tell me what's wrong."

"It's none of your business," Laura snapped.

"Wrong answer, toots. It is my business because you're my sister." Katie grabbed her by the shoulders and gave her a shake. "Now, dammit, I want to know what's wrong."

"Sweet heavens, Katie," Ali cried out as she rushed into the room. "What are you doing to poor Laura?" she demanded, and shoving Katie aside, she took Laura into her arms.

"I haven't done anything to poor Laura," Katie fired back. "She was like this when I got here, blubbering away like some idiot and making a grand mess of Grandmother's duvet with her mascara, I might add."

"There, there now," Ali soothed. She snatched the box of tissues from the bedside and handed a wad to Laura. "It's all right, Laura. Whatever it is, it can't be that bad."

"It is," Laura told her, and began to cry again.

Ali patted her back. "Shh, now. It'll be all right. Katie is going to get you a drink of water, and I'm going to get you a wet cloth to wipe your face. Then when you're feeling better, you can tell us what's wrong, and we'll see what we can do to fix it. All right?"

Laura nodded.

"Katie, the water?" Ali said as she handed Laura the facecloth.

"What do I look like, the maid?"

"No one would ever mistake you for a maid, Katherine," Ali told her in a voice that Laura thought sounded very much like their grandmother's. "You're much too foul-tempered. You'd be fired the first day."

Laura nearly chuckled as Katie stomped off to do her twin's bidding. Just as Ali had predicted, the water and cool towel had made her feel better. But what helped most was having her sisters crawl up to sit on the bed with her and listen while she told them everything that had happened beginning with the letter, her conversation with Elizabeth Sabrion and the fight with Josh.

"You're going to need to talk to Grandmother," Ali told her. "I know she can be demanding, but family means everything to her. She detested Derek from the start and never approved of my marrying him, but she accepted him as my choice. Things weren't good between us almost from day one, and we separated within the first year. But by then, I was two months pregnant. Mother wanted me to have an abortion, but Grandmother wouldn't hear of it. She said the baby was a Jardine, and part of the future. She said to even consider ending the pregnancy was a sin."

"Ali's right," Katie added. "Grandmother was the one who wrote the check to pay that snake Dawson off when he started making noises about joint custody of Tori. She said it was only money, and if Dawson was willing to sell his rights to be a father for a few dollars, then the loss was his."

As she listened to her sisters, Laura was finding it more and more difficult to reconcile Olivia as a woman who would not only suggest, but pay to have her own grandchild aborted. But if not Olivia, who? Even if Adrienne had lied and known about her mother being in New Orleans, she couldn't see her mother telling the other woman she was pregnant. The logical person to tell would have been Andrew Jardine, the baby's father. And that thought—that her own father might have sent the letter and check—left a sick feeling in her stomach.

"As for your problem with Josh, I think you were right. None of this is his business. The man has a lot of nerve, jumping on you like that and making you feel bad for not telling him about the letter," Katie told her. "That was personal. Where does he get off thinking you need to report to him?"

"It does sound a bit like arrogance on his part," Ali said diplomatically. "But from what you've said, it sounds to me like he was really hurting."

"Oh, don't go defending him," Katie jumped in. "As nice as Josh is, the man's always been too cocky by far. Just because he has that pretty face, he thinks women are going to fall at his feet."

"They do," Laura pointed out. She'd seen the way women looked at him without a lick of encouragement on his part. And hadn't she tripped over her tongue the first time he'd flashed her that smile and kissed her hand?

"He's a man. And we all know that men are arrogant, chauvinistic pigs who automatically assume that a woman is a brainless creature who will do what she's told," Katie said, obviously on a roll. "Just because the guy says he loves her, doesn't mean Laura has to fall into line with his plans for them, does it?"

"I think that depends on how Laura feels about

Josh," Ali replied. "How do you feel about him, Laura?"

She was in love with him. And she'd not only held the words back from him, she had hurt him terribly. "Oh, man," she murmured, and covered her face with her hands.

"Now look what you did," Katie accused Ali. "So help me, Laura, if you start blubbering again, I swear I'm going to hit you."

"I'm not going to cry," Laura told them. "Thank you. Thank you so much." She gave them both a hug and scrambled off the bed.

"Where are you going?" Katie asked.

"First to fix my face, and then to talk to Josh—if he'll speak to me." And after she told him she loved him, she would ask him to come with her to speak to her grandmother. It was time she put the past to rest. As she whirled around to start for the bathroom, she spied Adrienne in the doorway and stilled. How long had she been there? How much had she overheard? Laura wondered. "Adrienne, I didn't realize you were there. Did you need something?"

"Actually, I was looking for Ali. I wanted to speak with her about helping with a luncheon to benefit the symphony next month."

"Is this going to be another one of those luncheons where Ali supplies all the work and the hotel eats the food costs, but you get all the credit?" Katie asked.

Adrienne's eyes flashed a warning at her daughter. "Just because I choose to spend my time on charitable work and not working in the hotel as you do, that doesn't mean what I do is less important."

"Of course it's important, and I'll be happy to help," Ali said as she eased gracefully from the bed.

She looked at her watch, gasped. "I didn't realize how late it was. I need to pick up Tori now. Can this wait until this evening after dinner?"

"That will be fine. Thank you," Adrienne said politely.

"I'll walk out with you, Ali," Katie offered. "I need to get back to work and see if I can salvage that account."

"Are you coming down with us, Mother?" Ali asked when Adrienne made no attempt to leave.

"In a moment. I want to have a word with Laura."

Laura saw the protest form on Katie's lips and shook her head.

"Good luck, Laura," Ali said, and with Katie, she went racing down the stairs.

Laura knew that Adrienne didn't like her, even resented her presence, and she really couldn't blame her, all things considered. But like it or not, they would forever be linked because Adrienne's children were her siblings—siblings that she had begun to love. "Was there something you wanted to say to me?" Laura asked the other woman, eager to get this over with so that she could settle things with Josh.

"I couldn't help overhearing you say that Josh Logan had asked you to marry him."

Laura's mouth thinned. "Obviously you've been standing there quite some time."

"The three of you seemed so intent in your conversation, I didn't want to interrupt."

"Yes, I can see where you might not want to," Laura told her, making no effort to hide her sarcasm. "Is there a point to this discussion, Adrienne?"

"The point is since you have no mother and you are my children's half sister, I would hate to see you make the same mistake my Alison did and marry a man who is more interested in your bank account than he is in you.''

Laura laughed. "Adrienne, I can assure you that while I'm no pauper, Josh's interest in me could hardly be because of my bank account.''

"No, but I suspect his desire to marry you has a great deal to do with his wager with Olivia to win back the Princess Hotel. You do know that it was Josh's grandfather who built the hotel and that Olivia won it from him, don't you?''

"I know the story," Laura told her. "Josh has made no secret of it, and it's common knowledge.''

"Did Josh also tell you that he's tried unsuccessfully to get Olivia to sell him the hotel for the past ten years? Did he tell you that Olivia promised him that if he could convince you to take over management of the hotel for a trial period and successfully turn it around that she would give him the opportunity to win the hotel back?''

Laura narrowed her eyes. "Obviously, you know he didn't tell me. But I still don't see what that would have to do with Josh wanting to marry me.''

"Quite a lot, I suspect. You see, in the deal she made with Josh, Olivia agreed to reenact the wager in which she won the hotel from his grandfather. If you're successful in turning the hotel around by the end of the trial period, the two of you will draw cards. Whoever draws the high card wins, and to that person Olivia will sign over ownership of the hotel.''

"That's crazy," Laura whispered.

"I agree. But there's no stopping Olivia when she's determined about something. As for Josh, I don't have to tell you what a bright and ambitious young man he is. By marrying you, he ensures that whether or not he wins the card game, he'll reclaim the Princess Hotel for the Logans. And it won't cost him a dime.'' She gave Laura a sympathetic look. "I'm sorry. But I felt it was my duty to tell you.''

"Yes" was all Laura could manage. She pressed a hand to her chest as though it could ease the ache. She hadn't thought it possible for a heart to feel so battered, to feel so broken as hers did and to still go on beating. Yet hers did.

"I thought you might also want to know that Josh is downstairs right now waiting in the library for Olivia.''

Laura's head came up at that bit of news. And through the haze of pain and betrayal came the searing red heat of temper. He'd used her. He'd made her feel selfish and small, had made her fall in love with him, and all the while he'd been using her to get the hotel.

Ignoring Adrienne, she stormed out the door and headed for the library.

Josh turned from the window as the doors to the library burst open and watched in fascination as Laura came at him. She was a mess. Her hair looked like she'd just tumbled out of bed. Her skin was blotchy, and her smart navy suit looked like it had been slept in. But her eyes—those pale blue eyes that had always fascinated him—were blazing with the fire of battle. "You lousy son of a—"

Josh caught her hand before it connected with his face. "If you're here to try to stop me from saying anything to your grandmother about that letter, don't bother. As you pointed out, it's none of my concern. I'm here to see Olivia on business.''

"I'll just bet you are. I know—" she practically spat the words at him as she wrenched her wrist free "—I know all about your business arrangement with my grandmother. Did you think I wouldn't find out?"

"It wasn't any secret. And since you were present when I signed the consultant agreement with Olivia, I assumed you knew the terms of our contract."

"I'm not talking about any consultant agreement, and you know it," she shouted. "I'm talking about the wager! The one you made with Olivia and used me to try to get back the Princess."

Josh went still at her words. He'd already felt as though he'd been hit by a truck after that scene with her this morning. But because there was some truth in her accusation, he remained silent and waited for her to finish.

"At least you have the decency not to deny it," she accused, a world of hurt in her voice. "You accused me of keeping things from you. How could you keep that from me? How could you use me, pretend to be in love with me when all along it was the hotel you wanted, not me?"

Anger sparked in him. "You're right about one thing. I was a fool not to tell you about the deal Olivia came to me with. It was an idiotic idea to begin with, and I didn't think it had much of a prayer of succeeding. So by the time you'd decided to stay and take the job, I'd put it out of my mind. But I never used you," he told her firmly. "The only reason I took that consultant job was because I wanted you. Not the hotel, Laura. You."

"And you expect me to believe you? That this is all just a big mistake?"

"Believe whatever you want. But know this—I do

love you. There was never any pretending on my part about that. As for mistakes, the biggest one I made was in believing that you loved me, that we had begun to build something good together, that we could have a future together. Obviously, I was wrong. You made it quite clear earlier today just how little you trust me. That while I'm okay to have some fun with, to maybe tumble around on the sheets with, when it comes to things that really matter, when it comes to sharing something like finding that letter and telling me how it was tearing you up inside, you want me to back off. It's your business. Not mine.''

"Don't try to turn this around on me," she told him, but some of the stiffness went out of her stance. "I'm not the bad guy in this. You're the one who's been lying."

"The only one who's been lying, Laura, is you."

"Me?" she cried out in indignation. "I've never lied to you."

"No. You've been lying to yourself."

"That's ridiculous," she countered.

"Is it? You've been telling yourself since day one that the only thing between us is good sex, and that we shouldn't complicate things because you're only here temporarily. That this isn't your home, that these people aren't your family.''

"It's true," she insisted.

"Liar." He took a step toward, got in her face. "We both know that there's a hell of a lot more between us than good sex. Or at least there could have been. Just as you could have had a real home here, a real family who loves you and cares about you. But the truth is you don't want to let yourself believe that I love you, that your family loves you, because you're afraid.

You're afraid if you believe me that you won't be able to hold back your feelings.

"And that's the biggest risk of all, isn't it, Laura? If you were to let yourself love me or your family, you'd be leaving yourself wide open and risk being hurt," he accused. "Fine, that's your choice. Just as it's my choice not to settle for less than we could be together. Now, if you don't mind, I'd appreciate you getting the hell out of here. I'd like a minute alone before your grandmother arrives."

"I'm afraid you're a little late since I'm already here."

Josh whipped his gaze to the doorway where Olivia stood. He frowned as he noted her leaning heavily on the cane, and he couldn't help thinking that Olivia looked as though she'd aged ten years since that morning.

"I'll leave you alone to discuss your business," Laura told her grandmother. "But when the two of you are finished, I'd like to have a word with you."

"There's no need for you to go, Laura. What I have to say concerns you, too." She walked farther into the room and joined them. "I heard about what you did today for Clifford and Elizabeth Sabrion's anniversary. That was very thoughtful of you. I suspect you got that trait from your mother. As I recall, Juliet was thoughtful, too."

Laura nodded, but Josh didn't miss the flicker of surprise that crossed her features at the mention of her mother. As far as he knew, since the night of Laura's arrival, Olivia hadn't mentioned the other woman again. That she did now made him suspect that she'd somehow learned about the letter. "Duchess, are you all right?'' he asked, not liking her color or the way she was leaning so heavily on her cane.

"I'm just tired. If the two of you don't mind, I think I'll sit. What I have to say might take some time.'' She walked over to her desk, took the chair behind it.

When Olivia leaned her head back against the seat and closed her eyes a moment, Josh's concern grew. "Maybe you should rest, Duchess. I can come back tomorrow, and I'm sure whatever Laura has to say can wait, too,'' he offered, shooting Laura a look that said not to disagree with him.

"No,'' she said, opening her eyes. "I've waited too long already. After our meeting this morning, I decided it was time for me to come to terms with some of the decisions I've made in my life. And I'm afraid that when you've lived for eighty-one years as I have, you're forced to admit that not all the decisions you've made over the years were the right ones. One of those decisions that I regret most was my refusal to believe that Andrew was truly in love with your mother and not simply infatuated with her.''

"He loved her,'' Laura said defensively. "And she loved him.''

"So Andrew told me when he announced he intended to end his engagement to Adrienne and marry Juliet. Even when I threatened to disinherit him, he refused to back down. He said the money didn't matter, nothing mattered to him without Juliet. I didn't believe him. Not even when he brought Juliet here to meet me.''

"Is that why you went to the hotel to see my mother alone? So that you could convince her to leave?'' Laura asked, her voice bitter.

A pained expression crossed Olivia's face. "I suspected you'd figure that out when I'd heard you'd spoken to Elizabeth Sabrion. I wasn't sure she'd seen me. Obviously, she did. But you're right. When Andrew refused to listen to reason, I did go to see Juliet at the hotel to convince her to walk away.''

"My mother loved him. I know she did. She would never have walked away from him, kept me a secret from him, unless...unless you'd threatened her somehow.''

"Laura, child, I had nothing to threaten Juliet with. The only weapon I had was Juliet's feelings for Andrew. I told her she was forcing him to choose between her and his family, his heritage. I pleaded with her not to force him to make that choice.''

"And you knew how much importance my mother placed on family, didn't you?''

Olivia nodded. "Andrew told me that she'd been adopted. That her parents had been elderly, and they'd both passed away before she'd turned twenty.''

"How could you do that to her? To them? Why couldn't you just accept it?''

"Because twenty-nine years ago I was desperate,'' Olivia snapped. "I needed Andrew to marry Adrienne or I risked losing everything.''

"I—I don't understand,'' Laura said.

Olivia stood and walked over to the window. After a moment, she turned back to face them. "Twenty-nine years ago the hotel business wasn't a lot different than it is now. It was tough, and the owners that survived were the ones who were willing to fight for their piece of the business. I knew even back then how crucial it was that I get a foothold in the central business district if Jardine Enterprises was going to survive. The Duboises, Adrienne's parents, owned the Regent back

then. It wasn't anything like it is now. It was in need
of major work, but it was a prime location. The Duboises didn't have any idea what they had. They had
no idea how to make it work.''

"But you did," Josh added. He'd always respected
Olivia as a businesswoman. The fact that she would
have recognized the potential of the hotel's location
spoke volumes about her shrewdness.

"Yes. I knew I could turn it into a gold mine and
use it to feed business to the Princess.''

"So why not just buy it? Why push my father into
a marriage he didn't want?''

"Because I didn't have the money to buy it," Olivia
informed her. "And Franklin Dubois, Adrienne's father, had already received two other offers to buy the
property—offers that I couldn't match. Franklin agreed
to sell me the hotel at a price I could afford and to
carry a portion of the note, but only after our children
were married.''

"And without the wedding, there would be no
deal," Josh surmised.

Olivia nodded. "At the time, I had no reason to think
it wouldn't happen. Andrew and Adrienne had been
sweethearts since they were kids. They adored each
other, and Andrew had already given her an engagement ring.''

"But when he met my mother and changed his mind,
why did you insist he go through with the marriage to
Adrienne?" Laura argued.

"Because by the time Andrew met Juliet, I had already signed contracts, committing to the refurbish-
ment of the Regent, and had given deposits to the con-
tractors, the architects, the decorators. Back then every
cent I had was tied up in the Princess, and I'd used the

Princess as collateral for the loan to buy the Regent. It was too late to get my money back when Andrew came home and told me about Juliet. If my deal to buy the Regent didn't go through, I would not only have lost the money I'd already put up, but I would have lost the Princess, too. I'd already lost Simon. I couldn't lose his Princess, too.''

"Grandfather?" Josh asked, taken aback by Olivia's declaration. "You were in love with my grandfather?"

"Yes," she said simply. "He's the only man I ever loved. Even now that he's gone, I still love him."

"Then why didn't you marry him? I know he asked you. He told me he did. But you turned him down," Josh accused her. "You took his hotel from him, and then you married someone else."

"I didn't have any choice," she told him, her eyes filling with tears. "You don't know how it was back then. Fifty-six years ago, you didn't have the luxury of only marrying for love."

"It seems my father never had that luxury, either," Laura pointed out.

Olivia flushed. "You're right. I took that from him—which I regret more than you'll ever know."

"You didn't answer my question," Josh reminded her, still reeling from the idea that Olivia had been in love with his grandfather all these years—yet, she'd taken the Princess from him. "Why did you take grandfather's hotel and marry someone else?"

"Because I had a duty to my family," she explained. "I had to live up to my responsibility to them."

"By marrying a man you didn't love?" Laura asked.

"Judge me if you wish, but yes. That's exactly what I did. My father was a proud man, educated. He'd owned a small business, had done fairly well. And then the Depression hit, and he lost everything. He ended up going to work as a bookkeeper for Henry Jardine. Henry was near my father's age, but he was a kind man, and he was wealthy. He said he fell in love with me the first time he saw me. He asked my father for my hand in marriage and promised to provide for my family if I married him. I was the oldest of six. And I loved my father. I wanted to give him back some of his pride.''

''And then you met my grandfather.''

''Yes,'' Olivia said, a sad smile curving her lips. ''Simon Logan was a great deal like you, Joshua. He was so young, so handsome, and so full of life. He made me laugh. He made me glad to be alive. I loved him desperately. But he was just starting out then. He'd just built the Princess. Everything he owned was in her. He could barely support himself, let alone me and my family. He wanted me to break my engagement to Henry and marry him. I told him I couldn't, but he was determined to have me.''

''So he made the wager for the Princess,'' Josh supplied.

''Yes. He made that ridiculous wager in front of my father, Henry and half of the city. He challenged me to a game of cards, High-card draw. If he drew the high card, I would break my engagement to Henry and marry him. And if he lost, he would sign over the Princess to me and get out of my life forever.''

''And he lost,'' Josh said. ''And you took the Princess from him.''

''I had no choice,'' Olivia told him. ''My father and Henry would have insisted he honor the bet, but Simon didn't even argue. He simply signed over the deed to me and walked out of my life. I kept my end of the bargain and married Henry. Henry passed away a few years later, but by then it was too late. Simon had met your grandmother and married her, and they'd already had two babies. So I'd lost him forever. The only thing I had left of him was his hotel. I couldn't lose that. I couldn't lose Simon and the Princess, too.''

"The hotel meant that much to you?'' Laura asked, and there was no mistaking the raw fury in her tone. "You were willing to sacrifice your son's happiness, to condemn him to a marriage he didn't want and pay to have his bastard child aborted all to keep a piece of property?''

Olivia paled, and when her steps faltered, Josh rushed over to her. Taking her by the arm, he guided her back to the chair. "You didn't know?'' Josh asked.

Olivia shook her head.

"Are you saying you didn't know that my mother was paid fifty thousand dollars to get rid of me?''

Twenty-two

"Of course, I didn't know. How dare you accuse me of such a thing?" Olivia demanded.

Laura hesitated, taken aback by Olivia's outrage. "Are you going to deny that you're the one who sent my mother a note with a check telling her to take care of her little problem?"

Fire flashed in Olivia's eyes. "I most certainly do deny it. I never even knew Juliet was pregnant," she told her.

Was it possible she was telling the truth? Laura wondered. If Olivia hadn't been the one to send the money, then who had? Her heart constricted as she realized the answer. "Then if it wasn't you, it was Andrew."

"You're wrong," Olivia informed her, her voice firm. "Juliet never told Andrew she was pregnant. I'm as sure of that as I am of my own name."

"How do you know?" Laura asked.

"Because Andrew loved your mother. If he had known she was pregnant with his child, he would never have stopped searching for her. He would have searched the ends of the earth until he found you both."

"My father searched for my mother?" Laura asked, something inside her softening, healing at the thought that her father really would have wanted her, loved her.

"For weeks," Olivia told her. "But Juliet had disappeared without a trace."

"But if you didn't send the check and neither did Laura's father, who did?" Josh asked.

"I have no idea," Olivia told him.

"Could it have been Adrienne?" Josh asked. "Could she have known Juliet was pregnant?"

"I don't see how. When Juliet was here in New Orleans, Adrienne was in London with her mother. So I know she never met her. And since Juliet disappeared right after she left here, how would Adrienne have been able to find her when Andrew couldn't?" Olivia shook her head. "It had to be someone else."

"Someone your mother was close to," Josh added.

And Laura could think of only one person. The one person her mother would have turned to, the one person her mother had always considered her dearest friend. Uncle Paul. The realization left a sinking feeling in the pit of her stomach, and a new ache in her heart.

"After all this time, does it really matter who sent it?" Olivia asked her. "It can't be changed now. We can never go back and undo our mistakes. I can never go back and undo what my interference between Andrew and your mother caused. I can't get back all those years I missed being a part of your life.

"And when I think of all that I've cost you—the chance to know your father. For him to know you. And now I've even managed to mess things up with you and Joshua. I don't blame you for hating me, Laura. I've certainly earned your contempt."

She didn't want to be touched by Olivia's distress. She didn't want to care about her. But she did, Laura admitted. Reaching out, she touched the older woman's arm. A fresh sheen of tears came to Olivia's eyes, and Laura realized it was the first time she had ever touched the other woman. Her grandmother. She swallowed. "I don't hate you. And as you said, we can't go back and undo the past."

"No, we can't," Olivia told her. "I'm truly sorry, Laura. And I hope someday you'll be able to find it in your heart to forgive a foolish old woman."

But she had already forgiven Olivia, Laura admitted silently. From what she'd heard, her grandmother had suffered more than enough for her sins.

"I owe you an apology, too, Joshua. I should never have tried to manipulate you as I did, using your desire to get back Simon's Princess to get you to do what I wanted. It's just that I thought…I had hoped that maybe you and Laura might find your way to each other, unite our families, as Simon and I were never able to do." Olivia dropped her gaze. "Once again, I'm guilty of playing with people's lives. I had no right to interfere. If you still want to buy the Princess, I'll sell her to you."

"Then I guess there's really no need for me to stay now and complete the terms of my contract," Laura said. She waited, hoping Josh would tell her there was a reason for her to stay. That he loved her. That *he* wanted her to stay.

"But you don't have to leave," Olivia argued. "This is still your home. We're still your family."

"Thank you," Laura told her. "But I think it's time for me to go back to San Francisco." She had things there that she needed to resolve before she could finally put the past behind her and begin to think about the future.

"But, Laura—"

"Let her go, Duchess. I think Laura's made it clear that she doesn't want to stay here. And if there's one thing that I've learned these past six months, it's that just because you love someone doesn't mean that they necessarily love you.''

''And you would be the expert on what love is, wouldn't you?'' Laura charged back, hurt by his coldness.

''No, I'm not an expert. I'm simply a man who loves you. Who thought you loved me. But when you love someone, you love the good and the bad in them. When you love someone, you trust them with your heart. It doesn't mean they won't ever do or say something to hurt you, because they probably will. But when you love someone, you forgive them—even for hurting you. If you can't find it in your heart to forgive them, then what you had wasn't really love at all.''

Although she was already emotionally drained, Josh's words left her speechless. He made her feel petty and small, and she resented him for it and loved him at the same time. She wanted to explain to him that she wanted to go back to San Francisco to find the answers and finally put the past to rest so that she could begin to plan a future—a future she wanted with him. But before she could swallow past the fresh lump forming in her throat, he turned away from her.

He walked over to her grandmother, kissed her cheek. ''I'll give you a call later, Duchess.''

''Josh.'' She finally managed to get his name out. When he turned and looked at her with such cold green eyes, the words, the explanations, froze on her lips. ''Goodbye.''

''Goodbye, Laura. I hope you find whatever it is you're looking for in San Francisco.'' Then he walked out the door, shutting it quietly behind him, and took her heart with him.

What she found in San Francisco two days later were the answers about the past. Answers that she knew only

Uncle Paul could give her. Since she'd shown up on his doorstep that morning, he had aged ten years before her eyes. His shoulders were slumped. His face was ashen. And his eyes filled with guilt.

"How did you know it was me?" he asked her.

"It couldn't have been anyone else. You were the one person my mother loved and trusted, and you were my father's best friend. You were the one person they both would have turned to. It had to be you," Laura said, hurting for him, for herself, for her parents. "What I don't understand is why. Why did you do it, Uncle Paul?"

"Because I loved her," he said, his voice trembling with emotion. "I loved Juliet."

"Is that what you call love? Betraying her trust? Lying to her?"

He buried his face in his hands, wept.

And Laura waited. She waited while the man she had considered her beloved uncle, who had in essence been a father to her all her life, sobbed and suffered with the knowledge that she now knew of the sin he had committed against her mother, her father and her and had kept from all of them for nearly thirty years. Finally, when the worst of it seemed to be over and he had gotten some measure of control again, Laura asked, "Will you tell me what happened?"

"I can tell you what I know."

"All right."

"When Juliet came back from New Orleans, she didn't know she was pregnant at first. She never told me what happened in New Orleans between her and Olivia Jardine. Only that she couldn't marry Drew. She said she loved him too much to allow him to throw away everything for her. She was sure Drew would come after her, so she begged me to help her. She said she needed to move away quickly, to change her name, start a new life somewhere in another city where Drew couldn't find her. And she begged me to keep her secret.''

''And you helped her,'' Laura said.

''Yes. When Drew couldn't find her, naturally he came to me. I'd never seen him like that before—frantic, desperate, broken. But I'd sworn to Juliet that I wouldn't tell him where she was. And I kept my word. I lied to him, told him that I didn't know where she had gone, that I hadn't seen her.''

''So he went back to New Orleans?'' Laura asked.

''Eventually. He'd hired a detective, worked for a few weeks himself trying to find her. Finally, he gave up and went back home. He'd only been gone a couple of weeks when Juliet discovered she was pregnant. She was thrilled and terrified at the same time. She didn't know what to do. She wanted to tell Drew, but she didn't want him to feel he had to marry her because of the baby. Finally, after agonizing for nearly three months over what she should do, she decided she should tell him. That Drew had a right to know he was going to be a father.''

Laura's stomach fell at the news. ''Then my father knew she was pregnant with me?''

Her uncle's face flushed. ''No. Juliet hadn't been at her new job very long. She couldn't get time off or afford to fly down to New Orleans again. She was stressed and making herself sick with worry over how she was going to tell Drew about the baby over the phone. So I offered to go to New Orleans for her and tell him.''

''And?''

Her uncle hung his head a moment. When he lifted

his eyes to meet hers again, he said, "And I went to New Orleans with the intention of telling Drew. But when I got there, he had changed. He wasn't the same man I remembered. Juliet's leaving had taken its toll on him. He was harder, colder, sadder. Drew was seeing Adrienne again. He told me how she'd stood by him, seen him through the rough period after Juliet left. And he wasn't sure how it had happened, but their engagement was back on again."

"You never told him," Laura said, still unable to believe her uncle had done such a thing and how many lives had been changed because of it. "Why, Uncle Paul?"

"Because I loved Juliet. I always had. And I thought that if she didn't have Drew, if she thought he was lost to her forever, she would turn to me," he said, his voice hoarse, broken.

"So I took a sheet of stationery from the Princess Hotel, typed up that note to your mother and got a cashier's check. When I returned, I told Juliet that Drew was getting married. I even brought her clippings of the announcements. Then I lied to her, I told Juliet that I'd spoken to Olivia, told Olivia about the baby. I told her Olivia was convinced that if word were to get out about Juliet's pregnancy, both Drew and Adrienne's families would be disgraced and that Drew would be finished in New Orleans for good. Then I gave her the note and check and told her it was from Olivia. I knew by implying that Olivia wanted her to have an abortion that Juliet would never consider telling Drew again."

"And you were right. She never tried to contact him again, did she?"

"No. She didn't. But she never forgot him," her uncle said, sadness and a touch of pain in his voice.

"I thought she would eventually forget him. I even began supplying her with the news clippings and announcements to try to make her see that Drew had gone on with his life, that he had forgotten her, and that she should go on with hers. I kept hoping that she would eventually turn to me."

"She did turn to you, Uncle Paul," Laura pointed out.

"Yes. As a friend. Good old Paul—always Juliet's friend. But never the man she would love. Because the only man she would ever love was Drew." He laughed, but the sound held no humor. "You have no idea what a shock it was to see she'd kept all those clippings. The man had moved on with his life, married and had a family with another woman. And she loved him, anyway. She never stopped."

"She loved him, Uncle Paul. So she forgave him. I have it on good authority that's what you do when you love someone."

"I'm sorry," he said, openly weeping again. "I wasted so many years trying to win Juliet's love, and I never did. And now I've lost yours."

Watching him, Laura thought of all the months she'd wasted—angry with her mother, unjustly hating her father and grandmother, afraid to allow herself to trust and love her family, afraid to trust in Josh's love for her.

"You have every right to hate me, Laura. I hate myself for what I've done."

She should hate him for robbing her of her family, Laura conceded. But she didn't feel hate for him, she felt pity, she realized. Her uncle had paid for his sins, she decided. He'd lived his entire life loving a woman who would never love him as more than a friend. "I don't hate you, Uncle Paul,'' she whispered as she touched his shoulder.

"Can you forgive me, Laura? Can you ever forgive me for what I've done?''

"I still love you, Uncle Paul. So how can I not forgive you? After all, that's part of what love is—being able to forgive.''

And she could only hope that Josh loved her—at least enough to forgive her for being such a blind and stubborn fool, Laura thought three weeks later as she slid into the taxi at the New Orleans airport. "The Royal Princess Hotel, please,'' she told the driver, and pressed her hand to her nervous stomach.

"You here for a visit, ma'am?'' the driver asked as he pulled out onto the Interstate 10 and headed toward the city.

"No. This is home,'' she said, and smiled as she reflected on the words. It was home for her now, and here was where her family and her heart were.

When they pulled up in front of the hotel fifteen minutes later, Laura paid the driver and, after making arrangements with the hotel doorman to have someone deliver her bags to her grandmother's, she strode through the front doors of the Princess Hotel. "Good morning, Cliff,'' she told the elevator operator as she stepped inside the car.

"'Morning, Miss Harte,'' he said, tipping his hat and treating her to that infectious smile. "It's good to see you again.''

"The executive floor,'' she told him. "How's Elizabeth?''

"She's fine, ma'am. Just fine,'' he said as he punched the floor number. "She's still talking about our night in the honeymoon suite, been doing a bit of bragging to her sisters.''

Laura laughed. ''I'm glad to hear it. You be sure to tell her hello for me.''

''I'll do that, ma'am. I surely will.''

When she exited the elevator, Laura's stomach quivered. She thought of her sister Katie, her direct pipeline to the goings-on at the Princess, with her family and with Josh Logan. According to Katie, word on the grapevine was that the hotel's financials for May had shown a pitiful profit—but it was a profit, no less. Her grandmother was less demanding these days and even managed to smile occasionally. And Josh Logan was like a bear with a sore paw, Katie had said. The man was completely and totally miserable.

Laura smiled. When she reached the boardroom, she double-checked the slot in her briefcase for the deck of cards. They were there, wrapped with the same gold ribbon that Olivia had kept around them for fifty-six years. Drawing in a deep breath over what she was about to do, she straightened her shoulders and walked through the door. ''Good morning,'' she said.

Josh slopped coffee down the front of shirt. ''Damn!'' Scowling at her, he snatched a napkin from the bar area and wiped at the mess he'd made of his shirt. ''What are you doing here?'' he all but snarled.

''I'm here for the monthly financial meeting,'' she said sweetly as she leaned over and kissed Olivia's cheek. ''Hello, Grandmother.''

Olivia opened her mouth, closed it, and Laura grinned, unable to ever remember Olivia Jardine being at a loss for words. ''Am I late?'' Laura asked.

''No. No, not at all. We were just about to start,'' her grandmother said, and indicated for Laura to take a seat.

She chose the seat directly in Josh's line of vision, and crossed her legs. A trill of excitement sprinted along her nerves as she watched Josh's eyes heat. "Could I see a copy of the financials for May?"

Jerking his gaze to hers, he made a grunting sound and handed her one of the reports. Laura made a show of going through the various items indicating the departments expenses, profits, sales. Then she went to the bottom line. "Well, according to this, we made a profit for the month."

Olivia made a snorting sound. "I'd hardly call that a profit, my girl. It's not enough to pay for a decent steak dinner."

"But it's a profit all the same," Laura reminded her. "I believe if you refer to my management contract, it specified only that I had to put the hotel in the black by the end of the six-month trial period. Which is what I've done."

"You haven't even been here for the last three weeks," Josh challenged.

"Not physically. But I've kept my hand in the operations. And you'll recall that I was responsible for the marketing plan to push the operation in the black."

"All right, Laura, I'll agree you've fulfilled your obligations according to our contract. Are you saying that you want to stay on as the general manager at the Princess? Is that what you want?"

Laura paused. "That's part of it. I also would like for you to honor your agreement with Josh."

Olivia frowned. "Josh's services are very expensive. While he's done an excellent job for us these past six months, I hardly think we can continue to retain his services or that he would agree to stay on. Am I right, Josh?"

"I doubt that your granddaughter cares one way or

another whether I stay on here or not. What is it you want, Laura?'' he asked.

"I want my grandmother to honor her wager with you,'' she told him.

"Are you sure this is what you want, dear?'' her grandmother asked her.

"Absolutely,'' she replied.

"Very well, then. I'll call the front desk and ask for a deck of cards.''

"There's no need,'' Laura informed her, never taking her eyes from Josh. "If you look in my briefcase, you'll find what you need.''

She heard her grandmother's gasp. "H-how did you get these?''

"Katie. I asked her to send them to me and to let me know when you'd be holding this meeting.''

Josh narrowed his eyes. "What are you up to, Laura?''

"Honoring the terms of the wager you made with my grandmother. But to make it like the real wager, I think there has to be something else at stake here besides ownership of the Princess.''

"What do you suggest?'' he asked her.

"Do you remember telling me that you wanted to marry me?'' she asked.

"I remember. I also remember that you weren't interested.''

Ignoring the dig, Laura began, "As I recall, Grandmother, you said that in the original wager between you and Josh's grandfather, the game was high-card draw. Is that right?''

"Yes. That's right.''

"Then we'll do the same. If you win, I'll agree to marry you and you'll get the Princess,'' she told Josh.

"And if you lose, the Princess is signed over to me and you will get out of my life."

"Laura, we don't have to do it this way. This wager stuff, it was a stupid idea to begin with," he argued.

Oh, how she loved him, Laura thought. But no way did she intend to make this easy on the man. After all, he should have told her about the wager in the first place, she reasoned. But she had no intention of making the mistake their grandparents had. "Are you telling me you won't honor the wager you made with my grandmother?"

His eyes flashed. "I'll honor it."

"Then we're agreed on the stakes and the terms?"

"We're agreed," he said, his voice hard.

"Grandmother?" Laura called, and Olivia came forward with the deck. She placed it on the table between them.

Josh drew a card, turned it over and his expression fell. "Five of spades."

Laura drew from the deck—a Queen of Hearts. "Looks like I'll have to marry you, after all," she said as she tucked the card back into the deck without revealing it. Smiling, she went into his arms. "You win."

"Wrong," he told her, and scooped her up into his arms and kissed. "We both won."

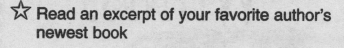

USA Today Bestselling Author

GINNA GRAY

THE
WITNESS

In the blink of
an eye, the life of
renowned concert pianist
Lauren Brownly changed forever.
She witnessed a grisly murder, and
discovered a devastating truth: *Her career
had been financed by the mob.* Now Lauren's
testimony against crime boss Carlo Giovessi
could finally bring him down.

Forced to trust FBI agent Wolf Rawlings,
she is put into protective custody. With mob
hitmen hot on their trail, Lauren and Wolf are
desperately fighting for survival....

*Available September 2001
wherever paperbacks are sold!*

Visit us at www.mirabooks.com   MGG832